ANTHOLOGY OF ISLAMIC LITERATURE

Anthology of Islamic Literature

*from the
rise of Islam
to modern
times*

*with an
introduction
and
commentaries
by*

James
Kritzeck

A MERIDIAN BOOK

MERIDIAN
Published by the Penguin Group
Penguin Books USA Inc., 375 Hudson Street,
New York, New York 10014, U.S.A.
Penguin Books Ltd, 27 Wrights Lane, London W8 5TZ, England
Penguin Books Australia Ltd, Ringwood, Victoria, Australia
Penguin Books Canada Ltd, 10 Alcorn Avenue, Toronto,
Ontario, Canada, M4V 3B2
Penguin Books (N.Z.) Ltd, 182–190 Wairau Road, Auckland 10, New Zealand

Penguin Books Ltd, Registered Offices: Harmondsworth, Middlesex, England

Published by Meridian, an imprint of New American Library, a division of
Penguin Books USA Inc.

This is an authorized reprint of a hardcover edition published by Holt,
Rinehart and Winston, a Unit of CBS Educational and Professional
Publishing. The hardcover edition was published simultaneously in Canada by
Holt, Rinehart and Winston of Canada, Limited.
First appeared in paperback as a Mentor edition.

First Meridian Printing, October, 1975
20 19 18 17 16 15 14 13 12 11 10

ACKNOWLEDGMENTS

I wish to thank my colleagues at Princeton and other universities for assisting me in the choice of selections for this anthology. My students in Oriental Studies 210 and 232 at Princeton have also helped me immeasurably in the course of our study of Islamic literature. I am particularly grateful to R. M. Rehder for his indications about Persian poets, and to Bruce Lawrence for able research assistance.

I also wish to thank the following for their kind permission to include in this anthology excerpts from the books listed:

George Allen & Unwin, Ltd., London, for excerpts from *The Faith and Practice of Al-Ghazzali*, translated by W. Montgomery Watt; and for "The Ode of Tarafah" from *The Seven Odes*, translated by A. J. Arberry, copyright by George Allen & Unwin, Ltd.; and for excerpts from *Tales from the Masnavi*, translated by A. J. Arberry, copyright © 1961 by George Allen & Unwin, Ltd.

George Allen & Unwin, Ltd., London, and The Macmillan Company, New York, for chapters from *The Koran Interpreted*, translated by A. J. Arberry, copyright © 1955 by George Allen & Unwin, Ltd.; and for the chapters "Tobacco" and "Coffee" from *The Balance of Truth* by Katib Chelebi, translated by G. L. Lewis, copyright 1957.

The American University of Beirut, for ten Lebanese proverbs from *Modern Lebanese Proverbs* by Anis Frayha (Nos. 25–26, 1953, in The Oriental Series).

A. J. Arberry, for excerpts from his translation of *The Doctrine of the Ṣūfīs*, published by the Cambridge University Press, Cambridge, copyright 1935 by A. J. Arberry.

Cambridge University Press for selections from Abu Nuwas, Abu al-Atahiyah, Al-Jahiz, Al-Mutanabbi, Al-Maarri, and Rumi, from *Translations of Eastern Poetry and Prose* (1921) by R. A. Nicholson; and for poems from *Moorish Poetry*, translated by A. J. Arberry (1953).

Jonathan Cape, Ltd., London, for extracts from *The Travels of Ibn Jubayr*, translated by J. R. C. Broadhurst (1952).

The Clarendon Press, Oxford, for excerpts from *The Mufaḍḍaliyāt*, translated by C. J. Lyall (1918).

Columbia University Press, New York, for excerpts from *Ancient Arabian Poetry*, translated by C. J. Lyall (1930).

The Cresset Press, Ltd., London, and E. P. Dutton & Co., Inc., New York, for the chapter "Purchase of Slaves," from Kai Kāᶜūs Ibn Iskandar's *A Mirror for Princes*, translated from the Persian by Reuben Levy. (First published by The Cresset Press, 1951.)

Helen B. Gadebush, as heir to the K. B. Jackson Estate, for two poems by Rudaki, from A. V. Williams Jackson's *Early Persian Poetry*, copyright 1920 by The Macmillan Company, New York.

The Trustees of the Gibb Memorial Trust, Cambridge, England, for passages from *Chahár Maqála*, translated by E. G. Browne (Luzac & Company, Ltd., London, 1921).

A. Guillaume, for excerpts from his translation of Ibn Ishaq's *Life of Muhammad*, published by the Oxford University Press, London, copyright 1955 by A. Guillaume.

Philip K. Hitti, for excerpts from his *An Arab-Syrian Gentleman and Warrior in the Period of the Crusades*, copyright 1929 by Philip K. Hitti.

University of Kentucky Press, Lexington, for five poems from *Dicbil b. ʿAlī*, translated by Leon Zolondek, copyright © 1961 by the University of Kentucky Press.

J. B. Lippincott Company, Philadelphia, successor to Frederick A. Stokes Company, for passages from *Stories from Saʿdī's Bústân and Gulistân*, translated by Reuben Levy.

Liveright Publishing Corp., New York, and Routledge & Kegan Paul, Ltd., London, for ten one-line proverbs from *Wit and Wisdom in Morocco* by Edward Westermarck (Liveright Publishing Corp., New York, 1931).

Luzac & Company, Ltd., for excerpts from *The Ring of the Dove* by Ibn Hazm, translated by A. J. Arberry (1953).

The Manchester University Press, Manchester, for the article "A Prose Translation of the *Moʿallaqah of Labīd* by William Wright," by Ursula Schedler, from *Journal of Semitic Studies*, Vol. VI, No. 1 (Spring, 1961).

John Murray, Ltd., London, for quotations from the following four volumes in their "Wisdom of the East" series: namely, the chapter "Group Solidarity," from *An Arab Philosophy of History*, translated by Charles Issawi (1950); excerpts from *The Awakening of the Soul* by Ibn Tufayl, translated by Paul Brönnle (1910); selected poems from *The Diwan of Abu'l-Ala*, translated by Henry Baerlein (1908); and passages from L. P. Elwell-Sutton's *Persian Proverbs* (1954).

The New Book Company, Bombay, for poems from *Court Poets of Iran and India*, translated by R. P. Masani.

Penguin Books Ltd., Harmondsworth, Middlesex, for chapters from *The Koran*, translated by N. J. Dawood (1956).

Phoenix Press, London, for six poems from *Arabic-Andalusian Casidas*, translated by Harold Morland, copyright 1949 by Phoenix Press.

Princeton University Press, Princeton, New Jersey, for excerpts from Sari Meḥmed Pasha's *Ottoman Statecraft*, translated by W. L. Wright, copyright 1935 by the Princeton University Press.

Routledge & Kegan Paul, Ltd., London, for extracts from Ibn Battúta's *Travels in Asia and Africa*, translated by H. A. R. Gibb (1929).

Routledge & Kegan Paul, Ltd., London, and Yale University Press, New Haven, Connecticut, for the piece "Advice" from Niẓām al-Mulk's *The Book of Government or Rules for Kings*, copyright © 1960 by Routledge & Kegan Paul, Ltd., London.

Routledge & Kegan Paul, Ltd., as successors to Janus Press, for extracts from *The Conference of the Birds* by Farid ud-Din Attar, translated by S. C. Nott. The Janus Press, London, 1954.

Eric Schroeder for passages from his *Muhammad's People* (Bond Wheelwright, Portland, 1955), copyright by Eric Schroeder.

Thames and Hudson Ltd., London, and Indiana University Press, Bloomington, for the chapter "Demon and Sage" from *The Tales of Marzuban*, translated by Reuben Levy, copyright 1960 by Thames and Hudson, London.

Theatre Arts Books, New York, for the play "The Bloody Poplar" from *The Turkish Theatre*, translated by Nicholas N. Martinovitch, copyright 1933 by Theatre Arts, Inc.

University of California Press, Berkeley, for passages from *Ibn Khaldun and Tamerlane* by Walter J. Fischel, copyright 1952 by the Regents of the University of California Press.

I should also like to acknowledge the fact that I have drawn upon the following for some of my source material:

Cambridge University Press, London, *Selected Poems from the Dīvāni Shamsi Tabrīz*, translated by R. A. Nicholson (1898).

The Clarendon Press, Oxford, *The Letters of Abu'l-Alá*, translated by D. S. Margoliouth (1898).

Longman and Cadell, London, *The Memoirs of Zehir-ed-Din Muhammad Baber*, translated by John Leyden and William Erskine (1826).

Luzac & Company, Ltd., London, *A History of Ottoman Poetry*, by E. J. W. Gibb, 6 vols. (1900–09).

John Murray, London, *Antar: A Bedoueen Romance*, translated by Terrick Hamilton (1819); *The Diary of H. M. The Shah of Persia*, translated by J. W. Redhouse (1874).

H. S. Nichols, London, *The Book of the Thousand Nights and a Night*, translated by Captain Sir R. F. Burton, 12 vols. (1894).

J. Parker, Longman, Hurst, Reese, Orme and Brown, London, *Kalila and Dimna: or The Fables of Bidpai*, translated by W. Knatchbull (1819).

Kegan Paul, Trench, Trübner & Co., London, *The Sháhnáma of Firdausi*, translated by A. G. Warner and E. Warner, 9 vols. (1906).

The Pilot Press, London, *Images from the Arab World*, translated by Herbert Howarth and Ibrahim Shukrallah (1944).

Grant Richards, London, *The Quatrains of Abu'l-Ala*, translated by D. S. Margoliouth (1898).

The Royal Asiatic Society, London, *The Assemblies of Al-Harīri*, Vol. 2, translated by Dr. F. Steingass (1898).

Trübner and Co., London, *Yúsuf and Zulaikha* by Jami, translated by Ralph T. H. Griffith (1882).

A. J. Valpy, London, *Lailí and Majnún* by Nizamí, tr. by James Atkinson (1836).

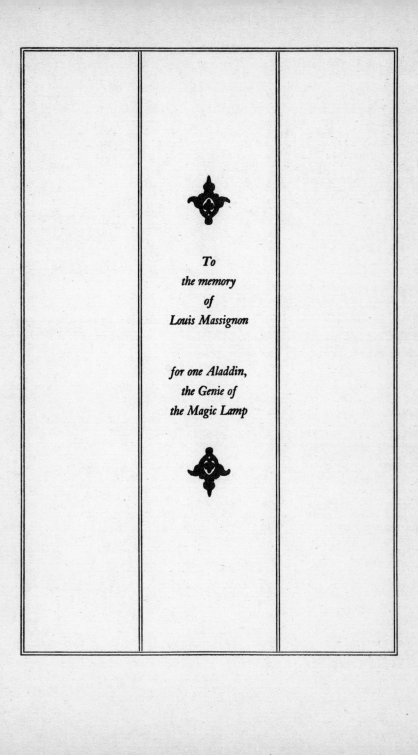

*To
the memory
of
Louis Massignon*

*for one Aladdin,
the Genie of
the Magic Lamp*

CONTENTS

CONTENTS

CONTENTS

ANTHOLOGY OF ISLAMIC LITERATURE

Nearly everyone literate in English has read parts of the *Arabian Nights* and the *Rubaiyat* of Umar Khayyam. These works have become standard favorites, classics of a sort, and to some extent deserve their fame. Yet they are rightly regarded by the Arabs and Persians as quite inferior morsels of what their rich literatures contain. Umar, though a very distinguished scientist in his day, has always been judged a minor poet by most Persians, while the *Arabian Nights* is considered by discerning Arabs as pulp literature of a rather vulgar sort. In recent years a considerable number of masterpieces of Islamic literature have individually displayed their merits through translation into Western languages, but few of them have become widely known.

The term "Islamic literature" requires an explanation, if not an apology. It is not a common term and may even be misleading. Islam is not the name of a language or group of languages. It is the name of a religion, the religion often but offensively called Mohammedanism, which was instituted in Arabia in the seventh century of our era and which today enjoys the adherence of nearly four hundred million persons calling themselves Moslems (or more accurately, Muslims), approximately one-seventh of the total estimated population of the earth. The world's Moslems are centered chiefly in the northern and eastern parts of Africa and the western and southern parts of Asia. Islam has also been used, more loosely, to denote this vast community of Moslems, the lands in which they live, their social and political institutions, and indeed the whole of their culture. It is in this last, most generous sense that the term is employed in the title of and, as far as possible, throughout this book.

Islamic culture is unquestionably one of the greater cultures in the history of mankind and of the world today. Few others have matched its extent and longevity, or its resiliency and tenacity. Few others have managed so consistently to incorporate and accommodate so many disparate elements and minds. Within Islamic culture, many ancient cultures have found a species of immortality; to it, many peoples, including non-Moslems, have contributed; from it, many ideas and other benefits have radiated to other cultures, including especially our own. Visually it is represented by many beautiful monuments, from the Alhambra in Spain to the Taj Mahal in India, from the crumbling domes of Samarkand to the rising domes of Kano. But visual art does not happen to represent, in the opinion of most experts, the greatest artistic expression of the Islamic genius. That role is customarily reserved for its literature.

Islamic literature can be, and usually is, subdivided according to languages. Principal among them are Arabic, Persian, and Turkish; but Berber, Hausa, Swahili, Somali, Albanian, Kurdish, Uzbek, Tadjik, Pashto, Baluchi, Urdu, Panjabi, Bengali, Gajarati, Sindhi, Telugu, Tamil, Malay, Javanese, Cham, and a good many others must be added. Many of these languages (including the three principal ones) have nothing, linguistically speaking, in common. Quite obviously, therefore, a tremendous number of forms and styles are comprehended under so general a rubric as "Islamic literature." At the same time, there is not only ample justification for, but a decided advantage in, approaching this immense body of literature as Islamic. Both the justification and the advantage are incomparably greater in this instance than they might be in approaching, say, an even larger body of literature as Christian or Buddhist. Separately, at this stage of affairs, many of these literatures would not justify anthologies of any great appeal outside the Islamic world. But taken together they comprise a meaningful entity which recommends itself highly as a basis for an anthology.

Richly diverse, like all great cultures and more so than most, Islamic culture has nonetheless evidenced a type of homogeneity which is truly striking. Although the religion of Islam has no doubt contributed the essential element in effecting that homogeneity, it has not been unique in its contribution. The spread of the Arabic and (to an almost equal extent) Persian languages over very wide areas of time and space helped also to effect that homogeneity. Throughout Islamic history many of its leading literary figures have been bilingual, and not a few of them have been trilingual.

These factors have immeasurably aided the dissemination and durability of certain standard Islamic literary forms. Students of comparative literature are likely to be the first, therefore, to perceive the value of conjoining these literatures in a single presentation.

It may be well to consider, first of all, some reasons why Islamic literature has for the most part remained so unappreciated in the West. To start with, Westerners have customarily brought to any consideration of Islam a whole set of preconceived notions which are almost entirely false; for that matter, the situation is mutual. During the thirteen centuries of their particular coexistence, Islam and Christendom have exhibited astonishingly little intellectual curiosity about one another. Through the contacts afforded them by history—contacts marked, to be sure, by other intellectual achievements such as the transmission of philosophical and scientific writings—a state of mutual understanding seldom better than elementary has persisted. Perhaps no Christian any longer believes that Mohammed was a renegade cardinal of the Colonna family, and few if any Moslems believe that the Virgin Mary is a Person of the Christian Trinity; but they have continued to accuse one another of polytheism, the very last thing of which either is guilty, down to the present time. Today the non-Moslem living outside the Islamic world who can distinguish Sunnites from Shiites is as rare as the Moslem who can distinguish among Protestant sects (many of them can distinguish Catholic and Orthodox from Protestant Christianity).

If it actually came to a test, one suspects that the Moslems would probably score higher. Consider, for instance, the following testimony:

During our first week at the Aramco[1] school on Long Island, questions were asked of us to ascertain our general knowledge about the Arab world.

---

[1] An abbreviation for the Arabian American Oil Company.

The questions "What is Islam?" and "Who was the Prophet Mohammed?" brought forth some interesting answers. One of our members thought that Islam was "a game of chance, similar to bridge." Another said it was "a mysterious sect founded in the South by the Ku Klux Klan." One gentleman believed it to be "an organization of American Masons who dress in strange costumes." The Prophet Mohammed was thought to be the man who "wrote the *Arabian Nights*." Another said he was "an American Negro minister who was in competition with Father Divine in New York City." One of the more reasonable answers came from one of our men who said, "Mohammed had something to do with a mountain. He either went to the mountain, or it came to him."[2]

Even supposing these answers to be no more than facetious guesses, they still reveal an appalling ignorance on the part of American adults of better than average educational backgrounds—who were, moreover, on their way to employment in Saudi Arabia.

Such ignorance, if inexcusable, is at least not inexplicable. It has, in fact, a long and fascinating history of its own, reaching back to the beginnings of contact between Islam and Christendom. Although its modern formulations may lack something of the range and piquancy which characterized those of earlier times, they still reflect to some extent an image of Islam (and to a great extent an attitude toward it) which was petrified in medieval times and which few persons have had the knowledge and intelligence to recognize for what it is, and even fewer the courage and patience to help supplant. In his important study of the making of that image, Norman Daniel has emphasized that ignorance of Islam was not the whole story anyway:

The essential differences that separate Christianity and Islam are about Revelation. For Christians the prophetic preparation of the Jews leads to a single event, the Incarnation, which is the inauguration of the Messianic Kingdom; for Catholics this Kingdom is the sacramental life of the Church. Any other scheme must seem a composite affair denying some and asserting other aspects of the single truth. For Muslims too there is just one Revelation, of the only religion, Islam, or submission to God; but it was made again

[2] Grant C. Butler, *Kings and Camels* (New York, 1960), pp. 16–17.

and again through successive prophets. Muhammad's was the final prophecy, but his was not more "Muslim" than that of Jesus, or Moses, or Abraham, "who was neither a Jew nor a Christian" (according to the Koran 3.60). For the Latin, it was an impossible imaginative effort so to suspend belief that this association of sacred names, which includes the most sacred of all, could seem anything but grotesque; yet it would be a mistake to imagine that medieval writers were ill-informed. There is evidence that they believed as much as they were willing to believe, and all who knew the Islamic reassessment of the familiar sequence of God's servants found it intolerable. As a result, Islam was often deformed when it was presented by Christians.[3]

As a direct result of that attitude and image, one imagines, the Islamic literatures have not, until comparatively recently, been widely studied in the West. Many of our universities still do not offer any courses in them or even elementary instruction in their languages. Recently there have been many encouraging improvements, however, along these lines; it may now be assumed that such improvements will continue and proliferate.

Which is not to say, either, that when the Islamic literatures have been studied, they were always studied badly. Quite the contrary. It might be said in general of the European Orientalists, from the so-called Age of Discovery to the turn of this present century, that they often appreciated those literatures more than some of the Islamic peoples themselves. Certainly their linguistic preparation in an age before tape recorders, their devotion, their breadth of vision, and their sheer achievements should inspire their modern progeny to envy, if nothing better. Had it not been for such men, it would still be impossible to put together an anthology of Islamic literature today.[4]

On the other hand, and at the risk of *lèse-majesté*, it must be said that some Western scholars of Islam and its literatures have themselves blocked the way to a wider and greater appreciation of these matters.

[3] *Islam and the West: The Making of an Image* (Edinburgh, 1960); cf. my "Moslem-Christian Understanding in Mediaeval Times," *Comparative Studies in Society and History*, Vol. IV (1962), pp. 388–401.
[4] See J. D. J. Waardenburg, *L'Islam dans le Miroir de l'Occident* (The Hague, 1961); and Raymond Schwab, *La Renaissance Orientale* (Paris, 1950).

Sometimes their studies have shown absolutely vicious prejudice against Islam, and palpable distaste for its literature. More often they have so concentrated on and limited themselves to minutiae communicated only to each other in the learned journals as to achieve the probably blissful state of total irrelevance.

The greatest damage of all has been done in the realm of translation. Sad to say, it has frequently been done by men who were for the most part innocent of the charges just mentioned. Of course, translation is at best a thankless task, and a haunting old proverb associates "translator" with "traitor." But the treachery which has been perpetrated against Islamic literature by means of translation has been nothing short of monstrous. No one who knows and loves the original texts of beautiful literary works wants them to be translated inaccurately, bowdlerized, or merely paraphrased. On the other hand, he does not want them emasculated by excessive literalism or made ridiculous by doggerel.

The worst examples of translations from Islamic literature are not worthy to be cited even in contempt. However, the point at hand may be strengthened by a few quotations of translations by experts whose more inspired performances appear throughout this anthology. R. A. Nicholson certainly advanced our knowledge of Islamic literature as much as anyone in the English-speaking world has ever done. In particular, his edition and translation of the *Masnavī* of Rumi is a noble monument of scholarship. Yet the translation sometimes reads like this:

(If) thou hast accepted (responded to) this (alluring cry), thou art left (unmoved) by the other, for a lover is deaf to the contrary of the object loved (by him).

(If) it (the World) has found the house (the heart) empty and taken abode (there), all else appears to him (the owner of the house) perverted or wonderful (extraordinary).

There is both the amber and the magnet (lodestone): whether thou art iron or straw thou wilt come to the hook (thou wilt be attracted).

The belly of the ass draws straw (to itself) at the (moment of) indrawing (deglutition); the belly of Adam (Man) is an attractor of wheat-broth.

If, on account of the darkness (of ignorance), thou dost not recognise a person (so as to discern his real nature), look at him whom he has made his *imám* (leader).

E. G. Browne, the great scholar of Persian literature, who left us the most compendious history of that literature in English, translated a passage from Hamd Allah Mustawfi as follows:

> The luck-forsaken land lay desolate.
> Many a fair one in that fearful hour
> Sought death to save her from th' invaders' power:
> Chaste maidens of the Prophet's progeny
> Who shone like asteroids in Virtue's sky,
> Fearing the lust of that ferocious host
> Did cast them down, and so gave up the ghost.

And Browne's and Nicholson's successor at Cambridge, A. J. Arberry, who has provided us with probably more translations of Islamic literature than anyone else, translated these lines from the Ode of Amru al-Qays:

> So with my companions I sat watching it between Dárij
> and El-Odheib, far-ranging my anxious gaze;
> over Katan, so we guessed, hovered the right of its deluge,
> its left dropping upon Es-Sitár and further Yadhbul.
> Then the cloud started loosing its torrent about Kutaifa,
> turning upon their beards the boles of the tall kanahbals.

Modern Islamic poets have not fared much better. Here is Arberry's rendition of a part of a poem by the modern Iraqi poet, Maruf al-Rusafi:

> Thou charmedst angels, ere that man was made,
>   The sun desired thee, while the moon yet slept,
> Ere sight descried, the ear in thee was glad,
>   The poem sang thee, ere the strings were swept:
> Maiden so lovely, and so nobly staid!

Few could be expected to develop an irresistible attraction to Islamic poetry from translations like those. In a large number of cases,

however, such translations are simply the only ones we have. This is
particularly true of poetry. But even in those cases where several
translations do exist, it is not always easy to choose one from among
them and establish persuasively that the one chosen is superior. Consider, for example, the opening lines of one of the most famous poems
in the Persian language, an ode by Hafiz, as translated by three different
and altogether competent translators:

My Shiraz Turk if she but deign
To take my heart into her hand,
I'll barter for her Hindu mole
Bukhara, yea, and Samarkand.

Wine, saki, wine! till all be gone;
Thou'lt never find in Eden's bowers
Such watered meads as Roknabad,
Nor fair Mosella's blood-rose flowers.

(Sir William Jones)

If that unkindly Shiraz Turk would take my heart within her hand,
I'd give Bukhara for the mole upon her cheek, or Samarqand!

Saqi, what wine is left for me pour, for in Heaven thou wilt not see
Musalla's sweet rose-haunted walks, nor Ruknabad's wave-dimpled strand.

(E. G. Browne)

Oh Turkish maid of Shiraz! in thy hand
If thou'lt take my heart, for the mole on thy cheek
I would barter Bokhara and Samarkand.

Bring, Cup-bearer, all that is left of thy wine!
In the Garden of Paradise vainly thou'lt seek
The lip of the fountain of Ruknabad,
And the bowers of Mosalla where roses twine.

(Gertrude Bell)

None of the three translations is really outstanding. In this anthology, a new and, I firmly believe, better translation has been provided. It is regrettable that the same thing cannot be said for all of the selections.

In fact, there are many great works of Islamic literature which have not yet been translated at all, and that is more the pity. Of course there remains the possibility that the fault lies with the works themselves—that they have not, in short, been judged to be worth translating. One should be cautioned against leaping to that conclusion. The fault lies, here again, more with the untutored and largely disinterested Westerner.

If the general reader normally has no acquaintance with the various Islamic languages, he does at least have some vague impression of their literatures as being sensuous, rambling, exotic, erotic, and fantastic. That impression, derived most likely from the *Arabian Nights* and from the innumerable Western imitations of the form which captured the imaginations and fantasies of eighteenth- and nineteenth-century Europeans, is not really as false as it deserves to be. Yet those who approach Islamic literature as novices are invariably surprised to discover within its unimagined bulk an equally unimagined wealth of form and content.

It is extremely unfortunate that the state of Western scholarly attention to Islamic literary criticism is almost antediluvian. Someone working in this field could almost be forgiven for despair, for example, at the sight of Ernst Robert Curtius' *Europäische Literatur und lateinisches Mittelalter*.[5] The deft and sure employment of philological techniques and literary theory on medieval Latin literature has no parallel for Islamic literature. Yet again there are rays of hope radiating both from some Western scholars and, particularly, from Near Eastern scholars.[6]

It has been customary to distinguish between two strains, easily recognized, within Islamic literature: a strain of popular "folk"

[5] Translated by W. R. Trask as *European Literature and the Latin Middle Ages*, Bollingen Series XXXVI (New York, 1953).
[6] See *Near Eastern Culture and Society*, edited by T. Cuyler Young (Princeton, 1951), pp. 48–82.

literature, and a strain of elegant "high" literature. Islamic literature is not unique in possessing two such strains, but it is unique in the manner in which their continuous interaction has shaped and nourished both. Poetry, the most beloved art of the Islamic peoples, rode quite freely between the two, although modern literature has succeeded to some degree in blurring the distinction between them.

Islamic literature is, at any rate, a literature of contrasts. It is a literature of skepticism and blind faith. It is a literature of asceticism and hedonism. It is a literature of economy and lavishness. It is a literature of strict form and hackneyed theme. Within so supple and even unwieldy a literature, the uninitiated reader will want to proceed cautiously and in possession of some maps.

He will want to be careful, for instance, of the florid verbosity of so many of the prose works. Naturally, literary tastes change from age to age, place to place, and person to person. In the twentieth century, we in the West are accustomed to enjoy a clipped and coldly antiseptic journalese which would have seemed even stranger to medieval Islamic writers than their apparent preciousness now seems to us. Indeed, stylistic differences which we seem to see within their works may have been less apparent to or intended by them than others which we overlook. On the other hand, their seeming lack of coherence or, better, discreteness in composition may not have been recognized at all by themselves.

An exclusive attention seems to be given to the individual verse, phrase, or paragraph, at the expense of the consistent layout of the whole. The Arab critics themselves have time and again demonstrated that the value of a poem to them would depend on the perfection of its individual lines. The critic encourages improved formulation of a traditional motif as a worthy goal of the poet, and frequently improved rendition is tantamount to a more concise one. Authors of prose works frequently profess their anxiousness to forestall a flagging of the reader's attention by quick shifts from one subject to another, or by a somewhat brusque transition from seriousness to jest; and they do not, by and large, concern themselves with maintaining the unity of their original or principal theme throughout a book. On the contrary, they seem to have taken a distinct delight in allowing themselves to be led away and astray by their associations, and the public appears to have been well satisfied with this procedure.[7]

The intimate connection between poetry and prose throughout Islamic literature, which helps to account for its apparent lavishness, is a crucial fact about that literature, and one which applies to nearly all of its prose genres. In recognizing this, however, one should not be misled into thinking that the creative spirit was consequently freer than it was, or that poetry was without its own strict conventions. Indeed, that would be almost the greatest mistake it is possible to make about Islamic poetry. The Arabs inherited from their desert ancestry an exceedingly elaborate and constraining corpus of poetic convention which in turn exerted an influence upon Persian and other later Islamic poetry. Referring to these conventions, Gustave von Grunebaum wrote: "In the two principal literatures of Islam, the Arabic and the Persian, the rigidity and the tenacity of genre conventions were extreme as they had been in classical antiquity. The critics, for the most part, made their influence felt on the conservative side. Theory desired the perpetuation of established tradition. The necessity of adapting expression to changes of impression was not generally recognized. Poetry, to those judges animated by an archaism, half-sentimental, half-philological, was primarily craftsmanship; its outstanding merit trueness to established form, not adequacy of self-expression."[8]

The reader should not miss, either, the thread of deep ethical concern intricately strung through all of Islamic literature. They malign it and misunderstand it who say that Islamic literature is meant only to gratify the ear and excite the idle imagination. In company with other literatures produced at times when ink and paper were at a greater premium than human memory, and when literacy was a prized gift, the written word was normally intended to profit fully as much as it was to please. Setting aside the Koran itself, which pervades

[7] G. E. von Grunebaum, "The Spirit of Islam as Shown in its Literature," *Islam* (London 1955), pp. 97–98.
[8] *Medieval Islam* (Chicago, 1947), pp. 259–260; cf. his *A Tenth-Century Document of Arabic Literary Theory and Criticism* (Chicago, 1950).

Islamic literature, the Sufi writers especially (members of that vast confraternity of religious contemplatives in Islam), and all of those many whom they influenced, dwelt single-mindedly upon the relationship between God and man. Asceticism was practiced early among the Moslems, and mysticism was experienced. It might even be said that after the initial stages of saints and theorists (not that either completely disappeared), Sufism became one of the greatest sources of literary inspiration in Islam. But the *adab* and *akhlāq* authors, too (who will be identified in due course), were constantly occupied with questions of morality. Even the otherwise engaged chronicler, the casual traveler, and the reckless, nonconformist poet gave frequent evidence of the importance they attached to basic ethical investigation.

It does not belie that point to admit, as one has to do, that many of the most cherished masterpieces of Islamic literature, particularly the models of style, are not what one would be inclined to call religious books; nay more, several of them have been accused of outright irreligious sentiment. That points to yet another trend in Islamic literature which the reader should notice: the many tones of alienation, anguish, and dissent. These, no less than the others, can be heard from the earliest to modern times. In the "New Poets" of the Abbasid period and the fables of Sadi, the tones are perhaps more muted, but in the lines of Al-Maarri and Umar Khayyam they resound as loudly and clearly as in those of Job and Ecclesiastes. Within Islam, surely one of the most comfortable and self-sufficient of cultures, the inquiring and self-searching mind of man was never lulled into total complacency.

Quite obviously, it is impossible to represent all of Islamic literature in satisfactory fashion in one volume of this size. After much negotiation and compromise, it has been decided to reduce this volume from its originally planned size and scope, and to follow it with another, *Modern Islamic Literature*, which will aim to give more adequate attention and coverage to that literature since 1800, when, in so very many ways, it changed its character and broke with tradition.

Several alternative methods of arrangement were considered for this anthology. One could, for instance, flinging history aside, have divided Islamic literature according to literary genres. Or one could, at greater risk, have divided it according to some bold new theory, speaking of a "pagan style," an "ornamental style," an "eclectic style," and so forth, still well within a fundamentally historical framework.[9] But finally it became apparent enough that a division according to more conventional historical periods was the only one which could possibly accommodate so tall an order. The problem of periodization of Islamic history is itself a knotty one, and the reader will certainly want to go beyond the brief historical summaries included at the beginning of each section in order to understand and appreciate more fully the selections which follow them.[10]

In theory the anthologist is the most unassailable of beings; he simply puts together his favorite passages under some rubric or other and deserves little acclaim—or disclaim—for doing so. In fact, of course, he is the most vulnerable of beings; since he plays Everyman, he invites criticism at every dotting of an "i." Some might assume that the anthologist of Islamic literature, granted its relative unfamiliarity to the nonspecialist, should be in a better position in this respect than others. That, too, is false. This anthology is most emphatically, even blatantly, not a book for specialists in Islamic literature. Yet since the anthologist will be presumed to be something of a specialist himself, it is by the specialists that his work will be judged most severely. He only deludes himself if he believes he is exonerated from his misdeeds by any general disclaimer. Wiser men have tried it for far less audacious works. Charles James Lyall, for one, insisted that his overpoweringly erudite *Translations of Ancient Arabian Poetry, Chiefly Prae-Islamic* was "not for the specialist."

It may partially engage the sympathy of the specialist critic to learn that I am far from satisfied with the results myself. The general aim of the anthology was to present writings of the most distinguished or representative Islamic authors in acceptable translations of sufficient

[9] I owe these terms to R. M. Rehder, and trust we have not heard the last of them.
[10] See H. A. R. Gibb, "An Interpretation of Islamic History," *Journal of World History*, Vol. I (1953), pp. 30–61; and M. G. S. Hodgson, "The Unity of Later Islamic History," *Journal of World History*, Vol. IV (1960), pp. 879–914.

length to permit them to make an impression upon the average, thoughtful reader. Many new translations were planned. Compromises began immediately. Some notable authors had to be omitted so as not to duplicate forms. Some were allowed to appear in Victorian (or even earlier) dress, while others were garbed in more modern clothing than really becomes them. Several whole classes of prose literature, such as history, philosophy, and law, were excluded on the grounds of incompatibility, while many poets had to be ruled out for no good reason. Selections from African and Southeast Asian Islamic literatures were left out owing to the difficulty of pleading their causes adequately within so narrow a scope. The most painful omissions were those of the Umayyad and Arab mystical poets of later date, as well as favorite passages from Al-Jahiz and Al-Hariri. In the same connection, it may be the better part of valor to admit a prejudice in favor of the Persian poets of the Mongol period.

The commentaries are brief, and annotation is sparse. It seemed much more important that the Islamic writers be allowed to speak for themselves. Some, it is true, speak longer than others; but that happens at every party. The names of the translators are mentioned at the end of each section of their translation; except where indicated, the notes are theirs. I have supplied English titles for most of the selections, but the titles of the original books have also been indicated.

In preference to imitating a few recent anthologies of segments of Islamic literature, I have patterned this one on Donald Keene's *Anthology of Japanese Literature* (New York, 1955)—even, as it has turned out, to the bifurcation of *Modern Japanese Literature* (New York, 1956). The result cannot aspire to be as successful as its model, but it is hoped that it will provide the reader with pleasant access to more of Islamic literature than he has yet found between two covers. That, at any rate, is what I set out to do.

J. K.

Cairo, 1963

All of the writers represented in this anthology wrote in languages which have employed, with some variations, the Arabic alphabet—an alphabet which is very different from the Roman and was in many respects unsuited to some of the languages which employed it.

T. E. Lawrence "of Arabia" made a classic comment on the problem of transliteration while he was reading the proofs of an abridgment of his *Seven Pillars of Wisdom*: "Arabic names won't go into English, exactly, for their consonants are not the same as ours, and their vowels, like ours, vary from district to district. There are some 'scientific systems' of transliteration, helpful to people who know enough Arabic not to need helping, but a wash-out for the world. I spell my names anyhow, to show what rot the systems are."

I do not myself believe that all of the systems are rot, but I readily admit that they are a wash-out for those who don't know the Arabic alphabet. Since this anthology is not intended for experts in Islamic languages, I have assumed that its readers neither need nor want a scientific transliteration throughout. It will be all the same to them, I imagine, to read Al-Jahiz for al-Jāḥiẓ and Attar for ʿAṭṭār.

But things are never that simple. Much copyrighted material has been reprinted in this anthology, and I have been powerless to tamper with it. For that matter, the task of respelling all the proper names in a single selection not in copyright, for example a story from *The Thousand and One Nights*, would be a gigantic undertaking. Presuming, too, a desire on the part of any reader not to err too badly in attempting to pronounce the foreign word he is reading, a word which is pronounced something like "koosoor" and best transliterated *quṣūr*, should probably not be left as "qusur."

The pattern I have adopted is not fanatically logical. I have fully transliterated, according to a system which is more or less standard among Islamicists writing in English, the titles of literary works and all technical terms in my own commentaries. All proper names and other words are left as they appear when transliterated according to the same system without the diacritical marks.

In recent times the modern Western custom of using personal and family names has increased in the Islamic world. Classical proper names, however, could be composed of as many as five parts:

(1) A personal name, usually (a) Arab names, as Muhammad, Ahmad, Ali, sometimes with the definite article, as Al-Hasan; (b) Biblical names in their Koranic forms, as Harun (Aaron), Ibrahim (Abraham), Sulayman (Solomon); (c) compound names, often a combination of Abd (slave) with one of the divine attributes, as Abd al-Aziz (slave of the Mighty), Abd al-Karim (slave of the Generous), or simply Abdullah (slave of God); or (d) Persian (Jamshid, Rustam), Turkish (Timur, Buri), and other names;

(2) A name compounded of Abu (father) or Umm (mother), as Abu Musa Ali (Ali, father of Moses) or Umm Ahmad (mother of Ahmad), which always preceded the personal name but did not necessarily indicate a real parental relationship and could be metaphorical, as Abu al-Fadl (father of merit) or even a nickname, as Abu al-Dawaniq (father of pennies, a name given to Caliph Al-Mansur);

(3) A list of ancestors, each introduced by Ibn (son) or Bint (daughter), often given for two generations, though sometimes many more (in extreme cases, back to Adam), or referring to a remote ancestor, as Ibn Sina, Ibn Khaldun, replaced by -i or -zadeh in Persian and -oghlu in Turkish;

(4) An honorific or descriptive epithet, sometimes a nickname but often a title, as (a) physical qualities, Al-Tawil (the tall), Al-Jahiz (the goggle-eyed); (b) virtues, Al-Rashid (the upright), Al-Mansur (the victorious); (c) professions, Al-Hallaj (the carder), Al-Khayyam (the tentmaker); (d) compounds of Din (religion) and other words,

Jalal al-Din (majesty of religion), Nizam al-Mulk (order of the kingdom), Sayf al-Islam (sword of Islam), the latter type preceding and sometimes replacing the personal name; and

(5) An adjective derived from place of birth, origin, or residence, sometimes from a sect, tribe, or family, and occasionally from a trade or profession, as Al-Misri (the Egyptian), Al-Isfahani (from Isfahan), Al-Wahhabi (the Wahhabite), often inherited and proudly multiplied.

Sometimes an author had, in addition, a pen name, as Firdawsi (of paradise).

ISLAMIC DATES

Instead of the Julian and Gregorian (the latter adopted in 1582) calendars used by the West, the Islamic world has used a calendar of its own, nowadays usually side by side with the Gregorian. Nearly all of the dates mentioned in this anthology are given according to the Gregorian calendar, but a few of them in some of the texts are given according to the Islamic calendar. That calendar begins with the first day (July 16) of the year (622) in which the *Hijrah* (or Hegira), Mohammed's move from Mecca to Medina, took place. It is a lunar calendar, which gains a year over the Gregorian every thirty-two or thirty-three years. There is a formula by which the two systems can be translated, but the nonspecialist and nonmathematical reader would doubtless prefer simply to consult one of the many available concordances, the best of which is H.-G. Cattenoz, *Tables de Concordance des Ères Chrétienne et Hégirienne*, 2nd ed. (Rabat, 1954).

"That inimitable symphony, the very sounds of which move men to tears and ecstasy," wrote Marmaduke Pickthall, describing the Koran. "As tedious a piece of reading as I ever undertook, a wearisome, confused jumble, crude, incondite—nothing but a sense of duty could carry any European through the Koran," was Thomas Carlyle's verdict. How could two sensitive and intelligent men of very similar backgrounds differ so markedly concerning a book which everyone knows is a world classic? The answer is complicated, but it can be made simple: Pickthall read Arabic and Carlyle did not.

For all of the world's Moslems, the Koran is the greatest work of literature. For almost everyone else it is, literally, a closed book. One would be hard pressed to find a single non-Moslem friend who has actually read it from cover to cover. Why is that? The Koran is not a long book; it is shorter than the New Testament. It is readily available in a variety of translations which are accurate enough, some of which have been issued in inexpensive editions. Is the Koran worth reading? To start with, what is it?

The Koran is the collection of formal utterances of·Mohammed, the prophet of Islam.[1] He was born in Mecca about 570 and was orphaned soon after his birth. The family into which he was born was part of a prominent tribe, but indications are that it was in straitened circumstances. Little reliable information has come down to us concerning Mohammed's youth. He became a trader, perhaps participated in caravans to Syria, and when he was about twenty-five, married a wealthy merchant's widow some years his senior.

[1] The best study of the Koran in a Western language is Theodor Nöldeke, et al., *Geschichte des Qorʾāns*, 3 vols. (Leipzig, 1909–38), but the average reader would be satisfied with Richard Bell, *Introduction to the Qurʾān* (Edinburgh, 1953). A convenient biography of Mohammed is W. Montgomery Watt, *Muhammad, Prophet and Statesman* (Oxford, 1961).

Mecca at that time, it is important to note, was no mere desert oasis, but a bustling and prosperous center of commerce on the major north-south caravan route, and its sanctuaries were places of religious pilgrimage for many neighboring tribes. Mohammed began by following the beliefs and customs which were commonly adhered to by his tribe and by most Arabians. However, he soon became disgusted with polytheism and the morality which went along with it and gave careful (but probably concealed) audience to the worship and disputation of Jews and Christians, who lived in Arabia in considerable numbers. He seems to have accepted their general religious tradition and pattern without feeling inclined to embrace either Judaism or Christianity. When he was about forty years old he experienced his first "revelation" and a call to prophethood. These revelations, which continued to occur at intervals during the rest of his life, constitute the Koran.

Mohammed proved himself a prophet in an important sense of the Hebrew term: he was not a man who *foretold*, but a man who *told forth*. He did not claim to be divine; that is the very last thing he would ever have claimed and the very last claim he would ever have recognized. Rather he claimed to be the reciter of a "recitation" (*qurʾān*, or Koran, means "recitation") unmistakably within the tradition of the Hebrew prophets. Mohammed preached; he did not write. Indeed, one of the principal bits of evidence adduced by Moslems for the divine origin of the Koran is the doubtful fact, and even more doubtful compliment, that their prophet was illiterate.

The Koran was not put together in written form until well after Mohammed's death. A special point must be made of the form in which it was put together, since that helps to explain why even well-meaning non-Moslems never get very far in reading it. Its one hundred fourteen chapters, except for the first, are arranged roughly in order of length; many of the chapters must themselves have been compilations. There was no good reason, apart from a rare rabbinical custom, for doing such a thing—and every reason for doing otherwise. The chapters vary in length from thousands of words to only a line or two, and generally speaking the longer ones are of a later period than the shorter ones. One is reading the Koran, therefore, in roughly the reverse order of that in which it was composed. This is a serious obstacle for any book to have to overcome.

For the Moslems, on the other hand, it is no obstacle at all, only a trivial complaint characteristic of infidels. The nature of their claim for the Koran (which is the Koran's claim for itself) fully accounts for this attitude. There is absolutely no doctrine of inspiration in Islam. The Koran must be believed to have no human author at all, but rather to be, syllable for syllable, the very dictation of God.[2] That dictation, through an angel customarily identified as Gabriel, was "taken" by Mohammed's memory and then confidently set adrift in other men's memories. From the evidence of the final text, it must be granted that those memories were excellent. Nevertheless, by comparison with the claims advanced for the Koran, those advanced by Jews and Christians for the books of the Bible seem very modest.

When the Moslem legists forbade translations of the Koran, they recognized something important for us to recognize. The most difficult things to translate from any language are those captivating little nuances, lying somewhere between prose and poetry, which catch perfectly the beauty of that language. The Koran was composed entirely of such prose-poetry, in a form called *saj^c*. Moslem sages contend that it is untranslatable, and they have no idea how right they are. It is regarded as a foolish cliché to say of a work that "it loses everything in translation." In the case of the Koran, this is true. No translation can convey more than the barest suggestion of what it is in the Koran that can "move men to tears and ecstasy."

So much for that. The Koran is still a book which can be read, if one is dogged enough, in a single day. One is likely to get further along with it, for the reason already given, if one starts at the back. Above all, one must bear in mind constantly while reading it that it is supposed to have been "spoken" by God to mankind through Mohammed. The *saj^c* and many individual features, which will be noted in due course, are common to the book as a whole. However, among the

[2] The Arabic "Allah" is translated "God" throughout.

chapters a distinction can be made between those composed at Mecca and those composed later at Medina. The distinction has sometimes been exaggerated by commentators but holds up well enough for the novice.

At Mecca, for some twelve years, Mohammed preached a religion which was quite simple and easy for anyone familiar with the Judaeo-Christian tradition to understand. For his polytheistic countrymen, of course, it was neither so simple nor so easy to understand. It was a religion of one God who created man, subsidized him with the goods of this world, revealed himself through the prophets and "messengers," and intends to judge him, rewarding good and punishing evil, in a life hereafter. Through Islam, this God wished to re-emphasize the fundamentals of what had become, in man's hands, a confused and contentious religious structure.

The themes and forms of the Meccan chapters are, from a literary standpoint, probably the most attractive in the book. The first chapter to be revealed, according to Islamic tradition, was "The Clot" (Koran 96). Each chapter has a title, usually taken from some striking reference within it, and all but one begin with the invocation, "In the name of God, the Merciful, the Compassionate":[3]

> Recite: In the name of your Lord who created,
> created man from a clot.
> Recite: And your Lord is most generous,
> who taught by the pen,
> taught man what he did not know.
>
> No, but man is rebellious
> because he sees himself grown rich.
> Indeed, the return is to your Lord.
>
> Have you seen him who forbids a servant to pray?
> Have you seen if he was rightly guided or ordered piety?
> Have you seen if he called [piety] a lie and turned his back on it?
> Did he know that God sees?

[3] These translations are the editor's.

No, if he does not desist, we shall seize him by the forelock,
a lying, sinful forelock!
So let him call his council.
We shall call the guards of hell.

No, do not obey him,
but fall down and draw near.

This chapter is obviously a conglomeration of editorial layers, and requires a great deal of explanation. It is more than likely that everything after the first five lines was added later, and everything after the first eight was aimed against a particular enemy. Most of the early Meccan chapters are simpler. Usually they begin with an interesting but harmless oath ("by the daylight," "by the fig and the olive," "by the city"), go on to indict some form of evil-doing, warn of judgment, frighteningly describe hell, and call men to repentance. "The Chargers" (100) is one of the most beautiful of them, though it, also, is difficult:

By the snorting chargers,
        the fire-strikers,
        the plunder-raiders at daybreak,
        the dust-raisers
        centering in it all together!

Man is indeed ungrateful to his Lord,
and he himself is a witness to that:
he is strong in his love of goods.

Does he not know that when
        what is in the graves will be torn out
        and what is in the breasts will be made to appear,
on that day their Lord will be an expert on them?

That chapter was chosen because it is an especially brilliant example of the rhythmic *saj*ᶜ. It sounds, insofar as its sound can be represented by the Roman alphabet, something like this:

> Waal aadiYAATi DAB-han,
>   faal mooriYAATi KAD-han,
>   faal mogheeRAATi SUB-han,
>   fa atharna beehee NAK-an
>   fa wasatna beehee JAM-an!
>
> Innal inSAANa lee rubbeehee la-kaNOOD,
> wa innahoo ala THAAlika la-shaHEED:
> wa innahoo lee hobbil khair la-shaDEED.
>
> Afalaa yalamoo itha
>   bothira maa fill koBOOR
>   wa hossila maa fiss soDOOR,
> inna rubbahom beehim yawma-ithin la-khaBEER?

Such clever combinations of repetition and variation of sound give these chapters their special lilt.[4] They are brief, lively, menacing, full of crisp and startling imagery. Some of them are built entirely around strange words, presumably as strange to their first audiences as they are to us. It has been shown that in this respect they resemble the oracular pronouncements of the Arabian soothsayers, although Mohammed took an extremely harsh stand against them—and, indeed, against all mere poets. "The Striking" (101) is an example:

> The "Striking"!—what is the "Striking"?
> What could convey to you what the "Striking" is?
> It is the day when people will be like scattered moths
> and the mountains will be like carded wool!
>
> Then, as for him whose scales [of merit] are heavy,
> he will be in a pleasing life.
> But as for him whose scales are light,
> he will be a son of—"Bereft"!
> And what could convey to you what "Bereft" is?—
> Raging fire!

[4] A. J. Arberry, in *The Holy Koran* (New York, 1953), pp. 20–26, has propounded an interesting theory about these combinations.

During this period, Mohammed liked to appeal, though somewhat
vaguely, to the authority of the Bible for his teachings: "All this is
written in earlier scriptures, the scriptures of Abraham and Moses"
(87.18). As he then saw it, his was mainly a confirming scripture for
the Arabs, who were without a scripture: "Before [the Koran], the
book of Moses was revealed, a guide and blessing to all men. This
book confirms it. It is revealed in the Arabic tongue" (46.12). Later,
when Jews and Christians proved unwilling to accept his claim in
sufficient numbers, he emphasized that they had deformed God's pure
religion and that the Koran invalidated their scriptures, which had
been corrupted. He represented Ishmael, the father of the Arabs according to Jewish lore, as coheir with Isaac to God's covenant with
Abraham.

The chapters of the later Meccan period already betray something
of this conflict. They also tend to be somewhat longer and to take
on more ambitious substance. Entire stories from the Old Testament
(such as that of Joseph, included later in full) are narrated in general
conformity with the Hebrew versions. Although there is only one
indisputable quotation from the Bible in the Koran (that of Psalm
37.29 in 21.105), the Bible is paraphrased in almost every chapter
after the early Meccan period. Some of the more trenchant chapters,
for example "Unity" (112), bespeak Islam's disassociation from
Christianity:

> Say: He is God—One!
> God—the eternally sought after!
> He did not have a son
> and was no one's son.
> And there is no one equal to Him.

In Mecca, Mohammed's message was first met with indifference,
then countered with opposition. The Meccans, and in particular
Mohammed's wealthier relatives who profited from the pilgrimage
trade to the pagan shrine of the Kaᶜbah, took his monotheistic warning
very much to heart, but not in the manner he intended. They planned
the elimination of his small sect. Some new material, aimed at coming
to terms with these opponents, was introduced into the Koran. Three

pagan goddesses, for instance, were acknowledged to be "daughters of God," whose cults might therefore be expected to continue. But such devices neither convinced nor placated the Meccans, and Mohammed himself soon regretted these "Satanic suggestions" and repudiated them. Ultimately a good many verses of the Koran were abrogated in this fashion. "The Unbelievers" (109) is said to have been revealed at this time:

> Say: O unbelievers!
>> I do not worship what you worship
>> and you do not worship what I worship;
>> and I shall not worship what you worship
>> and you will not worship what I worship.
> You have your religion and I have mine.

By 621, Islam's prospects seemed bleak. Mohammed had sent about eighty of his followers to Abyssinia, and indications are that some differences of opinion within his community, as well as the Meccan persecution, prompted that action. He had lost the encouraging presence of his first wife and the protective presence of his guardian, who, as chief of the Hashimite clan, had prevented violent steps being taken against him. Just as the situation was growing desperate, a miracle happened. Two of the principal tribes in Medina, a city some distance north of Mecca, had been feuding for years. Some of their members had heard Mohammed preach and sought him as mediator to end the feud. The Moslems left Mecca unobtrusively in small groups, and finally Mohammed himself fled.

The year of that "emigration" (*al-Hijrah*, or Hegira), 622, was later chosen as the commencement of the Islamic era. Although it might appear strange that it was selected in preference to the year of Mohammed's birth or that of his first revelation, it was actually an appropriate choice. For it was at Medina that Islam became a state— and ultimately a world empire and a world religion. That transformation did not, of course, take place overnight, but it took place rapidly. Mohammed proved himself a clever and farsighted statesman, as well as a religious leader. His conciliation was successful, and the expansion of his community began.

The style of the Meccan chapters of the Koran had been fitting for the blunt warnings and succinct preaching which were necessary there. At Medina, however, Mohammed became a lawgiver. The basic *saj*ᶜ form did not change in the Medinan chapters, but it was stretched tight to accommodate the lengthy and detailed prescriptions which now came forth. Certainly any legal portion of a typical Medinan chapter, such as the following from "Women" (4.11–12), provides a sharp contrast with any early Meccan chapter:

> God enjoins you [as follows] concerning [inheritance for] your children: A male shall get twice as much as a female. If there are more than two females, then they shall get two thirds of the estate; but if there is only one, then she shall get half. Parents shall get a sixth each, provided the deceased has a child; if he has no child and his parents are his only heirs, then his mother shall get a third. If he has more than one brother, then his mother shall get a sixth—after payment of legacies and debts.

It is really unfair to choose a passage like this one, but it was not chosen to typify the content of all the Medinan chapters. Several other Medinan chapters will be given in substantial extracts.

Mohammed tried to secure the support of Jewish communities in the vicinity of Medina by incorporating into Islam many elements of Jewish law and ritual. Those which remained within it (for example, the prohibition of pork, the regulations concerning fasting and circumcision) are too numerous to list. It is more important to note that at some point Mohammed broke violently with the past. Islam assumed its own direction of prayer, Mecca (previously it had been Jerusalem), and its own "sabbath," Friday.

Some authorities have professed to sense in this period a greater appreciation of Christianity on Mohammed's part. He regarded the Gospel (in the singular) as a book revealed to Christ, which would indicate that he knew very little about it. The position that he had taken concerning Christ seems to have prevented him from inquiring into the New Testament. He denied original sin, so the incarnation

became, in his eyes, the most wicked of blasphemies. Why he kept
referring to Jesus as "the Messiah" is therefore something of a mystery,
unless (as is quite possible) he had no idea of everything that title
implied. Surprisingly enough, he affirmed the virgin birth (19.17–26)
in words very similar to St. Luke's. According to one tradition, he
even asserted the immaculate conception. What is most surprising of
all, perhaps, is that he believed in the ascension of Jesus, while denying
his crucifixion:

> [The Jews] declared: "We have put to death the Messiah, Jesus the son
> of Mary, the apostle of God." But they did not kill him, nor did they crucify
> him. They only thought they did. . . . But God took him up to himself
> (4.156–158).

A clearer indication of greater friendliness toward Christians would
be the following verse:

> You will discover that those who are most implacable in their hatred of
> the [Moslems] are the Jews and the pagans, while those nearest to them in
> affection are those who profess to be Christians. That is because there are
> priests and monks among them, and they are free of pride (5.85).

Ultimately, however, both the Jews and the Christians, as "people of
the Book" (i.e., the Bible), were accorded a status as privileged
minorities within the Islamic state, or, more accurately, "protected"
minorities, in return for payment of special taxes.

Against other non-Moslems the Koran ordered warfare, a holy
warfare (*jihād*) against unbelievers. Mohammed spent much of the
rest of his life in directing military campaigns against trading caravans
and neighboring tribes, all with the general goals of consolidating and
extending his community and of forcing the Meccans, his most formidable enemies, into submission. Not all of these expeditions ended in
victory, and many of the victories were hard won. Tribal alliances
gradually emerged as almost as effective a means of attaining these
goals as warfare.

Mohammed's actions during these later years are usually regarded

by non-Moslems as, at best, unbecoming to him. In Islamic terms, on
the other hand, they appear both necessary and consistent. The fire
of warning had simply been translated, by Koranic direction, into the
fire of action. Toward the end, Mohammed was assured of final victory
in "The Assistance" (110):

> When God's assistance comes, and victory,
> and you see the people entering God's religion in droves,
> then glorify your Lord with praise and ask His forgiveness.
> Indeed, He is a forgiver.

In 631, Mecca capitulated and the way was prepared for further
expansion. A few months later, in 632, Mohammed died in the arms
of his favorite wife, Aishah, whose father succeeded him as his first
"successor" (*khalīfah*, hence caliph). Within a century, after one of
the most remarkable series of military conquests in history, Moslems
had carried the Koran into the valleys of France and the steppes of
Central Asia.

The Koran stands at the beginning of Islamic literature, but it
stands apart, pre-eminent without being dominant. All but a few of
the authors included in this anthology would have agreed that it represents divine truth as well as superlative literary style—the personal
style of God.

For Moslems the Koran is no more literature because it is scripture,
than it is scripture because it is literature. It is both scripture and
literature at the same time, in a manner absolutely unique to itself.
The classical legists formulated it in the concept of "inimitability"
(*i'jāz*), a formulation which in time found its way into several of the
Islamic creeds. The important thing, however, was not so much its
"inimitability" (its style was in fact consciously imitated by such poets
as Abu Nuwas and Al-Maarri and was even, upon occasion, criticized
by Moslems) as its singular claim, so unhesitatingly accepted by so
many persons. For them, first and foremost, the Koran is God's word.

By the same token, the literary style of the Koran has seldom engaged Moslem thinkers except in illustration of its divine nature or for ancillary purposes. For the Koran is everything to the devout Moslem: It is history, sacred and profane; it is prayer; it is a code of civil and religious law; it is a guide to conduct and meditation. "Everything is in a clear book" (11.6). When the first tortuous theological debates were over, the Koran was formally declared the "uncreated" Word of God, on a par with the divine presence itself. The non-Moslem may be captivated by its beauty, may discern its sharply characterized styles and manifold literary subtleties, but he can never fully understand or appreciate how the Koran has superintended all genuine Moslem thought and fashioned the Moslem soul.

The Opening[1]

In the name of God, the Merciful, the Compassionate

Praise be to God, the Lord of the Universe,
the Merciful, the Compassionate,
the Authority on Judgment Day.

It is You whom we worship
and You whom we ask for help.

Show us the upright way:
the way of those whom You have favored,
not of those with whom You have been angry
and those who have gone astray.

The Earthquake

In the name of God, the Merciful, the Compassionate

When the earth is shaken with its earthquake,
and the earth has brought up its burdens,
and man says, "What is happening to it?"
on that day it will tell its information,
because your Lord will have inspired it.

On that day the people will come forth
individually to be shown their deeds;
and he who does a particle of good will see it,
and he who does a particle of evil will see it.

[1] The first, or "opening," chapter of the Koran.

The Dawn

In the name of God, the Merciful, the Compassionate

Say: I take my refuge in the Lord of the dawn
from the evil in what He created,
and from the evil of the dusk when it envelops,
and from the evil of the witches who blow on knots,
and from the evil of the envier when he envies.

The People

In the name of God, the Merciful, the Compassionate

Say: I take my refuge in the Lord of the people,
the King of the people,
the God of the people,
from the evil of the furtive whisperer
who whispers in the breasts of the people,
of the genies and of the people.

The Mantled One

In the name of God, the Merciful, the Compassionate

O you enwrapped in your mantle,
rise up and warn!
Magnify your Lord!
Purify your clothing!
Shun pollution!
Do not favor in order to gain,
but be patient for your Lord.

For when the trumpet is sounded,
that day will be a difficult day,
far from easy for the unbelievers!

Leave Me with him whom I created unique,
on whom I bestowed ample wealth
and sons living in his presence,
and for whom I made everything smooth.

After that he wants Me to do more!
No!
He has been obstinate to Our revelations.
I shall impose on him a fearful doom!

The Quraysh[2]

In the name of God, the Merciful, the Compassionate

For uniting the Quraysh,
for uniting them the caravan of winter and summer.

So let them worship the Lord of this House.[3]
who fed them against hunger
and made them safe from fear.

TRANSLATED BY JAMES KRITZECK

The Night

In the Name of God, the Merciful, the Compassionate

By the night enshrouding
and the day in splendour
and That which created the male and the female,
surely your striving is to diverse ends.

As for him who gives and is godfearing
and confirms the reward most fair,
We shall surely ease him to the Easing.
But as for him who is a miser, and self-sufficient,
and cries lies to the reward most fair,
We shall surely ease him to the Hardship;
his wealth shall not avail him when he perishes.

Surely upon Us rests the guidance,
and to Us belong the Last and the First.

Now I have warned you of a Fire that flames,
whereat none but the most wretched shall be roasted,
even he who cried lies, and turned away;

[2] Mohammed's tribe.
[3] The Ka‘bah in Mecca.

and from which the most godfearing shall be removed,
even he who gives his wealth to purify himself
and confers no favour on any man for recompense,
only seeking the Face of his Lord the Most High;
and he shall surely be satisfied.

The Forenoon

In the Name of God, the Merciful, the Compassionate

By the white forenoon
and the brooding night!
Thy Lord has neither forsaken thee nor hates thee
and the Last shall be better for thee than the First.
Thy Lord shall give thee, and thou shalt be satisfied.

Did He not find thee an orphan, and shelter thee?
Did He not find thee erring, and guide thee?
Did He not find thee needy, and suffice thee?

As for the orphan, do not oppress him,
and as for the beggar, scold him not;
and as for thy Lord's blessing, declare it.

TRANSLATED BY A. J. ARBERRY

Joseph

In the Name of Allah, the Compassionate, the Merciful

Alif lam ra.[4] These are the verses of the Glorious Book. We have revealed the Koran in the Arabic tongue so that you may understand it.

In revealing this Koran We will recount to you the best of histories, though before We revealed it you were heedless of Our signs.

Joseph said to his father: "Father, I dreamt that eleven stars and the sun and the moon were prostrating themselves before me."

---

[4] Three unexplained letters of the alphabet. [Ed.]

"My son," he replied, "say nothing of this dream to your brothers, lest they should plot evil against you: Satan is the sworn enemy of man. You shall be chosen by your Lord. He will teach you to interpret visions and will perfect His favour to you and to the house of Jacob, as He perfected it to your forefathers Abraham and Isaac before you. Your Lord is wise and all-knowing."

Surely in the tale of Joseph and his brothers there are signs for doubting men.

They said to each other: "Joseph and his brother are dearer to our father than ourselves, though we are many. Truly, our father is much mistaken. Let us kill Joseph, or cast him away in some far-off land, so that we may have no rivals in our father's love, and after that be honourable men."

One of them said: "Do not kill Joseph. If you must get rid of him, cast him into a dark pit. Some caravan will take him up."

They said to their father: "Why do you not trust us with Joseph? Surely we are his friends. Send him with us tomorrow, that he may play and enjoy himself. We will take good care of him."

He replied: "It would much grieve me to let him go with you; for I fear lest the wolf should eat him when you are off your guard."

They said: "If the wolf could eat him despite our numbers, then we should surely be lost!"

And when they took Joseph with them, they decided to cast him into a dark pit. We addressed him, saying: "You shall tell them of all this when they will not know you."

At nightfall they returned weeping to their father. They said: "We went racing and left Joseph with our goods. The wolf devoured him. But you will not believe us, though we speak the truth." And they showed him their brother's shirt, stained with false blood.

"No!" he cried. "Your souls have tempted you to evil. But I will be patient: Allah alone can help me to bear the misfortune of which you speak."

And there passed by a caravan, who sent their waterman to the pit. And when he had let down his pail, he cried: "Rejoice! A boy!"

They took Joseph and concealed him among their goods. But Allah knew of what they did. They sold him for a trifling price, for a few pieces of silver. They cared nothing for him.

The Egyptian who bought him said to his wife: "Use him kindly. He may prove useful to us, or we may adopt him as our son."

Thus We found a home for Joseph, and taught him to interpret mysteries. Allah has power over all things, though most men may not know it. And when he reached maturity We bestowed on him wisdom and knowledge. Thus We reward the righteous.

His master's wife sought to seduce him. She bolted the doors and said: "Come!"

"Allah forbid!" he replied. "My lord has treated me with kindness. Wrongdoers never prosper."

She made for him, and he himself would have yielded to her had he not been shown a veritable sign by his Lord. Thus We warded off from him indecency and evil, for he was one of Our faithful servants.

He raced her to the door, but as she clung to him she tore his shirt from behind. And at the door they met her husband.

She cried: "Shall not the man who sought to violate your wife be thrown into prison or sternly punished?"

Joseph said: "It was she who sought to seduce me."

"If his shirt is torn from the front," said one of her people, "she is speaking the truth and he is lying. If it is torn from behind, then he is speaking the truth and she is lying."

And when her husband saw Joseph's shirt rent from behind, he said to her: "This is one of your tricks. Your cunning is great indeed! Joseph, say no more about this. Woman, ask pardon for your sin. You have done wrong."

In the city women were saying: "The Prince's wife has sought to seduce her servant. She has conceived a passion for him. It is clear that she has gone astray."

When she heard of their intrigues, she invited them to a banquet at her house. To each she gave a knife, and ordered Joseph to present himself before them. When they saw him, they were amazed at him and cut their hands, exclaiming: "Allah preserve us! This is no mortal, but a gracious angel."

"This is the man," she said, "on whose account you reproached me. I sought to seduce him, but he was unyielding. If he declines to do my bidding, he shall be thrown into prison and held in scorn."

"Lord," said Joseph, "sooner would I go to prison than give in to their advances. Shield me from their cunning, or I shall yield to them and lapse into folly."

His Lord heard his prayer and warded off their wiles from him. He hears all and knows all.

Yet though they were convinced of his innocence, the Egyptians thought it right to imprison him for a time.

Two young men went to prison with him. One of them said: "I dreamt that I was pressing grapes." And the other said: "I dreamt that I was carrying a loaf upon my head, and that the birds came and ate of it. Tell us the meaning of these dreams, for we can see you are a man of learning."

Joseph replied: "I can interpret them long before they are fulfilled. This knowledge my Lord has given me, for I have left the faith of those that disbelieve in Allah and deny the life to come. I follow the faith of my forefathers, Abraham, Isaac, and Jacob. We must never serve idols besides Allah. Such is the gift which Allah has bestowed upon us and all mankind. Yet most men do not give thanks.

"Fellow-prisoners! Are numerous gods better than Allah, the One, the Almighty? Those whom you serve besides Him are names which you and your fathers have invented and for which Allah has revealed no sanction. Judgement rests with Allah only. He has commanded you to worship none but Him. That is the true faith: yet most men do not know it.

"Fellow-prisoners, one of you shall serve his king with wine. The other shall be crucified, and the birds will peck at his head. That is the meaning of your dreams."

And Joseph said to the prisoner who he knew would be freed: "Remember me in the presence of your king."

But Satan made him forget to mention Joseph to his king, so that he stayed in prison for several years.

Now it so chanced that one day the king said: "I saw seven fatted cows which seven lean ones devoured; also seven green ears of corn and seven others dry. Tell me the meaning of this vision, my nobles, if you can interpret visions."

They replied: "It is but an idle dream; nor can we interpret dreams."

Thereupon the man who had been freed remembered Joseph after all those years. He said: "I shall tell you what it means. Give me leave to go."

He said to Joseph: "Tell us, man of truth, of the seven fatted cows which seven lean ones devoured; also of the seven green ears of corn and the other seven which were dry: for I would inform my masters."

Joseph replied: "You shall sow for seven consecutive years. Leave in the ear the corn you reap, except a little which you may eat. Then there shall follow seven hungry years which will consume all but little of that which you have stored for them. Then there will come a year of abundant rain, in which the people will press the grape."

The king said: "Bring this man before me."

But when the king's envoy came to him, Joseph said: "Go back to your master and ask him about the women who cut their hands. My master knows their cunning."

The king questioned the women, saying: "Why did you seek to entice Joseph?"

"Allah forbid!" they replied. "We know no evil of him."

"Now the truth must come to light," said the Prince's wife. "It was I who sought to seduce him. He has spoken the truth."

"From this," said Joseph, "my lord will know that I did not betray him in his absence, and that Allah does not guide the work of the treacherous. Not that I am free from sin: man's soul is prone to evil, except his to whom Allah has shown mercy. My Lord is forgiving and merciful."

The king said: "Bring him before me. I will make him my personal servant."

And when he had spoken with him, the king said: "You shall henceforth dwell with us, honoured and trusted."

Joseph said: "Give me charge of the granaries of the realm. I shall husband them wisely."

Thus We gave power to Joseph, and he dwelt at his ease in that land. We bestow Our mercy on whom We will, and never deny the righteous their reward. Better is the reward of the life to come for those who believe in Allah and keep from evil.

Joseph's brothers came and presented themselves before him. He recognized them, but they did not. And when he had given them their provisions, he said: "Bring me your other brother from your father. Do you not see that I give just measure and am the best of hosts? If you do not bring him, you shall have no corn, nor shall you come near me again."

They replied: "We will request his father to let him come with us. This we will surely do."

Joseph said to his servants: "Put their money into their packs, so that they may find it when they return to their people. Perchance they will come back."

When they returned to their father, they said: "Father, corn is henceforth denied us. Send our brother with us and we shall have our measure. We will take good care of him."

He replied: "Am I to trust you with him as I once trusted you with his brother? But Allah is the best of guardians: He is most merciful."

When they opened their packs, they found that their money had been returned to them. "Father," they said, "what more can we desire? Here is our money untouched. We will buy provisions for our people and take good care of our brother. We shall receive an extra camel-load; that should not be hard to get."

He replied: "I shall not let him go with you until you swear in Allah's name to bring him back to me, unless you are prevented."

And when they had given him their pledge, he said: "Allah is the witness of your oath. My sons, enter the town by different gates. If you do wrong, I cannot ward off from you the wrath of Allah: judgement is His alone. In Him I have put my trust. In Him alone let the faithful put their trust."

And when they entered as their father had advised them, his counsel availed them nothing against the decree of Allah. It was but a wish in Jacob's soul which he had thus fulfilled. He was possessed of knowledge which We had given him, though most men were unaware of it.

When they presented themselves before him, Joseph embraced his brother, and said: "I am your brother. Do not grieve at what they did."

And when he had given them their provisions, he hid a drinking-cup in his brother's pack.

Then a crier called out after them: "Travellers, you are thieves!"

They turned back and asked: "What have you lost?"

"The king's drinking-cup," he replied. "He that restores it shall have a camel-load of corn. I pledge my word for it."

"By Allah," they cried, "you know we did not come to do evil in this land. We are no thieves."

The Egyptians said: "What penalty shall we inflict on him that stole it, if you prove to be lying?"

They replied: "He in whose pack the cup is found shall be your bondsman. Thus we punish the wrongdoers."

Joseph searched their bags before his brother's, and then took out the cup from his brother's bag.

Thus We directed Joseph. By the king's law he had no right to seize his brother: but Allah willed otherwise. We exalt in knowledge whom We will: but above those that have knowledge there is One more knowing.

They said: "If he has stolen—know then that a brother of his has committed a theft before him."[5]

But Joseph kept his secret and did not reveal it to them. He thought: "Your crime was worse. Allah well knows that you are lying."

They said: "Noble prince, this boy has an aged father. Take one of us, instead of him. We can see you are a generous man."

He replied: "Allah forbid that we should seize any but the man with whom our property was found: for then we should be unjust."

When they despaired of him, they went aside to confer together. The eldest said: "Have you forgotten that you gave your father a solemn pledge, and that you broke your faith before this concerning Joseph? I shall not stir from this land until my father gives me leave or Allah makes known to me His judgement: He is the best of judges. Return to your father and say to him: 'Your son has committed a theft. We testify only to what we know. How could we guard against the unforeseen? Ask the townsfolk with whom we stayed and the caravan in which we travelled. We speak the truth.'"

"No!" cried their father. "Your souls have tempted you to evil. But I will be patient. Allah may bring them all to me. He alone is wise and all-knowing." And he turned away from them, crying: "Alas for Joseph!" His eyes went blind with grief and he was oppressed with silent sorrow.

His sons exclaimed: "By Allah, will you not cease to think of Joseph until you ruin your health and die?"

He replied: "I complain to Allah of my sorrow and sadness. He has made known to me things beyond your knowledge. Go, my sons, and seek news of Joseph and his brother. Do not despair of Allah's spirit; none but unbelievers despair of His spirit."

And when they presented themselves before Joseph, they said: "Noble prince, we and our people are scourged with famine. We have brought but little money. Give us some corn, and be charitable to us: Allah rewards the charitable."

"Do you know," he replied, "what you did to Joseph and his brother in your ignorance?"

They cried: "Can you indeed be Joseph?"

"I am Joseph," he answered, "and this is my brother. Allah has been

---

[5] Commentators say that Joseph had stolen an idol of his maternal grandfather's and broken it, so that he might not worship it.

gracious to us. Those that keep from evil and endure with fortitude, Allah will not deny them their reward."

"By the Lord," they said, "Allah has exalted you above us all. We have indeed been sinners."

He replied: "None shall reproach you this day. May Allah forgive you: He is most merciful. Take this shirt of mine and throw it over my father's face: he will recover his sight. Then return to me with all your people."

When the caravan departed their father said: "I feel the breath of Joseph, though you will not believe me."

"By Allah," said those who heard him, "this is but your old illusion."

And when the bearer of good news arrived, he threw Joseph's shirt over the old man's face, and his sight came back to him. He said: "Did I not tell you that Allah has made known to me things beyond your knowledge?"

His sons said: "Father, implore forgiveness for our sins. We have indeed been sinners."

He replied: "I shall implore my Lord to forgive you. He is forgiving and merciful."

And when they presented themselves before Joseph, he embraced his parents and said: "Welcome to Egypt, safe, if Allah wills!"

He helped his parents to a couch, and they all fell on their knees and prostrated themselves before him.

"This," said Joseph to his father, "is the meaning of my old vision: my Lord has fulfilled it. He has been gracious to me. He has released me from prison and brought you out of the desert after Satan had stirred up strife between me and my brothers. My Lord is gracious to whom He will. He alone is wise and all-knowing.

"Lord, You have given me power and taught me to interpret mysteries. You are the Creator of the heavens and the earth, my Guardian in this world and in the next. Let me die in submission and join the righteous."

That which We have now revealed to you is secret history. You were not present when Joseph's brothers conceived their plans and schemed against him. Yet strive as you may, most men will not believe.

You shall demand of them no recompense for this. It is an admonition to all mankind.

Many are the marvels of the heavens and the earth; yet they pass them by and pay no heed to them. The greater part of them believe in Allah only if they can worship other gods besides Him.

Are they confident that Allah's scourge will not fall upon them, or that the Hour of Doom will not overtake them unawares, without warning?

Say: "This is my path. With sure knowledge I call on you to have faith in Allah, I and all my followers. Glory be to Him! I am no idolater."

Nor were the apostles whom We sent before you other than mortals inspired by Our will and chosen from among their people.

Have they not travelled in the land and seen what was the end of those who disbelieved before them? Better is the world to come for those that keep from evil. Can you not understand?

And when at length Our apostles despaired and thought that none would believe in them, Our help came down to them, delivering whom We pleased. The evil-doers did not escape Our scourge. Their history is a lesson to men of understanding.

This is no invented tale, but a confirmation of previous scriptures, an explanation of all things, a guide and a blessing to true believers.

TRANSLATED BY N. J. DAWOOD

Repentance[1]

The Jews say, "Ezra is the Son of God";
the Christians say, "The Messiah is the Son of God."
That is the utterance of their mouths, conforming
with the unbelievers before them. God assail them!
How they are perverted!
They have taken their rabbis and their monks as lords
apart from God, and the Messiah, Mary's son—
and they were commanded to serve but One God;
there is no god but He; glory be to Him, above
that they associate—
desiring to extinguish with their mouths God's light;
and God refuses but to perfect His light, though
the unbelievers be averse.
It is He who has sent His Messenger with
the guidance and the religion of truth, that
He may uplift it above every religion, though
the unbelievers be averse.

O believers, many of the rabbis and monks indeed
consume the goods of the people in vanity
and bar from God's way. Those who treasure up
gold and silver, and do not expend them in
the way of God—give them the good tidings of
a painful chastisement,
the day they shall be heated in the fire of Gehenna
and therewith their foreheads and their sides and their
backs shall be branded: "This is the thing you have
treasured up for yourselves; therefore taste you now
what you were treasuring!"

[1] Although this is but an excerpt from the chapter, it should be noted that, uniquely, it does not begin with the invocation "In the name of God, the Merciful, the Compassionate." [Ed.]

The number of the months, with God, is twelve
in the Book of God, the day that He created
the heavens and the earth; four of them are sacred.
That is the right religion. So wrong not each other
during them. And fight the unbelievers totally
even as they fight you totally; and know that God
      is with the godfearing.
The month postponed is an increase of unbelief
whereby the unbelievers go astray; one year they make it
profane, and hallow it another, to agree with
the number that God has hallowed, and so profane
what God has hallowed. Decked out fair to them
are their evil deeds; and God guides not the people
      of the unbelievers.

O believers, what is amiss with you, that when
it is said to you, "Go forth in the way of God,"
you sink down heavily to the ground? Are you
so content with this present life, rather than
the world to come? Yet the enjoyment of this
present life, compared with the world to come,
      is a little thing.
If you go not forth, He will chastise you
with a painful chastisement, and instead of you
He will substitute another people; and you
will not hurt Him anything, for God is powerful
      over everything.

TRANSLATED BY A. J. ARBERRY

The Table

In the Name of Allah, the Compassionate, the Merciful

Believers, be true to your obligations. It is lawful for you to eat the flesh of all beasts other than that which is hereby announced to you. Game is forbidden while you are on pilgrimage. Allah decrees what He will.

Believers, do not violate the rites of Allah, or the sacred month, or the offerings or their ornaments, or those that repair to the Sacred House seeking Allah's grace and pleasure. Once your pilgrimage is ended, you shall be free to go hunting.

Do not allow your hatred for those who would debar you from the Holy Mosque to lead you into sin. Help one another in what is good and pious, not in what is wicked and sinful. Have fear of Allah, for He is stern in retribution.

You are forbidden the flesh of animals that die a natural death, blood, and pig's meat; also any flesh dedicated to any other than Allah. You are forbidden the flesh of strangled animals and of those beaten or gored to death; of those killed by a fall or mangled by beasts of prey (unless you make it clean by giving the death-stroke yourselves); also of animals sacrificed to idols.

You are forbidden to settle disputes by consulting the Arrows. That is a vicious practice.

The unbelievers have this day abandoned all hope of vanquishing your religion. Have no fear of them: fear Me.

This day I have perfected your religion for you and completed My favour to you. I have chosen Islam to be your faith.

He that is constrained by hunger to eat of what is forbidden, not intending to commit sin, will find Allah forgiving and merciful.

They ask you what is lawful to them. Say: "All good things are lawful to you, as well as that which you have taught the birds and beasts of prey to catch, training them as Allah has taught you. Eat of what they catch for you, pronouncing upon it the name of Allah. And have fear of Allah: swift is Allah's reckoning."

All good things have this day been made lawful to you. The food of those to whom the Scriptures were given[2] is lawful to you, and yours to them.

Lawful to you are the believing women and the free women from among those who were given the Scriptures before you, provided that you give them their dowries and live in honour with them, neither committing fornication nor taking them as mistresses.

He that denies the faith shall gain nothing from his labours. In the world to come he shall have much to lose.

Believers, when you rise to pray wash your faces and your hands as far as the elbow, and wipe your heads and your feet to the ankle. If you are polluted cleanse yourselves. But if you are sick or travelling the road; or if, when you have just relieved yourselves or had intercourse with women, you can find no water, take some clean sand and rub your hands and faces

[2] The Jews (but not the Christians).

with it. Allah does not wish to burden you; He seeks only to purify you and to perfect His favour to you, so that you may give thanks.

Remember the favours which Allah has bestowed upon you, and the covenant with which He bound you when you said: "We hear and obey." Have fear of Allah. He knows your inmost thoughts.

Believers, fulfil your duties to Allah and bear true witness. Do not allow your hatred for other men to turn you away from justice. Deal justly; justice is nearer to true piety. Have fear of Allah; He is cognizant of all your actions.

Allah has promised those that have faith and do good works forgiveness and a rich reward. As for those who disbelieve and deny Our revelations, they shall become the heirs of Hell.

Believers, remember the favour which Allah bestowed upon you when He restrained the hands of those who sought to harm you. Have fear of Allah. In Allah let the faithful put their trust.

Allah made a covenant with the Israelites and raised among them twelve chieftains. He said: "I shall be with you. If you attend to your prayers and pay the alms-tax; if you believe in My apostles and assist them and give Allah a generous loan, I shall forgive you your sins and admit you to gardens watered by running streams. But he that hereafter denies Me shall stray from the right path."

But because they broke their covenant We laid on them Our curse and hardened their hearts. They have perverted the words of the Scriptures and forgotten much of what they were enjoined. You will ever find them deceitful, except for a few of them. But pardon them and bear with them. Allah loves the righteous.

With those who said they were Christians We made a covenant also, but they too have forgotten much of what they were enjoined. Therefore We stirred among them enmity and hatred, which shall endure till the Day of Resurrection, when Allah will declare to them all that they have done.

People of the Book! Our apostle has come to reveal to you much of what you have hidden of the Scriptures, and to forgive you much. A light has come to you from Allah and a glorious Book, with which He will guide to the paths of peace those that seek to please Him; He will lead them by His will from darkness to the light; He will guide them to a straight path.

Unbelievers are those who declare: "Allah is the Messiah, the son of Mary." Say: "Who could prevent Allah from destroying the Messiah, the son of Mary, together with his mother and all the people of the earth? His is the kingdom of the heavens and the earth and all that lies between them. He creates what He will and has power over all things."

The Jews and the Christians say: "We are the children of Allah and His loved ones." Say: "Why then does He punish you for your sins? Surely you are mortals of His own creation. He forgives whom He will and punishes whom He pleases. His is the kingdom of the heavens and the earth and all that lies between them. All shall return to Him."

Followers of the Scriptures! Our apostle has come to reveal to you Our will after an interval during which there were no apostles, lest you should say: "No one has come to give us good news or to warn us." Now a prophet has come to give you good news and to warn you. Allah has power over all things.

Bear in mind the words of Moses to his people. He said: "Remember, my people, the favours which Allah has bestowed upon you. He has raised up prophets among you, made you kings, and given you that which He has given to no other nation. Enter, my people, the holy land which Allah has assigned for you. Do not turn back, or you shall be ruined."

"Moses," they replied, "a race of giants dwell in this land. We will not set foot in it till they are gone. Only then shall we enter."

Thereupon two God-fearing men whom Allah had favoured, said: "Go in to them through the gates, and when you have entered you shall surely be victorious. In Allah put your trust, if you are true believers."

But they replied: "Moses, we will not go in so long as *they* are in it. Go, you and your Lord, and fight. We will stay here."

"Lord," cried Moses, "I have none but myself and my brother. Do not confound us with these wicked people."

He replied: "They shall be forbidden this land for forty years, during which time they shall wander homeless in the earth. Do not grieve for these wicked people."

Recount to them in all truth the story of Adam's two sons: how they each made an offering, and how the offering of the one was accepted while that of the other was not. Cain said: "I will surely kill you." His brother replied: "Allah accepts offerings only from the righteous. If you stretch your hand to kill me, I shall not lift mine to slay you; for I fear Allah, the Lord of the Creation. I would rather you should add your sin against me to your other sins and thus incur the punishment of Hell. Such is the reward of the wicked."

Cain's soul prompted him to slay his brother; he killed him and thus became one of the lost. Then Allah sent down a raven, which dug the earth to show him how to bury the naked corpse of his brother. "Alas!" he cried. "Have I not strength enough to do as this raven has done and so bury my brother's naked corpse?" And he became repentant.

That was why We laid it down for the Israelites that whoever killed a human being, except as a punishment for murder or other wicked crimes, should be looked upon as though he had killed all mankind; and that whoever saved a human life should be regarded as though he had saved all mankind.

Our apostles brought them veritable proofs: yet it was not long before many of them committed great evils in the land.

Those that make war against Allah and His apostle and spread disorders in the land shall be put to death or crucified or have their hands and feet cut off on alternate sides, or be banished from the country. They shall be held to shame in this world and sternly punished in the next: except those that repent before you reduce them. For you must know that Allah is forgiving and merciful.

Believers, have fear of Allah and seek the right path to Him. Fight valiantly for His cause, so that you may triumph.

TRANSLATED BY N. J. DAWOOD

There is quite a large body of poetry in Arabic which is attributed to authors, known or anonymous, of the century or so before Islam. We possess no texts of this poetry antedating the Islamic period; most of the poems were written down for the first time in anthologies compiled in the eighth and ninth centuries.

In 1925, Taha Husayn, who was to become a prominent figure in modern Arabic literature and whose work will be represented in the sequel to this anthology, published a book entitled *Fī al-Shiᶜr al-Jāhilī* (Concerning Pre-Islamic Poetry), whose thesis was so astounding and downright offensive to Arab sentiment that it was promptly withdrawn from the market. Even in its revised form, published two years later, that thesis lost little of its bite.

"I have reached the conclusion," Husayn wrote, "that the general mass of what we call pre-Islamic literature has nothing whatever to do with the pre-Islamic period, but was just simply fabricated after the coming of Islam. It is therefore Islamic, and represents the life, the inclination, the desires of Muslims, rather than the life of the pre-Islamic Arabs. I now have hardly any doubt at all that what has survived of genuine pre-Islamic literature is very little indeed, representative of nothing and indicative of nothing. No reliance is to be placed in it for the purpose of elucidating the genuine literary picture of the pre-Islamic age."

European scholars had long expressed doubts about the authenticity of much of the pre-Islamic poetry, but the extreme statement of this thesis and the ensuing controversy remain linked to the name of Taha Husayn. To understand the outrage the thesis provoked, it is necessary, first of all, to realize that the body of poetry alleged to be pre-Islamic was not only accepted as authentic from the very start but was also regarded as the supreme canon and model of poetic excellence. To be sure, it was defied, assailed, and sometimes ridiculed in succeeding centuries, but its basic authenticity was not called into question.

The controversy is still far from closed, but the effect of more recent research has been to uphold the authenticity of much of the poetry as pre-Islamic, while recognizing that it was sometimes highly edited, supplemented, and even altered by its early editors (who were, incidentally, mainly philologists).[1]

On the surface, this poetry appears to express and to exalt that way of life and system of thought of the Arabs against which Islam fought. It extols the tribal virtues of revenge, fidelity to inherited feuds, and bravery in raids. Especially in the longer, highly developed, and much beloved form of the *qaṣīdah*, or ode, on the other hand, the subjects were tamer: recollections of love affairs (so to dignify them), descriptions of scenery and animals, and accounts of hunting exploits and other sports.

However wild the content might occasionally be, the form of the pre-Islamic poetry exhibits a complexity which is at first startling and easily convinces one that the poetic art had long been practiced and perfected among the Arabs. The meters and conventional sequences of the *qaṣīdah*, for instance, were exceedingly demanding, and even the shorter poems were stylistically very sophisticated.[2]

Recognized to be the greatest masterpieces of this poetry were the seven odes known as the *Muᶜallaqāt*, "the suspended ones," so titled, according to the traditional and suspect account, because they were the winners in an annual poetry competition, written in letters of gold, and suspended for all to read. Recently, scholars have found better etymologies for the term. The poets of the *Muᶜallaqāt* are Amru al-Qays, Tarafah, Zuhayr, Labid, Antarah, Amr, and Al-Harith.

The three translations from the *Muᶜallaqāt* which follow represent three very different dealings with their texts. The first is a free paraphrase by modern poets; the second is a literal translation by an

[1] For a fuller discussion of this controversy, see A. J. Arberry, *The Seven Odes* (London, 1957), pp. 228–254.
[2] The meters are described in detail by C. J. Lyall in *Translations of Ancient Arabian Poetry* (New York, 1930), pp. xlv–lii.

Arabist done more than a century ago; and the third is a translation
by a contemporary Arabist who has shown uncommon skill in the
translation of Islamic poetry.

The Ode of Amru al-Qays

> Beyond that reef of sand, recalling a house
> And a lady, dismount where the winds cross
> Cleaning the still extant traces of colony between
> Four famous dunes. Like pepper-seeds in the distance
> The dung of white stags in courtyards and cisterns,
> Resin blew, hard on the eyes, one morning
> Beside the acacia watching the camels going.
> And now, for all remonstrance and talk of patience
> I will grieve, somewhere in this comfortless ruin
> And make a place and my peace with the past.
>
> There were good days with the clover-smelling wenches.
> Best by the pool when I caught a clan drenching.
> I brought them in file to beg their things back,
> Playing for one that hung back; and paid them,
> All but her, with fat like tassels of satin,
> Chops from the fast camel I slaughtered. But her
> I forced to ride in a topheavy howdah,
> Tilting along with me by her, her tattling
> Of illegal burdening of beasts, and I tickling
> Her senses, and dropping the reins, and cropping the quinces.
>
> And sweet as her were the more complex raps
> At pregnant wives and mothers giving pap.
> An infant would scream, a woman half turning
> Roll an eyeball in a lolling head.
> There were jilts on spines of sand, a coquette
> Who carved my heart in brow-beating range,
> And no sauce of tears, till I disengaged
> The clung tissue. There was the pure ovoid
> In boudoir and ward and a watched ring.
> I went in at leisure and kept her happy.
>
> I passed the assassins and found the Pleiades.
> They surfaced round her with sash and beads.

She from her screen and chill gauze of shift
Turned and turned a phrase of bawdy men.
But we skirted the yards, she twitched her train
To a tail switching the sand on the tell-tale trace.
And under a whorl of crested dunes I pressed
Her temples back with her ankles and slender
Waist and shearings of flame for breast and sift
Of yolk for skin, a flamingo fledgling from the seas.

On account of laden trees I lost my friends,
Took their rebukes against beds with chips of incense,
Their cold looks for arms of eucalyptus
And snake fingers, meaning social intercourse
Such as I changed for other. Was not seduced
The eyeless way to totem bands. But pain
Came with a night like seawaves, a brine curtain
That moored its sting of stars on mountain masses.
Night lay long, I longed for it rising, it rose
With denser dawn between the thighs untensing.

I strapped a pouch, I walked where times of fire
Had gorged the passes. The wolf like a player
Was roaring the packs his losses. I answered:
"Our trades line no pockets. You and the lover
Thriftlessly eat what you win. We are leaner
By this ploughing." Next day the birds shut still in
The hills I rode early a roan stallion,
A new thing, a flux dancer,
After my cracked vases a crucible of the air.

The herds ripped away like cowries. I whipped
With my hands this turning top. We outstripped
The first riders and lunged at the buffalo
And the ruffled mates. Clashed till henna flecks
Of their blood, but no tired ooze, dashed his neck.
The cooks were busy that night jointing and broiling.
I sat watching his limbs as sleek as rollers
Of bridal oil. He stayed in my eyes, decked out
All night in his trappings, not sent away,
And webbed with decent tail his stride and dip.

My stretched arm burns in a flash, between shoals
Of crowned cloud, that lean on both flanks of the hills.

Rain pours on Katheitha, kisses the big trees
On Kanahbil, seizes the uplands of Qanan
Chasing the ibex, erasing the less than stone.
Only the major peaks, the bare spindles
Cap the deluge. Till dawn, and dwindling
It leaves tendrils like gay wares of Yemen
In sands where, drunk at the rim of vallies,
The thrushes tell the sun spiced folly.

Till evening, and far-off like sprigs of wild onion
The drowsy leopards at the limit of the vallies.

TRANSLATED BY HERBERT HOWARTH AND IBRAHIM SHUKRALLAH

The Ode of Labid

Sites of dwellings are these, over which, since they were last inhabited, many a long year has passed with its full tale of sacred and profane months.

They have been gifted with the showers of the constellations of spring, and the rains of the thunderclouds have fallen on them in torrents and in drizzle;
rains from every cloud of the night, and morning cloud that covers the sky, and evening cloud whose thunderpeals answer one another.

And so the shoots of the wild rocket have sprung up over them, and the gazelle and the ostrich have their young on the two sides of the valley;
and the antelopes lie quietly by their young, to which they have newly given birth, while their fawns roam in flocks over the plain.

And the torrents have newly laid bare the marks of the tents, as if they were lines of writing whose text the pens retrace;
or the lines which a woman tattooing traces afresh, rubbing in her lamp-black in circles, on which her pattern reappears.

And so I stood there questioning them—but why should we question the hard and lasting stones that have no clear speech to answer with?
They are tenantless, and yet the whole tribe was once here; but they set out from them at dawn, and nought was left but the trench and the thatch.
The women of the tribe filled thee with longing when they set out and entered within the cotton curtains, the framework whereof creaked;

litters all hung round, the woodwork of which is covered with a coarse
cloth, over which are fine curtains and embroiderys;

(those women) in bands, as if the deer of Tudih were on the litters and
the gazelles of Wajra, with their fawns lying around them.

They were started, and the mirage fell away from them as if they were
tamarisks or huge rocks at the place where the valley of Bisha opens out.

Does my camel resemble such a wild ass, or is she like an antelope that
has lost her calf by the wild beasts and loitered behind the herd, though the
leader of the herd is its chief stay; (*or,* that has left her calf and the leader of
the herd is her chief stay)

a flat-nosed antelope that has lost her fawn, and she quits not the sides
of the strips of pasture, wandering about or crying

for a white weanling, whose limbs have been rent by the ash-gray hunters
whose food is never lacking;

they found her off her guard and they killed it—verily the arrows of fate
do not miss the mark!

Night comes on her, and a drizzling rain descends steadily, drenching the
shrubs with its ceaseless downpour.

She makes her lair in the hollow trunk of a tree with high branches, standing apart on the skirts of the sandhills, whose fine sands are ever on the move.

The ceaseless rain reaches the stripe on her back in a night whose clouds
hide away the stars;

and she shines bright in the face of the darkness like a pearl from a sea-
shell that has dropped from its string;

until when the darkness rolls away and the morning dawns on her, she
comes forth with her legs slipping the mud.

She becomes distracted and wanders about the pools of Soʿaïd, for seven
nights coupled with seven whole long days;

until, when she lost all hope, the udder dried up, which all her suckling
and weaning had not drained;

and she heard the sound of man from a place of concealment, and it startled
her, for man is her bane.

And so she ran off, thinking that each of the two openings—what lay behind her and in front of her—was alike to be dreaded;

until, when the archers lost hope, they let loose trained dogs with hanging ears, and stiff collars on their necks.

And they overtook her, and she turned upon them with those horns of hers, like the spears of Semhar in sharpness and length,

to keep them off, for well she knew, if she did not keep them off, that her death was at hand among those decreed by fate.

And of them Wolf was run through and killed and drenched in blood, and Blackie was left in the place of his onset.

With such a camel then, when the glittering sands dance in the noonday and their hillocks put on the robes of the mirage,

I will accomplish my desire—not falling short of it through doubt or because revilers revile me for any desire of mine.

TRANSLATED BY WILLIAM WRIGHT

The Ode of Tarafah

A young gazelle there is in the tribe, dark-lipped, fruit-shaking,
flaunting a double necklace of pearls and topazes,
holding aloof, with the herd grazing in the lush thicket,
nibbling the tips of the arak-fruit, wrapped in her cloak.
Her dark lips part in a smile, teeth like a camomile
on a moist hillock shining amid the virgin sands,
whitened as it were by the sun's rays, all but her gums
that are smeared with collyrium — she gnaws not against them;
a face as though the sun had loosed his mantle upon it,
pure of hue, with not a wrinkle to mar it.

Ah, but when grief assails me, straightway I ride it off
mounted on my swift, lean-flanked camel, night and day racing,
sure-footed, like the planks of a litter; I urge her on
down the bright highway, that back of a striped mantle;
she vies with the noble, hot-paced she-camels, shank on shank
nimbly plying, over a path many feet have beaten.
Along the rough slopes with the milkless shes she has pastured
in Spring, cropping the rich meadows green in the gentle rains;
to the voice of the caller she returns, and stands on guard
with her bunchy tail, scared of some ruddy, tuft-haired stallion,
as though the wings of a white vulture enfolded the sides
of her tail, pierced even to the bone by a pricking awl;

anon she strikes with it behind the rear-rider, anon
lashes her dry udders, withered like an old water-skin.
Perfectly firm is the flesh of her two thighs—
they are the gates of a lofty, smooth-walled castle—
and tightly knit are her spine-bones, the ribs like bows,
her underneck stuck with the well-strung vertebrae,
fenced about by the twin dens of a wild lote-tree;
you might say bows were bent under a buttressed spine.
Widely spaced are her elbows, as if she strode
carrying the two buckets of a sturdy water-carrier;
like the bridge of the Byzantine, whose builder swore
it should be all encased in bricks to be raised up true.
Reddish the bristles under her chin, very firm her back,
broad the span of her swift legs, smooth her swinging gait;
her legs are twined like rope uptwisted; her forearms
thrust slantwise up to the propped roof of her breast.
Swiftly she rolls, her cranium huge, her shoulder-blades
high-hoisted to frame her lofty, raised superstructure.
The scores of her girths chafing her breast-ribs are water-
            courses
furrowing a smooth rock in a rugged eminence,
now meeting, anon parting, as though they were
white gores marking distinctly a slit shirt.
Her long neck is very erect when she lifts it up
calling to mind the rudder of a Tigris-bound vessel.
Her skull is most like an anvil, the junction of its two halves
meeting together as it might be on the edge of a file.
Her cheek is smooth as Syrian parchment, her split lip
a tanned hide of Yemen, its slit not bent crooked;
her eyes are a pair of mirrors, sheltering
in the caves of her brow-bones, the rock of a pool's hollow,
ever expelling the white pus mote-provoked, so they seem
like the dark-rimmed eyes of a scared wild-cow with calf.
Her ears are true, clearly detecting on the night journey
the fearful rustle of a whisper, the high-pitched cry,
sharp-tipped, her noble pedigree plain in them,
pricked like the ears of a wild-cow of Haumal lone-pasturing.
Her trepid heart pulses strongly, quick, yet firm
as a pounding-rock set in the midst of a solid boulder.
If you so wish, her head strains to the saddle's pommel
and she swims with her forearms, fleet as a male ostrich,

or if you wish her pace is slack, or swift to your fancy,
fearing the curled whip fashioned of twisted hide.
Slit is her upper lip, her nose bored and sensitive,
delicate; when she sweeps the ground with it, faster she runs.

Such is the beast I ride, when my companion cries
"Would I might ransom you, and be ransomed, from yonder
            waste!"
His soul flutters within him fearfully, he supposing
the blow fallen on him, though his path is no ambuscade.
When the people demand, "Who's the hero?" I suppose
myself intended, and am not sluggish, not dull of wit;
I am at her with the whip, and my she-camel quickens pace
what time the mirage of the burning stone-tract shimmers;
elegantly she steps, as a slave-girl at a party
will sway, showing her master skirts of a trailing white gown.
I am not one that skulks fearfully among the hilltops,
but when the folk seek my succour I gladly give it;
if you look for me in the circle of the folk you'll find me there,
and if you hunt me in the taverns there you'll catch me.
Come to me when you will, I'll pour you a flowing cup,
and if you don't need it, well, do without and good luck to
            you!
Whenever the tribe is assembled you'll come upon me
at the summit of the noble House, the oft-frequented;
my boon-companions are white as stars, and a singing-wench
comes to us in her striped gown or her saffron robe,
wide the opening of her collar, delicate her skin
to my companions' fingers, tender her nakedness.
When we say, "Let's hear from you," she advances to us
chanting fluently, her glance languid, in effortless song.

TRANSLATED BY A. J. ARBERRY

Poems from Early Anthologies

My love is ascending with the Yemen caravan
My body is in Mecca in chains.

But once she came eddying towards me
The bars were fast but she came
Came and gave me greeting, and rose
And turned and pivoted my life that way

My head is bent not for death or anything.
I am not tired of the gyves, my soul
Is immune from the loud promises

Only a longing for the days has disarmed me
The days when we met and I was free.

You are lost if the riddle approaches.
If it turns its back you guess it.
You see that you see no matter right
Unless you methodically reverse it.
To the lamp of noon night fetches
The obscure vehicle of its light.

TRANSLATED BY HERBERT HOWARTH AND IBRAHIM SHUKRALLAH

Abu al-Ata al-Sindi

I dreamt of you
as tawny spears
between us shook
with our twin bloods
spilling on the toasted sand.

By God, I do not know
the cause of that:
it must be either love or magic.

Supposing it is magic,
let us suppose that it is love;

and if not magic,
then, of course,
it is no fault of yours.

TRANSLATED BY JAMES KRITZECK

Malik Ibn al-Rayb

I thought who would weep for me, and none did I find to mourn
    but only my sword, my spear, the best of Rudainah's store,
And one friend, a sorrel steed, who goes forth with trailing rein
    to drink at the pool, since Death has left none to draw for him.

Yazid Ibn al-Khadhdhaq

I lie as though Time had shot my shape with darts unawares,
    winged sure to pierce me, unfeathered, sent from no bow-string.
What man can hope for a guard against the Daughters of Time?
    What spells avail to defeat the fated onset of Doom?
They closed my eyes — but it was not sleep that held them from sight:
    one who stood by—"He's gone, the son of al-Khadhdhaq!"
They combed my hair—but it was not because it hung unkempt,
    and then they clad me in clothes that bore no signs of wear.
They sprayed sweet odours on me, and said—"How goodly a man!"
    then wrapped my form in a white sheet closely folded around:
And then they sent of their best, young men of gentle descent,
    to lay my limbs in a grave dug deep out there in the dust.
Grieve not for me overmuch: let sorrow pass as it will:
    the wealth I left shall rejoice—why not?—the heart of my heir.

Rabiah Ibn Sufyan

I slew in my requital for Thaᶜlabah son of al-Khushām
    ᶜAmr son of ᶜAuf;
    and an end was thus put to distress of mind:
    Blood for blood—
    wiped out were the wounds;
and those who had gained a start in the race profited not by their advantage.

TRANSLATED BY C. J. LYALL

PROVERBS

Today, as throughout the centuries, proverbs come easily to the tongues of most Islamic peoples—more easily, it would seem, than to those of other peoples. In one small Lebanese village recently, a scholar recorded more than four thousand of them. Proverbs are very much on the surface of Islamic life and speech, but they are also deeply imbedded in Islamic literature. Some mention of them deserves to be made outside the historical framework of the anthology.[1]

During the last two centuries, in connection with the development of linguistic and ethnological sciences, scholars were more interested in proverbs than they are today. Many collections *de luxe* were printed, and there were even professors of proverbs in universities. If that interest was somewhat too exaggerated to last, at least it recognized and pointed up the fact that proverbs are noteworthy in any study of the history of old literatures.

Proverbs are sayings which are usually brief, concise, witty, and sage and which possess some element of style such as rhyme, alliteration, simile, metaphor, or simple wordplay. They are closely connected with the development of one of the oldest literary forms, the didactic story or fable. Most fables end with morals expressed in the form of proverbs, and all imply them. Which came first, the proverb or the fable, is often impossible to know. However, the literary value of fables in some of the early collections like Aesop's or Bidpai's was already very considerable. These fables indicate an age-old process of formation by oral repetition during which persons of talent improved upon them. Thus they emerge in their early written forms as quite polished productions. An example, "The Monkey and

[1] For more information on the role of proverbs in Islamic literature, see Anis Frayha, *Modern Lebanese Proverbs* (Beirut, 1953), pp. ix–xx; and Edward Westermarck, *Wit and Wisdom in Morocco* (New York, 1931), pp. 1–63.

the Tortoise," from Ibn al-Muqaffa's revised translation of Bidpai, is included in the next section.

Particularly among the Arabs, as we shall see, a very similar process was in the background of far lengthier and more sophisticated literary productions. Within the stream of folk literature, from which formal literature derived constant nourishment, the process went on and continues to go on. In the Islamic world you cannot escape the latest funny story about the Khoja, and you are virtually inundated by proverbs.

Moroccan Proverbs

The pumpkin gives birth and the fence has the trouble.
> A stone from the hand of a friend is an apple.

The tar of my country is better than the honey of others.
> If you are a peg, endure the knocking; if you are a mallet, strike.

Only its master stays in the grave.
> Salt will never be worm-eaten.

The falcon does not struggle when he is caught.
> Among walnuts only the empty one speaks.

The world has not promised anything to anybody.
> An old cat will not learn how to dance.

TRANSLATED BY EDWARD WESTERMARCK

Lebanese Proverbs

The son of a midwife knows everything.
> Lower your voice and strengthen your argument.

He who has money can eat sherbet in hell.
> If life is hard on you, dwell in cities.

He makes a wine cellar from one raisin.
> We traded in shrouds; people stopped dying.

His secret is at the tip of his tongue.
> Lock your door rather than accuse your neighbour.

The bride is a frog, but the wedding a cyclone.
> His brains hang at the top of his fez.

TRANSLATED BY ANIS FRAYHA

Persian Proverbs

The drowning man is not troubled by rain.
  No lamp burns till morning.
Walls have mice and mice have ears.
  Trust in God, but tie your camel.
A thief is a king till he's caught.
  What is brought by the wind will be carried away by the wind.
The doctor must heal his own bald head.
  He gives a party with bath-water.
You can't pick up two melons with one hand.
  At night a cotton-seed is the same as a pearl.

TRANSLATED BY L. P. ELWELL-SUTTON

THE AGE OF THE CALIPHS [632–1050]

HISTORICAL SUMMARY

Mohammed's sudden death in 632 created a crisis of the most serious order for his small state. He left no son and, it would appear, had made no definite plans for his succession. Within a matter of hours after his death, however, Islam had invented the religio-political office of the caliphate, which for more than six centuries remained the actual or at least the theoretical basis for its unity as a state. The first caliph was Abu Bakr, one of Mohammed's fathers-in-law. The problems of ruling the young community, difficult enough to start with, were immediately complicated by apostasy and attack. But Abu Bakr and his immediate successors (called the Orthodox Caliphs) proved themselves able not only to stabilize the community but also to mobilize it for expansion. Armies were dispatched into Syria, Mesopotamia, and Egypt, spearheading a program of conquest which was increasingly successful.

The fourth caliph, Ali, husband of Mohammed's daughter Fatimah, was destined to be the figure around whom the major, enduring schism between Moslems was to revolve. Elected to the caliphate in 656, he was opposed by two other contenders and, possibly on the basis of an old household grudge, by Mohammed's widow, Aishah. But his most important opposition came from Muawiyah, the governor of Syria. At the battle of Siffin, Ali agreed to arbitrate their dispute, a crucial tactical mistake. A few years later he was murdered. Part of his army had seceded and formed a terrorist organization. Ali's party (*shīʿat ʿAlī*), believing Ali's descendants to be the only rightful rulers of Islam, formed the Shiite sect. The rest of the Moslems came to be known as Sunnites (from *sunnah*, the "way" of the Prophet).

Muawiyah assumed the caliphate in 661. His victory was significant in a number of respects. It established in the caliphate a branch of Mohammed's family, the Umayyads, which had accepted Islam relatively late; it marked the beginning of a hereditary caliphate; and it permitted the capital of the Islamic empire to be moved from Arabia to Damascus in Syria. At first the Umayyads ruled ably enough. They set up an efficient administration patterned along Byzantine lines, and pursued most of the advantages along the frontiers. However, during the early years of the eighth century, opposition to their rule mounted. Despised from the outset by the Shiites, they were accused of worldliness and incompetence by others. Their principal disadvantages lay simply in their ancestry and their failure to recognize the importance of the increasing unrest on the eastern frontier in Khurasan. It was there that a revolt was launched in 749 which replaced them with a new Abbasid dynasty.

The Abbasid caliphs proclaimed the end of "secular Arab" rule and the commencement of a religious and international state. Under Caliph Al-Mansur a new capital was built at Baghdad in Iraq, which quickly became one of the most prosperous cities in the world. Influences from Persia, which regarded itself as culturally superior, abounded. Al-Mansur's grandson, the fabled Harun al-Rashid, ruled from 786 to 809. His reign was regarded by later generations, with good reason underlying the mystique, as the "Golden Age" of Islam. At the outset of his reign, certainly, his position could scarcely have been stronger. He was absolute spiritual and temporal ruler of an empire so vast that he himself could have possessed but imperfect knowledge of its dimensions. He was popular, limitlessly wealthy, and had able advisers. By the end of his reign, however, signs of decline in the whole structure of the empire had already made their appearance. A protracted civil war between two of his sons after his death accelerated the decline of the caliphal power.

The processes by which the Islamic empire disintegrated into many separate states were varied and complex. As for the caliphate itself, it began to delegate too much power and to place too much reliance upon a Turkish bodyguard, whose commandant eventually became ruler *de facto*. Sensing this crucial weakness, province after province assumed independent or semi-independent status and set about fighting against each other.

In two areas anti-caliphates were established. The first of them was in Spain, where a lone survivor of the Umayyad dynasty and his successors had welded together a respectable empire; the caliphate proper lasted from 929 to 1031, although Islamic power in Spain lasted for several more centuries. The second anti-caliphate, centered in Egypt and including neighboring countries, was that of the Shiite Fatimids, who ruled from 909 to 1171. The Shiite cause made great headway during this period. In addition to smaller dynasties elsewhere and the giant Fatimid empire, the Buwayhid dynasty subjugated the central caliphal holdings in 945. At the turn of the eleventh century, it might have seemed that Shiism was about to prevail, but by that time it was already too divided within itself to do so.

Most of the classical forms of Islamic literature originated during this period. At first the passion was for collecting and editing poetry from the oral tradition, which (together with the Koran, of course) represented what literature the Arabs were bequeathed. The phil- ologists in particular were fascinated by its wealth of rare words. But a number of Umayyad poets, generally following the same styles and techniques, produced some original and excellent poetry. The amatory prelude to the *qaṣīdah* fathered the love lyric as an inde- pendent form, and shorter *ghazals* were popular. Prose, on the other hand, was slower in developing distinctive literary styles. In the beginning, it was largely limited to unpolished historical accounts and traditions, including the *maghāzī* form (accounts of battles), most of which have survived to us only in fragmentary form.

The most original development of the early Abbasid period was the emergence of the "new style" in Arabic poetry. The "old style" of poetry "was not a suitable vehicle for the poetic tastes of the ᶜAbbāsids. The patronage of the court, the pietistic spirit fostered by the state, the needs of the governmental secretaries, the foreign in- fluence coming mainly from Persia, and the change in social condi- tions, all contributed to the popularity of the 'new style,' which was distinguished by the use of novel similes, praise and satire exceeding the limits of credibility, simplicity of expression, avoidance of strange words, and padding."[1] Many of the "new poets" were Shiite sympathizers.

More artful prose was fostered by translations into Arabic of foreign masterpieces, a growing desire for systematic accounts of early Islamic times, and the more sophisticated tastes of some neo-Moslem Persians. Indeed, the rise of an entirely new and ornate prose style is attributed to government scribes, who introduced into the Arabic they were forced to write the methods and modes of thought of their native traditions.

To serve the tastes of a new courtly society in which skill in Arabic literature was highly prized, the form known as *adab* was developed. It was a highly mannered, anecdotal, reservedly didactic, and vastly entertaining form, aimed at instilling "the pattern of cultivated living."[2] Al-Jahiz is usually credited with having established it in its paradigm form, but many other writers also deserve credit for their successful experiments with it. It spread far and wide, and for many centuries influenced nearly all forms of Islamic prose.

This period also saw the rise of modern (as distinct from Pahlavi) Persian literature. The nationalistic Samanid dynasty in Persia (874–999) encouraged the use of Persian as a medium of literary expression, and that policy was followed by the Ghaznavid dynasty (962–1186), despite the fact that the rulers of that dynasty were of Turkish blood. Firdawsi's *Book of Kings* (*Shāh-nāmeh*), the finest achievement of Persian poetry and the sole example of true epic form in all of Islamic literature, was written at that time.

---

[1] L. Zolondek, *Dicbil b. cAlī* (Lexington, 1961), p. 2.
[2] See M. G. S. Hodgson, *The Venture of Islâm*, Vol. I (Chicago, 1961), pp. 167–179, for a fuller discussion of *adab*.

IBN AL-MUQAFFA: THE MONKEY AND THE TORTOISE

[from *Kitāb Kalīlah wa-Dimnah*, The Book of Kalilah and Dimnah]

On the surface of the matter it may seem strange that the oldest work of Arabic prose which is regarded as a model of style is a translation from the Pahlavi (Middle Persian) of the Sanskrit work *Panchatantra*, or *The Fables of Bidpai*, by Ruzbih, a new convert from Zoroastrianism, who took the name Abdullah ibn al-Muqaffa. It is not quite so strange, however, when one recalls that the Arabs had much preferred the poetic art and were at first suspicious of and untrained to appreciate, let alone imitate, current higher forms of prose literature in the lands they occupied.

Leaving aside the great skill of its translation (which was to serve as the basis for later translations into some forty languages), the work itself is far from primitive, having benefited already at that time from a lengthy history of stylistic revision. *Kalilah and Dimnah* is in fact the patriarchal form of the Indic fable in which animals behave as humans—as distinct from the Aesopic fable in which they behave as animals. Its philosophical heroes through the interconnected episodes are the two jackals, Kalilah and Dimnah.

It seems unjust, in the light of posterity's appreciation of his work, that Ibn al-Muqaffa was put to death after charges of heresy, about 757.

When the former story was finished, King Dabschelim commanded Bidpai to relate the history of the man the success of whose pursuit in the fulfillment of his wishes is immediately followed by the loss of what he had obtained. The philosopher replied that the acquisition of a desired good is often attended with less difficulty than the means of preserving it, and whoever cannot secure the possession of what he has got into his power may be compared to the tortoise in the following fable:

It is told of a certain king of the monkeys, whose name was Mahir, that being very old and infirm through age, he was attacked by a young competitor

73

for his crown and was overcome and obliged to take flight; so he retired to the riverside, and discovered a fig-tree and climbed up into it, and determined to make it his home; and as he was one day eating of the fruit, a fig fell down, and the noise which it occasioned by falling into the water delighted him so much that he never ate without repeating the experiment; and a tortoise who was below, as often as a fig fell down, devoured it; and receiving during some days a regular supply, considered it as an attention towards him on the part of the monkey. Therefore he desired to become acquainted with him, and in a short time they grew so intimate that they often conversed familiarly together. Now it happened that the tortoise stayed a long time away from his wife, who grew impatient at his absence and complained of it to one of her neighbors, saying, "I fear something has happened unexpectedly to my husband." Her friend replied that if her husband was on the riverside he would probably have made acquaintance with the monkey and have been hospitably entertained by him.

Then after some days the tortoise returned to his home, and found his wife in a bad state of health and apparently suffering very much, and he could not conceal the uneasiness which the sight of her occasioned; and expressing aloud his distress, he was interrupted by her friend, who said to him, "Your wife is very dangerously ill, and the physicians have prescribed for her the heart of a monkey." The tortoise replied, "This is no easy matter, for living as we do in the water, how can we possibly procure the heart of a monkey? However, I will consult my friend about it." And he went to the shore of the river, and the monkey asked in terms of great affection what had detained him so long; and he answered, "The reluctance which I felt to repeat my visits was owing to my being at a loss how to make you any suitable return for the kindness you have shown me; but I beg of you to add to the obligations under which you have laid me, by coming and passing some days with me; and as I live upon an island, which moreover abounds in fruit, I will take you upon my back and swim over the water with you." The monkey accepted the invitation, and came down from the tree and got upon the back of the tortoise, who, as he was swimming along with him, began to reflect on the crime which he harbored in his breast, and from shame and remorse hung down his head. "What is the occasion," said the monkey, "of the sudden fit of sadness which is come upon you?" "It occurs to me," answered the tortoise, "that my wife is very ill and that I shall not therefore have it in my power to do the honors of my house in the manner I could wish." "The intimations," replied the monkey, "which your friendly behavior

has conveyed to me of your kind intentions, will supply the place of all un-
necessary parade and ostentation." Then the tortoise felt more at his ease,
and continued his course, but on a sudden he stopped a second time; upon
which the monkey, who was at a loss to account for this hesitation of the
tortoise, began to suspect that something more was intended by it than he
was able to discover; but as suddenly repressing every thought that was
injurious to the sincerity of his friend, he said to himself, "I cannot believe
that his heart has changed, that his sentiments towards me have undergone
an alteration, and that he intends to do me any mischief, however frequent
such appearances may be in the world; and it is the voice of experience which
directs the sensible man to look narrowly into the souls of those with whom
he is connected by ties of affinity or friendship, by attending closely to everything that passes without them; for a wink of the eye, an expression which
falls from the tongue, and even the motions of the body, are all evidences of
what is going on in the heart; and wise men have laid it down as a rule that
when anyone doubts the sincerity of his friend, he should, by unremittingly
observing every part of his conduct, guard against the possibility of being
deceived by him; for if his suspicions are founded, he is repaid for the violence
which they may have offered to his feelings, by the safety which they have
procured him; and if they have been entertained without good grounds, he
may at least congratulate himself on the measure of foresight which he
possesses, which in no instance can be otherwise than serviceable to him."

After having indulged himself in these reflections, he said to the tortoise,
"Why do you stop a second time and appear as if you were anxiously debating
some question with yourself?" "I am tormented," answered the tortoise,
"by the idea that you will find my house in disorder owing to the illness of
my wife." "Do not," said the monkey, "be uneasy on this account, for your
anxiety will be of no use to you, but rather look out for some medicine and
food which may be of service to your wife; for a person possessed of riches
cannot employ them in a better manner than either in works of charity during
a time of want or in the service of women." "Your observation," answered
the tortoise, "is just, but the physician has declared that nothing will cure her
except the heart of a monkey." Then the monkey reasoned with himself
thus: "Fool that I am! Immoderate desires, which are not suited to my age,
threaten me with destruction, and I now discover too late how true it is that
the contented man passes his life in peace and security, while the covetous
and ambitious live in trouble and difficulty; and I have occasion at this moment
for all the resources of my understanding, to devise a means of escaping from

the snare into which I have fallen." Then he said to the tortoise, "Why did you not inform me of this sooner, and I would have brought my heart with me; for it is the practice of the monkeys, when anyone goes out on a visit to a friend, to leave his heart at home, or in the custody of his family, that he may be able to look at the wife of him who has received him under his roof and be at the same time without his heart." "Where is your heart now?" said the tortoise. "I have left it in the tree," answered the monkey, "and if you will return with me thither I will bring it away." The proposal was accepted, and the tortoise swam back with the monkey, who, as soon as he was near enough, sprang upon the shore and immediately climbed up into the tree; and when the tortoise had waited for him some time, he grew impatient and called out to him to take his heart and come down, and not detain him any longer. "What," said the monkey, "do you think I am like the ass of whom the jackal declared that he had neither heart nor ears?" "How was this?" the tortoise asked.

"It is told," said the monkey, "that a lion in a forest was waited upon by a jackal who lived upon the food which he left; and it happened that the lion was attacked by a violent disease which brought on such a state of weakness that he was unable to hunt his prey; upon which the jackal asked him the reason of the change which he observed in his manner and appearance and was told that it was owing to the illness with which he was afflicted and for which there was no remedy except the heart and the ears of an ass. The jackal replied that there would be no difficulty in procuring them, for that he was acquainted with an ass who was in the service of a fuller and was employed in carrying his cloths; and he immediately set out and went to the ass, and as soon as he saw him he addressed him and told him how distressed he was to find him so thin and emaciated, which the ass accounted for by saying that his master gave him scarcely anything to eat. *Jackal*: 'Why do you remain any longer with him and submit to this treatment?' *Ass*: 'What can I do or whither can I go? Wherever I am, it is my fate to be ill used and starved.' *Jackal*: 'If you will follow me I will conduct you to a place uninhabited by men, who you say are your foes, and abounding in food, and where you will find a female ass whose equal in beauty and fatness was never seen and who is desirous of a male companion.' 'Let us not lose a moment in going to her,' said the ass, 'and I beg of you to show me the way.' Then the jackal led him to where the lion was, but entered alone into the forest to inform the lion of the spot where the ass was waiting; and the lion went out and immediately made an attempt to rush upon him but was unable through weakness; upon which the ass, being frightened, ran away.

"Then the jackal observed to the lion that he did not suppose he was so weak as to be unable to master the ass. 'Bring him to me a second time,' said the lion, 'and I promise you he shall not escape again.' So the jackal went to the ass and said, 'What was the reason of your sudden fright? A she ass, owing to the violence of her passion, gave you, to be sure, rather rude demonstrations of her affection, but you have only to remain quiet and undismayed and she will become gentle and submissive.' As soon as the ass heard her name mentioned his desire became uncontrollable, and he brayed through impatience and suffered himself to be conducted again to the lion; and the jackal preceded him as before and told the lion where he was, and cautioned him to be well upon his guard, for that if he escaped a second time he would never return. The eagerness of the lion not to be disappointed a second time of his prey was very great, and he went to the spot where the ass was, and no sooner saw him than, without leaving him time to prepare for his defense, he rushed upon him and killed him; then recollecting that the physicians had forbidden his flesh to be eaten before it had been washed and purified, he desired the jackal to take care that everything which was necessary was done and said that he would shortly come back and eat the heart and ears and leave him the rest.

"Now as soon as the lion was gone the jackal ate the heart and ears of the ass, hoping by this stratagem to deter the lion from eating any part of the remainder of the animal and that he should thereby have the whole for himself. Then the lion returned and asked for the heart and ears of the ass, and the jackal said to him, 'Do you think if he had had a heart and ears he would ever have suffered himself to be brought back after he had once escaped from destruction?'

"Now do not imagine," said the monkey in continuation to the tortoise, "that I am going to be guilty of the same folly as the ass in this fable. You have been endeavoring to deceive me by trick and contrivance, and I have therefore been obliged to practice, and with complete success, the same means in my defense, thereby showing that knowledge and talents can make good the error of a too easy and thoughtless compliance." "You are right," said the tortoise, "and an honest man will confess his crime; and if he has committed a fault he does not refuse instruction, that he may profit by the lesson which has been taught him if on any future occasion he should be entangled in difficulties, like the man who, when he has made a false step and fallen, supports himself on the ground against which he has stumbled, to raise himself again upon his feet."

TRANSLATED BY WYNDHAM KNATCHBULL

[from *Sīrat Rasūl Allāh*, The Life of the Messenger of God]

Though preceded and succeeded by many others, Ibn Ishaq's biography of Mohammed has had no serious rival as the standard biography. It was circulated almost exclusively in an edition by Ibn Hisham, but it appears likely that we possess the greater part of the original. The work was based upon widely circulating accounts of Mohammed's life already embodied in the *maghāzī* form, but it went some way beyond them in its selectivity and arrangement. Naturally it has aroused a great deal of comment and criticism throughout the centuries.

Composed as it is so largely of quotations from others, it offers but few stylistic impressions. One that it offers, however, is that of its author's clever use of transitions and cautionary phrases. The generous inclusion of poetry (most of it, one must assume, composed after the events related), too, points to a desire on the author's part to present his material in a pleasing literary fashion. To judge only by the success of the work, he did so.

Jewish rabbis, Christian monks, and Arab soothsayers had spoken about the apostle of God [Mohammed] before his mission, when his time drew near. As to the rabbis and monks, it was about his description and the description of his time which they found in their scriptures and what their prophets had enjoined upon them. As to the Arab soothsayers, they had been visited by satans from the jinn with reports which they had secretly overheard before they were prevented from hearing by being pelted with stars. Male and female soothsayers continued to let fall mention of some of these matters to which the Arabs paid no attention until God sent him and these things which had been mentioned happened and they recognized them. When the prophet's mission came the satans were prevented from listening, and they could not occupy the seats in which they used to sit and steal the heavenly tidings, for they were pelted with stars, and the jinn knew that that was due to an order which God had commanded concerning mankind. God said to His

79

prophet Muhammad when He sent him, as he was telling him about the jinn when they were prevented from listening and knew what they knew and did not deny what they saw: "Say, It has been revealed to me that a number of the jinn listened and said 'We have heard a wonderful Quran [Koran] which guides to the right path, and we believe in it and we will not associate anyone with our Lord and that He (exalted be the glory of our Lord) hath not chosen a wife or son. A foolish one among us used to speak lies against God, and we had thought men and jinn would not speak a lie against God and that when men took refuge with the jinn, they increased them in revolt,' ending with the words: 'We used to sit on places therein to listen; he who listens now finds a flame waiting for him. We do not know whether evil is intended against those that are on earth or whether their lord wishes to guide them in the right path.' "[1] When the jinn heard the Quran they knew that they had been prevented from listening before that so that revelation should not be mingled with news from heaven, so that men would be confused with the tidings which came from God about it when the proof came and doubt was removed; so they believed and acknowledged the truth. Then "They returned to their people, warning them, saying, O our people we have heard a book which was revealed after Moses confirming what went before it, guiding to the truth and to the upright path."[2]

When Muhammad the apostle of God reached the age of forty, God sent him in compassion to mankind "as an evangelist to all men."[3] Now God had made a covenant with every prophet whom he had sent before him, that he should believe in him, testify to his truth, and help him against his adversaries, and he required of them that they should transmit that to everyone who believed in them, and they carried out their obligations in that respect. God said to Muhammad, "When God made a covenant with the prophets (He said) this is the scripture and wisdom which I have given you, afterwards an apostle will come confirming what you know that you may believe in him and help him." He said, "Do you accept this and take up my burden?" i.e. the burden of my agreement which I have laid upon you. They said, "We accept it." He answered, "Then bear witness and I am a witness with you."[4] Thus God made a covenant with all the prophets that they should testify to his truth and help him against his adversaries and they transmitted

[1] Koran 72.1–10.
[2] Koran 46.29–30.
[3] Koran 34.28.
[4] Koran 3.81.

that obligation to those who believed in them among the two monotheistic religions.

After his companions had left, the apostle stayed in Mecca waiting for permission to migrate [to Medina]. Except for Abū Bakr and ʿAlī, none of his supporters were left but those under restraint and those who had been forced to apostatize. The former kept asking the apostle for permission to emigrate and he would answer, "Don't be in a hurry; it may be that God will give you a companion." Abū Bakr hoped that it would be Muhammad himself.

When the Quraysh saw that the apostle had a party and companions not of their tribe and outside their territory, and that his companions had migrated to join them, and knew that they had settled in a new home and had gained protectors, they feared that the apostle might join them, since they knew that he had decided to fight them. So they assembled in their council chamber, the house of Quṣayy b. Kilāb where all their important business was conducted, to take counsel what they should do in regard to the apostle, for they were now in fear of him.

According to what I have been told, none knew when the apostle left except ʿAlī and Abū Bakr and the latter's family. I have heard that the apostle told ʿAlī about his departure and ordered him to stay behind in Mecca in order to return goods which men had deposited with the apostle; for anyone in Mecca who had property which he was anxious about left it with him because of his well-known honesty and trustworthiness.

When the apostle decided to go he came to Abū Bakr, and the two of them left by a window in the back of the latter's house and made for a cave on Thaur, a mountain below Mecca. Having entered, Abū Bakr ordered his son ʿAbdullah to listen to what people were saying and to come to them by night with the day's news. He also ordered ʿĀmir b. Fuhayra, his freedman, to feed his flock by day and to bring them to them in the evening in the cave. Asmāʾ, his daughter, used to come at night with food to sustain them. The two of them stayed in the cave for three days. When Quraysh missed the apostle they offered a hundred she-camels to anyone who would bring him back.

When the apostle heard about Abū Sufyān coming from Syria, he summoned the Muslims and said, "This is the Quraysh caravan containing their property. Go out to attack it, perhaps God will give it as a prey."[5] The people

[5] The following is an account of the battle of Badr, fought in 624. [Ed.]

answered his summons, some eagerly, others reluctantly because they had not thought that the apostle would go to war. When he got near to the Hijaz, Abū Sufyān was seeking news, and questioning every rider in his anxiety, until he got news from some riders that Muhammad had called out his companions against him and his caravan. He took alarm at that and hired Ḍamḍam b. ʿAmr al-Ghifārī and sent him to Mecca, ordering him to call out Quraysh in defence of their property, and to tell them that Muhammad was lying in wait for it with his companions. So Ḍamḍam left for Mecca at full speed.

Quraysh, having marched forth at daybreak, now came on. When the apostle saw them descending from the hill ʿAqanqal into the valley, he cried, "O God, here come the Quraysh in their vanity and pride, contending with Thee and calling Thy apostle a liar. O God, grant the help which Thou didst promise me. Destroy them this morning!"

Then they advanced and drew near to one another. The apostle had ordered his companions not to attack until he gave the word, and if the enemy should surround them they were to keep them off with showers of arrows. He himself remained in the hut with Abū Bakr. . . . The apostle was beseeching his Lord for the help which He had promised to him, and among his words were these: "O God, if this band perish today Thou wilt be worshipped no more." But Abū Bakr said, "O prophet of God, your constant entreaty will annoy thy Lord, for surely God will fulfil His promise to thee." When the apostle was in the hut he slept a light sleep; then he awoke and said, "Be of good cheer, O Abū Bakr. God's help is come to you. Here is Gabriel holding the rein of a horse and leading it. The dust is upon his front teeth."

Then the apostle went forth to the people and incited them, saying, "By God in whose hand is the soul of Muhammad, no man will be slain this day fighting against them with steadfast courage, advancing, not retreating, but God will cause him to enter Paradise." ʿUmayr b. al-Ḥumām, brother of B. Salima, was eating some dates which he had in his hand. "Fine, Fine!" said he, "is there nothing between me and my entering Paradise save to be killed by these men?" He flung the dates from his hand, seized his sword, and fought against them till he was slain.

The total number of Quraysh slain at Badr as given to us is 50 men. . . . The total number [of prisoners] was 43 men.

The apostle took part personally in twenty-seven raids. . . . He actually fought in nine engagements.

When [Mohammed] had ended his words, Abū Bakr said to him: "O prophet of God, I see that this morning you enjoy the favor and goodness of God as we desire; today is the day of Bint Khārija [one of his wives]. May I go to her?" The apostle agreed and went indoors and Abū Bakr went to his wife in al-Sunḥ.

Al-Zuhrī said, and ᶜAbdullah b. Kaᶜb b. Mālik from ᶜAbdullah b. ᶜAbbās told me: That day ᶜAlī went out from the apostle and the men asked him how the apostle was and he replied that thanks be to God he had recovered. ᶜAbbās took him by the hand and said, "ᶜAlī, three nights hence you will be a slave. I swear by God that I recognized death in the apostle's face as I used to recognize it in the faces of the sons of ᶜAbduᵓl-Muṭṭalib. So let us go to the apostle; if authority is to be with us, we shall know it, and if it is to be with others we will request him to enjoin the people to treat us well."[6] ᶜAlī answered: "By God, I will not. If it is withheld from us none after him will give it to us." The apostle died with the heat of noon that day.

TRANSLATED BY ALFRED GUILLAUME

[6] The reference is to an enmity within Mohammed's family. Abu Bakr became the first caliph and Ali the fourth. [Ed.]

The poets of the Umayyad period hewed for the most part to the forms and themes which they had inherited and which had come to represent not only the ingredients but also the prerequisites and very definition of poetry. A few of them, it is true—Al-Farazdaq, Al-Akhtal, and Jarir—managed to assert their original talents, largely by the use of obscenity and the clever manipulation of the short *ghazal* form.[1]

With the Abbasid revolution, however, the mystique of the Arab desert lost status, and the so-called "new poets" were among the first to express the fact. It was Abu Nuwas, boon companion of Caliph Harun al-Rashid, who led and embodied the spirit of the movement. He voiced their common complaint that poets could not be expected to write about desert plants and animals which they had never seen, in poetic forms which they found tedious and sterile. His classic mimicry of the introduction to the *qaṣīdah* summed it up:

> The lovelorn wretch stopped at a desert camping ground to question it, and I stopped to inquire after the local tavern.
> May Allah not dry the eyes of him that wept over stones, and may he not ease the pain of him that yearns to a tent peg!
> They said, "Didst thou commemorate the dwelling places of the tribe of Asad?" Plague on thee! Tell me, who are the Banu Asad?

Abu al-Atahiyah (died 828) is often linked with Abu Nuwas, although temperamentally he was quite different from him. While Abu Nuwas wrote new poems of revelry, Abu al-Atahiyah wrote them in a rarely lifted fog of gloom. Another representative of the "new poets" was Dibil (died 872), who distinguished himself by

[1] See A. K. Kinany, *The Development of Gazal in Arabic Literature* (Damascus, 1951).

managing to attack nearly everything the Arabs held dearest. He was often obscene, sometimes vile, in his new styles of short poems, but his poetic genius was recognized even by his enemies. He carried both the theory and the practice of the "new poetry" farther than his more famous predecessors.

Abu Nuwas

A brook, a bottle, a bench, a way of waiting,
The body sweetens, the ghost stirs,
Golden four.

If you punish it you encourage it
It's a pharmacopoeia against itself
The yellow virus never lodged in it
The stone it touched maddened with delight
Came down the yards a sleepy bitch
With two lovers behind transpiring it
From flagon neck and turbid night
And around the house a glitter
Easy as sleep at first light
It was thinner thinner than water
Brittler and more delicate
And all light dipping under it
Made ingots and fire of it
And like time it circulated
From boy to boy and transmitted
His secret and itch

So my poems are always about it,
Motion's conduit,
Whose consistent simplicity
The agon and cathartics
The elegiacs of evening cattle
The fury of griffins and politics
Should be forbidden to contaminate

Tell the severe master of dialectic
You have learned something and we honour it
But your power exterminates itself
As long as you omit
Passion and compassion and charity,
The berry in love with itself.

Hurry, for the beergardens are blooming.
The war still a hill away. Earth
With all its aviary with the natural voices.
They sing, till your veins are strings
And a friction begins like recovery.
The soil has come into flower, and wine
(From the bed where an intact leek
And a Roman endlessly reproduce her)
Looks out. If you catch the instant
You will see her nodding.

TRANSLATED BY HERBERT HOWARTH AND IBRAHIM SHUKRALLAH

Youth and I, we ran
    a headlong race of pleasure;
No recorded sin
    but soon I took its measure.
Of the gifts of Time
    there's none to heaven nigher
Than when music wakes
    the string of lute and lyre.
O the girl whose song—
    I had it for the asking—
Oft at Dhī Ṭulūḥ
    rose where our tents were basking!
Make the most of Youth,
    it stayeth not for ever;
Let the wine flow round
    from eve to morn—one river!
Pour into thy cup
    a sparkling ruddy vintage
That will melt to ruth
    the miser's hardest mintage,

Sought and chosen out
    of old for Persia's ruler,
Dower'd with twin delights
    of fragrancy and colour.
Seest not thou that I
    have pawned my soul for liquor,
Kissed the mouth of fair
    gazelle and foaming beaker?
'Tis because I know,
    full well I know and fear it,
Far apart shall be
    my body and my spirit.

Ho! a cup and fill it up, and tell me it is wine,
For never will I drink in shade if I can drink in shine.
Curst and poor is every hour that sober I must go,
But rich am I whene'er well drunk I stagger to and fro.
Speak, for shame, the loved one's name, let vain disguises fall;
Good for naught are pleasures hid behind a curtain-wall.

    Come, Sulaimān, sing to me,
    And the wine, quick, bring to me!
    Lo, already Dawn is here
    In a golden mantle clear.
    Whilst the flask goes twinkling round,
    Pour me a cup that leaves me drowned
    With oblivion, ne'er so nigh
    Let the shrill muezzin[2] cry!

Abu al-Atahiyah

Get sons for death, build houses for decay!
All, all, ye wend annihilation's way.
For whom build we, who must ourselves return
Into our native element to clay?
O Death, nor violence nor flattery thou
Dost use; but when thou com'st, escape none may.
Methinks, thou art ready to surprise mine age,
As age surprised and made my youth his prey.

---

[2] The man who announces the hours of prayer from the minaret. [Ed.]

Surely shall Fate disjoint the proudest nose,
All wears away by movement and repose.
In long experience if wisdom be,
Less than my portion is enough for me.

O thou that gloriest in thy worldly state,
Mud piled on mud will never make thee great.
Nay, wouldst thou see the noblest man of all,
Look at a monarch in a beggar's pall!

TRANSLATED BY R. A. NICHOLSON

Every summary has a trend
Every question has an answer
Every event has an hour
Every action has its account
Every ascent has its limit
Every man has his book of fate.

Every guarantee is a symbol of death
Every building a promise of destruction
Every king and his domain the original of dust.

Upheavals and insurrection
And more than sweet surfeit provoke
Twitches of the eye. At beauty thrown
The fist clenches on itself.

Every day is a stage to death
You die while you play with arts and towers
Every door of the world you shut for safety
Opens a door on a new fang
You thought you were a husk when you found
The milk of life meant endless churning.

But you are not lust's conqueror
To hold it with effort and fret
All you see was planned by a dear king
Whose operations are like a presence
And he accessible with an excuse.

We have grown so old, old friends
We might never have been so young
Though our days were stalks of basil
Wet and waving and beaming
We spent long wanting a house
A place of violence and theft
We shall spend longer trying to be young
Tinkering with juvenilia
And a steady hole in the scalp.

Youth went out despite everything
There should be no cause when youth wears out
But death and the mountain.

TRANSLATED BY HERBERT HOWARTH AND IBRAHIM SHUKRALLAH

Vanity: To Harun al-Rashid

Live securely, as you wish;
    the palace heights are safe enough.
With pleasures flooding day and night,
    the smooth proves sweeter than the rough.

But when your breath begins to clog
    in sharp contractions of your lungs,
then know for certain, my dear sire,
    your life was vain as idle tongues.

TRANSLATED BY JAMES KRITZECK

Dibil

They sat and selected a pedigree which passed amongst the Arabs after dusk.
But when morning, the gold showed as counterfeit.
People have become money-changers who see something [false] in this quicksilvery
    lineage.

We attained the pleasures of life in Batyāthā,
When we were cheered thrice with the wine cup.
And thrice did I divorce my wife.

O you with the countenance of the scare-crow, depart and favor me with your prolonged absence.
Your face and my union with you have injured me with wounds which resist the
surgeon's probe.
A defective chin, a thick nose, and a forehead like the beam of the money-changer.
Throughout my protracted night with her I cried, "O avenge him who seeks the
light of day!"

Until calamity overtook her, Baghdād was the home of kings.
Gone is the joy of government, which was transferred to another land.
He who sees Sāmarrā is not rejoiced.[3] Nay! she is a sorrow for whoever sees her.
May my Lord hasten her shame and the humiliation of him who built her!

They announced my death. But it is an act of him who rejoices at my misfortune and
of a foe mortally wounded [by my satire].
They hold that if a poet experiences evil, his poetry dies. Far from it! The lifespan of
a poem is long.
I shall finish with a verse which people will praise—a verse which will have many
bearers among the Transmitters:
The bad poem dies before its author, but the excellent one lives, though its author dies.

TRANSLATED BY LEON ZOLONDEK

[3] A play on the name of the city *Surra Man Ra'a*, "he who sees [it] rejoices," usually in its
form derived from the Assyrian Samarra, the capital of the Islamic empire from 836 to
892. [Ed.]

[from *Kitāb al-Bayān*, The Book of Proof]

Credit for raising Arabic prose to its first heights of elegant expression is unanimously accorded to Al-Jahiz, a bold thinker who was deeply interested in all the sciences and who gave his name to a sect of rationalists. He is more important as the founder of a new ornamental style, identified eventually as *adab* literature. The form developed rapidly and underwent many permutations, some of which will be illustrated later in this anthology. Al-Jahiz, who died in 869, wrote many books, but the two from which these selections are taken were regarded, even in his own times, as his masterpieces.

Ghailān son of Kharasha said to Aḥnaf, "What will preserve the Arabs from decline?" He replied, "All will go well if they keep their swords on their shoulders and their turbans on their heads and ride horseback and do not fall a prey to the fools' sense of honour." "And what is the fools' sense of honour?" "That they regard forgiving one another as a wrong."

ᶜUmar said, "Turbans are the crowns of the Arabs."

An Arab of the desert was asked why he did not lay aside his turban. "Surely," said he, "a thing which contains the hearing and the sight ought to be prized."

ᶜAli said—God be well pleased with him!—"The elegance of a man is in his bonnet, and the elegance of a woman in her boots." And Ahnaf said, "Let your shoes be fine, for shoes are to men what anklets are to women."

ᶜAbdullah son of Jaᶜfar said to his daughter, "O little daughter, beware of jealousy, for it is the key of divorce; and beware of chiding, for it breeds hate. Always adorn and perfume thyself, and know that the most becoming adornment is antimony and the sweetest perfume is water."

ᶜAbdullah son of Jaᶜfar bestowed largesse of every kind on Nuṣaib Abu-ᵓl-Ḥajnā, who had made an ode in praise of him. "Why," they asked, "do you treat a fellow like this so handsomely—a negro and a slave?" "By God," he answered, "if his skin is black, yet his praise is white and his poem is truly Arabian. He deserves for it a greater reward than he has gotten. All he

91

received was only some lean saddle-camels and clothes which wear out and money which is soon spent, whereas he gave an ode fresh and brilliant and praise that will never die."

Mucāwiyah held an assembly at Kūfa to receive the oath of allegiance as Caliph. Those who swore loyalty to him were required to abjure allegiance to [the House of] cAli son of Abū Ṭālib—may God honour him! A man of the Banū Tamīm came to Mucāwiyah, who demanded that he should repudiate cAli. "O Prince of the Faithful," he replied, "we will obey those of you that are living, but we will not renounce those of you that are dead." Mucāwiyah turned to Mughīra and said, "Now, this is a man! Look after him well!"

cAuf said on the authority of Ḥasan: "The feet of a son of Adam will not stir [from the place of judgment] until he be asked of three things—his youth, how he wore it away; his life, how he passed it; and his wealth, whence he got it and on what he spent it."

Yūnus son of cUbaid said: "I heard three sayings more wonderful than any I have ever heard. The first is the saying of Ḥassān son of Abū Sinān—'Nothing is easier than abstinence from things unlawful: if aught make thee doubt, leave it alone.' The second is the saying of Ibn Sīrīn—'I have never envied any one any thing.' The third is the saying of Muwarriḳ al-cIjlī—'Forty years ago I asked of God a boon which He has not granted, and I have not despaired of obtaining it.' They said to Muwarriḳ, 'What is it?' He replied, 'Not to meddle with that which does not concern me.' "

Ziyād, the slave of cAiyāsh son of Abū Rabīca, said, "I am more afraid of being hindered from prayer than of being denied an answer to my prayer."

Some people said to Rābica of [the tribe] Ḳais: "We might speak to the men of thy family and they would purchase for thee a maid-servant who would relieve thee of the care of thy house." "By God," said she, "I am ashamed to beg aught of this world from Him who is the Lord of it all: how, then, should I beg it from one who is not the lord of it?"

A certain ascetic said: "Your dwellings are before you, and your life is after your death."

And Samuel son of cĀdiyā, the Jew, said in verse: "Being dead, I was created, and before that I was not anything that dies; but I died when I came to life."

Ḥasan son of Dīnār said: "Ḥasan [of Baṣra] saw a man in his death-struggle. 'Surely,' he exclaimed, 'a thing of which this is the end ought not to be desired at the first and ought to be feared at the last.' "

Two [ascetics] entered Ahwāz. One went towards the graveyard to satisfy a want of nature, and the other sat down near a goldsmith's shop. Meanwhile a woman came forth from one of the palaces with a small box containing precious stones. As she left the road to go up to the shop, she slipped and the box fell from her hand. There was an ostrich roaming to and fro, which belonged to the people of one of the houses in that neighbourhood. When the box fell, its lid came off and the contents were scattered, and the ostrich swallowed the largest and most valuable stone. All this was seen by the wanderer. The goldsmith and his lads sprang forward, collected the stones, and kept back the people with shouts, so that none of them approached the spot. On missing the jewel, the woman screamed. Those present made a thorough search and put their heads together, but the stone was not to be found. "By God," said one of them, "nobody was near us except this ascetic who is sitting here: he must have got it." So they questioned him. Now, he did not wish to inform them that it was in the ostrich's belly, for the ostrich would be slaughtered and he would then have had a share in shedding the blood of an animal. He said, therefore, "I have not taken anything." They searched him and carefully examined every article of his property and plied him hard with blows, until his companion came up and besought them to fear God. Then they seized him too, saying [to the other], "You have given it him to hide." He answered, "I have not given him anything." Whilst both were being beaten to death, an intelligent man passed by and heard from some of them what had happened. Seeing an ostrich roaming about the street, he enquired whether it was there when the jewel fell to the ground. "Yes," they said. "Then," said he, "this is the fellow you want." Accordingly, having compensated the owners of the ostrich, they slaughtered it and on ripping open its intestine discovered the stone. In that short time it had become reduced to something like half its former size, but the intestine had given it a tint which brought them a greater profit than they would have gained by selling it at its full weight, since the fire of the intestine is different from the [native] fire of the stone.

FLIES AND MOSQUITOES

[from *Kitāb al-Ḥayawān*, The Book of Animals]

In the fly there are two good qualities. One of these is the facility with which it may be prevented from causing annoyance and discomfort. For if any person wish to make the flies quit his house and secure himself from being troubled by them without diminishing the amount of light in the house, he has only to shut the door, and they will hurry forth as fast as they can and try to outstrip each other in seeking the light and fleeing from the darkness. Then no sooner is the curtain let down and the door opened than the light will return and the people of the house will no longer be harassed by flies. If there be a slit in the door, or if, when it is shut, one of the two folding leaves does not quite close on the other, that will serve them as a means of exit; and the flies often go out through the gap between the bottom of the door and the lintel. Thus it is easy to get rid of them and escape from their annoyance. With the mosquito it is otherwise, for just as the fly has greater power [for mischief] in the light, so the mosquito is more tormenting and mischievous and bloodthirsty after dark; and it is not possible for people to let into their houses sufficient light to stop the activity of the mosquito, because for this purpose they would have to admit the beams of the sun, and there are no mosquitoes except in summer when the sun is unendurable. All light that is derived from the sun partakes of heat, and light is never devoid of heat, though heat is sometimes devoid of light. Hence, while it is easily possible to contrive a remedy against flies, this is difficult in the case of mosquitoes.

The second merit of the fly is that unless it ate the mosquito, which it pursues and seeks after on the walls and in the corners of rooms, people would be unable to stay in their houses. I am informed by a trustworthy authority that Muḥammad son of Jahm said one day to some of his acquaintance, "Do you know the lesson which we have learned with regard to the fly?" They said, "No." "But the fact is," he replied, "that it eats mosquitoes and chases them and picks them up and destroys them. I will tell you how I learned this. Formerly, when I wanted to take the siesta, I used to give orders that the flies should be cleared out and the curtain drawn and the door shut an hour before noon. On the disappearance of the flies, the mosquitoes would collect in the house and become exceedingly strong and powerful and bite me violently as soon as I began to rest. Now on a certain day I came in and found the room open and the curtain up. And when I lay down to sleep, there were no mosquitoes and I slept soundly, although I was very angry with the slaves. Next day they cleared out the flies and shut the door as usual, and on my coming to take the siesta I saw a multitude of mosquitoes. Then on another day they forgot to shut the door, and when I perceived that it was open I reviled them. However, when I came for the siesta, I did not find a single mosquito and I said to myself, 'Methinks I have slept on the two days on which my precautions were neglected, and have been hindered from sleeping whenever they were carefully observed. Why should not I try today the effect of leaving the door open? If I sleep three days with the door open and suffer no annoyance from the mosquitoes, I shall know that the right way is to have the flies and the mosquitoes together, because the flies destroy them, and that our remedy lies in keeping near us what we used to keep at a distance.' I made the experiment, and now the end of the matter is that whether we desire to remove the flies or destroy the mosquitoes, we can do it with very little trouble."

TRANSLATED BY R. A. NICHOLSON

[from *Akhbār al-Ḥallāj*, Information about Al-Hallaj, and other sources]

One of the most controversial figures to arise in early Sufism was Al-Husayn ibn Mansur al-Hallaj, who is also, thanks to the devoted labors of a great modern Islamicist, one of the best known.[1] It is still no easy task to formulate Al-Hallaj's mystical doctrine, far less so to capsulate it. He embraced *fanā*, the extinction of personal consciousness, and other notions aimed at bridging the abyss between God and individual man in Islam. By the same token, to some he appeared blasphemously to contradict Islam's fundamental understanding of the transcendence of God and even to threaten the social order.

Al-Hallaj deliberately chose and taught the path of mystical union with God, comprehending but careless of the consequences of such a choice within a semi-theocratic state whose orthodox creed, though still in process of formulation, scorned and reproved it. He paid the supreme penalty for his choice. After many years of travel and teaching, he was arrested, imprisoned, and finally brutally executed in Baghdad in 922. The following selection comprises several reminiscences of his last days in which some of his ecstatic utterances are preserved.

I saw Hallaj in the Qatiᶜa Market once. He was weeping bitterly and crying: Hide me from God, you people! Hide me from God! Hide me from God! He took me from myself and has not given me back; and I cannot perform the service I should do in His Presence for my fear of His leaving me alone again. He will leave me deserted, abandoned! and woe for the man who knows himself outcast after that Presence!

People were weeping to hear him. Then Hallaj stopped by the gate that leads into the Attab Mosque, and began to speak—words some part of which we understood, but part was obscure.

[1] Louis Massignon, *La passion d'al-Hosayn-ibn-Mansour al Hallaj, martyr mystique de l'Islam*, 2 vols. (Paris, 1922).

Surely, said he in the clearer part, if He create creature of His, it must be in pure goodwill towards it. And if then He blazes upon it sometimes, and sometimes hides Himself from it behind a Veil, it is still always that the creature may go onward. If that Light never came, men would deny the very existence of God. If It was never veiled, all would be spellbound. That is why He will let neither state last forever. For me in this moment there is no Veil, not so much as a wink, between me and Him—a time for quiet, that my humanity die into His Deity while my body burns in the fire of His Power; that there be an end to trace and relic, face and word.

And then he said something which we could not understand: What you have to learn is this: that ordinary material things subsist atom by atom in His Godhead; that particular decrees are performed by Him as man.

Then he recited these verses:

> Prophecy is the Lamp of the world's light;
> But ecstasy in the same Niche has room.
> The Spirit's is the breath which sighs through me;
> And mine the thought which blows the Trump of Doom.
> Vision said it. In my eye
> Moses stood, on Sinai.

I entered unannounced into Hallaj's room one day (says Ibn Fatik); someone had been in before me. Hallaj was in prayer, and his brow pressed to the ground. He was saying: O Thou Whose Closeness girds my very skin, Whose Mystery spurns me far away as lie all things in time from the Eternal, Thou shinest so before me that I think Thou art all these things; and then Thou dost deny Thyself in me, till I declare Thou art nothing here. And this can neither be Thy Distance, for that would fortify my selfhood, nor Thy Closeness, for that would help me; neither Thy War, for that would destroy me, nor Thy Peace, for that would comfort me.

Then, noticing my presence, he raised himself. Come in, you do not disturb me, said he.

So I went farther in and sat down in front of him. His eyes glowed like burning coals, and they were bloodshot.

My dear son, he said, I hear people are going about saying I am a saint, and others saying that I am impious. I prefer those who call me impious; and so does God.

How so, master? I said.

They call me a saint because they respect me; but the others call me impious out of zeal for their religion. A man who is zealous for his religion is dearer to me, and dearer to God also, than a man who venerates a creature. What will you say yourself, Ibrahim, on the day when you see me hanging on the gibbet, and killed, and burned? Yet that will be the happiest day of all my life.

Well, don't stay here, he said presently. Go, and into the Grace of God.

> When the giving of Love is entire,
> And What Love cries to is bygone in the stress of its crying,
> Then a man verifies
> What passion testifies:
> Prayer is Unbelief
> Once one knows.

> Ay, go. Tell them I sailed for the deep Sea,
> And that my ship has foundered far offshore.
> By Holy Cross I must go on to death;
> To Holy Cities I can go no more.

> I have renounced the Faith of God.
> Obligatory on me
> It was to do what for Belief
> Would be iniquity.

Hallaj went one day into the Mosque of Mansur and cried: Gather round, and listen to what I have to tell.

And a great crowd assembled: lovers and followers of his, and haters and critics too.

You ought to know this, said Hallaj: God has made me your outlaw. Kill me.

People in the crowd began to weep; but Abd al-Wudud the Sufi pressed nearer to him and said: Shaykh, how could we kill a man who prays and fasts and recites the Word?

Shaykh, said Hallaj, the motive that really stays you from shedding my blood has nothing to do with Prayer or fasting or reciting the Word. So why not kill me? You will have your reward for it, and I shall come to my peace. For you it will be your Holy War; for me it will be my Martyrdom.

When Hallaj left the Mosque (says Abd al-Wudud) I followed him home and questioned him: Shaykh, what you have said troubles us. What did you mean?

Dear son, said he, no task is more urgent for the Muslims at this moment than my execution. Realize this, that my death will preserve the sanctions of the Law; he who has offended *must* undergo them.

His preaching went on. At last the Jurist Ibn Dawud gave this opinion: If what the Prophet—God's Prayer and Peace on him—brought us from God is true, then what Hallaj says is false. He concluded a violent attack with the words: He may lawfully be put to death.

Ibn Furat gave order for the arrest; but Hallaj left Baghdad with one of his disciples. This was in the year 297.

In the year 301 Hallaj was arrested at Susa and sent up to the capital. Evidence was collected in both Ahwaz and Baghdad that he had claimed divinity; he was also accused of asserting that the Deity took up His abode in members of the Alid House. For the time being he was committed to imprisonment in the Royal Palace.

In the euphoria of passion, said Hallaj, I have been exuberant. And the punishment for exuberance has overtaken me.

It was not till the year '9 that the affair came to a head, and to an end in his death and burning. All this time he was lodged in the Palace, well treated and allowed to receive visitors. His fraudulent pretensions made a complete dupe of Nasr the Chamberlain, who had charge of him; and Hamid ibn Abbas, then Vizier, heard tales that Hallaj had gained an ascendancy over various Attendants and other people about court by pretending that he could raise the dead and perform at pleasure any of the miracles attributed to the Prophets. Certain State Clerks, and even a member of the Hashimite family, were reported to be acting as his apostles and declaring that he, Hallaj, was God (the blasphemy of it!).

These persons were arrested, and confessed under cross-examination by Hamid that they were acting as the man's missionaries and were convinced that he was a god, with power to raise the dead. But when they repeated these statements in the presence of Hallaj himself, he repudiated them: God forbid, said he, that I should pretend to divinity, or to Prophecy—I am merely a man who worships God and practices prayer and fasting and good works; that is all.

By and by Hamid turned up a letter written by Hallaj which contained the following passage:

"If a man would go on Pilgrimage and cannot, let him set apart in his house some square construction, to be touched by no unclean thing, and let no one have access to it. When the day of the Pilgrimage rites comes, let him make his circuit round it, and perform all the same ceremonies as he would perform at Mecca. Then let him gather together thirty orphans, for whom he has prepared the most exquisite feast he can get; let him bring them to his house and serve them that feast; and after waiting on them himself, and washing their hands as a servant himself, let him present each of them with a new frock, and give them each seven dirhams. This will be a substitute for Pilgrimage."

My father (says Ibn Zanji) was reading this letter in evidence at a hearing; and as he finished this passage, Judge Abu Omar turned to Hallaj.

Where did you get that doctrine? he asked.

From Hasan of Basra's *Book of Devotion*, Hallaj replied.

That is false, said the Judge. Outlaw! we ourselves heard Hasan of Basra's *Devotion* when we were studying at Mecca, and there is nothing like that in it.

When Abu Omar used the term *Outlaw*, Hamid broke in, ordering him to put it in writing. The Judge went on trying to give his attention to Hallaj; in his opinion this doctrine was Atheism, and as such punishable with immediate death, for the atheist is given no chance of repentance. But Judge Ibn Buhlul gave his opinion that this in itself did not constitute a capital crime, unless Hallaj were to confess that he not only recorded this doctrine but also believed it—men sometimes record heretical doctrines without holding them. If Hallaj will declare, he went on, that he merely reports this doctrine, but does not himself believe it, then he should be summoned to recant; and if he recants there will be no case against him. If he refuses, then indeed he will deserve death.

But Hamid would not allow the examination to continue; he kept insisting—and finally in a tone which there was no gainsaying—that Abu Omar put in writing his opinion that Hallaj was an Outlaw. The Judge obeyed and signed; and the others present at the trial began to follow suit.

When Hallaj saw what was going on, he cried out: My blood must not be shed like this. You have no right to outlaw me by a quibble. My religion is Islam, my sect the True Way—there are books of mine maintaining the True Way in the bookstores at this moment. I adjure you in the Name of God, *do not shed my blood*.

During the whole time the people present at the hearing were putting their names to Abu Omar's opinion, he kept this up. When the signatures of all present were on the paper, Hamid sent it off to the Caliph Muqtadir.

Nasr the Chamberlain went to warn the Queen-Mother. I am afraid, he told her, that God's Vengeance will come on your son for the death of this devout teacher. So she went to Muqtadir and begged him to spare Hallaj. It was no use: the Caliph, ignoring her request, sent to Hamid the following rescript:

"Inasmuch as the judicial sentence is as you have transmitted it to us, have him taken to the Police Office and scourged with a thousand stripes; if he is not then dead, order his hands and feet amputated and his head then struck off; set his head on a stake and burn his body."

But that same day Muqtadir fell sick of a fever. This coincidence served to inflame the fancies of Nasr and the Queen-Mother; even Muqtadir felt uneasy, and sent Hamid a hurried order to put off the execution. So it was delayed for some days, until the Caliph recovered and his fears abated.

Hamid now urged that the prisoner be put to death without further delay. Muqtadir tried to put the question aside as unimportant.

Prince of the True Believers, said the Vizier, if this man is left to live, he will corrupt the Law and make apostates of your subjects. That will be the end of your dynasty. Let me carry out the sentence. If any trouble comes of it, you may order me to death myself.

Permission was granted. It was agreed that the Chief of Police should come after dark, for fear of a rescue, and bring a company of slaves and men mounted on mules, dressed as grooms, so that Hallaj might be set on one of the mules and huddled along in the middle of the crowd. Nazuk carried these instructions out, and conveyed Hallaj away that night, Hamid's retainers riding with them as far as the Bridge. The Chief of Police himself passed the night with his men, who lay picketed round the Session House building.

On the night before his delivery to execution (says his son Hamd), Hallaj stood up and performed the ordinary Prayer of two Bows. After that, he fell to repeating the word *Illusion, illusion, illusion* . . . to himself, and so continued till the night was more than half spent. Then for a long while he remained silent. Suddenly he gave a cry: *Truth! Truth!* and sprang to his feet. He bound on his turban, donned his cloak, stretched out his arms, and facing the Direction, fell into an ecstasy and talked with God.

Ibrahim ibn Fatik, his servant, and I, who were with him, both remembered some parts of what he then said: these:—

See, he said, we are ready to be called as Thy witnesses, and come for refuge into Thy Grace; into the splendor of Thy Glory, into the Brightness for Thy declaring of whatever Thou pleasest. *IN HEAVEN—GOD. ON EARTH—GOD.* O Setter of the Cycles and Shaper of Forms, O by Whose Decree these bodies are compounded! Thou wilt come shining to sight, when Thou wilt, on whom Thou wilt, and as Thou wilt, even as Thou didst blazon Thy Decree in the image of that *FAIREST FORM* of Adam, that Form which shall blazon forth the Word, the sole form gifted with knowledge and speech, and free power and proof.

Thou it was didst assign this Thy witness here his part to speak as Thyself. How then is it come to this? For Thou it was didst will my beginning, Thou Who didst seize my being to use it for Thy symbol, Thou Who didst proclaim it, at my last and highest, as My Divine Being, Who didst display the Reality of my knowledge, and those miracles I wrought. Thou it was didst raise me up at my ascensions to those thrones of my own pre-eternity, and didst cause me to speak the BE! of my own creation.

How is it come to this? that now I go to die, to suffer a felon's death, to hang on a gibbet, my body to be burned, my ashes given to the winds and streams for keeping? Ah!

Surely, surely the least portion of this flesh which has been Thine incense is promise for the body of my Rising, promise of reality more sure than the mightiest hills are real!

Then he began to speak in verse:

> For souls whose witness now departs, to go beyond Until,
>   into the Witness of Eternity,
>   Hear my sorrow, Thou!
> For those miracles whose dialectic shut the mouth of argument,
>   Hear my sorrow, Thou!
> In the name of Thy Love! for all the valiancy of that saintly
>   chivalry, who rode themselves as steeds,
>   Hear my sorrow, Thou!
> For them to be lost and gone, like unheeding Ad, or the
>   long-lost Worldly Garden!
> And then, the abandoned herd, wandering, stumbling,
> Blinder than beasts, blinder than flocking sheep.

He fell silent again. After a while his servant Ibrahim said: Master, give me some word for a keepsake.

Your self! he answered. Unless you enslave it, it will enslave you.

When the morning dawned, they came to fetch him out into the Square. As I watched him go, he was dancing in his chains.

A crowd beyond counting was assembled.

I was there (says Abu Hasan of Hulwan) the day they executed Hallaj. They brought him from his cell bound and chained; but he was laughing.

Master, said I, why are you like this?

He answered only with a verse:

> My Host, with His own ruthless courtesy,
> Passed me His Cup, and bade me drink. I drank.
> Round went the wine; sudden I heard Him cry:
> Headsman! the Mat and Sword! This is the end
> Of drink with Liodragon in July.

When they had brought him as far as the gibbet, and he saw the scaffold and the nails, he laughed till the tears ran from his eyes. Presently, turning to look at the crowd assembled, he saw Shibli among the rest.

Abu Bakr, said he, have you your prayer carpet with you?

Yes, said Shibli.

Will you lay it for me?

Shibli laid out his carpet. Hallaj performed a Prayer of two Bows, reciting the passage *WE SHALL TRY YOU* with the first and the passage *ALL SOULS TASTE DEATH* with the second. When his Prayer was finished, he spoke; I can only remember some of his words, the following:

O our God! Who dost glow in all places and art not in any place, I beseech Thee by the truth of Thy Word which declares that I am, by the truth of this my word which declares that Thou art, I beseech Thee, my Master, give me grace to be grateful for this happiness of Thy giving, that Thou didst hide from others what was unveiled to me, the raging fires of Thy Face, and forbid them to look, as I was permitted to look, into things hidden in the Mystery of Thee.

And these Thy servants who are gathered to slay me, in zeal for Thy Religion, longing to win Thy Favor, forgive them, Lord. Have mercy on them. Surely, if Thou hadst shown them what Thou hast shown me, they would never have done what they have done; and hadst Thou kept from me what Thou hast kept from them, I should not have suffered this tribulation. Whatsoever Thou wilt do, I praise Thee! Whatsoever Thou dost will, I praise Thee!

Then he was silent. The headsman stepped up to him and dealt him a smashing blow between the eyes; the blood poured from his nostrils. Shibli cried out, and rent his dress, and fell fainting.

The headsman was ordered to administer one thousand strokes with a scourge. It was done. Hallaj uttered no cry, nor did he plead for pardon.

Only according to one witness, when he had endured the six-hundredth blow, he cried out to the Chief of Police: Send for me! and I'll tell you what will more profit the Caliph than the storming of Constantinople!

They told me to expect some such offer, answered Nazuk, or a bigger one. It won't get you out of your stripes—nothing will.

After that Hallaj said nothing more until the thousandth blow came at last. His hand was then amputated, then his foot; and he was fastened on the gibbet.

There he hung till nightfall, when an order arrived from the Caliph Muqtadir giving permission for his beheading. However, the officer in charge said: It is late now — leave him till tomorrow.

When morning came he was taken down and dragged forward for decapitation. It was at this time that he spoke his last words: All who have known ecstasy long for this . . . the loneliness of the Only One . . . alone with the Alone.

He was set a little way in front of the gibbet, and his head struck off. The trunk was rolled up in a strip of reed-matting, and soaked in naphtha, then burned.

I was there (says the Clerk Ibn Zanji). I was standing up as tall as I could on the back of my mule—I had not been able to get into the Square. The trunk twisted on the coals as the flames burned it. When there was nothing left but ashes, they were collected and thrown from the Minaret over the Tigris. The head was set up on the Bridge for two days, and then sent to Khurasan to be exhibited in the various districts.

All booksellers were summoned to appear and obliged to take an oath that they would neither sell nor buy any work by Hallaj.

His disciples asserted that the person who had endured the scourging was not he, but some enemy of his on whom his likeness had been cast. Some of them even claimed to have seen him afterward, and to have heard something from him to that effect, along with more nonsense not worth the trouble of transcribing.

TRANSLATED BY ERIC SCHROEDER

[from *Dīvān*, Poetic Works]

Many of the greatest Persian poets are for us no more distinct than
shadows. They died without biographers, leaving only a residue of
anecdotes. We are not certain which words, which lines, which poems
are theirs, as their works remain scattered. Many of the minor poets
are, perhaps, irretrievably lost.

Rudaki is the first major poet who wrote Persian, the first for whom
we have a body of work. He was born and died in the district of
Rudak, near Samarkand, and in his later years was blind. He was the
court poet of the Samanids, and his musical poems gave him great
fame in his own time.

Perhaps his best-known lines, the *Jū-yi Mūliyān qaṣīdah*, are included in the passage concerning him from Samarqandi's *Chahār
Maqālah* in the next section.

Reunion after Separation

Of the pangs of separation I have suffered and borne more
Than, through all the distant ages, any mortal being bore;
And my heart had quite forgotten all the charms of union sweet;
But what joy 'tis, after severance, with one's idol dear to meet!
  So I turned me back in gladness, back unto the camp and tent,
Light in spirits and light-hearted, and my speech with lightness blent;
For there came enthralled to meet me—yet with bosom all unbraced—
A sweet maid with a cypress figure, tresses flowing to her waist.
  "How hath fared thy heart without me?" 'twas with coquetry she said,
"Yea, and how thy soul without me?" did she add, while blushing red.
  Then I spake and gave her answer, "O thou face of heavenly birth,
My soul's ruin, mischief-maker of all beauties of this earth!
Snared is my world in the circle of thy locks as amber sweet,
And 'tis caught like a ball with the mall-bat through thy curling ringlets neat!
Deeply filled am I with anguish by those eyes which arrows dart,

I am anguished by those tresses, which rich showers of musk impart.
Where were night without the moonbeam? where were day without the sun?
Where the rose that hath no water? where the mead that rain doth shun?"
    Then my bosom grew sweet through toying with her hyacinthine hair,
And my lips were sugared through kisses from that coral mouth so fair;
Now was she the ruby-buyer, and the ruby-seller I,
While the nectarous wine she poured me, and I drained the goblet dry.

Lament in Old Age

Every tooth, ah me! has crumbled, dropped and fallen in decay!
Tooth it was not, nay say rather, 'twas a brilliant lamp's bright ray;
Each was white and silvery-flashing, pearl and coral in the light,
Glistening like the stars of morning or the raindrop sparkling bright;
Not a one remaineth to me, lost through weakness and decay.

Many a desert waste existeth where was once a garden glad;
And a garden glad existeth where was once a desert sad.
    Ah, thou moon-faced, musky-tressed one, how canst thou e'er know or deem
What was once thy poor slave's station,—how once held in high esteem?
On him now thy curling tresses, coquettish thou dost bestow,
In those days thou didst not see him, when his own rich curls did flow.
Time there was when he in gladness, happy did himself disport,
Pleasure in excess enjoying, though his silver store ran short;
Always bought he in the market, countless-priced above the rest,
Every captive Turki damsel with a round pomegranate breast.

Ever was my keen eye open for a maid's curled tresses long,
Ever alert my ear to listen to the word-wise man of song.
House I had not, wife nor children, no, nor female family ties,
Free from these and unencumbered have I been in every wise.

Those the times when mine was fortune, fortune good in plenteous store.
    Now the times have changed,—and I, too, changed and altered must succumb,
Bring the beggar's staff here to me; time for staff and scrip has come!

TRANSLATED BY A. V. WILLIAMS JACKSON

AL-MUTANABBI: LAUDS

[from *Dīwān*, Poetic Works]

Unlike Al-Maarri, Al-Mutanabbi (915–965) took to the business
of panegyric with relish and success. He was the principal poetic
ornament of the Hamdanid dynasty in Syria, which distinguished
itself by literary patronage. Al-Mutanabbi was gifted with an almost
peerless talent and an almost demonic pride. When rebuffed, as he
occasionally was, he could loose verse as vicious and devastating as
has ever been written—verse at the same time so excellent that it
is considered among his masterpieces. Such verse is the first of the
following selections, written against Abu al-Misk Kafur, the Abyssinian
ruler of Egypt who had once befriended him.

Al-Mutanabbi did not follow the philosophy or art of the "new
poets." In fact he has been considered as a neoclassicist because he
went back to the older meters and forced them to bend to his art.
When he was free of patronage and most himself, his themes were
the decline of art and the beautiful variety of nature. Although one of
his rivals insisted "he strings pearls and bricks together," he is regarded by many Arabs as the greatest poet in their language.

> Promiscuous tags and liberal lip I hate,
> That gutter currency that swamps the state
> Where slaves who knock their masters down and clear
> The till, are certain of a great career.
> I went there as the guest of liars, who
> Would neither entertain nor let me go,
> Liars for whose putrid frames death would not function
> Unless equipped with a carbolic truncheon.
>
> I saw the land an orchard, the foxes creeping
> Between the crumbling walls and watchmen sleeping;
> On grapes perennial the foxes thrive.

I saw what I hoped never to see alive,
The dog that fouled me pampered and well-fed,
The nigger king in plumes, the good men dead.

I saw the cult of slaves, the rites imposed
On jailbirds by a eunuch in priest's clothes,
From which peeped out his servile origin:
The best-dressed leper cannot change his skin
A local proverb: when you buy your slave
Buy a stick too, and teach him to behave.

I saw the hole in the black lip that rules
The poltroons and the gluttons and the fools.
The nation governed by a pregnant pathic
Is either lunatic or astigmatic.
He picked my brain, forbade me to depart,
Postured abroad as patron of the arts.
I shouted death to escort me from pain
And would have relished it like sugar-cane,
But found a simpler way, this camel-crupper,
And ride, damning his midwife and his mother.

What howling sires, what genteel baboon set
Taught the tawny eunuch etiquette?
Did he learn manners from his auctioneer
When sold for twopence (discount for the tattered ear)?
Supremely sordid sir, in your defence
I'll be an advocate, and plead that since
The great white bulls at moments fail to rise
To the occasion, eunuchs can't do otherwise.

They went on, and left me long vague nights,
Longer than bridal nights, and showed me
The regular unwanted moon, and held
The new moon beyond the stretch of roads,
A journey away, and the way doubled
By a stop in existence like a wall.
And for their Hermes of calamity
They made me live when the lovers had gone.

The hot gardens sometimes heard voices
In migrant winds. Like a tree I waited

For the voice to come back. Touching a glass
I sometimes choked because the mind flashed
To fixed steel, that now catches the water
By the one-time camping-place of girls.
I watched the stars on their dark cruises.
Could they not lead to the high clearings?

Has the night not seen your eyes, I cried,
To grow thin and quiet and go?
By the last house I found dawn. The meeting
Healed my limbs and the night died
And the day stood in quick light,
Still wet with gelatine of birth, the sign
That hills were opening, and over lush roads
The sun advancing as your envoy.

Here is the final stretch, the instrument
That cuts short the reminiscence,
The chatter of what they did to death, the coil
Of it, and the paternal tube of it
And snakiness. At a long paean
The corpse turns over, quicker than hands,
Whose horns state the pain of earning,
Do for time and his slip. He passes
Imperiously, owning the air
And filigree of limbs and soul,
A trap in beauty's structure, that no lover
Could fathom and keep the manacles.
Galenus with his atabrine, the fluting moron
With his goats, went after him. They counted
A similar tally of hours, and the quiet
Was sweeter for the fool. Unbroken drive
Even for welfare is only warfare
And the metal weights on the lungs
Deny the blossoms to the stretch of need.

My songs gave eyes to the blind, ears to the deaf,
Set the critics flapping like nightbirds,
Set me at rest all night on my bed.

And pay me well if I write you a eulogy.
The flatterers will come to you mouthing it.
And desert every voice but mine, for I
Am the singing lark, the rest are echo.
Time is my scribe and my register
It follows me singing the words I drop.

From safe harbours they sailed away
Pre-occupied because of my poems.
The throats that had never spoken trilled
My scale, the moment before landfall.

TRANSLATED BY HERBERT HOWARTH AND IBRAHIM SHUKRALLAH

That which souls desire is too small a thing for them
    to fight about and perish by each other's hands,
Howbeit a true man will face grim Fate ere he suffer contumely.
If the life of aught that lives were lasting, we should reckon
    the brave the most misguided of us,
But if there is no escape from death, 'tis but weakness to be a coward.
All that the soul finds hard before it has come to pass
    is easy when it comes.

Men from their kings alone their worth derive.
But Arabs ruled by aliens cannot thrive:
Boors without culture, without noble fame,
Who know not loyalty and honour's name.
Go where thou wilt, thou seest in every land
Folk driven like cattle by a servile band.

TRANSLATED BY R. A. NICHOLSON

[from *Al-Ta'arruf li-Madhhab Ahl al-Taṣawwuf*, A Study of the
Ideology of the Sufis]

Al-Kalabadhi was a disciple of one of Al-Hallaj's friends and a native
of Bukhara. He produced a work which came to be recognized as
one of the three or four most important and best-loved compendiums
of Sufi theory and lore. It is especially characterized by an understand-
ably urgent zeal to establish the orthodoxy of Sufism in the eyes of
the theologians and legists. It was a worthy forerunner of the more
definitive and voluminous work in that same cause written by Al-
Ghazzali. A considerable part of its success is attributed by authorities
to its concise and orderly style.

I heard Abu ᵓl-Hasan Muhammad ibn Ahmad al-Fārisī[1] say: "The elements of Ṣūfism are ten in number. The first is the isolation of unification;
the second is the understanding of audition; the third is good fellowship;
the fourth is preference of preferring; the fifth is the yielding up of personal
choice; the sixth is swiftness of ecstasy; the seventh is the revelation of the
thoughts; the eighth is abundant journeying; the ninth is the yielding up of
earning; the tenth is the refusal to hoard."

Isolation of unification means that no thought of polytheism or atheism
should corrupt the purity of the belief in one God. The understanding of
audition implies that one should listen in the light of mystical experience,
not merely in the light of learning. The preference of preferring means that
one should prefer that another should prefer,[2] so that he may have the merit
of preferring. Swiftness of ecstasy is realised when the conscience is void of
anything that may disturb ecstasy, and not filled with thoughts which prevent
one from listening to the promptings of God. The revelation of the thoughts
means that one should examine every thought that comes into his conscience,
and follow what is of God, but leave alone what is not of God. Abundant
journeying is for the purpose of beholding the warnings that are to be found
in heaven and earth; for God says, "Have they not journeyed on in the land

---

[1] Nearly all of the authorities cited in this selection were renowned Sufis. Details of their
lives can be found in the standard biographical dictionaries of Sufism. [Ed.]
[2] That is, that one should be eager to teach others the more excellent way of self-abnegation.

and seen how was the end of those before them?"[3] and again, "Say, Journey ye on in the land, and behold how the creation appeared";[4] and the words "journey ye on in the land" are explained as meaning, with the light of gnosis, not with the darkness of agnosia, in order to cut the bonds (of materialism) and to train the soul. The yielding up of earning is with a view to demanding of the soul that it should put its trust in God. The refusal to hoard is only meant to apply to the condition of mystical experience, and not to the prescriptions of theology.

Al-Junayd said: "Ṣūfism is the preservation of the moments: that is, that a man does not consider what is outside his limits, does not agree with any but God, and only associates with his proper moment."[5] Ibn ᶜAṭā said: "Ṣūfism means being at ease with God." Abu Yaᶜqūb al-Sūsī said: "The Ṣūfi is the man who is never made uneasy when aught is taken from him, and never wearies himself with seeking (what he does not possess)." Al-Junayd was asked, "What is Ṣūfism?" He replied: "It is the cleaving of the conscience to God: and this is not attained, save when the soul passes away from secondary causes (*asbāb*), through the power of the spirit, and remains with God." Al-Shiblī was asked: "Why are the Ṣūfis called Ṣūfis?" He answered: "Because they have been stamped with the existence of the image and the affirmation of the attribute. If they had been stamped with the effacement of the image, only He would have remained, Who imposes the image and affirms the attribute, and poured their images upon them, but does not approve that any man who truly knows should have either image or attribute." Abū Yazīd said: "The Ṣūfis are children in the lap of God." Abū ᶜAbdillāh al-Nibājī said: "Ṣūfism is like the disease *birsām*:[6] in the first stages the patient raves, but when the disease takes a hold on him, it makes him dumb." He means, that the Ṣūfi at first describes his station and speaks as his state demands; but when revelation is granted to him, he is bewildered, and holds his tongue. I heard Fāris say: "So long as ideas appear in a man's thoughts, according to the dictates of the soul's vagaries, he finds it in his heart to esteem the former state higher, and so it comes that he divulges: but as for attainment, it throws a veil over the means of satisfaction, and so he is in the end

[3] Koran 30.8.
[4] Koran 29.19.
[5] "Moment" here has the mystical sense of the immediate spiritual condition: the mystic occupies himself only with the actual.
[6] A tumor of the stomach.

dumb to every appetite." When Al-Nūrī was asked about Ṣūfism, he said:
"It is a divulging of a station, and an attainment of a stature." Being asked to
describe their (*sc.* Ṣūfīs') characteristics, he said: "They bring joy into (the
hearts of) others, and turn away from (the desire of) harming them. God
says, 'Take to pardon, and order what is kind, and shun the ignorant.' "[7] By
"a divulging of a station" he means that the Ṣūfī, if he expresses himself at
all, does so in connection with his own spiritual state, and not with regard
to that of any other person, theoretically;[8] and by "an attainment of a stature"[9]
he signifies that such a man is transported by his own state through his own
state, away from the state of any other person. The following verses of Al-
Nūrī are also apposite:

> "Speak not of this," Thou saidst,
> Then into speechless mysteries Thou ledst
>   My wondering soul:
> Can utterance describe th'unutterable?

> Not every man that cries,
> "Lo, thus am I!" Thou tak'st at his surmise;
>   When deeds have shown
> That so he is, then claimest Thou thine own.

Now it is our intention to describe some of the stations in the language
of the Ṣūfīs themselves, but not at great length, for we have no love of long
speech. We will relate of the discourses of the Shaykhs only such as are easy
to understand, avoiding dark enigmas and fine-drawn allusions.

Union implies being inwardly separated from all but God, seeing inwardly—in the sense of veneration—none but God, and listening to none
but God. Al-Nūrī said: "Union is the revelation of the heart and the contemplation of the conscience." Revelation of the heart is illustrated by the
words of Ḥārithah: "It was as though I beheld the Throne of my Lord
coming forth," while contemplation of the conscience is indicated by the
Prophet's saying: "Worship God as if thou seest Him,"[10] and the words of
Ibn ʿUmar: "We were beholding God in that place." Another said: "Union

---

[7] Koran 8.198.
[8] *Sc.*, he talks only of personal experience, and does not presume to criticize others according to a preconceived theory.
[9] Or, "a stay."
[10] For this famous tradition, cf. Muslim, *Ṣaḥīḥ*, I, p. 158.

is when the conscience arrives at the station of oblivion," meaning that veneration for God distracts from the veneration of aught else. One of the great Ṣūfīs said: "Union is when the servant witnesses none but his Creator, and when no thought occurs to his conscience, save it be of his Maker." Sahl said: "They were moved by the affliction, and were therefore in commotion. If they had been at rest, they would have attained union."

Al-Junayd said: "Love is the inclination of the heart," meaning that the heart then inclines towards God and what is of God, without any effort. Another said: "Love is concord," that is, obedience in what God commands, refraining from what He forbids, and satisfaction with what He has decreed and ordained. Muḥammad ibn ᶜAlī al-Kattānī said: "Love means preferring the beloved." Another said: "Love means preferring what one loves for the person whom one loves." Abū ᶜAbdillāh al-Nibājī said: "Love is a pleasure if it be for a creature, and an annihilation if it be for the Creator." By "annihilation" he means that no personal interest remains, that such love has no cause, and that the lover does not persist through any cause. Sahl said: "Whoso loves God, he is life; but whoso loves, he has no life." By the words "he is life" he means that his life is agreeable, because the lover finds delight in whatever comes to him from the beloved, whether it be loathsome or desirable: while by "he has no life" he means that, as he is ever seeking to reach what he loves, and ever fearing that he may be prevented from attaining it, his whole life is lost. One of the great Ṣūfīs said: "Love is a pleasure, and with God there is no pleasure: for the stations of reality are astonishment, surrender and bewilderment. The love of man for God is a reverence indwelling in his heart, and not countenancing the love of any other than God. The love of God for man is, that He afflicts him, and so renders him improper for any but Him. This is the sense of God's words: 'And I have chosen thee for Myself.' "[11] By the words "renders him improper for any but Him" he means that there remains no part over in him wherewith he may attend to other things, or pay heed to material conditions. One of the Ṣūfīs said: "Love is of two kinds: the love of confession, which belongs to elect and common alike, and the love of ecstasy in the sense of attainment. With this latter there is no consideration of self or other creatures, or of secondary causes or conditions, for there is a total absorption in the consideration of what is with God and of God." One of the Ṣūfīs[12] composed these verses:

[11] Koran 20.43.
[12] The following verses are usually attributed to Rabiah, an eighth-century woman mystic of Baghdad; the translation is by R. A. Nicholson. [Ed.]

> Two ways I love Thee: selfishly,
> And next, as worthy is of Thee.
> 'Tis selfish love that I do naught
> Save think on Thee with every thought;
> 'Tis purest love when Thou dost raise
> The veil to my adoring gaze.
> Not mine the praise in that or this,
> Thine is the praise in both, I wis.

Ibn ʿAbd al-Ṣamad said: "Love is that which renders blind and deaf: it makes blind to all but the Beloved, so that one beholds no objective but Him. The Prophet said: Thy love is a thing which renders blind and deaf." He also recited the following verses:

> Love deafens me to every voice but His:
>   Was ever love so strange as this?
> Love blinds me, and on Him alone I gaze:
>   Love blinds and, being hidden, slays.

He also recited:

> There is a superfluity of love
> Which no man may endure: it soars above
> All judgment, when the so much dreaded thing
> Descends. Or let it equal anguish bring,
> He will be glad: or let it pass all measure,
> He will rejoice, and reckon it a pleasure.

Now the Ṣūfīs have certain peculiar expressions and technical terms which they mutually understand, but which are scarcely used by any others. We will set forth such of these as may be convenient, illustrating their meanings with word and phrase. In this we merely aim at explaining the meaning of the several expressions, not the experience which the expression covers: for such experience does not come within the scope even of reference, much less explanation. The real essence of the spiritual states of the Ṣūfīs is such that expressions are not adequate to describe it: nevertheless, these expressions are fully understood by those who have experienced these states.

TRANSLATED BY A. J. ARBERRY

[from *Shāh-nāmeh*, The Book of Kings]

Firdawsi is one of Iran's great heroes. His long epic poem, *Shāh-nāmeh*, is read by every school child in Iran and may still be heard recited in the coffeehouses and gymnasiums of the country. A. J. Arberry has printed an interesting letter which Mirza Muhammad Ali Furughi, a scholar and prime minister, wrote on the millenary of Firdawsi's birth, trying to explain his feelings about the poet and the poem.

He wrote in part: "Firdausī's *Shāh-nāma*, considered both quantitatively and qualitatively, is the greatest work in Persian literature and poetry; indeed, one can say that it's one of the world's literary masterpieces . . . [Firdawsi] rescued from oblivion and preserved for all time our national history . . . [and] our Persian language."[1]

Firdawsi was born in Tus. His family were rich landowners, and he lived most of his life on his estates. The poem was begun by Daqiqi, and when he died, Firdawsi took up his work, incorporated and acknowledged one thousand of his finished lines, and spent some twenty-five years completing it. The finished work contains over sixty thousand couplets; one standard edition of the Persian text fills ten volumes. Firdawsi deliberately tried to use Persian words and avoid the Arabic vocabulary which had already flooded his native tongue.

The subject of the *Shāh-nāmeh* is the history of Iran, its heroes and glory, from legendary times to those of the Sassanian kings.[2] It is decidedly not an Islamic work, although the general theme of the warfare between the descendants of Iraj (the Persians) and Tur (the Turks) had a very contemporary meaning. The major source for the poem, in which legend and history are almost inextricably mixed,

---

[1] *Classical Persian Literature* (London, 1958), pp. 45–50.

[2] In volume 9 of *The Sháhnáma of Firdausí*, tr. A. G. and Edmond Warner (London, 1906), there is a very useful "General Table of Contents," by means of which one can study the exceedingly complex arrangement of the poem and locate the following selection with respect to the whole.

seems to have been an old Pahlavi history of the early kings. Like most of the older epics, it is a fiercely patriotic work. The famous story of Firdawsi's experiences with Sultan Mahmud of Ghaznah in connection with the work has been included below in a selection from the *Chahār Maqālah* of Samarqandi. The poem was completed about 1010.

The following episode from the *Shāh-nāmeh* is already somewhat familiar to English readers because of its treatment by Matthew Arnold. It comes as close to genuine tragedy as anything in Islamic literature.

> The bright sun shone, the raven night flew low,
> Great Rustam donned his tiger-skin cuirass
> And mounted on his fiery dragon-steed.
> Two leagues divided host from host, and all
> Stood ready-armed. The hero with a casque
> Of iron on his head came on the field.
> Suhráb on his side revelling with comrades
> Had thus addressed Húmán: "That lion-man,
> Who striveth with me, is as tall as I am
> And hath a dauntless heart. He favoreth me
> In shoulder, breast, and arm, and thou wouldst say
> That some skilled workman laid us out by line.
> His very feet and stirrups move my love
> And make me blush, for I perceive in him
> The marks whereof my mother spake. Moreover
> My heart presageth that he must be Rustam,
> For few resemble him. I may not challenge
> My sire or lightly meet him in the combat."
>   Húmán said: "Rustam oft hath countered me:
> This charger is like his, except in action."
>   At sunrise, when they woke, Suhráb arrayed
> Himself in mail and mirthful though resolved
> Set forward shouting, ox-head mace in hand.
> He greeted Rustam smiling, thou hadst said
> That they had passed the night in company:
> "How went the night? How is't with thee to-day?
> Why so intent on strife? Fling down thine arrows
> And scimitar, and drop the hand of wrong.

Let us dismount and, sitting, clear our faces
With wine, and, leaguing in God's sight, repent
Our former strife. Until some other cometh
To battle, feast with me because I love thee,
And weep for shamefastness. In sooth thou comest
From heroes and wilt tell me of thy stock,
For as my foe thou shouldst not hide thy name.
Art thou the famous Rustam of Zábul,
The son of valiant Zál the son of Sám?"
    Then Rustam: "Young aspirant! heretofore
We talked not thus but spake last night of wrestling.
I am not to be gulled, attempt it not.
Though thou art young I am no child myself,
But girt to wrestle, and the end shall be
According to the will of Providence.
I have known ups and downs, and am not one
To practice guile upon."
                    Suhráb replied:
"Old man! if thou rejectest my proposals . . .!
I wished that thou shouldst die upon thy bed,
And that thy kin should tomb thy soulless corpse,
But I will end thee if it be God's will."
    They lighted, tied their chargers to a rock,
And cautiously advanced in mail and casque
With troubled hearts. They wrestled like two lions
Until their bodies ran with sweat and blood.
From sunrise till the shadows grew they strove
Until Suhráb, that maddened Elephant,
Reached out, up-leaping with a lion's spring,
Caught Rustam's girdle, tugged amain as though,
Thou wouldst have said, to rend the earth, and shouting
With rage and vengeance hurled him to the ground,
Raised him aloft and, having dashed him down,
Sat on his breast with visage, hand, and mouth
Besmirched with dust, as when a lion felleth
An onager, then drew a bright steel dagger
To cut off Rustam's head, who seeing this
Exclaimed: "Explain I must! O warrior
That takest Lions captive and art skilled
With lasso, mace, and scimitar! the customs
And laws of arms with us are not as yours.

In wrestling none may take a foeman's head
The first time that his back is on the ground,
But having thrown him twice and won the name
Of Lion then he may behead the foe:
Such is our custom."
                              Thus he sought to 'scape
The Dragon's clutches and get off with life.
The brave youth hearkened to the old man's words.
In part through confidence, in part through fate,
In part no doubt through magnanimity,
Suhráb let Rustam go, turned toward the plain,
Pursued an antelope that crossed his path,
And utterly forgot his recent foe.
When he was far away Húmán came up
As swift as dust and asked about the fight.
He told Húmán what had been said and done,
Who cried: "Alas! young man! art thou indeed
So weary of thy life? Woe for thy breast,
Mien, stature, stirrups, and heroic feet!
The mighty Lion whom thou hadst ensnared
Thou hast let go and all is still to do.
Mark how he will entreat thee on the day
Of battle owing to thy senseless act.
A king once spake a proverb to the point:
'Despise not any foe however weak.' "

    He took the very life out of Suhráb,
Who standing sorrowing and amazed replied:
"Let us dismiss such fancies from our hearts,
For he will come to fight with me tomorrow,
And thou shalt see a yoke upon his neck."

    He went to camp in dudgeon at his deed.
When Rustam had escaped his foeman's clutch
He was again as 'twere a mount of steel.
He went toward a rivulet as one
Who having fainted is himself again.
He drank and bathed, then prayed to God for strength
And victory, not knowing what the sun
And moon decreed, or how the turning sky
Would rob him of the Crown upon his head.

    The tale is told that Rustam had at first
Such strength bestowed by Him who giveth all

That if he walked upon a rock his feet
Would sink therein. Such puissance as that
Proved an abiding trouble, and he prayed
To God in bitterness of soul to minish
His strength that he might walk like other men.
According to his prayer his mountain-strength
Had shrunk, but face to face with such a task,
And pierced by apprehension of Suhráb,
He cried to God and said: "Almighty Lord!
Protect Thy slave in his extremity.
O holy Fosterer! I ask again
My former strength."

                       God granted him his prayer,
The strength which once had waned now waxed in him.
He went back to the field perturbed and pale
While, like a maddened elephant, Suhráb,
With lasso on his arm and bow in hand,
Came in his pride and roaring like a lion,
His plunging charger flinging up the soil.
When Rustam saw the bearing of his foe
He was astound and gazing earnestly
Weighed in his mind the chances of the fight.
Suhráb, puffed up with youthful arrogance,
On seeing Rustam in his strength and grace,
Cried: "Thou that didst escape the Lion's claws!
Why com'st thou boldly to confront me? Speak!
Hast thou no interests of thine own to seek?"

They tied their steeds while fate malignantly
Revolved o'erhead, and when dark fate is wroth
Flint rocks become like wax. The two began
To wrestle, holding by their leathern belts.
As for Suhráb thou wouldst have said: "High heaven
Hath hampered him," while Rustam reaching clutched
That warrior-leopard by the head and neck,
Bent down the body of the gallant youth,
Whose time was come and all whose strength was gone,
And like a lion dashed him to the ground;
Then, knowing that Suhráb would not stay under,
Drew lightly from his waist his trenchant sword
And gashed the bosom of his gallant son.

Whenever thou dost thirst for blood and stain
Therewith thy glittering dagger, destiny
    Will be athirst for thy blood, and ordain
Each hair of thine to be a sword for thee.
    Suhráb cried: "Ah!" and writhed. Naught recked
        he then
Of good or ill. "I am alone to blame,"
He said to Rustam. "Fate gave thee my key.
This hump-backed sky reared me to slay me soon.
Men of my years will mock me since my neck
Hath thus come down to dust. My mother told me
How I should recognise my father. I
Sought him in love and die of my desire.
Alas! my toils are vain, I have not seen him.
Now wert thou fish, or wrapped like night in gloom,
Or quit of earth wast soaring like a star,
My father would avenge me when he seeth
My pillow bricks. Some chief will say to Rustam:
'Suhráb was slain and flung aside in scorn
While seeking thee.' "
                Then Rustam grew distraught,
The world turned black, his body failed; o'ercome
He sank upon the ground and swooned away;
Till coming to himself he cried in anguish:
"Where is the proof that thou art Rustam's son?
May his name perish from among the great,
For I am Rustam! Be my name forgotten,
And may the son of Sám sit mourning me!"
    He raved, his blood seethed, and with groans he
        plucked
His hair up by the roots, while at the sight
Suhráb sank swooning till at length he cried:
"If thou indeed art Rustam thou hast slain me
In wanton malice, for I made advances,
But naught that I could do would stir thy love
Undo my breastplate, view my body bare,
Behold thy jewel, see how sires treat sons!
The drums beat at my gate, my mother came
With blood-stained cheeks and stricken to the soul
Because I went. She bound this on mine arm
And said: 'Preserve this keepsake of thy father's

And mark its virtue.' It is mighty now,
Now when the strife is over and the son
Is nothing to his sire."
                              When Rustam loosed
The mail and saw the gem he rent his clothes,
And cried: "Oh! my brave son, approved by all
And slain by me!"
                              With dust upon his head
And streaming face he rent his locks until
His blood ran down.
                              "Nay, this is worse and worse,"
Suhráb said, "Wherefore weep? What will it profit
To slay thyself? What was to be hath been."
    When day declined and Rustam came not back
There went forth twenty trusty warriors
To learn the issue. Both the steeds were standing
Bemoiled with dust, but Rustam was not there.
The nobles, thinking that he had been slain,
Went to Káús in consternation saying:
"The throne of majesty is void of Rustam!"
    A cry went up throughout the host and all
Was in confusion. Then Káús bade sound
The drums and trumpets, Tús came, and the Sháh
Said to the troops: "Dispatch a messenger
That he may find out what Suhráb hath done,
And if there must be mourning through Írán.
None will confront him with brave Rustam dead.
We must attack in force and speedily."
    While clamour raged Suhráb said thus to Rustam:
"The Turkmans' case is altered since my day
Is done. Use all thine influence that the Sháh
May not attack them. They approached Írán
Through trust in me, and I encouraged them.
How could I tell, O famous paladin!
That I should perish by my father's hand?
Let them depart unscathed, and treat them kindly.
I had a warrior in yonder hold
Caught by my lasso. Him I often asked
To point thee out: mine eyes looked ever for thee.
He told me all but this. His place is void.
His words o'er-cast my day, and I despaired.

See who he is and let him not be harmed.
I marked in thee the tokens that my mother
Described but trusted not mine eyes. The stars
Decreed that I should perish by thy hand.
I came like lightning and like wind I go.
In heaven I may look on thee with joy."
    Then Rustam choked, his heart was full of fire,
His eyes of tears. He mounted quick as dust
And came with lamentations to the host
In grievous consternation at his deed.
The Íránians catching sight of him fell prostrate
And gave God praise that Rustam had returned,
But when they saw the dust upon his head,
His clothes and bosom rent, they questioned him:
"What meaneth this? For whom art thou thus troubled?"
    He told the fearful deed, and all began
To mourn aloud with him. His anguish grew.
He told the nobles: "I have lost to-day
All strength and courage. Fight not with Túrán:
I have done harm enough."

TRANSLATED BY ARTHUR AND EDMOND WARNER

AL-MAARRI: DOUBTS

[from *Risālāt*, Letters, *Saqṭ al-Zand*, The Spark of Flint, and *Luzūm mā lā yalzam*, The Necessity of What Isn't Necessary]

In the course of his travels, which he recorded in a book regarded as an early masterpiece of Persian prose, Nasir-i Khosraw mentions visiting the Syrian town of Maarat al-Numan in 1047: "There was living there a certain personage called Abu al-Ala, who, though sightless, was the chief man of the city. He possessed great wealth and slaves and very numerous attendants, and it was as though all the inhabitants of the city were of his people. . . . There were continually with him some two hundred persons, come from all parts of the world, to attend his lectures on poetry and diction."

That is a picture of Al-Maarri which is unusual in every respect save his attachment to his native town. He was orphaned and blinded in his childhood. When he came to young manhood he perfected his already extraordinary mastery of the Arabic language and its prosody by traveling. He went to Baghdad, but found he had no taste for necessary panegyric, and arranged to return and spend the remainder of his life in Maarat al-Numan on conditions set forth in his letter included below. He died there in 1057.

Al-Maarri's poems are cynical and sad, but his is not the cynicism of Abu Nuwas or the sadness of Abu al-Atahiyah. His feelings and their expression are far more powerful. His skepticism had its own consistency and resonance, a consistency born no doubt of singular suffering and the resonance of an ear in a world of darkness. Yet one can detect now and then, mostly in his talk of love, dogged traces of a faith and hope in justice for men—whose miseries are not all by any means, as he knew better than most, self-inflicted.

124

Letter to the People of Maᶜarrat al-Nuᶜmān

In the name of God the merciful and clement! This letter is addressed to the people of Maᶜarrat (whom God encompass with happiness!) by Aḥmad son of ᶜAbdullah son of Sulaymān, and is meant for his acquaintance and kindred. God give peace to all these and abandon them not, and gather them and grieve them not!

This is my address to them at the time of my returning from ᶜIraḳ, the gathering place of wranglers and the home of the remainder of antiquity, after having ended my youth and bidden farewell to my springtime; after "milking all the udders of time," and proving its good and evil. I have found the best course for me to pursue in the days of my life is to go into retreat, such as shall make me stand towards mankind in the relation that the chamois in the plain stands in to the ostriches that are there. Nor have I been a bad counselor to myself, nor have I failed to secure my fair share of benefits. So I decided upon this course after asking God's help and revealing my idea to a few friends on whose characters reliance could be placed, all of whom thought it wise and considered it could be carried out with prudence. And it is a matter "over which night-journeys have been undertaken," which has been "settled at Baḳḳah," and "carried on the ostrich's back." It is no off-spring of the hour, no nursling of a month or a year; it is the child of past years and the product of reflection. I have hastened to inform you of this for fear that one of you out of courtesy might be fain to go to the house it is my custom to inhabit in order to meet me, and if he found this impossible, I might find myself afflicted with two bad things—bad manners and estrangement. And indeed "many people incur blame through no fault of their own"; and the proverb says "leave a man to his choice." And my soul did not consent to my returning till I had promised it three things—seclusion as complete as that of [the star] Al-Faniḳ in the constellation of the Bull; separation from the world like that of the egg-shell from the chick; and to remain in the city even though the inhabitants fled through fear of the [Byzantine] Greeks. And this, even though those who are attached to me, or profess attachment, flee like grey antelopes or white camels. And I swear that I did not travel to increase my means, nor to gain by interviewing my fellows.

What I wanted was to stay in a place of learning; and I found out the most precious of spots, only fate did not allow me to stay there, and only a fool will quarrel with destiny. So I abandoned all thought of the privilege which fate thought too dear to grant.

God grant that you may be able to abide in your homes and not have to
be always on your horses and stirrups; and God shed upon you His favour
as the full moonlight is shed upon the hare-brained gazelle. And may He give
good recompense to the people of Baghdad, for they praised me more than I
deserved, and testified to my merits before they knew them, and quite seriously
offered me their goods. Albeit they found me not fond of praise, neither eager
for other people's charity. And when I went away, it was against their will,
and "God is enough for me, and on Him let whoso will, rely."

TRANSLATED BY D. S. MARGOLIOUTH

The days are dressing all of us in white,
    For him who will suspend us in a row.
    But for the sun there is no death. I know
The centuries are morsels of the night.

Have I not heard sagacious ones repeat
    An irresistibly grim argument:
    That we for all our blustering content
Are as the silent shadows at our feet.

Now this religion happens to prevail
    Until by that one it is overthrown,—
    Because men dare not live with men alone,
But always with another fairy-tale.

God is above. We never shall attain
    Our liberty from hands that overshroud;
    Or can we shake aside this heavy cloud
More than a slave can shake aside the chain?

TRANSLATED BY HENRY BAERLEIN

Winter came on us. Under it
A beggar naked, the prince in his quilt.
The stars deny one a day's rations,
Feed the other the corpus of nations.
This earth, though often a bride, has killed
Her many grooms, and is still maiden.

Cup your right hand and drink clean.
The curve of the royal tusk is obscene.

Travellers, too, let us make provision
For a more exact destination.
Our best is no luckier than the surgeon
Who plotted growths in his own colon.
Let the fat swell. Cap or coronet,
Either may spin on that crossed ocean
Where featureless trunks face the infinite.

TRANSLATED BY HERBERT HOWARTH AND IBRAHIM SHUKRALLAH

The wants of my soul keep house, close-curtained, like modest wives,
While other men's wants run loose, like women sent back divorced.
A steed when the bit chafes sore can nowise for all his wrath
Prevail over it except he champ on the iron curb;
And never doth man attain to swim on a full-born tide
Of glory but after he was sunken in miseries.
It hindereth not my mind from sure expectations of
A mortal event, that I am mortal and mortal's son.
I swerve and they miss their mark, the arrows Life aims at me,
But sped they from bows of Death, not thus would they see me serve.
The strange camels jealously are driven from the pond of Death.
I vow, ne'er my watcher watched the storm where should burst its flood,
Nor searched after meadows dim with rain-clouds my pioneer.
And how should I hope of Time advantage and increment,
Since even as the branches he destroyed he hath rased the root?

My clothes are my winding-sheet, my dwelling my grave, my life
My doom; and to me is death itself resurrection.
Bedizen thee with splendidest adornment and get thee wealth!
Outshone, lady, are the likes of thee by a dust-stained
Unkempt little pilgrim-band who walk in the ways that lead
To Allah, be smooth the track they travel or rugged.
Nor bracelet nor anklet gleams amongst them on wrist or foot,
No head bears a diadem and no ear an earring.

And now I have lived to cross the border of fifty years,
Albeit enough for me in hardship were ten or five.

And if as a shadow they are gone, yet they also seem
Like heaped spoils, whereof no fifth for Allah was set apart.
The bale must on camel's back be corded, the world be loathed,
The body be laid in earth, the trace and the track be lost.
Make haste, O my heart, make haste, repenting, to do the deeds
Of righteousness — know'st thou not the grave is my journey's end?
And sometimes I speak out loud and sometimes I whisper low:
In sight of the One 'tis all the same, whether low or loud.
And still with adventurous soul I dive in the sea of Change,
But only to drown, alas, or ever I clutch its pearl.

TRANSLATED BY R. A. NICHOLSON

Tread lightly, for a thousand hearts unseen
Might now be beating in this misty green;
    Here are the herbs that once were pretty cheeks,
Here the remains of those that once have been.

Afearing whom I trust I gain my end,
But trusting, without fear, I lose, my friend;
    Much better is the Doubt that gives me peace,
Than all the Faiths which in hell-fire may end.

Among us some are great and some are small,
Albeit in wickedness, we're masters all;
    Or, if my fellow men are like myself,
The human race shall always rise and fall.

The air of sin I breathe without restraint;
With selfishness my few good deeds I taint;
    I come as I was moulded and I go,
But near the vacant shrine of Truth I faint.

A church, a temple, or a Käba Stone,
Koran or Bible or a martyr's bone—
    All these and more my heart can tolerate
Since my religion now is Love alone.

TRANSLATED BY AMEEN RIHANI

[from *Ṭawq al-Ḥamāmah*, The Dove's Necklace]

Ibn Hazm, who has been called "the greatest scholar and the most original thinker in Spanish Islam," was born in 994 at Cordova into a family recently converted from Christianity to Islam. After his family had fled Cordova at the time of its invasion by the Berbers, Ibn Hazm led a life of seclusion and study. Later he returned to become vizier to the caliph in Valencia, and occupied the same position at Cordova. He was imprisoned several times for his political associations and, toward the end of his life, abandoned politics to return to scholarship. He died in 1064.

His greatest work, beyond doubt, is a gigantic study of comparative religion, which exhibits an erudition and acumen rare for the times; but his most popular and beautiful work is a treatise "about love and lovers" called *The Dove's Necklace*. Apart from its being a perfect example of highly developed Arabic *adab*, it is considered important for its frank treatment of romantic love. It is also an anthology of the author's own love poetry. Although the inclusion of poetry is most characteristic of the *adab* style, in this particular selection it has been omitted in favor of more of the prose.

Love has certain signs which the intelligent man quickly detects and the shrewd man readily recognizes. Of these the first is the brooding gaze: the eye is the wide gateway of the soul, the scrutinizer of its secrets, conveying its most private thoughts and giving expression to its deepest-hid feelings. You will see the lover gazing at the beloved unblinkingly; his eyes follow the loved one's every movement, withdrawing as he withdraws, inclining as he inclines, just as the chameleon's stare shifts with the shifting of the sun.

The lover will direct his conversation to the beloved even when he purports, however earnestly, to address another: the affection is apparent to anyone with eyes to see. When the loved one speaks, the lover listens with rapt attention to his every word; he marvels at everything the beloved says, however extraordinary and absurd his observations may be; he believes him implicitly even when he is clearly lying, agrees with him though he is obviously in the wrong, testifies on his behalf for all that he may be unjust, follows after him however he may proceed and whatever line of argument he may adopt. The lover hurries to the spot where the beloved is at the moment, endeavours to sit as near to him as possible, sidles up close to him, lays aside all occupations that might oblige him to leave his company, makes light of any matter, however weighty, that would demand his parting from him, is very slow to move when he takes his leave of him.

Other signs of love are that sudden confusion and excitement betrayed by the lover when he unexpectedly sees the one he loves coming upon him unawares, that agitation which overmasters him on beholding someone who resembles his beloved or on hearing his name suddenly pronounced. A man in love will give prodigally, to the limit of his capacity, in a way that formerly he would have refused; as if he were the one receiving the donation, he the one whose happiness is the object in view; all this in order that he may show off his good points, and make himself desirable. How often has the miser opened his purse-strings, the scowler relaxed his frown, the coward leapt heroically into the fray, the clod suddenly become sharp-witted, the boor turned into the perfect gentleman, the stinker transformed into the elegant dandy, the sloucher smartened up, the decrepit recaptured his lost youth, the godly gone wild, the self-respecting kicked over the traces—and all because of love!

All these signs are to be observed even before the fire of love is properly kindled, ere its conflagration truly bursts forth, its blaze waxes fierce, its flames leap up. But when the fire really takes a hold and is firmly established, then you will see the secret whispering, the unconcealed turning away from all present but the beloved.

Other outward signs and tokens of love are the following, which are apparent to all having eyes in their heads: abundant and exceeding cheerfulness at finding oneself with the beloved in a narrow space, and a corresponding depression on being together in a wide expanse; to engage in a playful tug of war for anything the one or the other lays hold of; much clandestine winking; leaning sideways and supporting oneself against the object of one's affection; endeavouring to touch his hand and whatever part of his body one can reach, while engaged in conversation; and drinking the remainder of what the beloved has left in his cup, seeking out the very spot against which his lips were pressed.

There are also contrary signs that occur according to casual provocations and accidental incitements and a variety of motivating causes and stimulating thoughts. Opposites are of course likes, in reality; when things reach the limit of contrariety, and stand at the furthest bounds of divergency, they come to resemble one another. This is decreed by God's omnipotent power, in a manner that baffles entirely the human imagination. Thus, when ice is pressed a long time in the hand, it finally produces the same effect as fire. We find that extreme joy and extreme sorrow kill equally; excessive and violent laughter sends the tears coursing from the eyes. It is a very common phenomenon in the world about us. Similarly with lovers: when they love each other with an equal ardour and their mutual affection is intensely strong, they will turn against one another without any valid reason, each purposely contradicting the other in whatever he may say; they quarrel violently over the smallest things, each picking up every word that the other lets fall and wilfully misinterpreting it. All these devices are aimed at testing and proving what each is seeking in the other.

Now the difference between this sham, and real aversion and contrariness born of deep-seated hatred and inveterate contention, is that lovers are very quickly reconciled after their disputes. You will see a pair of lovers seeming to have reached the extreme limit of contrariety, to the point that you would reckon not to be mended even in the instance of a person of most tranquil spirit and wholly exempt from rancour, save after a long interval, and wholly irreparable in the case of a quarrelsome man; yet in next to no time you will observe them to have become the best of friends once more; silenced are those mutual reproaches, vanished that disharmony; forthwith they are laughing again and playfully sporting together. The same scene may be enacted several times at a single session. When you see a pair of lovers behaving in such a fashion, let no doubt enter your mind, no uncertainty invade your thoughts; you may be sure without hesitation, and convinced as by an unshakable certainty, that there lies between them a deep and hidden secret—the secret of true love. Take this then for a sure test, a universally valid experiment: it is the product only of an equal partnership in love and a true concord of hearts. I myself have observed it frequently.

Another sign is when you find the lover almost entreating to hear the loved one's name pronounced, taking an extreme delight in speaking about him, so that the subject is a positive obsession with him; nothing so much rejoices him, and he is not in the least restrained by the fear that someone listening may realize what he is about, and someone present will understand his true motives. Love for a thing renders you blind and deaf. If the lover could so contrive that in the place where he happens to be there should be no talk of anything but his beloved, he would never leave that spot for any other in the whole world.

It can happen that a man sincerely affected by love will start to eat his meal with an excellent appetite; yet the instant the recollection of his loved one is excited, the food sticks in his throat and chokes his gullet. It is the same if he is drinking or talking—he begins to converse with you gaily enough, then all at once he is invaded by a chance thought of his dear one. You will notice the change in his manner of speaking, the instantaneous failure of his conversational powers; the sure signs are his long silences, the way he stares at the ground, his extreme taciturnity. One moment he is all smiles, lightly gesticulating; the next he has become completely boxed up, sluggish, distrait, rigid, too weary to utter a single word, irritated by the most innocent question.

Love's signs also include a fondness for solitude and a pleasure in being alone, as well as a wasting of the body not accompanied by any fever or ache preventing free activity and liberty of movement. The walk is also an unerring indication and never-deceiving sign of an inward lassitude of spirit. Sleeplessness too is a common affliction of lovers; the poets have described this condition frequently, relating how they watch the stars, and giving an account of the night's interminable length.

Another sign of love is that you will see the lover loving his beloved's kith and kin and the intimate ones of his household, to such an extent that they are nearer and dearer to him than his own folk, himself, and all his familiar friends.

Weeping is a well-known sign of love, except that men differ very greatly from one another in this particular. Some are ready weepers; their tear-ducts are always overflowing, and their eyes respond immediately to their emotions, the tears rolling down at a moment's notice. Others are dry-eyed and barren of tears; to this category I myself belong. This is the result of my habit of eating frankincense to abate the palpitation from which I have suffered since childhood. I will be afflicted by some shocking blow, and at once feel my heart to be splitting and breaking into fragments; I have a choking sensation in my heart more bitter than colocynth, that prevents me from getting my words out properly, and sometimes well nigh suffocates me. My eyes therefore respond to my feelings but rarely, and then my tears are exceedingly sparse.

You will see the lover, when unsure of the constancy of his loved one's feelings for him, perpetually on his guard in a way that he never troubled to be before; he polishes his language, he refines his gestures and his glances, particularly if he has the misfortune and mischance to be in love with one given to making unjust accusations, or of a quarrelsome disposition.

Another sign of love is the way the lover pays attention to the beloved; remembering everything that falls from his lips; searching out all the news about him, so that nothing small or great that happens to him may escape his knowledge; in short, following closely his every movement. Upon my life, sometimes you will see a complete dolt under these circumstances become most keen, a careless fellow turn exceedingly quick-witted.

One of the strangest origins of passion is when a man falls in love through merely hearing the description of the other party, without ever having set eyes on the beloved. In such a case he will progress through all the accustomed stages of love; there will be the sending to and fro of messengers, the exchange of letters, the anxiety, the deep emotion, the sleeplessness; and all this without actual sight of the object of affection. Stories, descriptions of beautiful qualities, and the reporting of news about the fair one have a manifest effect on the soul; to hear a girl's voice singing behind a wall may well move the heart to love, and preoccupy the mind.

All this has occurred to more than one man. In my opinion, however, such a love is a tumbledown building without any foundations. If a man's thoughts are absorbed by passionate regard for one whom he has never seen, the inevitable result is that whenever he is alone with his own reflections, he will represent to himself a purely imaginary picture of the person whose identity he keeps constantly before his mind; no other being than this takes shape in his fantasy; he is completely carried away by his imagination, and visualizes and dreams of her only. Then if some day he actually sees the object of his fanciful passion, either his love is confirmed or it is wholly nullified. Both these alternatives have actually happened and been known.

This kind of romance usually takes place between veiled ladies of guarded palaces and aristocratic households, and their male kinsfolk; the love of women is more stable in these cases than that of men, because women are weak creatures and their natures swiftly respond to this sort of attraction, which easily masters them completely.

Often it happens that love fastens itself to the heart as the result of a single glance. This variety of love is divided into two classes. The first class is the contrary of what we have just been describing, in that a man will fall head over heels in love with a mere form, without knowing who that person may be, what her name is, or where she lives. This sort of thing happens frequently enough.

The second class is the contrary of what we shall be describing in the chapter next following, if God wills. This is for a man to form an attachment at first sight with a young lady whose name, place of abode and origin are known to him. The difference here is the speed or tardiness with which the affair passes off. When a man falls in love at first sight, and forms a sudden attachment as the result of a fleeting glance, that proves him to be little steadfast, and proclaims that he will as suddenly forget his romantic adventure; it testifies to his fickleness and inconstancy. So it is with all things; the quicker they grow, the quicker they decay; while on the other hand slow produced is slow consumed.

Some men there are whose love becomes true only after long converse, much contemplation, and extended familiarity. Such a one is likely to persist and to be steadfast in his affection, untouched by the passage of time; what enters with difficulty goes not out easily. That is my own way in these matters, and it is confirmed by Holy Tradition. For God, as we are informed by our teachers, when He commanded the Spirit to enter Adam's body, that was like an earthen vessel—and the Spirit was afraid, and sorely distressed—said to it, "Enter in unwillingly, and come forth again unwillingly!"

I have myself seen a man of this description who, whenever he sensed within himself the beginnings of a passionate attachment, or conceived a penchant for some form whose beauty he admired, at once employed the device of shunning that person and giving up all association with him, lest his feelings become more intense and the affair get beyond his control, and he find himself completely stampeded. This proves how closely love cleaves to such people's hearts, and once it lays hold of them never looses its grip.

I indeed marvel profoundly at all those who pretend to fall in love at first sight; I cannot easily prevail upon myself to believe their claims, and prefer to consider such love as merely a kind of lust. As for thinking that that sort of attachment can really possess the inmost heart and penetrate the veil of the soul's recess, that I cannot under any circumstances credit. Love has never truly gripped my bowels, save after a long lapse of time and constant companionship with the person concerned, sharing with him all that while my every occupation, be it earnest or frivolous. So I am alike in consolation and in passion; I have never in my life forgotten any romance, and my nostalgia for every former attachment is such that I well nigh choke when I drink and suffocate when I eat. The man who is not so constituted quickly finds complete relief and is at rest again; I have never wearied of anything once I have known it, and neither have I hastened to feel at home with it on first acquaintance. Similarly, I have never longed for a change for change's sake, in any of the things that I have possessed; I am speaking here not only of friends and comrades, but also of all the other things a man uses—clothes, riding-beast, food, and so on.

Life holds no joy for me, and I do nothing but hang my head and feel utterly cast down, ever since I first tasted the bitterness of being separated from those I love. It is an anguish that constantly revisits me, an agony of grief that ceases not for a moment to assail me. My remembrance of past happiness has abated for me every joy that I may look for in the future. I am a dead man, though counted among the living, slain by sorrow and buried by sadness, entombed while yet a dweller on the face of this mortal earth. God be praised, whatever be the circumstances that befall us; there is indeed no other God but He!

As for what transpires at first blush as a result of certain accidental circumstances—physical admiration, and visual enchantment which does not go beyond mere external forms—and this is the very secret and meaning of carnal desire; when carnal desire moreover becomes so overflowing that it surpasses these bounds, and when such an overflow coincides with a spiritual union in which the natural instincts share equally with the soul, the resulting phenomenon is called passionate love. Herein lies the root of the error which misleads a man into asserting that he loves two persons, or is passionately enamoured of two entirely different individuals. All this is to be explained as springing out of carnal desire, as we have just described; it is called love only metaphorically, and not in the true meaning of the term. As for the true lover, his yearning of the soul is so excessive as to divert him from all his religious and mundane occupations; how then should he have room to busy himself with a second love affair?

Know now—may God exalt you!—that love exercises an effective authority, a decisive sovereignty over the soul; its commands cannot be opposed; its ordinances may not be flouted; its rule is not to be transgressed; it demands unwavering obedience, and against its dominion there is no appeal. Love untwists the firmest plaits and looses the tightest strands; it dissolves that which is most solid, undoes that which is most firm; it penetrates the deepest recesses of the heart, and makes lawful things most strictly forbidden.

I have known many men whose discrimination was beyond suspicion, men not to be feared deficient in knowledge, or wanting in taste, or lacking in discernment, who nevertheless described their loved ones as possessing certain qualities not by any means admired by the general run of mankind or approved according to the accepted canons of beauty. Yet those qualities had become an obsession with them, the sole object of their passion, and the very last word (as they thought) in elegance. Thereafter their loved ones vanished, either into oblivion, or by separation, or jilting, or through some other accident to which love is always liable; but those men never lost their admiration for the curious qualities which provoked their approval of them, neither did they ever afterwards cease to prefer these above other attributes that are in reality superior to them.

Let me add a personal touch. In my youth I loved a slave-girl who happened to be a blonde; from that time I have never admired brunettes, not though their dark tresses set off a face as resplendent as the sun, or the very image of beauty itself. I find this taste to have become a part of my whole make-up and constitution since those early days; my soul will not suffer me to acquire any other, or to love any type but that. This very same thing happened to my father also (God be pleased with him!), and he remained faithful to his first preference until the term of his earthly life was done.

Were it not that this world below is a transitory abode of trial and trouble, and paradise a home where virtue receives its reward, secure from all annoyances, I would have said that union with the beloved is that pure happiness which is without alloy, and gladness unsullied by sorrow the perfect realization of hopes and the complete fulfillment of one's dreams.

I have tested all manner of pleasures, and known every variety of joy; and I have found that neither intimacy with princes, nor wealth acquired, nor finding after lacking, nor returning after long absence, nor security after fear, and repose in a safe refuge—none of these things so powerfully affects the soul as union with the beloved, especially if it come after long denial and continual banishment. For then the flame of passion waxes exceeding hot, and the furnace of yearning blazes up, and the fire of eager hope rages ever more fiercely.

The fresh springing of herbs after the rains, the glitter of flowers when the night clouds have rolled away in the hushed hour between dawn and sunrise, the plashing of waters as they run through the stalks of golden blossoms, the exquisite beauty of white castles encompassed by verdant meadows—not lovelier is any of these than union with the well-beloved, whose character is virtuous, and laudable her disposition, whose attributes are evenly matched in perfect beauty. Truly that is a miracle of wonder surpassing the tongues of the eloquent, and far beyond the range of the most cunning speech to describe: the mind reels before it, and the intellect stands abashed.

TRANSLATED BY A. J. ARBERRY

[from *Falsafat al-Akhlāq w-al-Siyar*, A Philosophy of Character and Conduct]

A Philosophy of Character and Conduct was written toward the end of Ibn Hazm's life in the more didactic *akhlāq* form, which is customarily distinguished from *adab*. It is a warm and personal work. Its discussion of anxiety as the basis for all action is original within Islamic thought and has a very modern sound now that the concept has been brought forward in psychology and philosophy.

I am a man who has always been uneasy about the impermanency and constant instability of fortune. Concerns of this sort have occupied me during the greater part of my life, and I have preferred to spend it in pursuing these matters studiously, rather than in looking for delights of the senses or the accumulation of great wealth, which most seem to prefer. In this book I have gathered teachings suggested by experience, in order that those into whose hands it should chance to fall may derive a little benefit from what has cost me so much anguish and meditation.

In my investigations I have constantly tried to discover an end in human actions which all men unanimously hold as good and which they all seek. I have found only this: the one aim of escaping anxiety. I have not only discovered that all humanity considers this good and desirable, but also that, notwithstanding the contradictory variety of opinions, designs, wishes, and purposes of men, no one is moved to act or resolves to speak who does not hope by means of action or word to release anxiety and drive it from his spirit. Now it is clear that some err in their choice of the right path leading to this end; others deviate from it; still others, and they are always in a minority, achieve it; yet escape from anxiety has always been the common purpose of men of all races and peoples since the world began and will be until it ends. All their desires have their unique foundation in this purpose.

Other ends do not seem to command the unanimous approbation of men. There are, for example, those who do not desire goodness, faith, or truth; there are those who prefer to satisfy their passions in a dark corner rather than to enjoy fame's flatteries; there are those who do not desire riches but prefer to be poor, as do most philosophers and devout people; there are those who, as if by natural inclination, detest sensual delights and hold as imperfect those who crave them; there are many who prefer ignorance to knowledge. One must reckon these things among the ends of human actions. Still, no one considers anxiety to be a good thing; every man seeks release from it.

Those who crave riches seek them only in order to drive the fear of poverty out of their spirits; others seek for glory to free themselves from the fear of being scorned; some seek sensual delights to escape the pain of privations; some seek knowledge to cast out the uncertainty of ignorance; others delight in hearing news and conversation because they seek by these means to dispel the sorrow of solitude and isolation. In brief, man eats, drinks, marries, watches, plays, lives under a roof, rides, walks, or remains still with the sole aim of driving out their contraries and, in general, all other anxieties.

Yet each of these actions is in turn an inescapable hotbed of new anxieties; unexpected obstacles to its realization raise difficulties according to the occasion . . . loss of what was gained, inability through misfortunes to reach a happy conclusion, unpleasant consequences which come with satisfaction, fear of competition, criticism of the jealous, theft by the covetous, aversion to seeing what we desire in the hands of an enemy, slanders, and the like.

After grasping this sublime truth and comprehending this weighty secret, I sought to find a sure method of arriving at this end which all men alike, ignorant and learned, holy and wicked, seek and hold as good. I discovered that this method consists in nothing else but directing one's self towards a Supreme Goodness by means of good works conducive to immortal life.

For, as I investigated, I observed that all things tended to elude me, and I reached the conclusion that the only permanent reality possible consists in good works useful for another, immortal life. Every other hope that I desired to see realized was followed by melancholy, sometimes because what was ardently desired escaped me, sometimes because I decided to abandon it. It seemed to me that nothing escaped these dangers but good works, directed by a Supreme Goodness. These alone were always followed by pleasure in the present and in the future: in the present because I was freed from numberless anxieties which disturbed my tranquility, and, moreover, friends and enemies concurred in commending me; and in the future because these works promised immortality.

The good work, one profitable for an immortal life, stands innocent of all defect, free of all imperfection, and is, moreover, a sure way to put aside every anxiety effectively. I have, indeed, observed that everyone who works for this end, even though he undergoes unpleasant tests on the road of life, not only is free of care but rejoices, because the hope which he holds for the end of his present life helps him to seek what he longs for and incites him to follow in this direction, the end in which he believes. And if any obstacle stands in his way, I have likewise observed he has no anxiety about it, because as he has not consecrated himself to what he sought, he does not consider the obstacle as a punishment inflicted on him. I have seen, too, that if anyone damages him he is joyful, and if any calamity comes about he is no less happy; and more, if he experiences sorrow or weariness in what he has done, he is still full of joy. He lives, in point of fact, in constant unending joy, while quite the contrary holds for other men.

The pleasure which the intelligent man experiences in the exercise of his reason, the learned man in his study, the prudent man in his discreet deliberation, and the devout man in his ascetic combat is greater than the delight which is felt by the glutton in his eating, the toper in his drinking, the lecher in his incontinence, the trader in his gainful bargaining, the gamester in his merriment, and the leader in the exercise of his authority. The proof of this lies in the fact that intelligent, learned, prudent, and devout men also experience those other delights which I have just enumerated in the same way as one who lives only to wallow in them, but they tend to abandon and separate themselves from them, preferring instead the quest for permanent release from anxiety through good and virtuous works.

It seems unworthy of a man to consecrate himself to something which is not higher than he is, that is to say, a Supreme Goodness. The intelligent person would account any lower price on himself as unworthy. Therefore he will consecrate himself to good works, to leading his brothers to truth, to the defense of sacred things, to avoiding any despicable humiliation which is not imposed on men by necessity of nature, and to protecting victims of injustice. One who consecrates himself to lesser things is like one who trades a precious gem for a pebble.

Do not forget, then, that only one thing deserves to be sought by all men, and that is the absence of care; and the unique avenue which leads to it is built of good works done for the sake of the Supreme Goodness. All else is a foolish waste of time.

TRANSLATED BY JAMES KRITZECK

The medieval Islamic *Maghrib* ("West"—meaning Spain and North Africa) often expressed a feeling of inferiority to East Islam. Even in the tenth century, when Cordova more than rivaled it, Baghdad was its symbol of elegance. Perhaps it was just as well that the Moors cherished that illusory ideal, for it lent constant incentive to their own artistic efforts.

Their achievements in the arts at least equaled those of East Islam during the same period, and among their major achievements was their poetry. Two poetic forms were brought to perfection in the West, the *muwashshah* and the *zajal*. Both forms were based on a refrain for chorus and so were undoubtedly meant to be sung. It is more than likely that these forms influenced Romance vernacular lyrics. Considered among the foremost Moorish poets were Ibn Zaydun, Ibn Quzman, and Al-Tutili.

Al-Husri: The Tress

A twisting curl
Hung down, to hurl
My heart of bliss
To the abyss.

The sable tress
Of faithlessness
Lent deadly grace
To faith's white face.

My heart doth fly,
Assaulted by
The mallet of
Your tress, my love,

141

I saw it smite
As black as night,
Its field of play
As white as day.

TRANSLATED BY A. J. ARBERRY

Mourning in Andalusia

In Andalusia clothes are white
That folk in mourning wear;
The custom's right. . . . I bear its truth
In every greying hair
That grieves for my lost youth.

Ibn Zaydun: Two Fragments

I

The world is strange
For lack of you;
Times change their common hue—
The day is black, but very night
With you was shining white.

II

Two secrets in the heart of night
We were until the light
Of busybody day
Gave both of us away.

Ibn Abra: The Beauty-Spot

A mole on Ahmad's cheek
Draws all men's eyes to seek
The love they swear reposes
In a garden there.
That breathing bed of roses
In a Nubian's care.

TRANSLATED BY HAROLD MORLAND

Ibn Ammar: Poet's Pride

I am Ben Ammar: my repute
Is not obscure to any one
Except the fool, who would dispute
The splendour of the moon and sun.

It is no wonder if I come
So late, when time is at an end;
The glosses that expound the tome
Are ever on the margins penned.

Ibn Wahbun: On Hearing Al-Mutanabbi Praised

Ibnul Husain wrote verses eloquent:
Of course: but princely gifts most excellent
Results achieve, and offerings open throats
To make delivery of their sweetest notes.

Exulting in the magic of his tone,
He called himself a prophet: had he known
That you some day would chant his poetry,
No doubt he would have claimed divinity!

Al-Tutili: Seville

I was bored with old Seville
And Seville was bored with me;
Had the city shared my skill
To invent abusive rhyme,
Rivals in invective, we
Would have had a lovely time.

So at last my weary heart
Could endure no more, and cried
It was time that we should part:
Water is much more purified
Than the dribble of a pool.

TRANSLATED BY A. J. ARBERRY

Ibn Sara: Pool With Turtles

Deep is the pool whose overflow
   In the cool bright showers
Is like an eye weeping below
Lashes of quivering flowers.

Look—the merry turtles sport
   Like Christians to the field
That sidle, frolic, and cavort
Bearing a casual shield.

The Shooting Star

The watch-star saw a devil-spy, that came
   On evil work,
   At heaven's gate lurk
And leapt against him in a path of flame;

And seemed a burning cavalier
   Whose swift career
Unbinds his turban till it streams
Behind, so jewelled that it gleams.

TRANSLATED BY HAROLD MORLAND

Ibn Hamdis: The Andalusian Fountains

And lions people this official wood
         encompass the pools with thunder
and profuse over aureate-banded
         bodies their skulls gush glass
Lions like stillness stirred
         questing mobility there
or trophies of carnivores
         proper those deployed haunches
Sun is tinder to the stirred
         colours, is light to long tongues,

is a hand to unsheathe the lunging

        blades that shiver out in a splash

By a zephyr damp and thread

        are woven and corsleted

on a branch sits sorcery netted

        like incandescent birds from space

That lest they fall to freedom

        are forcibly propped, lest their songs

start a whistling on the ponds

        and a warbling in the mercurial trees

And they dipped in cascades

        of chrysolite and tossed pearl

and they chatter an astral

        mischief: while expert armourers

Garnish with gilt hoods

        the gates: and an invert

terrace of stalactites

        glows in a submarine recess.

This specialist brocade

        is a mere hallucination

its azure and sun and plantation

        ephemeral as fine skies

Some with beasts in the wood

        some with the fowl in disaster

are the antique lineal masters

        hunting their sperm down ornate galleries.

TRANSLATED BY HERBERT HOWARTH AND IBRAHIM SHUKRALLAH

Ibn Quzman: The Radish

The radish is a good
And doubtless wholesome food,
But proves, to vex the eater,
A powerful repeater.

This only fault I find:
What should be left behind
Comes issuing instead
Right from the eater's head!

Mutarrif: Love's Code

I am a youth as passionate
As you might ever wish to see,
A poet glorious and great,
Sublime in generosity.

Iraq upon her ample breast
Has suckled me with fond desire;
Baghdad has fed me with the best
Refreshment lover could require.

When weary sickness on me lies
Unending, and successive grief
Revisits my unsleeping eyes,
In passion's pangs I find relief.

Such is the code of chivalry
Jamil discovered long ago,
Whereunto others like to me
Have added newly what they know.

TRANSLATED BY A. J. ARBERRY

TURKS, FRANKS, AND MONGOLS [1050–1350]

By the middle of the eleventh century, the political fragmentation of the Islamic empire had weakened it to such a point that it almost invited the series of invasions which marked its history for the next three centuries and which changed its complexion so radically.

The first of the invaders came from Central Asia through the funnel of Khurasan. They were Turks of the Seljuk tribes. Hardened by life and inescapable warfare on the Kirghiz steppes, they had gradually descended to the lands surrounding the Oxus River and had participated not only in their own intertribal struggles but also, as mercenaries, in the complicated border wars which eventually apprized them of the golden opportunity which was theirs. They accepted Sunnite Islam and assembled enough forces and equipment to invade Persia. As they did so, they acquired a cause (or rationale) for their invasion—the liberation of the caliph from his Shiite Buwayhid captors. In 1055, they entered Baghdad, and their rule was legitimized by the caliph, who settled down to a new type of captivity. But Tughril Beg and his son Alp Arslan carried the Seljuk conquest beyond Baghdad to the frontiers of Byzantium and Fatimid Egypt. Under Alp Arslan's son, Malikshah (1072–92), a valiant attempt was made to solidify the new order along recognizably traditional Islamic lines. But the many Seljuk commanders and their soldiers were not inclined to obey a single centralized authority, and the extent of their conquests made it easy for them to subdivide according to loyalties and geographical positions.

It was at this point that there appeared on the scene an unexpected second wave of invaders, the crusaders from Europe. The memory of the destruction of the Holy Sepulcher in Jerusalem by the Fatimid Caliph Al-Hakim in 1009 (it had been rebuilt, after a fashion, later) and, more immediately, Alp Arslan's victory at Manzikert in 1071, where the Emperor Romanus Diogenes was taken prisoner, impelled Emperor Alexius Comnenus to seek military assistance from Europe against the Turks. Pope Urban II preached the crusade at Clermont in 1095. The ensuing expedition was not only a response to the Seljuk threat, of course, but a result of political, economic, and social factors in Europe as well. The success of the First Crusade, culminating in the capture of Jerusalem in 1099, was indeed spectacular. A sizable European enclave was established within the Islamic world.

Then came the Moslem reaction. Zangi, the *atabeg* of Mosul and soon the greatest ruler in Syria, destroyed the most annoying of the Latin possessions, the county of Edessa. His son Nur al-Din took Damascus and continued the offensive. It was left to the son of one of his commanders, whose name was Saladin (Salah al-Din), to turn the tide decisively against the crusaders. Saladin prepared his way methodically. First of all, he put an end to the Fatimid caliphate of Egypt in 1171; then he took over its Syrian possessions; then he neutralized the extremist Shiite stronghold at Masyad; and only then did he pursue his attacks on the Franks. In 1187 he captured Jerusalem. An agreement reached at the conclusion of the Third Crusade in 1192 gave pilgrims access to the city. Saladin's heirs did not pursue the matter much further, for they were too busy dividing his empire among themselves. In 1250 his sultanate passed into the hands of one of his successor's military slaves, the Turkish Mamluks, who began one of the longest and most effective dynastic rules in all of Islamic history.

The Eastern realms of the Islamic world were scarcely affected by the crusades but were soon to experience the third and most fatal of the invasions, that of the Mongols. It is said that the Caliph Al-Nasir actually invoked the aid of the hordes of Genghis Khan in destroying the power of the Khwarizm Shah, a threatening rival in Persia. If he did so, he was ill advised. The Mongols recognized weakness and planned their conquest. Genghis' great-nephew, Hulagu Khan, left Mongolia in 1253, intent upon the destruction of the caliphate and every force surrounding it. In 1258 his armies entered Baghdad, killed the caliph and his heirs, and moved on to the borders of Mamluk territory. There they were repulsed. After several later attempts at conquering the Mamluks, they retired to a spacious and comfortable domain in Persia and Iraq, where they were converted to Islam en masse toward the end of the century. Their empire was known as the Il-Khanid empire; it endured for a century. The Mamluks, in the meantime, drove out the last of the crusaders from their stronghold at Acre in 1291 and busied themselves in consolidating their holdings in Syria, Arabia, and Upper Egypt.

It might appear incredible that some of the finest Islamic literature was produced during those centuries in which the Islamic world was suffering its cruelest defeats and undergoing its most agonizing transformations. The fact is not, in reality, so difficult to explain. The crusaders were never much more than an annoyance. Both the Turkish and Mongol invaders, by accepting Islam, acknowledged the superiority of its culture. They did so, moreover, at the very time when that culture could be regarded as firmly forged and ready for challenge. Fortunately, the ferocious conquerors became the most docile and appreciative of pupils and the most lavish of patrons.

This period saw the production of some of the greatest masterpieces of Arabic prose, although it was less favorable to Arabic poetry. For centuries the Arabs had been entertained by itinerant storytellers called *rāwīs*. The *rāwī* was a living library; he had committed to memory a large repertoire of poems and stories. But he had also to be a poet himself and, above all, an improviser. The more skillful and original he was, obviously, the more enthusiastic and generous his audiences were likely to be. Like all performers of the sort, the *rāwī* chose to repeat his most successful performances and to arrange occasions at which they could be delivered. Many of these works became part of common lore. Practitioners of the literary art, now fortified with the niceties of *adab* and a strong sense of structure, drew upon this vast raw material to create elegant forms of belles-lettres. The most clever of the forms was the *maqāmah*, brought to perfection by Al-Hariri. At the same time, Arabic prose manifested a general new narrative versatility, stemming no doubt from centuries of usage in such fields as theology, philosophy, law, and history. The autobiographies of

Al-Ghazzali and Usamah, the philosophical romance of Ibn Tufayl, and the travelogue of Ibn Jubayr all represent a new handling of the compliant language.

For all the advance of Arabic prose, however, this period must in justice be marked down as an age of Persian literature. Masterpieces of Persian prose and poetry followed one another in rapid succession, owing especially to the prior claim of Islamic Persian culture upon the interest and patronage of the Turks and Mongols. Even basically Arabic forms of poetry and prose were adapted with talent and sometimes with genius to Persian, and original forms were not rare. In the hands and on the tongues of Umar Khayyam, Al-Warawini, Nizami, Attar, Rumi, and Sadi, the quatrain, the literary fable, the *masnavi*, and *adab* reached the highest stages of their development.

[from *Siyāsat-nāmeh*, The Book of Government]

The first decades of Seljuk rule were, as might be imagined, a time of extreme chaos for the eastern Islamic world. The greater part of it was now ruled by warrior chieftains through their slaves, in delicate co-operation with the former landowners. By an incredible stroke of fortune, the "central" Seljuk sultan, Alp Arslan, and his son Sultan Malikshah (whose full name conjoins the royal titles of the Turks, the Arabs, and the Persians) brought into their service as vizier a Persian who proved himself uniquely capable of dealing with this complicated situation. He is known by his honorific title Nizam al-Mulk.

Nizam al-Mulk set out to reform the administration, and he saw much around him which stood in need of reformation. His aim was to build up the central power and prestige of his monarch. One contemporary asserts, "For twenty years covering the reign of Malikshah, Nizam al-Mulk had all the power concentrated in his own hands, while the sultan had nothing to do but sit on the throne or enjoy the chase."

But Nizam al-Mulk was a cultured man and a Persian, and he evidently wished to smooth the rough edges of his Turkish overlords, while to some extent serving the cause of Persian nationalism. He effected many reforms and founded many institutions of learning, but even after thirty years of service he correctly concluded that there was still a long way to go. Fortunately there is preserved to us a remarkable document in which he spelled out in detail his picture of the ideal toward which he was working, the *Book of Government*, written in the form of advice to governors and composed, so we are told, at Sultan Malikshah's invitation.

There is an earnestness in this book which outweighs its purely literary value. That value, nevertheless, is great—as great as its message is studied and passionate. In the following selections, many of the literary graces have been clipped in favor of the message. "No king or emperor can afford not to possess and know this book, especially in these days," wrote one of the first scribes, who also recorded the fact that Nizam al-Mulk felt the need to revise the work and add eleven new chapters dealing with "the enemies of the state." That action was grimly prophetic, for Nizam al-Mulk was soon afterwards assassinated by one of the chief enemies he designated.

It is the king's duty to enquire into the condition of his peasantry and army, both far and near, and to know more or less how things are. If he does not do this he is at fault and people will charge him with negligence, laziness and tyranny, saying, "Either the king knows about the oppression and extortion going on in the country, or he does not know. If he knows and does nothing to prevent it and remedy it, that is because he is an oppressor like the rest and acquiesces in their oppression; and if he does not know then he is negligent and ignorant." Neither of these imputations is desirable. Inevitably therefore he must have postmasters; and in every age in the time of ignorance and of Islam, kings have had postmasters, through whom they have learnt everything that goes on, good and bad. For instance, if anybody wrongly took so much as a chicken or a bag of straw from another—and that five hundred farsangs away—the king would know about it and have the offender punished, so that others knew that the king was vigilant. In every place they appointed informers and so far checked the activities of oppressors that men enjoyed security and justice for the pursuit of trade and cultivation. But this is a delicate business involving some unpleasantness; it must be entrusted to the hands and tongues and pens of men who are completely above suspicion and without self-interest, for the weal or woe of the country depends on them. They must be directly responsible to the king and not to anyone else; and they must receive their monthly salaries regularly from the treasury so that they may do their work without any worries. In this way the king will know of every event that takes place and will be able to give his orders as appropriate, meting out unexpected reward, punishment or commendation to the persons concerned. When a king is like this, men are always eager to be obedient, fearing the king's displeasure, and nobody can possibly have the audacity to disobey the king or plot any mischief. Thus the employment of intelligence agents and reporters contributes to the justice, vigilance and prudence of the king, and to the prosperity of the country.

Spies must constantly go out to the limits of the kingdom in the guise of merchants, travellers, sufis, pedlars (of medicines), and mendicants, and bring back reports of everything they hear, so that no matters of any kind remain concealed, and if anything [untoward] happens it can in due course be remedied. In the past it has often happened that governors, assignees, officers, and army-commanders have planned rebellion and resistance, and plotted mischief against the king; but spies forestalled them and informed the king, who was thus enabled to set out immediately with all speed and, coming upon them unawares, to strike them down and frustrate their plans; and if any foreign king or army was preparing to attack the country, the spies informed the king, and he took action and repelled them. Likewise they brought news, whether good or bad, about the condition of the peasants, and the king gave the matter his attention, as did cAdud ad Daula on one occasion.

A king cannot do without suitable boon-companions with whom he can enjoy complete freedom and intimacy. The constant society of nobles [such as] margraves and generals tends to diminish the king's majesty and dignity because they become too arrogant. As a general rule people who are employed in any official capacity should not be admitted as boon-companions, nor should those who are accepted for companionship be appointed to any public office, because by virtue of the liberty they enjoy in the king's company they will indulge in high-handed practices and oppress the people. Officers should always be in a state of fear of the king, while boon-companions need to be familiar. If an officer is familiar he tends to oppress the peasantry; but if a boon-companion is not familiar the king will not find any pleasure or relaxation in his company. Boon-companions should have a fixed time for their appearance; after the king has given audience and the nobles have retired, then comes the time for their turn.

There are several advantages in having boon-companions: firstly, they are company for the king; secondly, since they are with him day and night, they are in the position of bodyguards, and if any danger (we take refuge with Allah!) should appear, they will not hesitate to shield the king from it with their own bodies; and thirdly, the king can say thousands of different things, frivolous and serious, to his boon-companions which would not be suitable for the ears of his wazir or other nobles, for they are his officials and functionaries; and fourthly, all sorts of sundry tidings can be heard from boon-companions, for through their freedom they can report on matters, good and bad, whether drunk or sober; and in this there is advantage and benefit.

A boon-companion should be well-bred, accomplished, and of cheerful face. He should have pure faith, be able to keep secrets, and wear good clothes. He must possess an ample fund of stories and strange tales both amusing and serious, and be able to tell them well. He must always be a good talker and a pleasant partner; he should know how to play backgammon and chess, and if he can play a musical instrument and use a weapon, so much the better. He must always agree with the king, and whatever the king says or does, he must exclaim, "Bravo!" and "Well done!" He should not be didactic, with "Do this" and "Don't do that," for it will displease the king and lead to dislike. Where pleasure and entertainment are concerned, as in feasting, drinking, hunting, polo and wrestling—in all matters like these it is right that the king should consult with his boon-companions, for they are there for this purpose. On the other hand, in everything to do with the country and its cultivation, the military and the peasantry, warfare, raids, punishments, gifts, stores and travels, it is better that he should take counsel with the ministers and nobles of the state and with experienced elders, for they are more skilled in these subjects. In this way matters will take their proper course.

When ambassadors come from foreign countries, nobody is aware of their movements until they actually arrive at the city gates; nobody gives any information [that they are coming] and nobody makes any preparation for them; and they will surely attribute this to our negligence and indifference. So officers at the frontiers must be told that whenever anyone approaches their stations, they should at once despatch a rider and find out who it is who is coming, how many men there are with him, mounted and unmounted, how much baggage and equipment he has, and what is his business. A trustworthy person must be appointed to accompany them and conduct them to the nearest big city; there he will hand them over to another agent who will likewise go with them to the next city (and district), and so on until they reach the court. Whenever they arrive at a place where there is cultivation, it must be a standing order that officers, tax-collectors and assignees should give them hospitality and entertain them well so that they depart satisfied. When they return, the same procedure is to be followed. Whatever treatment is given to an ambassador, whether good or bad, it is as if it were done to the very king who sent him; and kings have always shewn the greatest respect to one another and treated envoys well, for by this their own dignity has been enhanced. And if at any time there has been disagreement or enmity between kings, and if ambassadors have still come and gone as occasion requires, and discharged their missions according to their instructions, never have they been molested or treated with less than usual courtesy. Such a thing would be disgraceful, as God (to Him be power and glory) says [in the Quran 24.53], "The messenger has only to convey the message plainly."

It should also be realized that when kings send ambassadors to one another their purpose is not merely the message or the letter which they communicate openly, but secretly they have a hundred other points and objects in view. In fact they want to know about the state of roads, mountain passes, rivers and grazing grounds, to see whether an army can pass or not; where fodder is available and where not; who are the officers in every place; what is the size of that king's army and how well it is armed and equipped; what is the standard of his table and his company; what is the organization and etiquette of his court and audience hall; does he play polo and hunt; what are his qualities and manners, his designs and intentions, his appearance and bearing; is he cruel or just, old or young; is his country flourishing or decaying; are his troops contented or not; are the peasants rich or poor; is he avaricious or generous; is he alert or negligent in affairs; is his wazir competent or the reverse, of good faith and high principles or of impure faith and bad principles; are his generals experienced and battle-tried or not; are his boon-companions polite and worthy; what are his likes and dislikes; in his cups is he jovial and good-natured or not; is he strict in religious matters and does he shew magnanimity and mercy, or is he careless; does he incline more to jesting or to gravity; and does he prefer boys or women. So that, if at any time they want to win over that king, or oppose his designs or criticize his faults, being informed of all his affairs they can think out their plan of campaign, and being aware of all the circumstances, they can take effective action, as happened to your humble servant in the time of The Martyr Sultan Alp Arslan (may Allah sanctify his soul).

The troops must receive their pay regularly. Those who are assignees of course have their salaries to hand independently as assigned; but in the case of pages who are not fit for holding fiefs, money for their pay must be made available. When the amount required has been worked out according to the number of troops, the money should be put into a special fund until the whole sum is in hand, and it must always be paid to them at the proper time. Alternatively the king may summon the men before him twice a year, and command that they be paid, not in such a way that the task be delegated to the treasury and they receive their money from there without seeing the king; rather the king should with his own hands put it into their hands (and skirts), for this increases their feelings of affection and attachment, so that they will strive more eagerly and steadfastly to perform their duties in war and peace.

Enlightened monarchs and clever ministers have never in any age given two appointments to one man or one appointment to two men, with the result that their affairs were always conducted with efficiency and lustre. When two appointments are given to one man, one of the tasks is always inefficiently and faultily performed; and in fact you will usually find that the man who has two functions fails in both of them, and is constantly suffering censure and uneasiness on account of his shortcomings. And further, whenever two men are given a single post each transfers [his responsibility] to the other and the work remains forever undone. On this point there is a proverb which runs, "The house with two mistresses remains unswept; with two masters it falls to ruins." One of the two thinks to himself, "If I take pains to do the work expediently, and take care not to let anything go wrong, our master will think that this is due to the capability and skill of my partner, not to my own diligent and patient efforts." The other one has the same idea and thinks, "Why should I take trouble for nothing when it will go without praise or thanks? Whatever efforts and exertions I make, my master will suppose that my partner has done it." Actually there will be constant confusion in the work, and if the manager says, "What is the cause of this inefficiency?" each man will say that it is the other's fault. But when you go to the root of the matter and think intelligently, it is not the fault of either of them. It is the fault of the man who gave one appointment to two persons. And whenever a single officer is given two posts by the divan it is a sign of the incompetence of the wazir and the negligence of the king. Today there are men, utterly incapable, who hold ten posts, and if another appointment were to turn up, they would spend their efforts and money to get it; and nobody would consider whether such people are worthy of the post, whether they have any ability, whether they understand secretaryship, administration, and business dealings, and whether they can fulfill the numerous tasks which they have already accepted. And all the time there are capable, earnest, deserving, trustworthy, and experienced men left unemployed, sitting idle in their homes; and no one has the interest or judgment to enquire why one unknown, incapable, base-born fellow should occupy so many appointments, while there are well-known, noble, trusted, and experienced men who have no work at all, and are left deprived and excluded, particularly men to whom this dynasty is greatly indebted for their satisfactory and meritorious services. This is all the more extraordinary because in all previous ages a public appointment was given to a man who was pure alike in religion and in origin; and if he was averse and refused to accept it, they used compulsion and force to make him take the responsibility. So naturally the revenue was not misappropriated, the peasants were unmolested, assignees enjoyed a good reputation and a safe existence, while the king lived a life of mental and bodily ease and tranquillity. But nowadays all distinction has vanished; and if a Jew administers the affairs of Turks or does any other work for Turks, it is permitted; and it is the same for Christians, Zoroastrians and Qarmatis. Everywhere indifference is predominant; there is no zeal for religion, no concern for the revenue, no pity for the peasants. The dynasty has reached its perfection; your humble servant is afraid of the evil eye and knows not where this state of affairs will lead.

TRANSLATED BY HUBERT DARKE

The *Qābūs-nāmeh* is a book of counsel written by Kai Kaus ibn Iskandar for his son Gilanshah, who became the last ruling member of a small princely house, the Ziyarids, which ruled in the mountainous provinces of Gilan, Mazandaran, and Gurgan on the south shore of the Caspian Sea in the tenth and eleventh centuries. Kai Kaus himself ruled for twenty years, to 1069, leaving the throne for reasons which are now unknown, and says he wrote the book when he was sixty-three, in 1082.

The book is divided into forty-four chapters and gives advice on a wide range of subjects, including love, politics, astrology, polo, chess, and "the procedure when visiting the warm baths." It was intended as a manual to help the young prince in the right direction of his life and the maintenance of his power. It is one of the finest examples of the form of literature known as the "mirror for princes," which was very popular in court circles and heavily endowed with the graces of *adab*. It is considered, together with the *Siyāsat-nāmeh* and the *Chahār Maqālah*, one of the three greatest works of early Persian prose.

When you set out to buy slaves, be cautious. The buying of men is a difficult art; because many a slave may appear to be good, who, regarded with knowledge, turns out to be the opposite. Most people imagine that buying slaves is like any other form of trading, not understanding that the buying of slaves, or the art of doing so, is a branch of philosophy. Anyone who buys goods of which he has no competent understanding can be defrauded over them, and the most difficult form of knowledge is that which deals with human beings. There are so many blemishes and good points in the human kind, and a single blemish may conceal a myriad good points, while a single good point may conceal a myriad faults.

Human beings cannot be known except by the science of physiognomy and by experience, and the science of physiognomy in its entirety is a branch of prophecy that is not acquired to perfection except by the divinely directed apostle. The reason is that by physiognomy the inward goodness or wickedness of men can be ascertained.

Now let me describe to the best of my ability what is essential in the purchasing of slaves, both white and black, and what their good and bad points are, so that they may be known to you. Understand then that there are three essentials in the buying of slaves; first is the recognition of their good and bad qualities, whether external or internal, by means of physiognomy; second is the awareness of diseases, whether latent or apparent, by their symptoms; third is the knowledge of the various classes and the defects and merits of each.

With regard to the first requirement, that of physiognomy, it consists of close observation when buying slaves. (The buyers of slaves are of all categories: there are those who inspect the face, disregarding body and extremities; others look to the corpulence or otherwise of the slave.) Whoever it may be that inspects the slave must first look at the face, which is always open to view, whereas the body can only be seen as occasion offers. Then look at eyes and eyebrows, followed by nose, lips and teeth, and lastly at the hair. The reason for this is that God placed the beauty of human beings in eyes and eyebrows, delicacy in the nose, sweetness in the lips and teeth and freshness in the skin. To all these the hair of the head has been made to lend adornment, since [God] created the hair for adornment.

You must, consequently, inspect everything. When you see beauty in the eyes and eyebrows, delicacy in the nose, sweetness in the lips and teeth and freshness in the skin, then buy the slave possessing them without concerning yourself over the extremities of the body. If all of these qualities are not present, then the slave must possess delicacy; because, in my opinion, one that is delicate without having beauty is preferable to one that is beautiful but not possessed of delicacy.

The learned say that one must know the indications and signs by which to buy the slaves suited for particular duties. The slave that you buy for your private service and conviviality should be of middle proportions, neither tall nor short, fat nor lean, pale nor florid, thickset nor slender, curly-haired nor with hair overstraight. When you see a slave soft-fleshed, fine-skinned, with regular bones and wine-coloured hair, black eyelashes, dark eyes, black eyebrows, open-eyed, long-nosed, slender-waisted, round-chinned, red-lipped, with white regular teeth, and all his members such as I have described, such a slave will be decorative and companionable, loyal, of delicate character, and dignified.

The mark of the slave who is clever and may be expected to improve is this: he must be of erect stature, medium in hair and in flesh, broad of hand and with the middle of the fingers lengthy, in complexion dark though ruddy, dark-eyed, open-faced and unsmiling. A slave of this kind would be competent to acquire learning, to act as treasurer or for any other [such] employment.

The slave suited to play musical instruments is marked out by being soft-fleshed (though his flesh must not be over-abundant, especially on the back), with his fingers slender, neither lean nor fat. (A slave whose face is over-fleshy, incidentally, is one incapable of learning.) His hands must be soft, with the middles of the fingers lengthy. He must be bright-visaged, having the skin tight; his hair must not be too long, too short or too black. It is better, also, for the soles of the feet to be regular. A slave of this kind will swiftly acquire a delicate art of whatever kind, particularly that of the instrumentalist.

The mark of the slave suited for arms-bearing is that his hair is thick, his body tall and erect, his build powerful, his flesh hard, his bones thick, his skin coarse and his limbs straight, the joints being firm. The tendons should be tight and the sinews and blood-vessels prominent and visible on the body. Shoulders must be broad, the chest deep, the neck thick and the head round; also for preference he should be bald. The belly should be concave, the buttocks drawn in and the legs in walking well extended. And the eyes should be black. Any slave who possesses these qualities will be a champion in single combat, brave and successful.

The mark of the slave suited for employment in the women's apartments is that he should be dark-skinned and sour-visaged and have withered limbs, scanty hair, a shrill voice, little [slender] feet, thick lips, a flat nose, stubby fingers, a bowed figure, and a thin neck. A slave with these qualities will be suitable for service in the women's quarters. He must not have a white skin nor a fair complexion; and beware of a ruddy-complexioned man, particularly if his hair is limp. His eyes, further, should not be languorous or moist; a man having such qualities is either over-fond of women or prone to act as a go-between.

The mark of the slave who is callous [insensitive] and suited to be a herdsman or groom is that he should be open-browed and wide-eyed, and his eyelids should be flecked with red. He should, further, be long in lips and teeth and his mouth should be wide. A slave with these qualities is extremely callous, fearless and uncivilized.

The mark of the slave suited for domestic service and cookery is that he should be clean in face and body, round-faced, with hands and feet slender, his eyes dark inclining to blue, sound in body, silent, the hair of his head wine-colored and falling forward limply. A slave with these qualities is suitable for the occupations mentioned.

Each then, should have the essential characteristics which I have recounted. But I will also mention the defects and virtues which should be known in respect of each separate race. You must understand that Turks are not all of one race, and each has its own nature and essential character. Amongst them the most ill-tempered are the Ghuzz[1] and the Qipchāqs; the best-tempered and most willing are the Khutanese, the Khallukhīs, and the Tibetans; the boldest and most courageous are the Turghay (?), the most inured to toil and hardship and the most active are the Tatars and the Yaghmā, whereas the laziest of all are the Chigil.

It is a fact well-known to all that beauty or ugliness in the Turks is the opposite of that in the Indians. If you observe the Turk feature by feature [he has] a large head, a broad face, narrow eyes, a flat nose, and unpleasing lips and teeth. Regarded individually the features are not handsome, yet the whole is handsome. The Indian's face is the opposite of this; each individual feature regarded by itself appears handsome, yet looked at as a whole the face does not create the same impression as that of the Turk. To begin with, the Turk has a personal freshness and clearness of complexion not possessed by the Indian; indeed the Turks win for freshness against all other races.

Without any doubt, what is fine in the Turks is present in a superlative degree, but so also is what is ugly in them. Their faults in general are that they are blunt-witted, ignorant, boastful, turbulent, discontented, and without a sense of justice. Without any excuse they will create trouble and utter foul language, and at night they are poor-hearted. Their merit is that they are brave, free from pretense, open in enmity, and zealous in any task allotted to them. For the [domestic] establishment there is no better race.

Slavs, Russians, and Alans are near in their temperament to the Turks, but are more patient. The Alans are more courageous than the Turks at night and more friendly disposed towards their masters. Although in their

---

[1] On the identity of the Ghuzz and of the other tribes mentioned in this section, see *Ḥudūd al-ʿĀlam*, translated by V. Minorsky, E. J. W. Gibb Memorial Series, N. S. XI (London, 1937), pp. 311 ff.

craftsmanship they are nearer to the Byzantines, being artistic, yet there are faults in them of various kinds; for example they are prone to theft, disobedience, betrayal of secrets, impatience, stupidity, indolence, hostility to their masters, and escaping. Their virtues are that they are soft-natured, agreeable, and quick of understanding. Further they are deliberate in action, direct in speech, brave, good road-guides, and possessed of good memory.

The defect of the Byzantines is that they are foul-tongued, evil-hearted, cowardly, indolent, quick-tempered, covetous, and greedy for worldly things. Their merits are that they are cautious, affectionate, happy, economically-minded, successful in their undertakings, and careful to prevent loss.

The defect of the Armenians is that they are mischievous, foul-mouthed, thieving, impudent, prone to flight, disobedient, babblers, liars, friendly to misbelief, and hostile to their masters. From head to foot, indeed, they incline rather towards defects than to merits. Yet they are quick of understanding and learn their tasks well.

The defect of the Hindu is that he is evil-tongued and in the house no slave-girl is safe from him. But the various classes of the Hindus are unlike those that prevail amongst other peoples, because in other peoples the classes mingle with each other, whereas the Hindus, ever since the time of Adam (Upon whom be peace!), have practiced the following custom: namely, no trade will form an alliance with any outside it. Thus, grocers will give their daughters only to grocers, butchers to butchers, bakers to bakers, and soldiers to soldiers.

Each of these groups therefore has its own special character, which I cannot describe one by one because that would entail a book in itself.

However, the best of them, people benevolent, brave or skilled in commerce, are [respectively] the Brahman, the Rāwat and the Kirār. The Brahman is clever, the Rāwat brave, and the Kirār skilled in commerce, each class being superior to the one after. The Nubian and the Abyssinian are freer of faults, and the Abyssinian is better than the Nubian because many things were said by the Prophet in praise of the former.

These then are the facts concerning each race and the merits and defects of each.

Now the third essential is being completely alive to defects both external and internal through knowledge of symptoms, and this means that at the time of buying you may not be careless. Do not be content with a single look; many a good slave may appear vile at first sight and many an extremely vile one appear to be good. Further there is the fact that a human being's visage does not continually bear the same complexion. Sometimes it is more inclined to be handsome, at other times to be ugly. You must carefully inspect all the limbs and organs to ensure that nothing remains hidden from you. There are many latent diseases which are on the point of coming but have not yet appeared and will do so within a few days; such diseases have their symptoms.

Thus, if there is a yellowness in the complexion, the lips being changed [from the normal] in colour, and dry, that is the symptom of haemorrhoids. If the eyelids are continuously swollen, it is a symptom of dropsy. Redness in the eyes and a fullness of the veins in the forehead are the mark of epilepsy. Tearing out the hair, flickering of the eyelashes and chewing of the lips are the signs of melancholia. Crookedness in the bone of the nose or irregularity in it are the symptoms of fistula; hair that is extremely black, but more so in one place than another, shows that the hair has been dyed. If here and there upon the body you perceive the marks of branding where no branding should be, examine closely to ensure that there is no leprosy under it. Yellowness in the eyes and a change [from the ordinary] in the colour of the face are the symptoms of jaundice.

When you buy a slave, you must take and lay him down, press him on both sides and watch closely that he has no pain or swelling. If he has, it will be in the liver or spleen. Having looked for such hidden defects, seek further for the open ones, such as smells from the mouth and nose, hardness of hearing, hesitation in utterance, irregularity of speech, walking off the [straight] road, coarseness of the joints, and hardness at the base of the teeth, to prevent any trickery being practised on you.

When you have seen all that I have mentioned and have made certain, then if you should buy, do so from honest people, and so secure a person who will be of advantage to your household. As long as you can find a non-Arab do not buy an Arabic-speaking slave. You can mould a non-Arab to your ways, but never the one whose tongue is Arabic. Further, do not have a slave-girl brought before you when your appetites are strong upon you; when desire is strong, it makes what is ugly appear good in your eyes. First abate your desires and then engage in the business of purchasing.

Never buy a slave who has been treated with affection in another place. If you do not hold him dear, he will show ingratitude to you, or will flee, or will demand to be sold, or will nourish hatred in his heart for you. Even if you regard him with affection, he will show you no gratitude, in view of what he has experienced elsewhere. Buy your slave from a house in which he has been badly treated, so that he will be grateful for the least kindness on your part and will hold you in affection. From time to time make your slaves a gift of something; do not allow them to be constantly in need of money in such a way that they are compelled to go out seeking it.

Buy slaves of a good price, for each one's value is in accordance with his price. Do not buy a slave who has had numerous masters; a woman who has had many husbands and a slave who has had many masters are held in no esteem. Let those you buy be well-favoured. And when a slave truly desires to be sold, do not dispute with him, but sell; when a slave demands to be sold or a wife to be divorced, then sell or divorce, because you will have no pleasure from either.

If a slave is deliberately (and not through inadvertence or mistake) lazy or neglectful in his work, do not teach him under compulsion to improve; have no expectation of that, for he will in no wise become industrious or capable of improvement. Sell him quickly; you may rouse a sleeping man with a shout, but a dead body cannot be roused by the sound of a hundred trumpets and drums. Further, do not assemble a useless family about you; a small family is a second form of wealth.

Provide for your slaves in such fashion that they will not escape, and treat them that you have well, as befits your dignity; if you have one person in good condition it is better than having two in ill condition. Do not permit your male slave to take to himself in your household someone whom he calls "brother," nor permit slave-girls to claim sisterhood with each other; it leads to great trouble. On bond and free impose the burdens which they are able to bear, that they may not be disobedient through sheer weakness. Keep yourself ever adorned with justice, that you may be included amongst them that are honoured as such.

The slave must recognize your brother, sister, mother or father as his master. Never buy a dealer's exhausted slave; he is as fearful of the dealer as the ass is of the farrier. Set no store by the slave who always, when called to any work, demands to be sold and never has any fears with regard to being bought and sold; you will gain nothing good from him. Change him quickly for another, seeking out one such as I have described. Thus you will achieve your purpose and suffer no troubles.

TRANSLATED BY REUBEN LEVY

The most famous lines of Islamic literature in English translation, no doubt, are these:

> A Book of Verses underneath the Bough,
> A Jug of Wine, a Loaf of Bread—and Thou
> Beside me singing in the Wilderness—
> Oh, Wilderness were Paradise enow!

As everyone knows, they are Edward Fitzgerald's translation of a quatrain of Omar (let us call him Umar) Khayyam. But are they Umar himself? It is true that there is a Persian quatrain attributed to Umar which might be translated literally as follows:

> If hand should give of the pith of the wheat a loaf,
> and of wine a two-maunder jug, of sheep a thigh,
> with a little sweetheart seated in a desolation,
> a pleasure it is that is not the attainment of any sultan.

Fitzgerald translated this quatrain, and all the others, very freely. By the simple substitution of a book of poems for a thigh of mutton and a bough for a sultan, he translated us straight into a Victorian picnic. Still, one would have to be insensitive to prefer the literal translation (and some would include the original) to Fitzgerald's.

The accuracy of attributing the *Rubāᶜiyyāt* to Umar has also been questioned. He lived his life in Khurasan and was well known as a scientist, working on the specific weights of gold and silver, on third-degree equations, and on the reform of the calendar. One authority has suggested that his quatrains may have been written as pithy summaries of his lectures on science and philosophy. Be that as it may, it is impossible to determine with any certainty which of the hundreds of quatrains attributed to him are, in fact, his own. Each of these four-line poems, with its own particular meter, is meant to stand by itself.

The philosophy of the *Rubāᶜiyyāt* is a philosophy of skepticism, but not of despair. The poet is incredulous, but not defiant; disillusioned, but compassionate.

> Come, fill the Cup, and in the fire of Spring
> Your Winter-garment of Repentance fling:
>   The Bird of Time has but a little way
> To flutter—and the Bird is on the Wing.
>
> With me along the strip of Herbage strown
> That just divides the desert from the sown,
>   Where name of Slave and Sultān is forgot—
> And Peace to Mahmūd on his golden Throne![1]
>
> I sometimes think that never blows so red
> The Rose as where some buried Caesar bled;
>   That every Hyacinth the Garden wears
> Dropt in her Lap from some once lovely Head.
>
> For some we loved, the loveliest and the best
> That from his Vintage rolling Time hath prest,
>   Have drunk their Cup a Round or two before,
> And one by one crept silently to rest.
>
> Myself when young did eagerly frequent
> Doctor and Saint, and heard great argument
>   About it and about; but evermore
> Came out by the same door where in I went.
>
> With them the seed of Wisdom did I sow,
> And with mine own hand wrought to make it grow
>   And this was all the Harvest that I reap'd—
> "I came like Water, and like Wind I go."
>
> Perplext no more with Human or Divine,
> Tomorrow's tangle to the winds resign,
>   And lose your fingers in the tresses of
> The Cypress-slender Minister of Wine.

[1] The line refers to Sultan Mahmud of Ghaznah. [Ed.]

A Hair perhaps divides the False and True;
Yes; and a single Alif[2] were the clue—
    Could you but find it—to the Treasure-house,
And peradventure to The Master too.

You know, my Friends, with what a brave Carouse
I made a Second Marriage in my house;
    Divorced old barren Reason from my Bed,
And took the Daughter of the Vine to Spouse.

I sent my Soul through the Invisible,
Some letter of that After-life to spell:
    And by and by my Soul return'd to me,
And answer'd "I Myself am Heav'n and Hell."

Heav'n but the Vision of fulfill'd Desire,
And Hell the Shadow from a Soul on fire,
    Cast on the Darkness into which Ourselves,
So late emerged from, shall so soon expire.

The Moving Finger writes; and, having writ,
Moves on: nor all your Piety nor Wit
    Shall lure it back to cancel half a Line,
Nor all your Tears wash out a Word of it.

Oh Thou, who didst with pitfall and with gin
Beset the Road I was to wander in,
    Thou wilt not with Predestined Evil round
Enmesh, and then impute my Fall to Sin!

Indeed, indeed, Repentance oft before
I swore—but was I sober when I swore?
    And then and then came Spring, and Rose-in-hand
My thread-bare Penitence apieces tore.

Ah Love! could you and I with Him conspire
To grasp this sorry Scheme of Things entire,
    Would not we shatter it to bits—and then
Remould it nearer to the Heart's Desire!

TRANSLATED BY EDWARD FITZGERALD

---

[2] The first letter of the Arabic alphabet, a single vertical stroke. [Ed.]

For a sensitive and intelligent tradition-minded Moslem living in the East, the second half of the eleventh century must have offered a very unsettling world. Just such a person was Al-Ghazzali, who advanced himself rapidly in that world—to a professorship of religious sciences at the Nizamiyyah in Baghdad—and even more rapidly renounced it in order to be true to himself.

Al-Ghazzali found his answer in Sufism, and he saw his answer as a universally applicable one, demanding expression. In his *Iḥyāʾ ʿUlūm al-Dīn* (The Renaissance of Religious Sciences), he set forth his system of harmony between mysticism and theology. He died in Tus, the city of his birth, in 1111.

In *Deliverance from Error*, Al-Ghazzali recorded the period of his interior trial from the hindsight of its solution. Even today, with our meager abilities to place ourselves exactly in his position but with plentiful abilities to place ourselves in a similar one, his account is strangely moving.

The different religious observances and religious communities of the human race, and likewise the different theological systems of the religious leaders, with all the multiplicity of sects and variety of practices, constitute ocean depths in which the majority drown and only a minority reach safety. From my early youth, since I attained the age of puberty before I was twenty, until the present time when I am over fifty, I have ever recklessly launched out into the midst of these ocean depths; I have ever bravely embarked on this open sea, throwing aside all craven caution; I have poked into every dark recess; I have made an assault on every problem; I have plunged into every abyss; I have scrutinized the creed of every sect; I have tried to lay bare the inmost doctrines of every community. All this have I done that I might distinguish between true and false, between sound tradition and heretical innovation.

To thirst after a comprehension of things as they really are was my habit and custom from a very early age. It was instinctive with me, a part of my God-given nature, a matter of temperament and not of my choice or contriving. Consequently as I drew near the age of adolescence the bonds of mere authority (*taqlīd*) ceased to hold me, and inherited beliefs lost their grip upon me, for I saw that Christian youths always grew up to be Christians, Jewish youths to be Jews, and Muslim youths to be Muslims.

I therefore said within myself: "To begin with, what I am looking for is knowledge of what things really are, so I must undoubtedly try to find what knowledge really is." It was plain to me that sure and certain knowledge is that knowledge in which the object is disclosed in such a fashion that no doubt remains along with it, that no possibility of error or illusion accompanies it, and that the mind cannot even entertain such a supposition. Certain knowledge must also be infallible; and this infallibility or security from error is such that no attempt to show the falsity of the knowledge can occasion doubt or denial, even though the attempt is made by someone who turns stones into gold or a rod into a serpent. Thus I know that ten is more than three. Let us suppose that someone says to me: "No, three is more than ten, and in proof of that I shall change this rod into a serpent"; and let us suppose that he actually changes the rod into a serpent and that I witness him doing so. No doubts about what I know are raised in me because of this. The only result is that I wonder precisely how he is able to produce this change. Of doubt about my knowledge there is no trace.

After these reflections I knew that whatever I do not know in this fashion and with this mode of certainty is not reliable and infallible knowledge; and knowledge that is not infallible is not certain knowledge.

Thereupon I investigated the various kinds of knowledge I had, and found myself destitute of all knowledge with this characteristic of infallibility except in the case of sense-perception and necessary truths. So I said: "Now that despair has come over me, there is no point in studying any problems except on the basis of what is self-evident, namely, necessary truths and the affirmations of the senses. I must first bring these to be judged in order that I may be certain on this matter. Is my reliance on sense-perception and my trust in the soundness of necessary truths of the same kind as my previous trust in the beliefs I had merely taken over from others, and as the trust most men have in the results of thinking? Or is it a justified trust that is in no danger of being betrayed or destroyed?"

I proceeded therefore with extreme earnestness to reflect on sense-perception and on necessary truths, to see whether I could make myself doubt them. The outcome of this protracted effort to induce doubt was that I could no longer trust sense-perception either. Doubt began to spread here and say: "From where does this reliance on sense-perception come? The most powerful sense is that of sight. Yet when it looks at the shadow (*sc.* of a stick or the gnomon of a sundial), it sees it standing still, and judges that there is no motion. Then by experiment and observation, after an hour it knows that the shadow is moving and, moreover, that it is moving not by fits and starts but gradually and steadily by infinitely small distances in such a way that it is never in a state of rest. Again, it looks at the heavenly body (*sc.* the sun) and sees it small, the size of a shilling;[1] yet geometrical computations show that it is greater than the earth in size."

In this and similar cases of sense-perception the sense as judge forms his judgments, but another judge, the intellect, shows him repeatedly to be wrong; and the charge of falsity cannot be rebutted.

To this I said: "My reliance on sense-perception also has been destroyed. Perhaps only those intellectual truths which are first principles (or derived from first principles) are to be relied upon, such as the assertion that ten are more than three, that the same thing cannot be both affirmed and denied at one time, that one thing is not both generated in time and eternal, nor both existent and nonexistent, nor both necessary and impossible."

Sense-perception replied: "Do you not expect that your reliance on intellectual truths will fare like your reliance on sense-perception? You used to trust in me; then along came the intellect-judge and proved me wrong; if it were not for the intellect-judge you would have continued to regard me as true. Perhaps behind intellectual apprehension there is another judge who, if he manifests himself, will show the falsity of intellect in its judging, just as, when intellect manifested itself, it showed the falsity of sense in its judging. The fact that such a supra-intellectual apprehension has not manifested itself is no proof that it is impossible."

My ego hesitated a little about the reply to that, and sense-perception heightened the difficulty by referring to dreams. "Do you not see," it said, "how, when you are asleep, you believe things and imagine circumstances, holding them to be stable and enduring, and, so long as you are in that dream-condition, have no doubts about them? And is it not the case that when you

[1] Literally *dīnār*.

awake you know that all you have imagined and believed is unfounded and ineffectual? Why then are you confident that all your waking beliefs, whether from sense or intellect, are genuine? They are true in respect of your present state; but it is possible that a state will come upon you whose relation to your waking consciousness is analogous to the relation of the latter to dreaming. In comparison with this state your waking consciousness would be like dreaming! When you have entered into this state, you will be certain that all the suppositions of your intellect are empty imaginings. It may be that that state is what the Sufis claim as their special 'state' (*sc.* mystical union or ecstasy), for they consider that in their 'states' (or ecstasies), which occur when they have withdrawn into themselves and are absent from their senses, they witness states (or circumstances) which do not tally with these principles of the intellect. Perhaps that 'state' is death; for the Messenger of God (God bless and preserve him) says: 'The people are dreaming; when they die, they become awake.' So perhaps life in this world is a dream by comparison with the world to come; and when a man dies, things come to appear differently to him from what he now beholds, and at the same time the words are addressed to him: 'We have taken off thee thy covering, and thy sight today is sharp (Koran 50:21).' "

When these thoughts had occurred to me and penetrated my being, I tried to find some way of treating my unhealthy condition; but it was not easy. Such ideas can only be repelled by demonstration; but a demonstration requires a knowledge of first principles; since this is not admitted, however, it is impossible to make the demonstration. The disease was baffling, and lasted almost two months, during which I was a sceptic in fact though not in theory nor in outward expression. At length God cured me of the malady; my being was restored to health and an even balance; the necessary truths of the intellect became once more accepted, as I regained confidence in their certain and trustworthy character.

This did not come about by systematic demonstration or marshalled argument, but by a light which God most high cast into my breast. That light is the key to the greater part of knowledge. Whoever thinks that the understanding of things divine rests upon strict proofs has in his thought narrowed down the wideness of God's mercy.

I commenced, then, with the science of theology (ʿ*ilm al-kalām*), and obtained a thorough grasp of it. I read the books of sound theologians and myself wrote some books on the subject. But it was a science, I found, which, though attaining its own aim, did not attain mine. Its aim was merely to preserve the creed of orthodoxy and to defend it against the deviations of heretics.

Now God sent to His servants by the mouth of His messenger, in the Koran and traditions, a creed which is the truth and whose contents are the basis of man's welfare in both religious and secular affairs. But Satan too sent, in the suggestions of heretics, things contrary to orthodoxy; men tended to accept his suggestions and almost corrupted the true creed for its adherents. So God brought into being the class of theologians, and moved them to support traditional orthodoxy with the weapon of systematic argument, by laying bare the confused doctrines invented by the heretics, at variance with traditional orthodoxy. This is the origin of theology and theologians.

In due course a group of theologians performed the task to which God invited them; they successfully preserved orthodoxy, defended the creed received from the prophetic source, and rectified heretical innovations. Nevertheless in so doing they based their arguments on premises which they took from their opponents and which they were compelled to admit by naïve belief (*taqlīd*), or the consensus of the community, or bare acceptance of Koran and traditions. For the most part their efforts were devoted to making explicit the contradictions of their opponents and criticizing them in respect of the logical consequences of what they admitted.

This was of little use in the case of one who admitted nothing at all save logically necessary truths. Theology was not adequate to my case and was unable to cure the malady of which I complained. It is true that, when theology appeared as a recognized discipline and much effort had been expended in it over a considerable period of time, the theologians, becoming very earnest in their endeavours to defend orthodoxy by the study of what things really are, embarked on a study of substances and accidents with their nature and properties. But since that was not the aim of their science, they did not deal with the question thoroughly in their thinking, and consequently did not arrive at results sufficient to dispel universally the darkness of confusion due to the different views of men. I do not exclude the possibility that for others than myself these results have been sufficient; indeed, I do not doubt that this has been so for quite a number. But these results were mingled with naïve belief in certain matters which are not included among first principles.

My purpose here, however, is to describe my own case, not to disparage those who sought a remedy thereby, for the healing drugs vary with the disease. How often one sick man's medicine proves to be another's poison!

After I had done with theology I started on philosophy. I was convinced that a man cannot grasp what is defective in any of the sciences unless he has so complete a grasp of the science in question that he equals its most learned exponents in the appreciation of its fundamental principles, and even goes beyond and surpasses them, probing into some of the tangles and profundities which the very professors of the science have neglected. Then and only then is it possible that what he has to assert about its defects is true.

So far as I could see none of the doctors of Islam had devoted thought and attention to philosophy. In their writings none of the theologians engaged in polemic against the philosophers, apart from obscure and scattered utterances so plainly erroneous and inconsistent that no person of ordinary intelligence would be likely to be deceived, far less one versed in the sciences.

I realized that to refute a system before understanding it and becoming acquainted with its depths is to act blindly. I therefore set out in all earnestness to acquire a knowledge of philosophy from books, by private study without the help of an instructor. I made progress towards this aim during my hours of free time after teaching in the religious sciences and writing, for at this period I was burdened with the teaching and instruction of three hundred students in Baghdad. By my solitary reading during the hours thus snatched, God brought me in less than two years to a complete understanding of the sciences of the philosophers. Thereafter I continued to reflect assiduously for nearly a year on what I had assimilated, going over it in my mind again and again and probing its tangled depths, until I comprehended surely and certainly how far it was deceitful and confusing, and how far true and a representation of reality.

When I had finished with these sciences, I next turned with set purpose to the method of mysticism (or Sufism). I knew that the complete mystic "way" includes both intellectual belief and practical activity; the latter consists in getting rid of the obstacles in the self and in stripping off its base characteristics and vicious morals, so that the heart may attain to freedom from what is not God and to constant recollection of Him.

The intellectual belief was easier to me than the practical activity. There is a difference between knowing the true nature and causes and conditions of the ascetic life, and actually leading such a life and forsaking the world.

I apprehended clearly that the mystics were men who had real experiences, not men of words, and that I had already progressed as far as was possible by way of intellectual apprehension. What remained for me was not to be attained by oral instruction and study, but only by immediate experience and by walking in the mystic way.

Now from the sciences I had laboured at, and the paths I had traversed in my investigation of the revelational and rational sciences (that is, theology and philosophy), there had come to me a sure faith in God most high, in prophethood (or revelation), and in the Last Day. These three credal principles were firmly rooted in my being, not through any carefully argued proofs, but by reason of various causes, coincidences, and experiences which are not capable of being stated in detail.

It had already become clear to me that I had no hope of the bliss of the world to come save through a God-fearing life and the withdrawal of myself from vain desire. It was clear to me too that the key to all this was to sever the attachment of the heart to worldly things, by leaving the mansion of deception and returning to that of eternity, and to advance towards God most high with all earnestness. It was also clear that this was only to be achieved by turning away from wealth and position and fleeing from all time-consuming entanglements.

Next I considered the circumstances of my life, and realized that I was caught in a veritable thicket of attachments. I also considered my activities, of which the best was my teaching and lecturing, and realized that in them I was dealing with sciences that were unimportant and contributed nothing to the attainment of eternal life.

After that I examined my motive in my work of teaching, and realized that it was not a pure desire for the things of God, but that the impulse moving me was the desire for an influential position and public recognition. I saw for certain that I was on the brink of a crumbling bank of sand and in imminent danger of hell-fire unless I set about to mend my ways.

I reflected on this continuously for a time, while the choice still remained open to me. One day I would form the resolution to quit Baghdad and get rid of these adverse circumstances; the next day I would abandon my resolution. I put one foot forward and drew the other back. If in the morning I had a genuine longing to seek eternal life, by the evening the attack of a whole host of desires had reduced it to impotence. Worldly desires were striving to keep me by their chains just where I was, while the voice of faith was calling, "To the road! To the road! What is left of life is but little and the journey before you is long. All that keeps you busy, both intellectually and practically, is but hypocrisy and delusion. If you do not prepare *now* for eternal life, when will you prepare? If you do not *now* sever these attachments, when will you sever them?" On hearing that, the impulse would be stirred and the resolution made to take to flight.

Soon, however, Satan would return. "This is a passing mood," he would say; "do not yield to it, for it will quickly disappear; if you comply with it and leave this influential position, these comfortable and dignified circumstances where you are free from troubles and disturbances, this state of safety and security where you are untouched by the contentions of your adversaries, then you will probably come to yourself again and will not find it easy to return to all this."

For nearly six months beginning with Rajab 488 A.H. (=July, 1095 A.D.), I was continuously tossed about between the attractions of worldly desires and the impulses towards eternal life. In that month the matter ceased to be one of choice and became one of compulsion. God caused my tongue to dry up so that I was prevented from lecturing. One particular day I would make an effort to lecture in order to gratify the hearts of my following, but my tongue would not utter a single word nor could I accomplish anything at all.

Much confusion now came into people's minds as they tried to account for my conduct. Those at a distance from Iraq supposed that it was due to some apprehension I had of action by the government. On the other hand, those who were close to the governing circles and had witnessed how eagerly and assiduously they sought me, and how I withdrew from them and showed no great regard for what they said, would say, "This is a supernatural affair; it must be an evil influence which has befallen the people of Islam and especially the circle of the learned."

I left Baghdad, then. I distributed what wealth I had, retaining only as much as would suffice myself and provide sustenance for my children. This I could easily manage, as the wealth of Iraq was available for good works, since it constitutes a trust fund for the benefit of the Muslims. Nowhere in the world have I seen better financial arrangements to assist a scholar to provide for his children.

I continued at this stage for the space of ten years, and during these periods of solitude there were revealed to me things innumerable and unfathomable. This much I shall say about that, in order that others may be helped: I learnt with certainty that it is, above all, the mystics who walk on the road of God; their life is the best life; their method the soundest method; their character the purest character; indeed, were the intellect of the intellectuals, and the learning of the learned, and the scholarship of the scholars who are versed in the profundities of revealed truth, brought together in the attempt to improve the life and character of the mystics, they would find no way of doing so; for to the mystics all movement and all rest, whether external or internal, bring illumination from the light of the lamp of prophetic revelation; and behind the light of prophetic revelation there is no other light on the face of the earth from which illumination may be received.

I had persevered thus for nearly ten years in retirement and solitude. I had come of necessity, from reasons which I do not enumerate—partly immediate experience, partly demonstrative knowledge, partly acceptance in faith—to a realization of various truths. I believed that it was permissible for me in the sight of God to continue in retirement, on the ground of my inability to demonstrate the truth by argument. But God most high determined Himself to stir up the impulse of the sovereign of the time, though not by any external means; the latter gave me strict orders to hasten to Naysābūr (Nīshāpūr) to tackle the problem of this lukewarmness in religious matters. So strict was the injunction that, had I persisted in disobeying it, I should at length have been cut off! I came to realize, too, that the grounds which had made retirement permissible had lost their force. "It is not right that your motive for clinging to retirement should be laziness and love of ease, the quest for spiritual power and preservation from worldly contamination. It was not because of the difficulty of restoring men to health that you gave yourself this permission."

On this matter I consulted a number of men skilled in the science of the heart and with experience of contemplation. They unanimously advised me to abandon my retirement and leave the *zāwiyah* (hospice). My resolution was further strengthened by numerous visions of good men, in all of which alike I was given the assurance that this impulse was a source of good, was genuine guidance, and had been determined by God most high for the beginning of this century; for God most high has promised to revive His religion at the beginning of each century.[2] My hope became strong, and all these considerations caused the favourable view of the project to prevail.

God most high facilitated my move to Naysābūr to deal with this serious problem in Dhuʾl-Qaʿdah, the eleventh month of 499 (=July, 1106). I had originally left Baghdad in Dhuʾl-Qaʿdah, 488 (=November, 1095), so that

[2] There was a well-known tradition to the effect that at the beginning of each century God would send a man to revive religion. The events in question took place a few months before the beginning of the sixth century A.H.

my period of retirement had extended to eleven years. It was God most high who determined this move, and it is an example of the wonderful way in which He determines events, since there was not a whisper in my heart while I was living in retirement. In the same way my departure from Baghdad and withdrawal from my position there had not even occurred to my mind as a possibility. But God is the upsetter of hearts[3] and positions. As the tradition has it, "The heart of the believer is between two of the fingers of the Merciful."

In myself I know that, even if I went back to the work of disseminating knowledge, yet I did not go back. To go back is to return to the previous stage of things. Previously, however, I had been disseminating the knowledge by which worldly success is attained; by word and deed I had called men to it, and that had been my aim and intention. But now I am calling men to the knowledge whereby worldly success is given up and its low position in the scale of real worth is recognized. This is now my intention, my aim, my desire; God knows that this is so. It is my earnest longing that I may make myself and others better. I do not know whether I shall reach my goal or whether I shall be taken away while short of my object. I believe, however, both by certain faith and by intuition, that there is no power and no might save with God, the high, the mighty, and that I do not move of myself but am moved by Him, I do not work of myself but am used by Him. I ask Him first of all to reform me and then to reform through me, to guide me and then to guide through me, to show me the truth of what is true and to grant of His bounty that I may follow it, and to show me the falsity of what is false and to grant of His bounty that I may turn away from it.

TRANSLATED BY W. MONTGOMERY WATT

---

[3] *Muqallib al-qulūb*—a play on words. [Ed.]

[from *Al-Maqāmāt*, The Assemblies]

The twin strains of Arabic folk literature and more sophisticated *adab* never came closer to fusion than they did in the *maqāmah* form. What the *maqāmah* did, one authority explains, "was to invest with the literary graces of *saj*ᶜ [rhymed prose] and the glamour of impromptu composition the old-time tale in alternate prose and verse . . . and, by a stroke of genius, to adopt as the mouthpiece of [its] art that familiar figure in popular story, the witty vagabond."

The greatest writer in the *maqāmah* form, and one of the most respected figures in Arabic literature, was Al-Hariri of Basrah, who was born in 1054 and died in 1122. He produced a set of *maqāmah*s in which his *rāwī*, Al-Harith, meets Abu Zayd Seruj, a clever trickster, who appears in many situations and guises to display his talent. Unabashed imitations of the work of Al-Hamadhani a century before, they clearly surpass their predecessors in all respects. It is, in fact, difficult to imagine that the Arabic language has ever been handled with more consummate skill under such restrictions. There are sections composed exclusively of words with double meanings, series of sentences ending in rhyming syllables or with regular combinations of consonants throughout, and poems utilizing only certain letters of the alphabet.

The following selections may serve at least to illustrate the fact that the rigidity of form did not prevent amusing stories from being told. For all their cleverness, indeed, they did not escape outcries of moral indignation over their cavalier plots and favoritism toward the trickster. It is easily granted that they were not intended to be edifying, but they are certainly far from frivolous.

Samarkand

Al Ḥârith, son of Hammâm, related: In one of my journeys I chose sugar-candy for a merchandise, making with the same for Samarcand, and in those days I was upright of build, brimful of sprightliness, taking sight from the bow of enjoyment at the target of pleasures, and seeking in the sap of my youth help against the glamours of the water-semblance [mirage]. Now I reached her on a Friday morn, after I had endured hardship, and I bestirred myself without tarrying, until a nightstead was got, and when I had carried there my sugar-candy, and was entitled to say "at home with me," I wended forthwith towards a bath, when I put from me the weariness of travel, and took to the washing of the congregation-day conformably to tradition. Then I hastened with the bearing of the humble to the cathedral mosque, so as to join those who were near the prayer-leader, and offer [as it were] the fattened camel, and happily I was foremost in the race, and elected the central place for hearing the sermon. Meanwhile people ceased not to enter in troops into the faith of Allah, and to arrive singly and in pairs, until, when the mosque was crowded with its assembly, and a person had waxed equal with his shadow, the preacher sallied forth, swaggering in the wake of his acolyths, and straightway mounted the steps of the pulpit of the [divine] call, until he stood at its summit, when he gave blessing with a wave of his right hand, sitting down thereafter until the ritual of the cry to prayer was completed. Then he rose and spoke: "Praise be to Allah, the exalted of names, the praised for His bounties, the abundant in gifts, the called upon for the rescinding of calamity;—king of the nations, restorer of rotten bones, honourer of the folks of forbearance and generosity, destroyer of ᶜÂd and Irem;— whose cognizance comes up with every secret, whose compassion encompasses every obdurate in sin, whose munificence comprises all the world, whose power breaks down every revolter.—I praise Him with the praise of one who proclaims [God's] unity and professes Islâm, I pray to Him with the prayer of the hopeful, the trusting, for He is the God, there is no God but He, the unique, the one, the just, the eternal, there is none begotten to Him, and no begetter, no companion with Him and no helpmate.— He sent forth Mohammed to spread about Islâm, to consolidate religion, to confirm the guidance of the apostles, to straighten the black-hued and the red.—He united womb-connections, he taught the fundamentals of truth, he set a stamp on the lawful and the forbidden, he regulated [laid down the rules for] the doffing and the donning of the pilgrim-cloak.—May Allah exalt his place, and perfect the blessing and benediction upon him, may He have compassion on his race, the worthy, and on his progeny, the uterine, as long as the pile-cloud pours, as long as the dove coos, as long as the cattle graze, as long as the sword assaults.—Work ye, may Allah have mercy upon you, the work of the pious, exert yourselves towards your return [on the resurrection day] with the exertion of the sound, curb your lusts with the curbing of enemies, make ready for your departure with the readiness of the blissful.—Put ye on the robes of abstinence, and put away the ailings of greed, make straight the crookedness of your dealings, and resist the whisperings of hope.—Portray ye to your imaginings the vicissitudes of circumstances, and the alighting of terrors, and the attacks of sickness, and the cutting off from pelf and kin:— Bethink ye yourselves of death, and the agony of its throwing-place, of the tomb and the awfulness of that which is sighted there, of the grave-niche and the loneliness of the one deposed in it, of the angel and the frightfulness of his questioning and of his advent.—Look ye at fortune and the baseness of its onslaught, and the evil of its deceit and cunning:—How many road-marks has it effaced, how many viands embittered! how many a host has it scattered, how many an honoured king has it overthrown.—Its striving is to strike deaf the ears, to make flow the tear-founts, to baffle desires, to destroy the songster and the listener to the song. Its decree is the same for kings and subjects, for the lord and the henchman, for the envied and the envier, for serpents and for lions.—It enriches not, but to turn away, and reverse hopes; it bestows not, but to outrage and cut into the limbs; it gladdens not, but to sadden, and revile, and injure; it grants no health, but to engender disease and frighten friends.—Fear ye Allah! fear ye Allah! May Allah keep you! How long this persistency in levity, this perseverance in thoughtlessness, this stubbornness in sin, this loading yourselves with crime, this rejection of the word of the wise, this rebellion against the God of heaven?—Is not senility your harvest, and the clod your couch? Is not death your capturer, and [the bridge] Ṣirât your path? Is not the hour [of resurrection] your tryst, and the plain [or hell] your goal? Are not the terrors of doomsday laid in ambush for you? Is not the abode of transgressors Al-Ḥuṭamah, the firmly [safely] locked?—Their warder Mâlik, their comeliness raven blackness, their food poison, their breathing-air the scorching blast!—No wealth prospers them, no offspring; no numbers protect them, and no equipments.—But lo, Allah has mercy upon the man who rules his passion, and who treads the paths of His guidance; who makes firm his obedience towards his Lord, and strives for the restfulness of his place of refuge; who works while life lasts obedient, and fortune at truce with him, and health perfect and welfare at hand;—Lest he be overtaken by the frustration of his wish, by the faltering of speech, by the alighting of afflictions, by the fulfilment of fate, by the blunting of senses, by the remedy of the sepulchres. Alack on them for a misery whose woefulness is assured, whose term is infinite! He who is remedied thereby is wretched, his distractedness has none to allay it, his regret none to pity it; there is no one to ward off that which befalls him. May then Allah inspire you with the praiseworthiest of inspirations! May He robe you with the robe of glory! May He cause you to alight in the abode of peace! Of Him I ask mercy upon you and on the people of the religion of Islâm, for He is the most forgiving of the generous, the saviour, and peace be with you."—Said Al Ḥârith, son of Hammâm: Now, when I saw that the sermon was a choice thing without a flaw, and a bride without a spot, the wonderment at its admirable strain urged me on to look at the preacher's face, and I began to scan it narrowly, and to let my glance range over him carefully, when it became clear to me by the truth of tokens, that it was our Shaykh, the author of the Assemblies.— There was, however, no help from keeping silent for the time being; so I withheld until he had left off praying, and "the dispersing on the earth" had come. Then I turned towards him, and hastened to meet him, and when he spied me he quickened his pace, and was profuse in doing me honour, bidding me to accompany him to his abode and making me a confidant of the particulars of his intimate affairs.—Now, when the wing of darkness had spread, and the time for sleep had come, he brought forth wineflasks secured with plug, whereupon I said to him: "Dost thou quaff it before sleep, and thou the prayer-leader of the people?" But he replied: "Hush! I by day am preacher, but by night make merry."—Said I: "By Allah, I know not whether to wonder more at thy unconcernedness as to thy kinsfolk and thy birthplace, or at thy preacher-office with thy foul habits, and the rotation of thy wine-cup."—Thereupon he turned his face in disgust from me, and presently he said:—Listen to me:

"Weep not for a friend that is distant, nor for an abode, but turn thyself about with fortune as it turns about.

Reckon thou all mankind thy dwelling-place, and fancy all the earth thy home.

Forbear with the ways of him with whom thou dealest, and humor him, for it is the wise that humors.

Miss thou no chance of enjoyment, for thou knowest not if thou live a day, or if an age.

Know thou that death is going round, and the moon-halos circle above all created beings,

Swearing that they will not cease chasing them, as long as morn and even turn and re-turn.

How then mayest thou hope to escape from a net from which neither Kisrá escaped, nor Dârâ."

Said he [the narrator]: And when the cups went between us from hand to hand, and the vital spirits waxed gleeful, he dragged from me the oath that allows no exception, that I would screen his repute [secret]. So I complied with his wish, and kept faith with him, and ranked him before the great in the rank of Al Fuẓail, and let down the skirt over the turpitudes of the night; and this continued to be his wont and my wont, until the time for my return came, when I took leave from him, while he persisted in hypocrisy and in secretly quaffing old wine.

Tiflis

I had covenanted with Allah, be He exalted, since I was of the age of about a score, that I would not delay prayer as far as it was in my power, so that with my roaming in deserts, and in spite of the sport of leisure-hours, I kept the stated times of prayer and guarded myself from the sin of letting them slip by, and when I joined in a journey and alighted in any place, I welcomed the summoner to it, and took pattern from him, who observed it religiously. Now it happened at a time when I had come to Tiflis, that I prayed together with a number of poorly-off people, and when we had finished prayer and were about to go, there sallied forth an old man, with a face plainly contorted by palsy, worn of garments and strength, who said: "I conjure him who has been made of the clay of liberality and suckled of the milk of good fellowship, that he but spare me a moment's hurrying, and listen to a few words from me, whereafter the choice belongs to him, and it rests with his hand to spend or refuse." Then the people fastened their hoops to him [locked their knees together to him], and sat still like the hillocks. Now when he perceived how nicely they kept silent and how considerate they showed themselves in their demeanor [deportment] he said: "O ye, endowed with eyes clear of sight, and visions bright of perception, does not eye-witnessing dispense with hearsay? and does not the smoke tell of the fire? Hoariness is apparent, and weakness oppressive, and disease manifest, and the inward state thus laid bare. Yet erewhile I was one of those who possess and bestow, who exercise authority and rule, who grant help and gifts, who assist and assault. But calamities ceased not to subvert, nor vicissitudes to take away scrap by scrap, till the nest was despoiled and the palm empty; privation became my raiment and bitterness my life-stay, my little ones whined from hunger and craved for the sucking of a date-stone. Yet withal I came not to stand in this place of ignominy and to disclose to you things [to be] hidden, but after I had suffered and was palsy-stricken, and had waxed grey from all I met with, and, oh! would that I had not been spared!" Then he sighed the sigh of the sorrowful, and indited with a feeble voice:

"I cry to the Compassionate, be praise to Him, for fortune's fickleness and hostile rancour

And for calamities that have shattered my rock, and overthrown my frame and its foundations,

Have broken down my stem, and woe to him whose boughs adversities pull down and break.

My dwelling they have wasted even as to banish from the wasted spot the rats themselves;

They left me bewildered and dazed, to bear the brunt of poverty and all its pangs,

While heretofore I was a lord of wealth, who trailed his sleeves along in luxury,

Whose leaves the supplicants beat freely down, whose hospitable fires night-farers praised;

But who is now, as though the world, that casts the evil eye on him, had never smiled on him,

From whom he turns who was his visitor, and whom he scorns to know who sought his gift.

So if a good man mourns the evil plight he sees an old man in, betrayed by fortune,

Then let him ease the sorrow that afflicts him, and mend the state that puts him thus to shame."

Said the narrator: Now the company inclined to ascertain his condition, so
as to find out what he might have concealed, and to sift the truth of his affair.
So they said to him: "We know by this time the excellence of thy degree,
and the abundance of thy rain-cloud, but make now known to us the tree of
thy branch, and withdraw the veil from thy descent." Then he showed himself averse with the reluctancy of one whom misfortunes have befallen or
to whom the tidings of daughters [born to him] have been brought, and he
indited with emphatic utterance, although in a low voice:

"By thy life, I assure thee, not showeth the branch by the zest of its fruit
from what root it has sprung,
So eat what is sweet, when it cometh to hand, and ask not the honey
where swarmeth the bee!
And learn to discern, when thou pressest thy grapes, the must of thy
press from the acid it yields,
That by testing thou value the costly and cheap, to buy and to sell all
things by their likes;
For blame would accrue to the witty, the wise, if error of judgment were
fastened on him."

Then the people were roused by his sagacity and subtleness, and beguiled
by the beauty of his delivery, along with his disease, so that they collected
for him the hidden treasures of their belts and whatever was secreted in their
breast-pockets, saying to him: "Thou hast drifted to a shallow well and repaired to an empty hive; so take this trifle [pittance] and reckon it neither
a miss nor a hit." Then he made much of their little, and accompanied its
acceptance with thanks, whereupon he turned away, dragging half his body,
and made off, stumbling on his road. Said the narrator of this tale: Now the
fancy struck me, that he had disguised his appearance, and shammed in his
gait, so I rose to thread his path and to track his traces, while he glanced at
me askance and gave me a wide berth, until, when the road was clear and
identification [the disclosure of the truth] became possible, he looked at me
with the look of him who is friendly and glad of the meeting, and shows his
true colours after he had dissembled, saying to me: "I imagine thou art a
brother of peregrination, and looking out for companionship. Wouldst thou
then fain have a mate who is kind to thee and helps thee, and is indulgent with
thee and shares in thy expenses?" Said I to him: "If such a mate came forward, providence, indeed, would favour me." He replied: "Thou hast found,

so rejoice, and hast encountered the generous, so cleave to him." Then he had a long laugh, and stood before me, a sound man, when lo! it was our Shaykh of Serûj, with no ailment in his body and nothing doubtful in his outward tokens. Then I rejoiced at meeting with him, and at the feignedness of his palsy, and bethought me of rebuking him for the evilness of his ways, but he opened his mouth and indited before I could chide him:

"I show me in rags, so that people may say, a wretch that forbears with the hardships of times.

I feign to the world to be palsied of face, for often my heart thus obtaineth its wish;

Ay, but for my raggedness find I compassion, and but for the palsy I meet with my wants."

Thereupon he said: "No pasture is left me in these parts, nor anything to be hoped for from their people, and if thou wilt be my mate, on our way with us, on our way!" So we fared forth from the place, we twain by ourselves, and I kept company with him for full two years, nay, I would fain have associated with him while my life lasts, but time, the disperser, forbade me.

TRANSLATED BY F. STEINGASS

[from *Chahār Maqālah*, Four Discourses]

The *Four Discourses*, completed about 1156, stands as a monument of early Persian prose. Nizami Arudi Samarqandi, the author, had tried his hand unsuccessfully at poetry, and traveled extensively in the traces of its masters. He became a master himself simply by recording what he had heard of the poets—and of civil servants, astrologers, and doctors (the titles of the *Four Discourses*). Evidently he cared less about the absolute accuracy of his accounts than about the elegance of their expression, for E. G. Browne, in a preface to one edition of the Persian text, lists fifteen "egregious" errors of fact in the work. This has never deterred the Persians, nor could it ever deter them, from drawing on the *Four Discourses* for their most cherished stories about their early poets.

Rudaki

They relate thus, that Naṣr ibn Aḥmad, who was the most brilliant jewel of the Sāmānid galaxy, whereof the fortunes reached their zenith during the days of his rule, was most plenteously equipped with every means of enjoyment and material of splendour—well-filled treasuries, a far-flung army, and loyal servants. In winter he used to reside at his capital, Bukhārā, while in summer he used to go to Samarqand or some other of the cites of Khurāsān. Now one year it was the turn of Herāt. He spent the spring season at Bādghīs, where are the most charming pasture-grounds of Khurāsān and ᶜIrāq, for there are nearly a thousand water-courses abounding in water and pasture, any one of which would suffice for an army.

When the beasts had well enjoyed their spring feed, and had regained their strength and condition, and were fit for warfare or to take the field, Naṣr ibn Aḥmad turned his face toward Herāt, but halted outside the city at Margh-i-Sapīd and there pitched his camp. It was the season of spring; cool breezes from the north were stirring, and the fruit was ripening in the districts of Mālin and Karūkh—such fruit as can be obtained in but few places, and nowhere so cheaply. There the army rested. The climate was charming, the breeze cool, food plentiful, fruit abundant, and the air filled with fragrant scents, so that the soldiers enjoyed their life to the full during the spring and summer.

When Mihrgān [the festival of the autumnal equinox] arrived, and the juice of the grape came into season, and the basil, rocket, and feverfew were in bloom, they did full justice to the delights of youth and took tribute of their juvenile prime. Mihrgān was protracted, for the cold did not wax severe, and the grapes ripened with exceptional sweetness. For in the district of Herāt one hundred and twenty different varieties of the grape occur, each sweeter and more delicious than the other; and amongst them are in particular two kinds which are not to be found in any other region of the inhabited world, one called *Parniyān* and the other *Kalanjarī*, thin-skinned, small-stoned, and luscious, so that you would say they contained no earthly elements. A cluster of Kalanjarī grapes sometimes attains a weight of five maunds, and each individual grape five dirhams' weight; they are black as pitch and sweet as sugar, and one can eat many by reason of the lusciousness that is in them. And besides these there were all sorts of other delicious fruits.

So the Amīr Naṣr ibn Aḥmad saw Mihrgān and its fruits, and was mightily pleased therewith. Then the narcissus began to bloom, and the raisins were plucked and stoned in Mālin, and hung up on lines, and packed in store-rooms; and the Amīr with his army moved into the two groups of hamlets called Ghūra and Darwāz. There he saw mansions of which each one was like highest paradise, having before it a garden or pleasure ground with a northern aspect. There they wintered, while the Mandarin oranges began to arrive from Sīstān and the sweet oranges from Māzandarān; and so they passed the winter in the most agreeable manner.

When [the second] spring came, the Amīr sent the horses to Bādghīs and moved his camp to Mālin [to a spot] between two streams. And when summer came and the fruits again ripened, Amīr Naṣr ibn Aḥmad said, "Where shall we go for the summer? For there is no pleasanter place of residence than this. Let us wait till Mihrgān." And when Mihrgān came, he said, "Let us enjoy Mihrgān at Herāt and then go"; and so from season to season he continued to procrastinate, until four years had passed in this way. For it was then the heyday of the Sāmānian prosperity, and the land was flourishing, the kingdom unmenaced by foes, the army loyal, fortune favourable, and heaven auspicious; yet withal the Amīr's attendants grew weary, and desire for home arose within them, while they beheld the king quiescent, the air of Herāt in his head and the love of Herāt in his heart; and in the course of conversation he would compare, nay, prefer Herāt to the Garden of Eden, and would exalt its charms above those of a Chinese temple.

So they perceived that he intended to remain there for that summer also. Then the captains of the army and nobles of the kingdom went to Master Abū ᶜAbdiᵓllāh Rūdagī, than whom there was none more honoured of the king's intimates, and none whose words found so ready an acceptance. And they said to him, "We will present thee with five thousand *dīnārs* if thou wilt contrive some artifice whereby the king may be induced to depart hence, for our hearts are craving for our wives and children, and our souls are like to leave us for longing after Bukhārā." Rūdagī agreed; and, since he had felt the Amīr's pulse and understood his temperament, he perceived that prose would not affect him, and so had recourse to verse. He therefore composed a *qaṣīda*; and, when the Amīr had taken his morning cup, came in and sat down in his place; and, when the musicians ceased, he took up the harp, and, playing the "Lover's Air," began this elegy:

> The Jū-yi-Mūliyān[1] we call to mind,
> We long for those dear friends long left behind.

Then he strikes a lower key, and sings:

> The sands of Oxus, toilsome though they be,
> Beneath my feet were soft as silk to me.
> Glad at the friends' return, the Oxus deep
> Up to our girths in laughing waves shall leap.
> Long live Bukhārā! Be thou of good cheer!
> Joyous towards thee hasteth our Amīr!
> The Moon's the Prince, Bukhārā is the sky;
> O Sky, the Moon shall light thee by and by!
> Bukhārā is the mead, the Cypress he;
> Receive at last, O Mead, thy Cypress-tree!

When Rūdagī reached this verse, the Amīr was so much affected that he descended from his throne, all unbooted bestrode the horse which was on

---

[1] A stream and series of plantations along its banks near Bukhara. [Ed.]

sentry-duty, and set off for Bukhārā so precipitately that they carried his leggings and riding-boots after him for two parasangs, as far as Burūna, and only then did he put them on; nor did he draw rein anywhere till he reached Bukhārā, and Rūdagī received from the army the double of that five thousand *dīnārs*.

Firdawsi

Master Abuʾl-Qāsim Firdawsī was one of the Dihqāns (landowners) of Ṭūs, from a village called Bāzh in the district of Ṭabarān, a large village capable of supplying a thousand men. There Firdawsī enjoyed an excellent position, so that he was rendered quite independent of his neighbours by the income which he derived from his lands, and he had but one child, a daughter. His one desire in putting the Book of Kings (*Shāhnāma*) into verse was, out of the reward which he might obtain for it, to supply her with an adequate dowry. He was engaged for twenty-five years on this work ere he finished the book, and to this end he left nothing undone, raising his verse as high as heaven, and causing it in sweet fluency to resemble running water. What genius, indeed, could raise verse to such a height as he does in the letter written by Zāl to Sām, the son of Narīman in Māzandarān, when he desired to ally himself with Rūdāba, the daughter of the King of Kābul:

> Then to Sām straightway sent he a letter,
> Filled with fair praises, prayers, and good greeting.
> First made he mention of the World-Maker,
> Who doom dispenseth and doom fulfilleth.
> "On Nīram's son Sām," wrote he, "the sword-lord,
> Mail-clad and mace-girt, may the Lord's peace rest!
> Hurler of horse-troops in hot-contested fights,
> Feeder of carrion-fowls with foemen's flesh-feast,
> Raising the roar of strife on the red war-field,
> From the grim war-clouds grinding the gore-shower,
> Who by his manly might merit on merit
> Heaps, till his merit merit outmeasures."

In eloquence I know of no poetry in Persian which equals this, and but little even in Arabic.

When Firdawsī had completed the *Shāhnāma*, it was transcribed by ʿAlī Daylam and recited by Abū Dulaf, both of whom he mentions by name in tendering his thanks to Ḥuyayy-i-Qutayba, the governor of Ṭūs, who had conferred on Firdawsī many favours.... [He] was the revenue-collector of Ṭūs, and deemed it his duty at least to abate the taxes payable by Firdawsī; hence naturally his name will endure till the Resurrection, and Kings will read it.

So ʿAlī Daylam transcribed the *Shāhnāma* in seven volumes, and Firdawsī, taking with him Abū Dulaf, set out for the Court of Ghazna. There, by the help of the great Minister Aḥmad ibn Ḥasan, the secretary, he presented it, and it was accepted, Sulṭān Maḥmūd expressing himself as greatly indebted to his Minister. But the Prime Minister had enemies who were continually casting the dust of misrepresentation into the cup of his rank, and Maḥmūd consulted with them as to what he should give Firdawsī. They replied, "Fifty thousand *dirhams*, and even that is too much, seeing that he is in belief a Rāfiḍī and a Muʿtazilite.... Now Sulṭān Maḥmūd was a zealot, and he listened to these imputations and caught hold of them, and in all only twenty thousand *dirhams* were paid to Ḥakīm Firdawsī. He was bitterly disappointed, went to the bath, and on coming out bought a draft of sherbet, and divided the money between the bath-man and the sherbet-seller. Knowing, however, Maḥmūd's severity, he fled from Ghazna by night, and alighted in Herāt at the shop of Azraqī's father, Ismaʿīl the bookseller, where he remained in hiding for six months, until Maḥmūd's messengers had reached Ṭūs and had turned back thence, when Firdawsī, feeling secure, set out from Herāt for Ṭūs, taking the *Shāhnāma* with him. Thence he came to Ṭabaristān, to the Sipahbad Shahriyār of the House of Bāwand, who was King there; and this is a noble house which traces its descent from Yazdigird [the last Sasanian king].

Then Firdawsī wrote a satire of a hundred couplets on Sulṭān Maḥmūd in the Preface, and read it to Shahriyār, saying, "I will dedicate this book to you instead of to Sulṭān Maḥmūd, for this book deals wholly with the legends and deeds of thy forebears." Shahriyār treated him with honour and shewed him many kindnesses, and said, "O Master, Maḥmūd was induced to act thus by others, who did not submit your book to him under proper conditions, and misrepresented you. Moreover you are a Shīʿite, and whosoever loves the Family of the Prophet, his worldly affairs will prosper no more than theirs. Maḥmūd is my liege-lord: let the *Shāhnāma* stand in his name, and give me the satire which you have written on him, that I may expunge it and give you some little recompense; and Maḥmūd will surely summon thee and seek to satisfy thee fully, for the labour spent on such a book must not be wasted." And next day he sent Firdawsī 100,000 *dirhams*, saying, "I buy each couplet at a thousand *dirhams*; give me those hundred couplets, and be reconciled to Maḥmūd." So Firdawsī sent him these verses, and he ordered them to be expunged; and Firdawsī also destroyed his rough copy of them, so that this satire was done away with and only these six verses of it remained:[2]

> They cast imputations on me, saying, "That man of many words
> Hath grown old in the love of the Prophet and ᶜAli."
> If I speak of my love for these
> I can protect a hundred such as Maḥmūd.
> No good can come of the son of a slave,
> Even though his father hath ruled as King.
> How long shall I speak on this subject?
> Like the sea I know no shore.
> The King had no aptitude for good,
> Else would he have seated me on a throne.
> Since in his family there was no nobility,
> He could not bear to hear the names of the noble.

In truth good service was rendered to Maḥmūd by Shahriyār, and Maḥmūd was greatly indebted to him.

When I was at Nīshāpūr in the year A.H. 514 (A.D. 1120–1121), I heard Amīr Muᶜizzī say that he had heard Amīr ᶜAbduᵓr-Razzāq at Ṭūs relate as follows: "Maḥmūd was once in India, and was returning thence towards Ghazna. On the way, as it chanced, there was a rebellious chief possessed of a strong fortress, and next day Maḥmūd encamped at the gates of it, and sent an ambassador to him, bidding him come before him on the morrow, do homage, pay his respects at the Court, receive a robe of honour, and return to his place. Next day Maḥmūd rode out with the Prime Minister on his right hand, for the ambassador had turned back and was coming to meet the King. 'I wonder,' said the latter to the Minister, 'what answer he will have given?' Thereupon the Minister recited this verse of Firdawsī's:

> Should the answer come contrary to my wish,
> Then for me the mace, and the field [of battle], and Afrāsiyāb.

[2] According to others, more of it survived; a satirical preface circulated as Firdawsi's work is translated in *Persian Poems*, edited by A. J. Arberry (London and New York, 1954), pp. 183–185. [Ed.]

'Whose verse,' enquired Maḥmūd, 'is that, for it is one to inspire courage?' 'Poor Abuʾl-Qāsim Firdawsī composed it,' answered the Minister; 'he who laboured for five-and-twenty years to complete such a work, and reaped from it no advantage.' 'You have done well,' said Maḥmūd, 'to remind me of this, for I deeply regret that this noble man was disappointed by me. Remind me at Ghazna to send him something.'

So when the Minister returned to Ghazna, he reminded Maḥmūd, who ordered Firdawsī to be given sixty thousand *dīnārs*' worth of indigo, and that this indigo should be carried to Ṭūs on the King's own camels, and that apologies should be made to Firdawsī. For years the Minister had been working for this, and at length he had achieved his work; so now he despatched the camels, and the indigo arrived safely at Ṭabarān.³ But as the camels were entering through the Rūdbār Gate, the corpse of Firdawsī was being borne forth from the Gate of Razān. Now at this time there was in Ṭabarān a preacher whose fanaticism was such that he declared that he would not suffer Firdawsī's body to be buried in the Musulmān Cemetery, because he was a Rāfiḍī (Shīʿa); and nothing that men could say served to move this doctor. Now within the Gate there was a garden belonging to Firdawsī, and there they buried him, and there he lies to this day." And in the year A.H. 510 (A.D. 1116–1117) I visited his tomb.

They say that Firdawsī left a daughter of very lofty spirit, to whom they would have given the King's gift; but she would not accept it, saying, "I need it not." The Postmaster⁴ wrote to the Court and represented this to the King, who ordered that doctor to be expelled from Ṭabarān as a punishment for his officiousness, and to be exiled from his home, and the money to be given to the Imām Abū Bakr ibn Isḥāq-i-Kirāmī⁵ for the repair of the rest-house of Chāha, which stands on the road between Merv and Nīshāpūr on the boundaries of Ṭūs. When this order reached Ṭūs it was faithfully carried out; and the restoration of the rest-house of Chāha was effected by this money.

---

³ A district of the city of Tus. [Ed.]
⁴ The postmasters in Abbasid times were important government agents.
⁵ The head of the Kirami sect at Nishapur.

Umar Khayyam

In the year A.H. 506 (A.D. 1112–1113), Khwāja Imām ᶜUmar-i-Khayyāmī and Khwāja Imām Muẓaffar-i-Isfizārī⁶ had alighted in the city of Balkh, in the Street of the Slave-sellers, in the house of Amīr Abū Saᶜd Jarrah, and I had joined that assembly. In the midst of our convivial gathering I heard that Argument of Truth ᶜUmar say, "My grave will be in a spot where the trees will shed their blossoms on me twice a year." This thing seemed to me impossible, though I knew that such a one would not speak idle words.

When I arrived at Nīshāpūr in the year A.H. 530 (A.D. 1135–1136), it being then four years since that great man had veiled his countenance in the dust, and this nether world had been bereaved of him,⁷ I went to visit his grave on the eve of a Friday (seeing that he had the claim of a master on me), taking with me one to point out to me his tomb. So he brought me out to the Ḥīra Cemetery; I turned to the left, and found his tomb situated at the foot of a garden wall over which pear-trees and peach-trees thrust their heads, and on his grave had fallen so many flower-leaves that his dust was hidden beneath the flowers. Then I remembered that saying which I had heard from him in the city of Balkh, and I fell to weeping, because on the face of the earth and in all the regions of the habitable globe, I nowhere saw one like unto him. My God (blessed and exalted is He!) have mercy upon him, by His Grace and His Favour! Yet although I witnessed this prognostication on the part of that Proof of the Truth ᶜUmar, I did not observe that he had any great belief in astrological predictions; nor have I seen or heard of any of the great [scientists] who had such belief.

TRANSLATED BY E. G. BROWNE

---

⁶ A notable astronomer who collaborated with Umar Khayyam and others in the computation of the Jalali calendar. [Ed.]
⁷ That would place Umar's death in A.H. 526 (A.D. 1132), while most authorities place it between A.H. 515 and 517 (A.D. 1121–1124). [Ed.]

[from *Ḥayy ibn Yaqẓān*, Alive, Son of Awake]

Ḥayy ibn Yaqẓān has one of the most carefully constructed plots in Arabic literature, yet it is not usually counted among the works of belles-lettres, but rather as a book of philosophy. Certainly its author, Ibn Tufayl, born near Granada in the early years of the twelfth century, was a gifted philosopher. He became physician and adviser to the philosophically inclined Caliph Abu Yaqub of the Almohad dynasty, and it was he who introduced into the court circle young Ibn Rushd, or Averroës, the most influential of all the Moslem philosophers. In *Ḥayy ibn Yaqẓān*, on the other hand, Ibn Tufayl translated his philosophical system into the form of a romance based upon two current stories which happened, for his purposes, to fit very well together.

Every thinking person must have wondered at some time or another what his intellect would be like if it had been formed within a different society and environment. *Ḥayy ibn Yaqẓān* is the story of an infant boy washed up on an unpopulated island and nursed by a roe, who learns as he lives, and reasons methodically toward an ordered cosmology and eventually a philosophical contemplation of God. The second story begins when Hayy is visited by another human being, a hermit from another island, who is astounded by Hayy's grasp of these matters and easily converts him to Islam. The two set off to convert mankind to their system and way of life, but come to realize that it is suited only to a chosen few.

Granted that Hayy's reasoning closely follows the philosophical manuals of the time and that the plot is too often cement rather than brick, Ibn Tufayl's work is a masterpiece of economically elegant prose. It was translated into English just a few years before Daniel Defoe wrote *Robinson Crusoe*, and has been suggested as having an influence upon that work.

By the time he [Hayy] had attained to the end of his *third septenary*, viz. to the twenty-first year of his age, he had found out many things which were of great use to him for the conveniences of life. He made himself clothes and shoes of the skins of wild beasts after he had dissected them for use. He made himself thread of their hair, as also of the rind of the stalks of althea mallows and other plants that could be easily parted asunder and drawn into threads. And he learned the making of these threads from the use he had made of the rushes before. He made a sort of bodkin of the strongest thorns he could get and splinters of cane, sharp-pointed with stones.

The art of building he was taught by the observations he made upon the swallows' nests. He built himself a room to repose and rest therein, and also a store-house and pantry to lay up the remainder of his victuals. He guarded it with a door made of canes twisted together to prevent any of the beasts from getting in when he happened to be away. He got hold of certain birds of prey which he made use of for hawking, and others of the tamer sort which he bred up, and fed upon their eggs and chickens. He also took to him the horns of wild bulls, which he fastened upon the strongest canes he could get and the staves of the tree Alzan and others of similar kind.

Thus by the help of fire and of sharp-edged stones he so fitted them that they served him as spears. He made himself also a shield of the skins of beasts, folded and compacted together. And thus he tried to provide himself with artificial weapons, being destitute of natural arms.

When he saw that his hand supplied all those defects quite well, and that none of the various kinds of wild beasts ventured to stand up against him, but fled away from him and only excelled him in their swiftness, he bethought himself of contriving some art how to be even with them, and finally decided there would be nothing so convenient as to chase some of the strongest and swiftest beasts of the island, nourishing them with food until they might let him get on the backs of them, so that he might pursue other kinds of wild beasts.

There were in that island wild horses and asses, out of which he chose some that seemed fittest for the purpose, and by dint of exercise he made them so tractable that he became complete master of his wishes. And when he had made out of the skins of beasts something that served him instead of bridles and saddles, it was an easy matter for him to overtake beasts which he scarcely could have taken in any other way.

He made all these discoveries whilst he busied himself in the study of anatomy, studiously searching after the properties of the component parts of animals and their differences, and all this he did, as we mentioned above, by the time he was twenty-one years of age.

After this he proceeded further to examine the nature of bodies that were subject to generation and corruption, as the different kinds of animals, plants, minerals, and different sorts of stones, earth, water, exhalations and vapours, ice, snow, hail, smoke, fire, and hoar-frost.

In all these he observed different qualities and a diversity of actions and motions, agreeing in some respects and differing in others. He found that, so far as they agreed, they were *one*; where they disagreed, *a great many*; and when he looked into the properties whereby they were distinguished from one another, he found them so manifold that he could not comprehend them.

As to himself, he knew that his spirit was one in essence, and was really the substance of his being, and that the other parts served only as so many instruments. So he perceived his own essence to be but one.

Then attentively considering the different kinds of animals, he perceived that the one thing common to them all was sensation and nutrition and the faculty of moving of their own accord wheresoever they pleased, all of which actions he was assured were the proper effects of the animal spirit, and that those lesser things in which they differed were not so proper to that spirit.

For he considered that the animal spirit may differ with regard to some qualities, according to the variety of constitutions in several animals. And so he looked upon the whole species of living creatures as one.

Then, on contemplating the different species of plants, he perceived that the individuals of every species were like one another in their boughs, branches, leaves, fruits; and so, taking a view of all the different kinds of plants, he decided within himself that they were all *one* and the same in respect of that agreement between themselves in their actions, viz. their nourishment and growth.

He then contemplated those bodies which have neither sense, nourishment, nor growth, such as stones, earth, water, air, and fire; which he saw had all of them three dimensions, viz. *length, breadth*, and *thickness*; and that their differences only consisted in this, that some of them were coloured, others not; some were hot, others cold, and similar differences.

He noticed also that hot bodies grew cold, and, on the contrary, cold ones grew warm. He saw further that water rarefied into vapours, and vapours again thickened and turned into water. Then he observed that the bodies which were burnt turned into coals, ashes, flame, and smoke; and that the smoke, when in its ascent it was intercepted by an arch of stones, thickened them into soot and became like other earthly substances. From whence he concluded that all things were in reality *one*, like the animals and plants, though multiplied and diversified in some respects.

Now after he had attained thus far, so as to have a general and indistinct notion of an *Agent*, a vehement desire seized him to get a more distinct knowledge of him. But since he had not yet withdrawn himself from the sensible world, he began to look for this voluntary Agent among things sensible; nor did he know, as yet, whether it were one Agent or many. Therefore he took a view of all the bodies that were near him, viz. which his thoughts had been continually fixed upon; which he found all successively liable to generation and corruption, either completely or in parts, as *water* and *earth*, parts of which are consumed by *fire*.

He perceived likewise that the air was changed into snow by extremity of cold, and then again into water; and among all the other bodies which he had near him, he could find none which had not its existence anew and required some voluntary Agent to give it a being. Therefore he laid all those sublunary bodies aside, and transferred his thoughts to the consideration of the heavenly bodies.

Thus far had he arrived with his reflections about the *fourth septenary* of his age. He recognised that the heavens and all the stars contained therein were bodies, because they are extended according to the three dimensions: length, breadth, and thickness.

Then he began to ask himself whether their extension was infinite, whether they extended to an endless length and breadth, or whether they were circumscribed by any bounds and terminated by certain limits.

This problem continually occupied his mind. But soon, owing to the power of his reflection and the penetration of his thought, he perceived that the idea of an infinite body was an absurdity, an impossibility, a notion quite unintelligible. And he confirmed himself in this way of thinking by numerous arguments that presented themselves to his mind.

Now, whereas it appeared to him that the whole world was only one Substance which stood in need of a voluntary Agent, and that its various parts seemed to him but one thing in like manner as the bodies of the lower world which is subject to generation and corruption, he took a broad view of the whole world, and debated within himself whether it existed in time after it had been, and came to be out of nothing; or whether it was a thing that had existed from eternity and never wanted a beginning.

In respect to this matter, he had many and grave doubts within himself, so that neither of these opinions prevailed over the other. For when he proposed to himself the belief of eternity, there arose many objections in his mind with regard to the impossibility of an *infinite being*, just as the existence of an *infinite body* had seemed impossible to him.

He saw, furthermore, that any substance that was not void of *qualities* produced anew, but always endued with them, must also itself be produced anew, because it cannot be said to be before them; and that which cannot exist before qualities newly produced, must needs itself be newly produced.

On the other hand, however, when he proposed to himself to believe in a new production thereof, other objections occurred to him—in particular this, that the notion of its being produced after non-existence could in no wise be understood, unless it was supposed there was some time antecedent to its existence; whereas time was amongst the number of those things that belonged to the world and was inseparable therefrom, wherefore the world cannot be understood to be later than time.

He then reasoned within himself: if the world be produced anew, it must needs have a producer or creator; and if so, why did this creator create the world now and not before?

Was it because some motive supervened which it had not before? But there was nothing besides him, the Creator.

Was it, then, owing to some change in his own nature? If so, what has caused this change?

Thus he did not cease to consider these things within himself for some years, and to ponder over its different bearings; and a great many arguments offered themselves on both sides, so that neither of those opinions preponderated in his judgment over the other.

Since it seemed difficult to him to make a definite decision on this question, he began to consider within himself what would be the necessary consequence which did follow from either of those opinions, and that they might both be alike. And he perceived that, if he supposed the world to be created in time, and to have had an existence after non-existence, it would necessarily follow therefrom that the world could not come forth into existence by its own power, but required some agent to produce it; but this agent could not be perceived by any of the senses; for if it were an object of the senses, it would be *body*, and if *body*, part of the world, and would have had its existence anew; so that it would have stood in need of some other cause which should have produced it anew. And if this second creator were also a body, he would depend upon a third, and that third upon a fourth, and so on *ad infinitum*, which, however, would be absurd and irrational.

The world, therefore, must necessarily have a creator that has not a bodily substance; and as the creator is, indeed, without such a bodily substance, it is quite impossible for us to apprehend him by any of our senses; for we perceive nothing by the help of the five senses but bodies or such qualities as adhere to bodies.

Thus far he had advanced in his knowledge by the end of the *fifth septenary* from his birth, that is, when he was thirty-five years old. And the consideration of this supreme being was then so fixed in his mind that it hindered him to think of any other thing, so that he forgot altogether the consideration of their existence and of their nature, until in the end it came to this, that as soon as he cast his eyes upon anything of any kind whatsoever, he at once saw in it the prints of this Agent, and in a moment his thoughts were diverted from the Creature and transferred to the Creator, so that his heart was altogether withdrawn from thinking on this inferior world, which contains the objects of sense (inferior sensible world), and entirely taken up with the contemplation of the superior intellectual world.

As to the end of his story, I will tell you all about it, with the help of God.

When *Hayy* returned to the Sensible World, after his digression into the Divine World, he began to loathe the burden and troubles of this mortal life on earth, and to be filled with a most earnest and passionate desire of the life to come; and he strove to return to the same state in the same way as at first, until he attained thereto with less labour than he had done formerly. And he continued in it the second time longer than at the first.

Then he returned to the Sensible World; and then again he sought to re-enter into that state of speculation, and found it easier than the first and second time, and continued therein much longer.

In this way it grew easier and easier unto him, and his remaining therein became longer and longer, until at last he could attain it whenever he desired, and remain therein as long as he pleased, except when the necessity of his body required it. Those necessities, however, he had restrained within so narrow a compass that a narrower could hardly be imagined.

And while in this state he often wished that God, the Almighty and Glorious, would altogether detach him from this body of his that called him away from that place, so that he might wholly and continually give himself up to his delight, and might be freed from all that pain and grief with which he was afflicted, as often as he was forced to turn his mind from that state to attend on his bodily necessities.

TRANSLATED BY PAUL BRÖNNLE

Usamah ibn Munqidh was born in 1095, the year the crusades began.
He was a nephew of the prince of Shayzar in Syria and was raised to
be a warrior and a gentleman. He was a witness to the end of the
Fatimid caliphate in Egypt, and a friend of Saladin. When he was
in late middle age, the Islamic frontier with the Franks was already
sufficiently nonbelligerent to permit close association between the two
peoples. Usamah was one of those Moslems whose position and
education permitted and encouraged such association, and he took
advantage of them.

Many years later, when he was more than ninety years old, he
wrote his memoirs. As an example of candid autobiography and informal *adab* style—perhaps one might say *adab* as lived—his work is
much appreciated. Naturally his reminiscences of the Franks take
second place to accounts of his hunting exploits, but they constitute
some of the most fascinating sections of his book.

"If any book is the man," his translator writes, "*Kitāb al-Iᶜtibār*
is certainly Usāmah. Shaken by years, amiably rambling in his talk
and reminiscences, our nonagenarian spins one anecdote after another,
slipping into his story bits of his philosophy of life couched in such
homely and poignant, often naïve, phrases as to be remembered. More
delectable stories can be had nowhere else in Arabic literature."

Mysterious are the works of the Creator, the author of all things! When
one comes to recount cases regarding the Franks, he cannot but glorify Allah
(exalted is he!) and sanctify him, for he sees them as animals possessing the
virtues of courage and fighting, but nothing else, just as animals have only
the virtues of strength and carrying loads. I shall now give some instances of
their doings and their curious mentality.

In the army of King Fulk, son of Fulk, was a Frankish reverend knight
who had just arrived from their land in order to make the holy pilgrimage

and then return home. He was of my intimate fellowship and kept such
constant company with me that he began to call me "my brother." Between
us were mutual bonds of amity and friendship. When he resolved to return
by sea to his homeland, he said to me:

"My brother, I am leaving for my country and I want thee to send with
me thy son (my son, who was then fourteen years old, was at that time in
my company) to our country, where he can see the knights and learn wisdom
and chivalry. When he returns, he will be like a wise man."

Thus there fell upon my ears words which would never come out of the
head of a sensible man; for even if my son were to be taken captive, his captivity could not bring him a' worse misfortune than carrying him into the
lands of the Franks. However, I said to the man:

"By thy life, this has been exactly my idea. But the only thing that prevented me from carrying it out was the fact that his grandmother, my mother,
is so fond of him that she did not this time let him come out with me until
she exacted an oath from me to the effect that I would return him to her."

Thereupon he asked, "Is thy mother still alive?" "Yes," I replied. "Well,"
said he, "disobey her not."

A case illustrating their curious medicine is the following:
The lord of al-Munayṭirah[1] wrote to my uncle asking him to dispatch
a physician to treat certain sick persons among his people. My uncle sent
him a Christian physician named Thābit. Thābit was absent but ten days when
he returned. So we said to him, "How quickly hast thou healed thy patients!"
He said:

They brought before me a knight in whose leg an abscess had grown,
and a woman afflicted with imbecility.[2] To the knight I applied a small
poultice until the abscess opened and became well; and the woman I put on
diet and made her humor wet. Then a Frankish physician came to them and
said, "This man knows nothing about treating them." He then said to the
knight, "Which wouldst thou prefer, living with one leg or dying with two?"
The latter replied, "Living with one leg." The physician said, "Bring me a
strong knight and a sharp ax." A knight came with the ax. And I was standing

---

[1] In Lebanon near Afqah, the source of Nahr-Ibrāhīm, i.e., ancient Adonis.
[2] Ar. *nashāf*, "dryness," is not used as a name of a disease. I take the word therefore to be
Persian *nishāf*—"imbecility."

by. Then the physician laid the leg of the patient on a block of wood and bade the knight strike his leg with the ax and chop it off at one blow. Accordingly he struck it—while I was looking on—one blow, but the leg was not severed. He dealt another blow, upon which the marrow of the leg flowed out and the patient died on the spot. He then examined the woman and said, "This is a woman in whose head there is a devil which has possessed her. Shave off her hair." Accordingly they shaved it off and the woman began once more to eat their ordinary diet—garlic and mustard. Her imbecility took a turn for the worse. The physician then said, "The devil has penetrated through her head." He therefore took a razor, made a deep cruciform incision on it, peeled off the skin at the middle of the incision until the bone of the skull was exposed, and rubbed it with salt. The woman also expired instantly. Thereupon I asked them whether my services were needed any longer, and when they replied in the negative I returned home, having learned of their medicine what I knew not before.

I have, however, witnessed a case of their medicine which was quite different from that.

The king of the Franks[3] had for treasurer a knight named Bernard [*barnād*], who (may Allah's curse be upon him!) was one of the most accursed and wicked among the Franks. A horse kicked him in the leg, which was subsequently infected and which opened in fourteen different places. Every time one of these cuts would close in one place, another would open in another place. All this happened while I was praying for his perdition. Then came to him a Frankish physician and removed from the leg all the ointments which were on it and began to wash it with very strong vinegar. By this treatment all the cuts were healed and the man became well again. He was up again like a devil.

Another case illustrating their curious medicine is the following:

In Shayzar we had an artisan named abu-al-Fath, who had a boy whose neck was afflicted with scrofula. Every time a part of it would close, another part would open. This man happened to go to Antioch on business of his, accompanied by his son. A Frank noticed the boy and asked his father about him. Abu-al-Fath replied, "This is my son." The Frank said to him, "Wilt thou swear by thy religion that if I prescribe to thee a medicine which will cure thy boy, thou wilt charge nobody fees for prescribing it thyself? In that

[3] Fulk of Anjou, king of Jerusalem.

case, I shall prescribe to thee a medicine which will cure the boy." The man took the oath and the Frank said:

"Take uncrushed leaves of glasswort, burn them, then soak the ashes in olive oil and sharp vinegar. Treat the scrofula with them until the spot on which it is growing is eaten up. Then take burnt lead, soak it in ghee butter [*samn*] and treat him with it. That will cure him."

The father treated the boy accordingly, and the boy was cured. The sores closed, and the boy returned to his normal condition of health.

I have myself treated with this medicine many who were afflicted with such disease, and the treatment was successful in removing the cause of the complaint.

Everyone who is a fresh emigrant from the Frankish lands is ruder in character than those who have become acclimatized and have held long association with the Moslems. Here is an illustration of their rude character.

Whenever I visited Jerusalem I always entered the Aqsa Mosque, beside which stood a small mosque which the Franks had converted into a church. When I used to enter the Aqsa Mosque, which was occupied by the Templars [*al-dāwiyyah*], who were my friends, the Templars would evacuate the little adjoining mosque so that I might pray in it. One day[4] I entered this mosque, repeated the first formula, "Allah is great," and stood up in the act of praying, upon which one of the Franks rushed on me, got hold of me and turned my face eastward, saying, "This is the way thou shouldst pray!" A group of Templars hastened to him, seized him and repelled him from me. I resumed my prayer. The same man, while the others were otherwise busy, rushed once more on me and turned my face eastward, saying, "This is the way thou shouldst pray!" The Templars again came in to him and expelled him. They apologized to me, saying, "This is a stranger who has only recently arrived from the land of the Franks and he has never before seen anyone praying except eastward." Thereupon I said to myself, "I have had enough prayer." So I went out, and have ever been surprised at the conduct of this devil of a man, at the change in the color of his face, his trembling, and his sentiment at the sight of one praying towards the *qiblah*.[5]

I saw one of the Franks come to al-Amīr Muՙīn-al-Dīn (may Allah's mercy rest upon his soul!) when he was in the Dome of the Rock,[6] and say

[4] About 1140.
[5] The direction of the Kaՙbah in the holy city, Mecca.
[6] *al-sakhrah*, the mosque standing near al-Aqsa in Jerusalem.

to him, "Dost thou want to see God as a child?" Mu‘īn-al-Dīn said, "Yes." The Frank walked ahead of us until he showed us the picture of Mary with Christ (may peace be upon him!) as an infant in her lap. He then said, "This is God as a child." But Allah is exalted far above what the infidels say about him!

The Franks are void of all zeal and jealousy. One of them may be walking along with his wife. He meets another man who takes the wife by the hand and steps aside to converse with her while the husband is standing on one side waiting for his wife to conclude the conversation. If she lingers too long for him, he leaves her alone with the conversant and goes away.

Here is an illustration which I myself witnessed:

When I used to visit Nāblus,[7] I always took lodging with a man named Mu‘izz, whose home was a lodging house for the Moslems. The house had windows which opened to the road, and there stood opposite to it on the other side of the road a house belonging to a Frank who sold wine for the merchants. He would take some wine in a bottle and go around announcing it by shouting, "So and so, the merchant, has just opened a cask full of this wine. He who wants to buy some of it will find it in such and such a place." The Frank's pay for the announcement made would be the wine in that bottle. One day this Frank went home and found a man with his wife in the same bed. He asked him, "What could have made thee enter into my wife's room?" The man replied, "I was tired, so I went in to rest." "But how," asked he, "didst thou get into my bed?" The other replied, "I found a bed that was spread, so I slept in it." "But," said he, "my wife was sleeping together with thee!" The other replied, "Well, the bed is hers. How could I therefore have prevented her from using her own bed?" "By the truth of my religion," said the husband, "if thou shouldst do it again, thou and I would have a quarrel." Such was for the Frank the entire expression of his disapproval and the limit of his jealousy.

Another illustration:

We had with us a bath-keeper named Sālim, originally an inhabitant of al-Ma‘arrah,[8] who had charge of the bath of my father (may Allah's mercy rest upon his soul!). This man related the following story:

"I once opened a bath in al-Ma‘arrah in order to earn my living. To this

[7] Neapolis, ancient Shechem.
[8] Ma‘arrat-al-Nu‘mān, between Ḥamāh and Aleppo.

bath there came a Frankish knight. The Franks disapprove of girding a cover around one's waist while in the bath. So this Frank stretched out his arm and pulled off my cover from my waist and threw it away. He looked and saw that I had recently shaved off my pubes. So he shouted, "Sālim!" As I drew near him he stretched his hand over my pubes and said, "Sālim, good! By the truth of my religion, do the same for me." Saying this, he lay on his back and I found that in that place the hair was like his beard. So I shaved it off. Then he passed his hand over the place and, finding it smooth, he said, "Sālim, by the truth of my religion, do the same to madame [*al-dāma*]" (*al-dāma* in their language means the lady), referring to his wife. He then said to a servant of his, "Tell madame to come here." Accordingly the servant went and brought her and made her enter the bath. She also lay on her back. The knight repeated, "Do what thou hast done to me." So I shaved all that hair while her husband was sitting looking at me. At last he thanked me and handed me the pay for my service."

Consider now this great contradiction! They have neither jealousy nor zeal, but they have great courage, although courage is nothing but the product of zeal and of ambition to be above ill repute.

Here is a story analogous to the one related above:

I entered the public bath in Ṣūr [Tyre] and took my place in a secluded part. One of my servants thereupon said to me, "There is with us in the bath a woman." When I went out, I sat on one of the stone benches and behold! the woman who was in the bath had come out all dressed and was standing with her father just opposite me. But I could not be sure that she was a woman. So I said to one of my companions, "By Allah, see if this is a woman," by which I meant that he should ask about her. But he went, as I was looking at him, lifted the end of her robe and looked carefully at her. Thereupon her father turned toward me and said, "This is my daughter. Her mother is dead and she has nobody to wash her hair. So I took her in with me to the bath and washed her head." I replied, "Thou hast well done! This is something for which thou shalt be rewarded [by Allah]!"

A curious case relating to their medicine is the following, which was related to me by William of Bures [*kilyām dabūr*], the lord of Ṭabarayyah [Tiberias], who was one of the principal chiefs among the Franks. It happened that William had accompanied al-Amīr Muꜥīn-al-Dīn (may Allah's mercy rest upon his soul!) from ꜥAkka to Ṭabarayyah when I was in his company too. On the way William related to us the following story in these words:

"We had in our country a highly esteemed knight who was taken ill and was on the point of death. We thereupon came to one of our great priests and said to him, 'Come with us and examine so and so, the knight.' 'I will,' he replied, and walked along with us, while we were assured in ourselves that if he would only lay his hand on him the patient would recover. When the priest saw the patient, he said, 'Bring me some wax.' We fetched him a little wax, which he softened and shaped like the knuckles of fingers, and he stuck one in each nostril. The knight died on the spot. We said to him, 'He is dead.' 'Yes,' he replied, 'he was suffering great pain, so I closed up his nose that he might die and get relief.'

Let this go and let us resume the discussion regarding Harim.[9]

We shall now leave the discussion of their treatment of the orifices of the body to something else.

I found myself in Ṭabarayyah at the time the Franks were celebrating one of their feasts. The cavaliers went out to exercise with lances. With them went out two decrepit, aged women whom they stationed at one end of the race course. At the other end of the field they left a pig which they had scalded and laid on a rock. They then made the two aged women run a race while each one of them was accompanied by a detachment of horsemen urging her on. At every step they took, the women would fall down and rise again, while the spectators would laugh. Finally one of them got ahead of the other and won that pig for a prize.

I attended one day a duel in Nāblus between two Franks. The reason for this was that certain Moslem thieves took by surprise one of the villages of Nāblus. One of the peasants of that village was charged with having acted as guide for the thieves when they fell upon the village. So he fled away. The king[10] sent and arrested his children. The peasant thereupon came back to the king and said, "Let justice be done in my case. I challenge to a duel the man who claimed that I guided the thieves to the village." The king then said to the tenant who held the village in fief, "Bring forth someone to fight the duel with him." The tenant went to his village, where a blacksmith lived, took hold of him and ordered him to fight the duel. The tenant became thus sure of the safety of his own peasants, none of whom would be killed and his estate ruined.

[9] A hemistich quoted from the pre-Islamic poet Zuhayr ibn-abi-Sulma al-Muzani.
[10] Fulk of Anjou, king of Jerusalem (1131–1142).

I saw this blacksmith. He was a physically strong young man, but his heart failed him. He would walk a few steps and then sit down and ask for a drink. The one who had made the challenge was an old man, but he was strong in spirit and he would rub the nail of his thumb against that of the forefinger in defiance, as if he was not worrying over the duel. Then came the viscount [*al-biskund*], i.e., the seignior of the town, and gave each one of the two contestants a cudgel and a shield and arranged the people in a circle around them.

The two met. The old man would press the blacksmith backward until he would get him as far as the circle, then he would come back to the middle of the arena. They went on exchanging blows until they looked like pillars smeared with blood. The contest was prolonged and the viscount began to urge them to hurry, saying, "Hurry on." The fact that the smith was given to the use of the hammer proved now of great advantage to him. The old man was worn out and the smith gave him a blow which made him fall. His cudgel fell under his back. The smith knelt down over him and tried to stick his fingers into the eyes of his adversary, but could not do it because of the great quantity of blood flowing out. Then he rose up and hit his head with the cudgel until he killed him. They then fastened a rope around the neck of the dead person, dragged him away and hanged him. The lord who brought the smith now came, gave the smith his own mantle, made him mount the horse behind him, and rode off with him. This case illustrates the kind of jurisprudence and legal decisions the Franks have—may Allah's curse be upon them!

I once went in the company of al-Amīr Mu'īn-al-Dīn (may Allah's mercy rest upon his soul!) to Jerusalem. We stopped at Nāblus. There a blind man, a Moslem, who was still young and was well dressed, presented himself before al-Amīr carrying fruits for him and asked permission to be admitted into his service in Damascus. The Amīr consented. I inquired about this man and was informed that his mother had been married to a Frank whom she had killed. Her son used to practice ruses against the Frankish pilgrims and co-operate with his mother in assassinating them. They finally brought charges against him and tried his case according to the Frankish way of procedure.

They installed a huge cask and filled it with water. Across it they set a board of wood. They then bound the arms of the man charged with the act, tied a rope around his shoulders, and dropped him into the cask, their idea being that in case he was innocent, he would sink in the water and they would then lift him up with the rope so that he might not die in the water; and in case he was guilty, he would not sink in the water. This man did his best to sink when they dropped him into the water, but he could not do it. So he had to submit to their sentence against him—may Allah's curse be upon them! They pierced his eyeballs with red-hot awls.

Later this same man arrived in Damascus. Al-Amīr Muᶜīn-al-Dīn (may Allah's mercy rest upon his soul!) assigned him a stipend large enough to meet all his needs and said to a slave of his, "Conduct him to Burhān-al-Dīn al-Balkhī (may Allah's mercy rest upon his soul!) and ask him on my behalf to order somebody to teach this man the Koran and something of Moslem jurisprudence." Hearing that, the blind man remarked, "May triumph and victory be thine! But this was never my thought." "What didst thou think I was going to do for thee?" asked Muᶜīn-al-Dīn. The blind man replied, "I thought thou wouldst give me a horse, a mule and a suit of armor and make me a knight." Muᶜīn-al-Dīn then said, "I never thought that a blind man could become a knight."

Among the Franks are those who have become acclimatized and have associated long with the Moslems. These are much better than the recent comers from the Frankish lands. But they constitute the exception and cannot be treated as a rule.

Here is an illustration. I dispatched one of my men to Antioch on business. There was in Antioch at that time al-Raᵓīs Theodoros Sophianos [*tādrus ibn-al-ṣaffī*], to whom I was bound by mutual ties of amity. His influence in Antioch was supreme. One day he said to my man, "I am invited by a friend of mine who is a Frank. Thou shouldst come with me so that thou mayest see their fashions." My man related the story in the following words:

"I went along with him and we came to the home of a knight who belonged to the old category of knights who came with the early expeditions of the Franks. He had been by that time stricken off the register and exempted from service, and possessed in Antioch an estate on the income of which he lived. The knight presented an excellent table, with food extraordinarily clean and delicious. Seeing me abstaining from food, he said, "Eat, be of good cheer! I never eat Frankish dishes, but I have Egyptian women cooks and never eat except their cooking. Besides, pork never enters my home." I ate, but guardedly, and after that we departed.

As I was passing in the market place, a Frankish woman all of a sudden hung to my clothes and began to mutter words in their language, and I could not understand what she was saying. This made me immediately the center of a big crowd of Franks. I was convinced that death was at hand. But all of a sudden that same knight approached. On seeing me, he came and said to that woman, "What is the matter between thee and this Moslem?" She replied, "This is he who has killed my brother Hurso [ʿurs]." This Hurso was a knight in Afāmiyah who was killed by someone of the army of Ḥamāh. The Christian knight shouted at her, saying, "This is a bourgeois [burjāsi] (i.e., a merchant) who neither fights nor attends a fight." He also yelled at the people who had assembled, and they all dispersed. Then he took me by the hand and went away. Thus the effect of that meal was my deliverance from certain death."

TRANSLATED BY PHILIP K. HITTI

[from *Al-Riḥlah*, Travels]

In repentance for having drunk wine, so we are told, Ibn Jubayr left his post in Valencia in 1183 and set out on a pilgrimage to Mecca. During his pilgrimage he kept a journal of his experiences, which was unusual not only in the abundance of its detail but also in the vividness of its descriptions. The pilgrimage also inspired him to write several poems, notably one in praise of Saladin, whom he came to hero-worship. But his literary renown, which has been surprisingly great, is due exclusively to this account of his journey, which he gave to copyists after his return to Spain in 1185.

On landing at Jiddah, happy in the safety which Great and Glorious God had granted us, we earnestly beseeched Him that our return should not be by this accursed sea, unless some necessity arose preventing our going by other ways. God in His power acts with beneficence in all that He decrees and disposes.

This Jiddah is a village on the coast we have mentioned.[1] Most of its houses are of reeds, but it has inns built of stone and mud, on the top of which are reed structures serving as upper chambers, and having roofs where at night rest can be had from the ravages of the heat. In this village are ancient remains which show that it is old. Traces of the walls that encompassed it remain to this day. In it is a place having an ancient and lofty dome, which is said to have been the lodging place of Eve, the mother of mankind—God's blessing upon her—when on her way to Mecca. This edifice was erected to illustrate its blessedness and excellence. God best knows concerning it. The city has a blessed mosque attributed to ᶜUmar ibn al-Khattab[2]—may God hold him in His favour—and another with two pillars of ebony wood, also attributed to him—may God hold him in His favour—although some attribute it to Harun al-Rashid[3]—may God have mercy on him.

[1] That is, the eastern coast of the Red Sea. [Ed.]
[2] The second caliph, who ruled from 634 to 644. [Ed.]
[3] The fifth Abbasid caliph, who ruled from 786 to 809. [Ed.]

Most of the inhabitants of this town and the surrounding desert and mountains are Sharifs, ᶜAliites, Hasanites, Husaynites, and Jaᶜfarites—may God hold in His favour their noble ancestors.[4] They lead a life so wretched as to break the hardest stone in compassion. They employ themselves in all manner of trades, such as hiring camels should they possess any, and selling milk or water and other things like dates which they might find, or wood they might collect. Sometimes their women, the Sharifahs themselves, share in this work. Glory to the Determiner in what He decrees. Beyond peradventure they are of a house to which God is pleased to give the life to come and not of this world; and He has made us amongst those who it is proper should love the family of the Prophet, from whom He has removed impurity, and whom He has cleansed.

Outside the city are ancient constructions which attest the antiquity of its foundation. It is said that it was a Persian city. It has cisterns hewn from the hard rock, connected with each other, and beyond count for their number. They are both within and without the town, and men say that there are three hundred and sixty outside the town, and the same within. We indeed saw a great number, such as could not be counted. But in truth the things of wonder are many. Glory to Him whose knowledge encompasses them all.

The greater number of the people of these Hejaz and other lands are sectaries and schismatics who have no religion, and who have separated into various doctrines. They treat the pilgrims in a manner in which they do not treat the Christians and Jews under tribute, seizing most of the provisions they have collected, robbing them, and finding cause to divest them of all they have. The pilgrim in their lands does not cease to pay dues and provide foods until God helps him to return to his native land. Indeed, but for what God has done to mend the affairs of Muslims in these parts by means of Saladin,[5] they would suffer the most grievous oppression, with no remission of its rigours. For Saladin lifted from the pilgrim the customs duty, and in its stead provided money and victuals, with orders that they should be sent to Mukthir, Emir of Mecca. But when this consignment allotted to the pilgrims was somewhat delayed, this Emir returned to intimidating them and made show to imprison them for the dues.

---

[4] These groups are branches of Mohammed's descendants through Ali and Fatimah, the first two being more general designations. [Ed.]
[5] Salah al-Din, sultan of Egypt from 1171 to 1193. [Ed.]

In this regard, it happened that when we arrived at Jiddah the matter was under discussion with Mukthir, this Emir, and we had been arrested. His order came that the pilgrims should guarantee each other (for payment) and might then enter the Haram [Holy Mosque] of God. Should the money and victuals due for him from Saladin arrive it would be well; otherwise he would not forgo his dues from the pilgrims. Such was his speech, as if God's Haram were an heirloom in his hand and lawfully his to let to the pilgrims. Glory to God who alters and changes laws.

That which Saladin has substituted for the pilgrim's customs dues was two thousand dinars and two thousand and two *irdabb* of wheat, which is about eight hundred *qafiz* in our Seville measure, and this was exclusive of the land-rents granted to them by this ordinance in Upper Egypt and in the Yemen. And but for the absence of this just Sultan, Saladin, at the wars against the Franks in Syria, these actions of the Emir against the pilgrims would never have occurred.

The lands of God [i.e., Islamic lands] that most deserve to be purified by the sword and cleansed of their sins and impurities by blood shed in holy war, are these Hejaz lands, for what they are about in loosening the ties of Islam and dispossessing the pilgrims of their property and shedding their blood. Those of the Andalusian jurisprudents who believe that the pilgrims should be absolved from this religious obligation believe rightly for that reason, and for the way, unpleasing to Great and Glorious God, in which the pilgrims are used. The traveller by this way faces danger and oppression. Far otherwise has God decreed the sharing in that place of His indulgence. How can it be that the House of God should now be in the hands of people who use it as an unlawful source of livelihood, making it a means of illicitly claiming and seizing property, and detaining the pilgrims on its account, thus bringing them to humbleness and abject poverty. May God soon correct and purify this place by relieving the Muslims of these destructive schismatics with the swords of the Almohades, the defenders of the Faith, God's confederates, possessing righteousness and truth, the protectors of the Haram of Great and Glorious God, the abstainers from what is unlawful, the zealous raisers of His name, the proclaimers of His message and the upholders of His creed.[6] Truly He can do as He wishes. He is the best of Protectors, the best of Helpers.

---

[6] *Al-Muwaḥḥidūn*, "the Unitarians," a reforming dynasty in northwestern Africa and southern Spain, which ruled from the mid-twelfth century to the mid-thirteenth. [Ed.]

Let it be absolutely certain and beyond doubt established that there is no Islam save in the Maghrib lands.[7] There they follow the clear path that has no separations and the like, such as there are in these eastern lands of sects and heretical groups and schisms, save those of them whom Great and Glorious God has preserved from these things. There is no justice, right, or religion in His sight except with the Almohades—may God render them powerful. They are the last just imams of this time; all the other Kings of the day follow another path, taking tithes from the Muslim merchants as if they were of the community of the *dhimmah*,[8] seizing their goods by every trick and pretext, and following a course of oppression the like of which, oh my God, has never been heard of. All of them, that is, except this just Sultan, Saladin, whom we have mentioned for his conduct and virtues. If he but had a helper in the cause of righteousness . . .[9] of what I desire. May Great and Glorious God mend the affairs of the Muslims with His beneficent attention and kind works.

The blessed Black Stone is encased in the corner [of the Kaʿbah] facing east. The depth to which it penetrates it is not known, but it is said to extend two cubits into the wall. Its breadth is two-thirds of a span, its length one span and a finger joint. It has four pieces, joined together, and it is said that it was the Qarmata[10]—may God curse them—who broke it. Its edges have been braced with a sheet of silver whose white shines brightly against the black sheen and polished brilliance of the Stone, presenting the observer a striking spectacle which will hold his gaze. The Stone, when kissed, has a softness and moistness which so enchants the mouth that he who puts his lips to it would wish them never to be removed. This is one of the special favours of Divine Providence, and it is enough that the Prophet—may God bless and preserve him—declare it to be a covenant of God on earth. May God profit us by the kissing and touching of it. By His favour may all who yearn fervently for it be brought to it. In the sound piece of the stone, to the

[7] That is, northwestern Africa. [Ed.]

[8] The Christian and Jewish minorities, which were granted formal protection by the Islamic state, subject to certain conditions. [Ed.]

[9] The Arabic text is defective at this point. [Ed.]

[10] The Qarmata, or Carmathians, were a sect of Ismaili Shiites who dominated the Arabian peninsula during the first half of the tenth century, captured Mecca, and carried off the Black Stone to al-Bahrayn. It was restored in 951 by order of the Fatimid Caliph al-Mansur. [Ed.]

right of him who presents himself to kiss it, is a small white spot that shines and appears like a mole on the blessed surface. Concerning this white mole, there is a tradition that he who looks upon it clears his vision, and when kissing it one should direct one's lips as closely as one can to the place of the mole.

The sacred Mosque is encompassed by colonnades in three (horizontal) ranges on three rows of marble columns so arranged as to make it like a single colonnade. Its measurement in length is four hundred cubits, its width three hundred, and its area is exactly forty-eight *maraja* [sing. *maraj*, a measure of area amongst the western Arabs equaling fifty square cubits]. The area between the colonnades is great, but at the time of the Prophet— may God bless and preserve him—it was small and the dome of Zamzam was outside it. Facing the Syrian corner, wedged in the ground, is the capital of a column which at first was the limit of the Haram. Between this capital and the Syrian corner are twenty-two paces. The Kacbah is in the center (of the Haram) and its four sides run directly to the east, south, north, and west. The number of the marble columns, which myself I counted, is four hundred and seventy-one, excluding the stuccoed column that is the Dar al-Nadwah (House of Counsel), which was added to the Haram. This is within the colonnade which runs from the west to the north and is faced by the Maqam and the Iraq corner. It has a large court and is entered from the colonnade. Against the whole length of this colonnade are benches under vaulted arches where sit the copyists, the readers of the Koran, and some who ply the tailor's trade.

The Haram enfolds rings of students, sitting around their teachers, and learned men. Along the wall of the colonnade facing it are also benches under arches in the same fashion. This is the colonnade which runs from the south to the east. In the other colonnades, the benches against the walls have no arches over them. The buildings now in the Haram are at the height of perfection.

The new moon of this month [the month of pilgrimage, Dhū al-Ḥijjah, in 1184] rose on the night of Thursday, corresponding with the 15th of March. In the watching for it the people were involved in a strange circumstance and a remarkable fabrication; and a false utterance almost provoked the stones, not to mention other things, to rebut and deny it. It happened in this wise. They were watching for the appearance of the new moon on the night of Thursday, the 30th of the month. On the horizon the air had thickened and the clouds had piled up, when, with the sunset, a faint glimmering of red appeared. Eagerly the people yearned for some break in the clouds that their eyes might catch a glimpse of the new moon. While they were about this, one of them cried, "God is Great," and the vast concourse followed him and cried, "God is Great," rising to behold what they could not see, and pointing at what they only imagined, such was their eagerness that the "standing" on Mount ᶜArafat should fall on Friday. As if the pilgrimage must be tied to that precise day!

They therefore forged the false testimonies; and a party of Maghrabis— may God prosper their affairs—together with some Egyptians and their chiefs, went to the Qadi and testified that they had seen it. He answered them most harshly, and peremptorily rejected their evidence; and in declaring their statements spurious he put them to the greatest shame, saying "Wonder of wonders! Did one of you affirm that he had seen the sun under such thickly woven clouds I would not accept his affirmation. How then can I believe that you saw a new moon that is twenty-nine nights old?"[11] Amongst other things he said was: "The Maghrabis are disordered. A hair from the eyebrow comes in sight, and with fancy's eye they deem it to be the new moon." This Qadi, Jamal al-Din, displayed in this matter of the false testimony firmness and prudence, so that the learned praised him and the wise thanked him. And well might they do so, for the rights of the pilgrimage are of great consequence to Muslims who come to them "from every remote path" [Koran 22.27]. If complaisance were shown, zeal would be impaired and unsound thought admitted. May God by His favour raise all obscurities and their evils.

On the night of this Friday the new moon appeared during a break in the clouds, clothed in the radiance of the thirtieth night. The crowds then raised tremendous shouts and proclaimed the "standing" (on Mount ᶜArafat) would take place on Friday, crying, "Praise be to God who did not render vain our efforts, or bring to nought our proposals," as if it were a truth with them that if the "standing" did not fall upon a Friday it would not be acceptable to God, nor could God's mercy be hoped for or expected. But God is above that. On Friday they met before the Qadi and . . . [he] let them know that he had asked leave of the Emir Mukthir that the ascent to ᶜArafat be made on the morning of Friday. They would stand on ᶜArafat in the evening and on the morning of the following Saturday, and would pass the night at Muzdalifah.

[11] The Arabs believed that each new moon's crescent took thirty nights to form before it appeared to sight. [Ed.]

If the "standing" were done on Friday, there would be no objection to their delaying the passing of the night in Muzdalifah, this being permitted by Muslim imams. . . . All those present thanked the Qadi for his conduct of the enquiry and prayed for him, and the laity who were there revealed their approval and departed in peace. Praise be to God for that.

This blessed month is the third of the sacred months. The first ten days are those in which the people assemble. It is the great period of the pilgrimage, the month of cries [of *labbayka*, "Here am I, O Lord"] and of the flowing of blood [sacrifice], and the time when from all lands and ways the deputations to God [pilgrims] do meet. It is the target of God's mercy and blessings, and (the month) in which occurs the solemn "standing" on ʿArafat. May God by His favour and bounty grant that we be of those who during it win benefits, and divest us of the raiment of sin and transgressions. For He is at once the All-Powerful and the Forgiving.

A manifest miracle is that this Safe City [Mecca], which lies in a valley bed that is a bow-shot or less in width, can contain this vast host; a host such that, were it brought into the greatest of cities, could not be contained. This venerated city, in what concerns it of manifest miracles, namely its expansion for multitudes beyond count, is described only by the true analogy of the *ulema* [learned doctors of divinity], that its enlargement for newcomers is that of a uterus for the fetus. So it is with ʿArafat and the other great shrines in this sacred land. May God with His grace and bounty increase its sanctity, and in it grant to us His mercy.

TRANSLATED BY R. J. C. BROADHURST

[from *Laylā u Majnūn*, Layla and Majnun]

Nizami is so incredibly ponderous a poet that one most likely does him an injustice by anthologizing him at all. The lone alternative of omitting him altogether, however, is so much more unjust that even he himself might agree that something of his work is better than nothing.

It happens that Nizami is remarkable in the respect that he treats his themes and his characters in a fashion that we think of as contemporary. He was born about 1140 in Ganja in the Caucasus. His genius is now acclaimed and venerated by many races; among other honors, he is regarded as a hero of the Soviet people. Soviet scholarship on his works, granted the essential caveats, is unquestionably the best. The fact of the matter is, however, that Nizami, though no Sufi and most certainly no mystic, was a devout Moslem and a poet securely planted in the Persian tradition. It is presumed that his life was uneventful, or, more precisely, that its major events were his poems.

His short poems are few and not especially interesting. His greatness was established by five long poems: *Makhzan al-Asrār*, The Treasury of Secrets; *Khusraw u Shīrīn*, Khosraw and Shirin; *Laylā u Majnūn*, Layla and Majnun; *Iskandar-nāmeh*, The Book of Alexander; and *Haft Paykar*, The Seven Beauties. All of these poems are difficult and original in style. One translator states: "Nizami is unconventionally obscure. He employs images and metaphors to which there is no key save in the possession of the poetic sense and of sound judgment." Most importantly, Nizami established the *masnavi* as a form for long and continuous narrative, thereby setting a pattern which was to be imitated well into the seventeenth century and never, save perhaps by Jami, equaled.

> And now remote from peopled town,
> Midst tangled forest, parch'd and brown,

219

The maniac roams; with double speed
He goads along his snorting steed
Till, in a grove, a sportsman's snare
Attracts his view, and, struggling there,
Its knotted meshes dast between,
Some newly-prison'd deer are seen;
And as the sportsman forward springs
To seize on one, and promptly brings
The fatal knife upon its neck,
His hand receives a sudden check;
And looking upwards, with surprise,
(A mounted chief before his eyes!)
He stops — while thus exclaims the youth:—
"If e'er thy bosom throbb'd with ruth,
Forbear! for 'tis a crime to spill
A gazelle's blood—it bodeth ill;
Then set the pleading captive free;
For sweet is life and liberty.
That heart must be as marble hard,
And merciless as wolf or pard,
Which clouds in death that large black eye,
Beaming like Laili's, lovingly.
The cruel stroke, my friend, withhold;
Its neck deserves a string of gold.
Observe its slender limbs, the grace
And winning meekness of its face.
The musk-pod is its fatal dower,
Like beauty, still the prey of power;
And for that fragrant gift thou'rt led
The gentle gazelle's blood to shed!
O, seek not gain by cruel deed,
Nor let the innocent victim bleed."
"But," cried the sportsman, "these are mine;
I cannot at my task repine:
'Tis the sportsman's task, and free from blame,
To watch and snare the forest-game."

Majnūn, upon this stern reply,
    Alighted from his steed, and said—
"O, let them live! they must not die.
    Forbear! and take this barb instead."

The sportsman seized it eagerly.
　　And, laughing, from the greenwood sped.

Majnūn, delighted, view'd his purchased prize,
And in the gazelle's sees his Lailī's eyes;
But soon, freed from the snare, with nimble feet
The tremblers bound to some more safe retreat.
The simple maniac starts, and finds, amazed,
The vision vanish'd which his fancy raised.

'Tis night—and darkness, black as Lailī's tresses,
Veils all around, and all his soul oppresses;
No lucid moon like Lailī's face appears;
No glimpse of light the gloomy prospect cheers:
In a rude cavern he despairing lies,
The tedious moments only mark'd with sighs.

Now, shielded by the harem screen,
The sweet Narcissus sad is seen:
Listening she hears, disconsolate,
Her father's words, which seal her fate;
And what has Lailī now to bear,
But loneliness, reproach, despair,
With no congenial spirit to impart
One single solace to her bursting heart!

Meanwhile the spicy gale on every side
Wafts the high vaunting of her beauty's pride
Through all the neighbouring tribes, and more remote
Her name is whisper'd and her favor sought.
Suitors with various claims appear—the great,
The rich, the powerful—all impatient wait
To know for whom the father keeps that rare
But fragile crystal with such watchful care.
Her charms eclipse all others of her sex,
Given to be loved, but rival hearts to vex;
For when the lamp of joy illumines her cheeks,
The lover smiles, and yet his heart it breaks:
The full-blown rose thus sheds its fragrance round;
But there are thorns, not given to charm, but wound.

Among the rest that stripling came,
Who had before avow'd his flame;
His cheerful aspect seem'd to say,
For him was fix'd the nuptial-day.

His offerings are magnificent;
    Garments, embroider'd every fold,
And rarest gems, to win consent,
    And carpets work'd with silk and gold:
Amber, and pearls, and rubies bright,
And bags of musk, attract the sight;
And camels of unequall'd speed,
And ambling nags of purest breed;—
These (resting for a while) he sends
Before him, and instructs his friends,
With all the eloquence and power
Persuasion brings in favoring hour,
To magnify his worth, and prove
That he alone deserves her love.
"A youth of royal presence, Yemen's boast,
Fierce as a lion, powerful as a host;
Of boundless wealth, and valor's self, he wields
His conquering sword amid embattled fields.
Call ye for blood? 'tis shed by his own hand.
Call ye for gold? he scatters it like sand."

And when the flowers of speech their scent had shed,
Diffusing honors round the suitor's head;
Exalting him to more than mortal worth,
In person manly, noble in his birth;
The sire of Lailī seem'd oppressed with thought,
As if with some repulsive feeling fraught;
Yet promptly was the answer given—he soon
Decreed the fate of Yemen's splendid moon;
Saddled the steed of his desire, in sooth,
Flung his own offspring in the dragon's mouth.
Forthwith the nuptial pomp, the nuptial rites,
    Engage the chieftain's household—every square
Rings with the rattling drums—whose noise excites
    More deafening clamor through the wide bazār.

The pipe and cymbal, shrill and loud,
    Delight the gay assembled crowd;
And all is mirth and jollity,
With song, and dance, and revelry.

But Lailī, mournful, sits apart,
The shaft of misery through her heart;
And black portentous clouds are seen
Darkening her soft expressive mien:
Her bosom swells with heavy sighs,
Tears gush from those heart-winning eyes,
Where Love's triumphant witchery lies.
In blooming spring a wither'd leaf,
She drops in agony of grief;
Loving her own—her only one—
Loving Majnūn, and him alone;
All else from her affections gone;
And to be joined, in a moment's breath,
To another!—Death, and worse than death!

TRANSLATED BY JAMES ATKINSON

[from *Marzubān-nāmeh*, The Book of Marzuban]

Although the *Marzubān-nāmeh* was compiled in its present form by Al-Warawini in the early years of the thirteenth century, it appears to embody material which is much earlier, supposedly and conceivably first compiled in Middle Persian.

It is to be classified in the fable and apologue genre which we have already sampled in the *Kalīlah wa-Dimnah* in Arabic. Stylistically, the *Marzubān-nāmeh* is a great advance over its Arabic forerunner. Al-Warawini regarded the stories before him as too simple and monotonous in style, so he introduced numerous literary decorations in the form of proverbs and poetry, and refashioned the stories to suit the *adab* style. His work is, in fact, a striking example of the success with which that style could be applied to common raw material. The *Marzubān-nāmeh* is in its way a milestone, because, like Al-Hariri's *Maqāmāt*, it is unsurpassable in its genre. The selection chosen is the mid-point in the work.

The prince said:

In times past and in bygone ages, the demons, who have now withdrawn their faces behind the curtain of mystery and are concealed from eyes which behold only the apparent, went about the world openly. They mingled and associated closely with human beings and by seduction and delusion beguiled them from the path of truth and salvation, and they displayed fanciful images tricked out with meretricious ornaments before the eyes of men.

In the course of time there appeared in the land of Babylon a man of true piety, who came to dwell upon a mountain top and there built a cell, in which he spread out his rug for worship. From there he summoned the people to follow the highroad of a pure life, and within a short space of time the carpet of his preaching was spread far and wide, so that many men adopted his wise practices. Numberless disciples arose, taking upon themselves the laws of his holy creed and forsaking the heresy of misbelief in order to enter the way of the faith. These now turned their faces away from the demons and all their works, and turned in the true direction for the worship of God.

The fame of the man became diffused throughout every clime in the world, where men spoke of him almost as though he knew the secret of the prophetic tradition: "The realm of my people shall attain to a position of which something remains hidden from me myself." The demons, bewildered and perturbed at the decline in their fortunes, presented themselves before their chief, the demon Ox-foot, who was one of their proudest afreets and one of the foulest of their objects of worship and their sources of miscreance. He was one who, when incantation was being practised, fled like Iblis [the Devil] from the sacred formula "There is no might (save in Allah)," but persisted in his adherence to evil like iron to a magnet. The army of the devils was under his command and he was leader of the troops of the accursed, marshal of the caravan of miscreance and chief highwayman upon the road of delusion and fantasy. He could pass through the door of the treasure-house of human purity, could break the seal of Solomon, and fix in impotence the talisman of Pharaoh's magicians. To him, then, the demons came in a body and with one tongue cried out to him for succour.

"This man Dīni," they said, "has seated himself upon this rock and cast a stone shattering the crystal goblet of our lives, so that he has banished the fear of us from out of men's hearts. If we do not today stop this breach and destroy this affliction, then tomorrow, when he performs the five-fold act of worship ordained by his law (the parasol of his authority then spreading its protection over the regions of the world as the sun of his power raises its head above the summit of that mountain), we shall have no recourse open to us but submission and compliance with his will."

The hearing of this disquisition had wondrous effect upon Ox-foot. The fire of his devilry stirred up the flames of rage, yet he would not permit the reins of haste to slacken in his hands.

"I ask you for time," he said. "For although such affairs as these tolerate no delay, they cannot be conducted without due deliberation; and although no deferment can be permitted, there is no plunging into them without first indulging in deep thought."

He then caused three of the principal demons to be stationed before him, each of them advisor of the state and an aid in days of anxiety, and with them began to take counsel. To the eldest he said:

"What action is in your view required by the events which have occurred?"

He answered:

"From the eye of men of wisdom and experience it is not concealed that two things there are which do not permanently remain in the same state; one is fortune at its height and the other the life in the body, each having its recognized limit and appointed term. Just as, by the doctrine of the transmigration of souls, a spirit is transferred out of the frame which it occupies into another, so also fortune is moved from one height which is agreeable to it to another one. In the days of his prosperity a man is not afflicted by troubles, and the foundations of his good fortune are susceptible to no injury. During that period he can be likened to a mountain which suffers no breach from the slings of the thunder, the naphtha-bottles of the lightning, the mangonels of the thunderbolts, the stone-showers of the hail, or the flying arrows of the rain. But when the days of his good fortune come to an end, he resembles a tree from which the sap and freshness have departed, allowing it to wither and flag, so that in the gentlest breeze its branches are torn away and it may be unrooted by the feeblest hand. It may then collapse almost without a cause. The revolution of treacherous chance and the law of the turning skies have ever worked thus.

"Today, when fortune is contained within the measure of this man's capacity and fate lies where agreeable to him, the arrow of any contrivance which we could shoot would go astray of the mark, and any scheme which we could concoct in order to frustrate his progress would remain crudely ineffectual. We must therefore allow the weakness inherent in his constitution to take its course, while we remain on the alert, watchful for the moment when the sun of his fortunes begins to decline and the lord of his ascendant star moves away from the house of felicity, and luck throws its protection over our affairs. Then, if we make a stand to oppose him, we may emerge triumphant, with success on our side and adversity and failure on his."

Ox-foot then signed to the second counsellor and asked him the substance of his opinion on the question. He replied:

"What the minister has said is approved by justice and applauded by reason, but it would be contrary to every advantage if we were to hold our hands from hostile action in any respect or to place the fetters of neglect or procrastination upon the hands and feet of our powers and will. While he is strong, any delay in attacking him means a reinforcement of his strength and an increase proportionately in our weakness. No wise man, even seeing that fortune is the ally of the enemy, fails to exert his full powers to combat him, striving at the same time to conserve and ensure the perpetuation of the forces which he perceives to be left within himself. So a physician, to take a parallel, even when failing to restore a patient to full health, conserves by a careful regimen and scientific devices the remaining natural powers possessed by the invalid. And were he not to do so, death would inevitably ensue. Consequently we must undertake, with all the force at our disposal, to destroy the foundations of this man's work, so that, even though he has affixed the bridle of his authority to the heads of a whole people and taken the keys of authority over them into his own sleeve, it is our duty to go out into the field of combat, casting off all fear of death. The reply to a foeman can be given only with the tongue of the sword, and not with the shield of amiability placed over the face of self-preservation."

Ox-foot then turned to the third counsellor, inquiring what his opinion demanded before the ideas of the others were put into execution. His reply was:

"What the others have proposed has already taken root in your mind. It is in the nature of everyone created to be disposed to the eager reception of what is agreeable and in harmony with the spirit. And it is especially probable that if the words uttered are pleasantly modulated, the phrases well turned and the language steeped in sugar, the style will find a home in the very heart of one's liking. There is a saying that just as one may, with iron smoothly tempered into steel, break up the other kinds of iron, so may one with delectably sweet words strip off the outward integument of men's behaviour. Thus there have been affecting poems and shafts of finely-pointed wit that have made avaricious men generous, cowards brave, depraved men good, troubled men tranquil, and simpletons noble.

"It is my view that, even if it were possible, it would render us little service to shed the blood of this man Dīnī, for the evil of it would soon attach itself to us. The scheme is alien to all discretion and foresight, for if he were to be destroyed without some patent reason, some dishonouring accusation, some obvious charge or some clear argument, then another religious pretender would arise in his place to become his successor. The trouble of it would harass us continually until doomsday and matters would pass beyond all retrieving, because the generality of created beings have a natural partiality for the weak and an antipathy to the powerful.

"The course which is to be recommended, and the scheme, then, to be preferred, is this: for you by satanic whisperings and magical cunning to lay the foundations of worldliness in his breast, so that he may become occupied and infatuated with the trivialities of this abode of illusion. Place before his eyes a glittering picture of the gaily-frescoed walls of the house of pleasures and delights, and let the honeyed droplets of lust so trickle from the branches of anticipation that he will fail to see the serpent of destiny waiting open-jawed at his feet. In the end all his people will see how he has forsaken his ascetic habits and studious chastity and become engrossed with the world; they will believe you when you loosen your tongue to demonstrate his vicious-ness and publish abroad his infamies. Then they will turn from him, and the market for his pretensions will fall."

Ox-foot regarded this discourse as being least contaminated with self-interest and nearest to what was expedient. He said:

"You have given us admirable advice and demonstrated the right path. It is now my own opinion that we should in a general assembly discuss with Dīnī the secrets of the sciences and the verities of all things, so that he may be defeated in argument with me and the nakedness of his ignorance be un-covered by me before all the people. It is then that I shall spill his blood, for if his slaying were deferred until after the completion of these preliminary steps which you have described, the result would be nothing but time wasted."

Turning to the eldest counsellor, Ox-foot now inquired of him what his view was with regard to putting this plan into execution. He answered:

"When a course of action lies between two opposing sides, it would not be reason's choice to adhere to one side and have regard to one possibility only. Many are the falsehoods which fancy his painted in the colours of verac-ity, and many the lies which imagination has displayed in the robes of truth, as occurred in the incident of the double-sighted son of the hospitable man."

Ox-foot having inquired what the story of that was, he replied:

There once lived a certain man of liberal disposition who delighted in hospitality. He would seize travellers by the rein, empty his purse for them, and entertain all strangers lavishly. Indeed every laudable quality clung to him, and all noble attributes were particular to his nature, except his generosity, which was universal. What he expended came from the purse of his own earnings, not from income produced by extortion from others. (The custom is different to-day, when smoke only rises from men's kitchens after they have set on fire the grain-stacks of a hundred Musulmans, when they place a tiny loaf upon their tables only after flooding other men's houses with treachery, and when they only add a handful of salt to their dish after sprinkling a load of it on the wounds of the poor. To-day, also, two sticks are added to a brazier only after helpless people have been dealt two hundred blows with sticks upon their sides.)

From him the world's noblest learnt the ways in which to dispense generosity, and hospitable manners in particular. Those lines which ungenerous men bring to their brows when guests descend at their door, he reserved for the ornamentation of his goblets and for the engraving of his culinary vessels; the vinegar which miserly curmudgeons accumulate in their faces when they emerge to greet visitors was used by him for flavouring his ragout.

One day a treasured guest alighted at his door. With all courtesy and respect he came forward to meet him, offering him in every particular the attention and welcome which the occasion demanded. When they had ended their partaking of food, the host in apology spoke of his difficulty in obtaining wine.

"It cannot be doubted," said he, "that when the mirror of life's enjoyment becomes clouded, there is no polish for it equal to wine. For the unhappy spirit seated amongst his fellows, when there is a silence during the conversation, it is always proper to call for a flagon of wine; and when, as part of the fulfilment of the host's duties, an anthology of verse is being recited to the company assembled, there is nothing which provides the solitary man with a more congenial ally against the disagreeable activities of destiny than wine. In the past few evenings, for one cause or another, we have drunk a great deal with friends, so that only one bottle is left. But if it is to your liking, we will pass a little time in the enjoyment of it."

The guest answered that it was for his host to decide, and at that he told his son to go to a particular place, from which he was to fetch a bottle that he would find lying there. Now the unhappy youth was afflicted with double vision in his eye and a deficiency of brains. When his eye fell upon the bottle, its outline cast a two-fold reflection upon the distorting mirror of his sight, so he returned to his father and said:

"There are two bottles. Which shall I bring?"

What had occurred was clear to the father; nevertheless the sweat broke out on his forehead in his embarrassment at the thought that his guest might imagine he had been holding back a second bottle and thus charge him either with stupidity or lack of due consideration. Seeing no other way out of his dilemma, he said to the boy:

"Break one of the two and bring the other here."

In accordance with his father's instruction, the boy took a stone, which he dashed against the bottle. But then, not being able to discover another, he returned disappointed and unhappy at his failure, to tell his father of what had occurred. To the guest it was clearly apparent that any defect there might be lay not in the father's regard but in the boy's vision.

"I have told you this story in order that you may realize that even the sense of sight, which is the most perfect of the senses in the perception of phenomena, is not secure from the accidents of error. The faculty of insight, then, which, as one of the inner faculties, must look behind the veils of fancy and imagination, is even less able to maintain freedom from the fluctuations of accuracy and error. It behoves you to look into this matter with profound thought, taking no step towards the accomplishment of the project without consideration and the certainty of being on the right course.

"The Creator fashioned man's essence to be the purest amongst those of the animals, granting to him a greater share of knowledge, perception and intelligence than to any of the others. He also provided each individual person with a star from amongst the upper and lower orbs to be the guardian of his fortunes, so that it may keep and foster him in the bosom of care as nurses rear children. He further appointed for each an angel from the sacred world of the heavenly courts to be his preceptor, who shall set before him the tablets providing wisdom and instruction.

"Possessed even of these advantages, as man in the pursuit of his lusts takes a step forward, he promptly becomes the bondsman of us demons, and is overwhelmed and conquered by us. What, then, would be the condition of us, the demons, whose essence consists of the thick smoke of darkness compounded with barbarism, if we were to place the reins of our heart into the hands of lust, without either thought or deliberation? How should we overcome mankind, which possesses so many resources and weapons and is endowed with so many great qualities? I fear that in your quest for this superiority and supremacy greater ill may befall you."

"I have listened to what you have to say," said Ox-foot, "and it has hit the target of truth. Yet it is still possible to prevail against our adversary by a clever application of skill, by an abundance of wisdom and serviceable knowledge, as the mouse did against the serpent."

"What," inquired the counsellor, "was that story?"

TRANSLATED BY REUBEN LEVY

ATTAR: THE BIRD PARLIAMENT

[from *Manṭiq al-Ṭayr*, The Conference of the Birds]

Even the dates of Attar's life cannot be fixed with any certainty, and in his works the editorial problem appears like the very devil. Recently it has been shown that eight of the twenty-five works believed to have been his were forgeries. Hellmut Ritter, the European scholar who has done the most work on Attar, wrote: "The works attributed to him fall into three groups which differ so considerably in content and style that it is difficult to ascribe all three to the same person."

Overlooking this perplexing situation, let us say that Attar was by early trade a druggist, as his name would indicate, who lived in Khurasan during the second half of the twelfth century and well into the thirteenth, a Sufi master who wrote much and well concerning the mystical search for God. That is more than we know about many Persian poets.

The Bird Parliament is Attar's most famous work. It is an allegory, of course, of man's contemplative journey—if he chooses to take it—toward union with God. The main story is clear and well-constructed, and it is interspersed throughout with a variety of subsidiary tales. It is this combination of the planned and the random, in fact, which lends the book its distinctive character within Sufi literature.

All of the birds of the world, known and unknown, were assembled together. They said: "No country in the world is without a king. How comes it, then, that the kingdom of the birds is without a ruler? This state of things cannot last. We must make effort together and search for one; for no country can have a good administration and a good organization without a king."

So they began to consider how to set out on their quest. The Hoopoe, excited and full of hope, came forward and placed herself in the middle of the assembled birds. On her breast was the ornament which symbolized that she had entered the way of spiritual knowledge; the crest on her head was as the crown of truth, and she had knowledge of both good and evil.

"Dear Birds," she began, "I am one who is engaged in divine warfare, and I am a messenger of the world invisible. I have knowledge of God and of the secrets of creation. When one carries on his beak, as I do, the name of God, Bismillah, it follows that one must have knowledge of many hidden things. Yet my days pass restlessly and I am concerned with no person, for I am wholly occupied by love for the King. I can find water by instinct, and I know many other secrets. I talk with Solomon and am the foremost of his followers. It is astonishing that he neither asked nor sought for those who were absent from his kingdom, yet when I was away from him for a day he sent his messengers everywhere, and, since he could not be without me for a moment, my worth is established forever. I carried his letters, and I was his confidential companion. The bird who is sought after by the prophet Solomon merits a crown for his head. The bird who is well spoken of by God, how can he trail his feathers in the dust? For years I have travelled by sea and land, over mountains and valleys. I covered an immense space in the time of the deluge; I accompanied Solomon on his journeys, and I have measured the bounds of the world.

"I know well my King, but alone I cannot set out to find him. Abandon your timidity, your self-conceit and your unbelief, for he who makes light of his own life is delivered from himself; he is delivered from good and evil in the way of his beloved. Be generous with your life. Set your feet upon the earth and step out joyfully for the court of the King. We have a true King, he lives behind the mountains called Kāf. His name is Simurgh and he is the King of birds. He is close to us, but we are far from him. The place where he dwells is inaccessible, and no tongue is able to utter his name. Before him hang a hundred thousand veils of light and darkness, and in the two worlds no one has power to dispute his kingdom. He is the sovereign lord and is bathed in the perfection of his majesty. He does not manifest himself completely even in the place of his dwelling, and to this no knowledge or intelligence can attain. The way is unknown, and no one has the steadfastness to seek it, though thousands of creatures spend their lives in longing. Even the purest soul cannot describe him, neither can the reason comprehend: these two eyes are blind. The wise cannot discover his perfection nor can the man of understanding perceive his beauty. All creatures have wished to attain to this perfection and beauty by imagination. But how can you tread that path with thought? How measure the moon from the fish? So thousands of heads go here and there, like the ball in polo, and only lamentations and sighs of longing are heard. Many lands and seas are on the way. Do not imagine that the journey is short; and one must have the heart of a lion to follow this unusual road, for it is very long and the sea is deep. One plods along in a state of amazement, sometimes smiling, sometimes weeping. As for me, I shall be happy to discover even a trace of him. That would indeed be something, but to live without him would be a reproach. A man must not keep his soul from the beloved, but must be in a fitting state to lead his soul to the court of the King. Wash your hands of this life if you would be called a man of action. For your beloved, renounce this dear life of yours, as worthy men. If you submit with grace, the beloved will give his life for you.

"An astonishing thing! The first manifestation of the Simurgh took place in China in the middle of the night. One of his feathers fell on China and his reputation filled the world. Everyone made a picture of this feather, and from it formed his own system of ideas, and so fell into a turmoil. This feather is still in the picture-gallery of that country; hence the saying, 'Seek knowledge, even in China!'

"But for his manifestation there would not have been so much noise in the world concerning this mysterious Being. This sign of his existence is a token of his glory. All souls carry an impression of the image of his feather. Since the description of it has neither head nor tail, beginning nor end, it is not necessary to say more about it. Now, any of you who are for this road, prepare yourselves, and put your feet on the Way."

When the Hoopoe had finished, the birds began excitedly to discuss the glory of this King, and seized with longing to have him for their own sovereign, they were all impatient to be off. They resolved to go together; each became a friend to the other and an enemy to himself. But when they began to realize how long and painful their journey was to be, they hesitated, and in spite of their apparent good will began to excuse themselves, each according to his type.

One bird said to the Hoopoe: "O you who know the road of which you have told us and on which you wish us to accompany you, to me the way is dark, and in the gloom it appears to be very difficult, and many parasangs in length."

The Hoopoe replied: "We have seven valleys to cross, and only after we have crossed them shall we discover the Simurgh. No one has ever come back into the world who has made this journey, and it is impossible to say how many parasangs there are in front of us. Be patient, O fearful one, since all those who went by this road were in your state.

"The first valley is the Valley of the Quest, the second the Valley of

Love, the third is the Valley of Understanding, the fourth is the Valley of Independence and Detachment, the fifth of Pure Unity, the sixth is the Valley of Astonishment, and the seventh is the Valley of Poverty and Nothingness, beyond which one can go no farther."

When the birds had listened to this discourse of the Hoopoe their heads dropped down, and sorrow pierced their hearts. Now they understood how difficult it would be for a handful of dust like themselves to bend such a bow. So great was their agitation that numbers of them died then and there. But others, in spite of their distress, decided to set out on the long road. For years they travelled over mountains and valleys, and a great part of their life flowed past on this journey. But how is it possible to relate all that happened to them? It would be necessary to go with them and see their difficulties for oneself, and to follow the wanderings of this long road. Only then could one realize what the birds suffered.

In the end, only a small number of all this great company arrived at that sublime place to which the Hoopoe had led them. Of the thousands of birds, almost all had disappeared. Many had been lost in the ocean; others had perished on the summits of the high mountains, tortured by thirst; others had had their wings burnt and their hearts dried up by the fire of the sun; others were devoured by tigers and panthers; others died of fatigue in the deserts and in the wilderness, their lips parched and their bodies overcome by the heat. Some went mad and killed each other for a grain of barley; others, enfeebled by suffering and weariness, dropped on the road, unable to go farther; others, bewildered by the things they saw, stopped where they were, stupefied; and many who had started out from curiosity or pleasure, perished without an idea of what they had set out to find.

So then out of all those thousands of birds, only thirty reached the end of the journey. And even these were bewildered, weary and dejected, with neither feathers nor wings. But now they were at the door of this Majesty that cannot be described, whose essence is incomprehensible—that Being who is beyond human reason and knowledge. Then flashed the lightning of fulfilment, and a hundred worlds were consumed in a moment. They saw thousands of suns, each more resplendent than the other, thousands of moons and stars all equally beautiful, and seeing all this they were amazed and agitated like a dancing atom of dust, and they cried out: "O Thou who art more radiant than the sun! Thou who hast reduced the sun to an atom, how can we appear before Thee? Ah, why have we so uselessly endured all this suffering on the

Way? Having renounced ourselves and all things, we now cannot obtain that for which we have striven. Here it little matters whether we exist or not."

Then the birds, who were so disheartened that they resembled a cock half-killed, sank into despair. A long time passed. When, at a propitious moment, the door suddenly opened, there stepped out a noble Chamberlain, one of the courtiers of the Supreme Majesty. He looked them over and saw that out of thousands, only these thirty birds were left.

He said: "Now then, O Birds, where have you come from, and what are you doing here? What is your name? O you who are destitute of everything, where is your home? What do they call you in the world? What can be done with a feeble handful of dust like you?"

"We have come," they said, "to acknowledge the Simurgh as our King. Through love and desire for him we have lost our reason and our peace of mind. Very long ago, when we started on this journey, we were thousands, and now only thirty of us have arrived at this sublime court. We cannot believe that the King will scorn us after all the sufferings we have gone through. Ah, no! He cannot but look on us with the eye of benevolence!"

The Chamberlain replied: "O you whose minds and hearts are troubled, whether you exist or do not exist in the universe, the King has his being always and eternally. Thousands of worlds of creatures are no more than an ant at his gate. You bring nothing but moans and lamentations. Return then to whence you came, O vile handful of earth!"

At this the birds were petrified with astonishment. Nevertheless, when they came to themselves a little, they said: "Will this great King reject us so ignominiously? And if he really has this attitude to us, may he not change it to one of honour? Remember Majnūn, who said: 'If all the people who dwell on earth wished to sing my praises, I would not accept them; I would rather have the insults of Laila. One of her insults is more to me than a hundred compliments from another woman!' "

"The lightning of his glory manifests itself," said the Chamberlain, "and it lifts up the reason of all souls. What benefit is there if the soul be consumed by a hundred sorrows? What benefit is there at this moment in either greatness or littleness?"

The birds, on fire with love, said: "How can the moth save itself from the flame when it wishes to be one with the flame? The friend we seek will content us by allowing us to be united to him. If now we are refused, what is there left for us to do? We are like the moth who wished for union with the flame of the candle. They begged him not to sacrifice himself so foolishly and for such an impossible aim, but he thanked them for their advice and told them that since his heart was given to the flame forever, nothing else mattered."

Then the Chamberlain, having tested them, opened the door; and as he drew aside a hundred curtains, one after the other, a new world beyond the veil was revealed. Now was the light of lights manifested, and all of them sat down on the masnad, the seat of the Majesty and Glory. They were given a writing which they were told to read through; and reading this, and pondering, they were able to understand their state. When they were completely at peace and detached from all things, they became aware that the Simurgh was there with them, and a new life began for them in the Simurgh. All that they had done previously was washed away. The sun of Majesty sent forth his rays, and in the reflection of each other's faces these thirty birds (*si-murgh*) of the outer world contemplated the face of the Simurgh of the inner world. This so astonished them that they did not know if they were still themselves of if they had become the Simurgh. At last, in a state of contemplation, they realized that they were the Simurgh and that the Simurgh was the thirty birds. When they gazed at the Simurgh they saw that it was truly the Simurgh who was there, and when they turned their eyes toward themselves they saw that they themselves were the Simurgh. And perceiving both at once, themselves and Him, they realized that they and the Simurgh were one and the same being. No one in the world has ever heard of anything to equal it.

Then they gave themselves up to meditation, and after a little they asked the Simurgh, without the use of tongues, to reveal to them the secret of the mystery of the unity and plurality of beings. The Simurgh, also without speaking, made this reply: "The sun of my majesty is a mirror. He who sees himself therein sees his soul and his body, and sees them completely. Since you have come as thirty birds, *si-murgh*,[1] you will see thirty birds in this mirror. If forty or fifty were to come, it would be the same. Although you are now completely changed, you see yourselves as you were before.

"Can the sight of an ant reach to the far-off Pleiades? And can this insect lift an anvil? Have you ever seen a gnat seize an elephant in its teeth? All that you have known, all that you have seen, all that you have said or heard—all this is no longer that. When you crossed the valleys of the Spiritual Way and when you performed good tasks, you did all this by my action; and you were able to see the valleys of my essence and my perfections. You, who are only thirty birds, did well to be astonished, impatient and wondering. But I

---

[1] *Simurgh*, as "God," and *sī murgh*, "thirty birds," although not a very subtle play on words, determined the plot of the work. [Ed.]

am more than thirty birds. I am the very essence of the true Simurgh. Annihilate then yourselves gloriously and joyfully in me, and in me you shall find yourselves."

Thereupon the birds at last lost themselves forever in the Simurgh—the shadow was lost in the sun, and that is all.

All that you have heard or seen or known is not even the beginning of what you must know, and since the ruined habitation of this world is not your place you must renounce it. Seek the trunk of the tree, and do not worry about whether the branches do or do not exist.

When a hundred thousand generations had passed, the mortal birds surrendered themselves spontaneously to total annihilation. No man, neither young nor old, can speak fittingly of death or immortality. Even as these things are far from us, so the description of them is beyond all explanation or definition. If my readers wish for an allegorical explanation of the immortality that follows annihilation, it will be necessary for me to write another book. So long as you are identified with the things of the world you will not set out on the Path, but when the world no longer binds you, you enter as in a dream, and knowing the end, you see the benefit. A germ is nourished among a hundred cares and loves so that it may become an intelligent and acting being. It is instructed and given the necessary knowledge. Then death comes and everything is effaced, its dignity is thrown down. This that was a being has become the dust of the street. It has several times been annihilated; but in the meanwhile it has been able to learn a hundred secrets of which previously it had not been aware, and in the end it receives immortality, and is given honour in place of dishonour. Do you know what you possess? Enter into yourself and reflect on this. So long as you do not realize your nothingness and so long as you do not renounce your self-pride, your vanity and your self-love, you will never reach the heights of immortality. On the Way you are cast down in dishonour and raised in honour.

And now my story is finished; I have nothing more to say.

TRANSLATED BY S. C. NOTT

[from *Dīvān-i Shams-i Tabrīz*, Poems of Shams of Tabriz]

A Persian scholar who has given much of his life to the study of Rumi, using all the evidence he could, drew a portrait of the man: "[Rumi] was a man of sallow complexion. His body was thin and lean, while his eyes flashed with a hypnotic brightness daunting to those who looked upon him. In his earlier years he wore a scholar's turban and a wide-sleeved gown, but after his encounter with Shams al-Dīn he changed these habits for a blue robe and a smoke-coloured turban, which he never altered to the end of his days. In his conduct he was peaceful and tolerant towards men of all sects and creeds . . . [and] was never heard to utter one bitter reply."

That is a portrait, far from fanciful, of the greatest mystical poet in Persian. Rumi was born in Balkh in 1207. His father was a Sufi and a noted preacher who was forced to leave Balkh for political reasons. The family traveled across western Asia to Konya in Anatolia, where Rumi ("the Roman," referring to the former Byzantine territory) stayed the rest of his life and succeeded to his father's professorship. He died in 1273.

His meeting with the wandering dervish Shams al-Din of Tabriz changed his whole way of life. He gave up the Islamic religious sciences, founded the Mevlevi order of dervishes, and composed the two works for which he is rightly called great: the *Dīvān-i Shams-i Tabrīz*, a group of lyric poems, or *ghazals*, signed with the name of his friend; and the *Masnavī*, an exceedingly long religious poem (its English translation fills three large volumes) which is regarded by Persians as "the Persian Koran" and second only to the *Shāh-nāmeh* as a masterwork of their literature.

> What is to be done, O Moslems? for I do not recognize myself.
> I am neither Christian, nor Jew, nor Gabr,[1] nor Moslem.

[1] A Zoroastrian.

I am not of Nature's mint, nor of the circling heavens.
I am not of earth, nor of water, nor of air, nor of fire;
I am not of the empyrean, nor of the dust, nor of existence, nor of entity.
I am not of India, nor of China, nor of Bulgaria, nor of Saqsīn;[2]
I am not of the kingdom of ʿIrāqain,[3] nor of the country of Khorāsān.
I am not of this world, nor of the next, nor of Paradise, nor of Hell;
I am not of Adam, nor of Eve, nor of Eden and Riẓwān.[4]
My place is the Placeless, my trace is the Traceless;
'Tis neither body nor soul, for I belong to the soul of the Beloved.
I have put duality away, I have seen that the two worlds are one;
One I seek, One I know, One I see, One I call.
He is the first, He is the last, He is the outward, He is the inward;
I know none other except 'Yā Hū' and 'Yā man Hū.'[5]
I am intoxicated with Love's cup, the two worlds have passed out of my ken;
I have no business save carouse and revelry.
If once in my life I spent a moment without thee,
From that time and from that hour I repent of my life.
If once in this world I win a moment with thee,
I will trample on both worlds, I will dance in triumph forever.
O Shamsi Tabrīz, I am so drunken in this world
That except of drunkenness and revelry I have no tale to tell.

Thee I choose, of all the world, alone;
Wilt thou suffer me to sit in grief?
My heart is as a pen in thy hand,
Thou art the cause if I am glad or melancholy.
Save what thou willest, what will have I?
Save what thou showest, what do I see?
Thou mak'st grow out of me now a thorn and now a rose;
Now I smell roses and now pull thorns.
If thou keep'st me that, that I am;
If thou would'st have me this, I am this.
In the vessel where thou givest colour to the soul
Who am I, what is my love and hate?

---

[2] A city in the Caucasus, or, perhaps, another of the same name in East Turkestan.
[3] Literally "the two ʿIrāqs," i.e., the region between the Tigris and Euphrates rivers and that of west central Persia.
[4] In Islamic tradition, the angel who keeps the keys of paradise.
[5] "O He" and "O He who is," familiar dervish invocations.

Thou wert first, and last thou shalt be;
Make my last better than my first.
When thou art hidden, I am of the infidels;
When thou art manifest, I am of the faithful.
I have nothing, except thou hast bestowed it;
What dost thou seek from my bosom and sleeve?

Make yourself like to the community, that you may feel spiritual joy;
Enter the street of the tavern, that you may behold the wine-bibbers.
Drain the cup of passion, that you may not be shamed;
Shut the eyes in your head, that you may see the hidden eye.
Open your arms, if you desire an embrace;
Break the idol of clay, that you may behold the face of the Fair.
Why, for an old woman's sake, do you endure so large a dowry,
And how long, for the sake of three loaves, will you look on the sword and
      the spear?
Always at night returns the Beloved: do not eat opium tonight;
Close your mouth against food, that you may taste the sweetness of the moutn.
Lo, the cup-bearer is no tyrant, and in his assembly there is a circle:
Come into the circle, be seated; how long will you regard the revolution
      (of time)?
Look now, here is a bargain: give one life and receive a hundred.
Cease to behave as wolves and dogs, that you may experience the Shepherd's
      love.
You said: "My foe took such a one away from me":
Go, renounce that person in order to contemplate the being of Him.
Think of nothing except the creator of thought;
Care for the soul is better than feeling care for one's bread.
Why, when God's earth is so wide, have you fallen asleep in a prison?
Avoid entangled thoughts, that you may see the explanation in Paradise.
Refrain from speaking, that you may win speech hereafter;
Abandon life and the world, that you may behold the Life of the world.

Look on the face of Love, that you may be properly a man.
Do not sit with the frigid, for you will be chilled by their breath.
Seek from the face of Love something other than beauty;
It is time that you should consort with a sympathetic companion.
Since you are properly a clod, you will not rise into the air;
You will rise into the air if you break and become dust;
If you break not, He who moulded you will break you.

When death breaks you, how should you become a separate substance?
When the leaf grows yellow, the fresh root makes it green;
You are complaining of Love thro' which you become pale.
And, O friend, if you reach perfection in our assembly,
Your seat will be the throne, you will gain your desire in all things.
But if you stay many more years in this earth,
You will pass from place to place, you will be as the dice in backgammon.
If Shamsi Tabrīz draws you to his side,
When you escape from captivity you will return to that orb.

This is Love: to fly heavenward,
To rend, every instant, a hundred veils.
The first moment, to renounce life;
The last step, to fare without feet.
To regard this world as invisible,
Not to see what appears to one's self.
"O heart," I said, "may it bless thee
To have entered the circle of lovers,
To look beyond the range of the eye,
To penetrate the windings of the bosom!
Whence did this breath come to thee, O my soul,
Whence this throbbing, O my heart?
O bird, speak the language of birds:
I can understand thy hidden meaning."
The soul answered: "I was in the (divine) factory
While the house of water and clay was a-baking.
I was flying away from the (material) workshop
While the workshop was being created.
When I could resist no more, they dragged me
To mould me into shape like a ball."

Happy the moment when we are seated in the palace, thou and I,
With two forms and with two figures but with one soul, thou and I.
The colours of the grove and the voice of the birds will bestow immortality
At the time when we come into the garden, thou and I.
The stars of heaven will come to gaze upon us;
We shall show them the moon itself, thou and I.
Thou and I, individuals no more, shall be mingled in ecstasy,
Joyful, and secure from foolish babble, thou and I.
All the bright-plumed birds of heaven will devour their hearts with envy

In the place where we shall laugh in such a fashion, thou and I.
This is the greatest wonder, that thou and I, sitting here in the same nook,
Are at this moment both in ᶜIrāq and Khorāsān, thou and I.

> I died as mineral and became a plant,
> I died as plant and rose to animal,
> I died as animal and I was man.
> Why should I fear? When was I less by dying?
> Yet once more I shall die as man, to soar
> With angels blest; but even from angelhood
> I must pass on: all except God doth perish.
> When I have sacrificed my angel soul,
> I shall become what no mind e'er conceived.
> Oh, let me not exist! for Non-existence
> Proclaims in organ-tones, "To Him we shall return."[6]

TRANSLATED BY R. A. NICHOLSON

ILLUSTRATIONS

[from the *Masnavī*]

The Greek and the Chinese Artists, on the Difference
Between Theologians and Mystics

If you desire a parable of the hidden knowledge, tell the story of the
Greeks and the Chinese.

"We are the better artists," the Chinese declared.

"We have the edge on you," the Greeks countered.

"I will put you to the test," said the Sultan. "Then we shall see which
of you makes good your claim."

"Assign to us one particular room, and you Greeks another," said the
Chinese.

The two rooms faced each other, door to door, the Chinese taking one
and the Greeks the other. The Chinese demanded of the king a hundred colours,
so that worthy monarch opened up his treasury and every morning the Chinese
received of his bounty their ration of colours from the treasury.

ᶜKoran 2.156.

"No hues or colours are suitable for our work," said the Greeks. "All we require is to get rid of the rust."

So saying, they shut their door and set to work polishing; smooth and unsullied as the sky they became.

There is a way from multicolority to colourlessness; colour is like the clouds, colourlessness is a moon. Whatever radiance and splendour you see in the clouds, be sure that it comes from the stars, the moon, and the sun.

When the Chinese had completed their work they began drumming for joy. The king came in and saw the pictures there; the moment he encountered that sight, it stole away his wits. Then he advanced toward the Greeks, who thereupon removed the intervening curtain so that the reflexion of the Chinese masterpieces struck upon the walls they had scoured clean of rust. All that the king had seen in the Chinese room showed lovelier here, so that his very eyes were snatched out of their sockets.

The Greeks, my father, are the Sufis; without repetition and books and learning, yet they have scoured their breasts clean of greed and covetousness, avarice and malice. The purity of the mirror without doubt is the heart, which receives images innumerable. The reflexion of every image, whether numbered or without number, shines forth forever from the heart alone, and forever every new image that enters upon the heart shows forth within it free of all imperfection. They who have burnished their hearts have escaped from scent and colour; every moment, instantly, they behold Beauty.

The Sufi, the Fakih and the Sharif, and How Their Solidarity Was Destroyed

A gardener one day saw in his orchard three men, seemingly come to rob it—a Fakih, a Sharif, and a Sufi, each one an insolent and perfidious rogue.

"I have a hundred proofs of their rascality," he murmured. "But they are united, and in union is strength. I cannot single-handed overcome the three of them; so first I must divide them one from the other. I will isolate each one of them from the others, then, when he is alone, I can pluck out his beard."

By a trick he got the Sufi away from the other two, intending to set his colleagues against him.

"Go into the house," he said to him. "Fetch a rug for your comrades."

The Sufi went. Then the gardener said to his two companions, "You are a Fakih, and you are an eminent Sharif. It is in accordance with your legal judgment"—this to the Fakih—"that we eat bread; it is by the wings of your wisdom that we fly. And the other of you, he is our prince and sovereign; he is a Sayyid of the family of the Prophet. Who, pray, is this gluttonous, ignoble Sufi, that he should sit with kings like yourselves? When he returns, you two shake him off and have the freedom of my orchard and villa for a week. What is an orchard after all? My life is at your disposal. You have always been as dear to me as my right eye."

His devilish whispers duped them completely. They drove the Sufi off, and when he was gone the gardener, their common foe, followed after him with a thick stick.

"You dog!" he cried. "Is it part of your Sufism that you hop into my orchard in my despite? Did Junaid and Bayazid show you this way? From which Shaikh and Pir did you get this instruction?"

Having got the Sufi by himself he gave him such a beating that he cracked his head and half killed him.

"My troubles are over!" exclaimed the Sufi. "But now you, my comrades, look out for yourselves! You considered me an outsider; but beware! I am no more of an outsider than this cuckold. What I have tasted you will also have to taste; such a draught as this is the recompense of every rotter."

The gardener, having finished with the Sufi, hit upon the same kind of pretext as before.

"O Sharif," he called, "pray go to the house. I have baked some delicious wafers for breakfast. Shout to Qaimaz from the door to fetch the wafers— and the goose as well."

Having got him out of the way, the gardener said to the Fakih, "Far-sighted sir, it is clear and sure that you are a Fakih. But he—a Sharif? What a ridiculous claim he makes! Who knows who made his mother? Many a fool has attached himself to Ali and the Prophet!"

The Fakih fell under his spell. Off at once the rascal went in the wake of the Sharif.

"You ass!" he cried. "Who invited you into this orchard? Is thievery all that you have inherited from the Prophet? The lion-cub takes after the lion, but tell me, in what respect do you take after the Prophet?"

That mightily resourceful man then dealt with the Sharif as a Khariji rebel would deal with the family of Muhammad. The Sharif was devastated by the scoundrel's blows.

"One dip is enough for me!" he cried to the Fakih. "You paddle there alone if you like, all on your own. Give him your belly to beat like a drum! If I am no Sharif and unworthy, unfit to be your comrade, at least I am no worse for you than such a scoundrel."

The gardener, having finished with the Sharif, addressed himself to the Fakih.

"What sort of a Fakih do you call yourself? You put to shame every fool alive. Is this your legal judgment, you amputated thief, that you may enter my garden without so much as a by-your-leave? Did you read such a licence in the *Intermediate*? Is this problem so resolved in the *Comprehensive*?"

"You are perfectly right," said the Fakih. "Beat me: I am in your power. This is the due recompense for one who breaks with friends."

Whoever the Devil cuts off from the men of nobility, finding him isolated, he proceeds to devour him. To quit the congregation of the saints for so much as a moment—that is the chance for Satan's cunning. Know this well.

The Policeman and the Drunkard, on Spiritual Intoxication

A policeman on his beat at midnight saw a man lying asleep at the base of a wall.

"Hi, you are drunk," he called to him. "Tell me, what have you been drinking?"

"The contents of the bottle," the man replied.

"Well, what may the contents of the bottle be?" the policeman asked.

"Some of what I have drunk," said the man.

"Ah, but that is out of sight," said the policeman. "Come on, what have you been drinking?"

"What is out of sight in the bottle."

The questions and answers went round and round. The policeman remained like a donkey stuck in the mud.

"Say *ah* now," the policeman ordered.

"*Hu, hu,*" the drunkard stammered.

"I said, 'Say *ah*,' and you are saying *hu*," the policeman said.

"That is because I am happy, while you are bent double with grief," the drunkard replied. "People say *ah* when they are in pain or sorrow or when they have been wronged. Winebibbers shout *hu hu* out of happiness."

"I know nothing about that," said the policeman. "Get up, get up. Enough chiseling high notions. Stop this wrangling!"

"Go away!" the man retorted. "What business have you with me?"

"You are drunk," the policeman said. "Up with you now. Come along to the lockup."

"Officer, leave me alone," said the drunkard. "Go away. How can you carry off a pledge from a naked man? If I had the power to walk I would have gone to my own home, and then how would all this have happened? If I had been in my right reason and human contingency, I would still be sitting on the bench, holding forth like the shaikhs."

TRANSLATED BY A. J. ARBERRY

[from *Būstān*, The Fruit Garden, and *Gulistān*, The Rose Garden,
and *Dīvān*, Poetic Works]

Sadi's morals sometimes turn out to be a wink. He had, like many storytellers, a sharp sense of the dishonest turnings of human behavior, particularly of that dishonesty which is often associated with exaggerated Oriental manners. This was combined in his work with a sincere reverence for the mystical, with admirable common sense, and with a charming simplicity of style.

He is perhaps the most beloved author of Iran, and the classic writer of Persian *adab*. The *Gulistān*, his book of stories in prose mixed with verses, is one of the country's most popular and familiar books; and his other major book, the *Būstān*, a *masnavī*, is almost as famous. His *ghazals*, an important part of his work and fame, are highly praised in the East and rarely read in the West. He also wrote poems in Arabic.

Like Hafiz, he is closely associated with Shiraz, but unlike Hafiz, he may have traveled widely across the Near East and was for several years a student in the Nizamiyyah of Baghdad. He spent the last years of his life, to 1292, in Shiraz, and it is there that he is buried.

It was told me that a certain old man on the road to [holy] Hejaz said two prayers for every step he took, and walked so zealously in the path of God that he did not stop even to pluck the thorns from his foot. But there came a time when, by the instigation of a seducer, his conduct found favour in his own eyes. Through the Devil's cunning he fell into the pit of saying that no better road than his own was possible; and, if he had not found God's mercy, false pride would have turned his head from the true path. A voice from Heaven came to him out of the void and said:

"O fortunate man of blessed spirit, think not that if you have obeyed God's will you have found a footing at his court. To compose your heart by well-doing were better than a thousand prayers in every stage [of your road]."

A dog bit the foot of a Bedouin with such fury that poison dripped from its teeth and the pain at night was so great that sleep could not comfort him.

Now in his household he had a little daughter who upbraided him and was very angry. "Did you too not have teeth?" she asked. The unhappy man ceased his wailing and said, laughing: "My darling little mother, even though I had the power and a spear too, yet it would revolt me to use my own jaws and teeth. It would be impossible for me to apply my teeth to a dog's leg even if a sword were held at my head." The nature of dogs is evil, but man cannot [in defence] act like a dog.

A thief got into the house of a religious man, but after the most diligent search had the mortification not to find anything. The good man, discovering his situation, threw the blanket on which he had slept in the way which the thief had to pass, in order that he might not be disappointed. "I have heard that those who are truly pious distress not the hearts of their enemies. How canst thou attain to this dignity, who art in strife and contention with thy friends?" The affection of the righteous is the same in presence as in absence; not like those who censure you behind your back, but before your face are ready to die for you. "When you are present, meek as a lamb; but when absent, like the wolf, a devourer of mankind." "Whosoever recounts to you the faults of your neighbour will doubtless expose your defects to others."

Speak no ill of any man, good or evil, O generous man, if you are wise; for you make the evil man your enemy and turn the good man into an evil one. When a man tells you that so-and-so is evil, know that he is within the slanderer's own skin; for so-and-so's explanation of his doings is necessary, and demonstration of his evil deed is demanded. Once you have spoken a word of ill against your fellow men, even if what you say is true, you too are evil.

A man once elongated his tongue in slander against an absent person. A sage of noble character said to him:

"Mention no ill of anyone to me, and thereby you will prevent my thinking ill of you. I understand his dignity is diminished, but that fact will never increase the importance of you."

A man once said to me:

"I thought there was a jest which runs that thieving is better than slander?"

I replied:

"O my friend of scattered wits, the saying astonishes me. What good can you see in dishonesty that you give it a higher status than slander?"

"Well," he replied, "thieves show courage, and by the strength of their arms acquire enough for their bellies. What does a fool want with slander; blackening a man's record and deriving no enjoyment from doing so?"

At the Nizámíya (College) I had a stipend, and night and day I was engaged in instructing and repetition. Once I said to the professor:

"O sage, my colleague so-and-so is jealous of me. If I were to tell the essential truth about him, his vile soul would be destroyed."

The learned principal blazed up in anger and said:

"How wonderful! You do not approve of your colleague's envy. Who has informed you then that slander is good? If he has gone to hell by the path of meanness, you will overtake him by this other path."

TRANSLATED BY REUBEN LEVY

Is that full moon veiled,
Or does the houri have her hand in dye?
And is it indigo on her eyebrows
Which tie the heart,
Or a bow of rainbows across the sun?
The flood has passed over my head, my friend.
Limit your unkindness, leash your cruelty.
Return, because sorrowing over you,
My eyes are a thousand springs of water.
You are oppression, a hot temper and bad habits,
However often you do good.
May I follow your command, whatever you say,
My soul on your lips, my eyes on your speech.
Your face is a gate to Paradise,
Hearts are meat for your salty lips.
I said, throw water on the fire,
But this fiery heart is not dampened by water.
No one has the patience to endure you,
Your violence transports no sleep to my eyes.
There is no doubt that in the torrent's course
Whatever one builds is ruin.
By day and by night your face
Is notoriety of the city,
The anarchy of the crowd.

Whoever does not turn toward you
Is an animal in the form of a man.
O heart-curing drug of my pain,
I am fixed in your slavery.
You know I cannot turn from you,
Your errors are my truth.
Although you are ruler and we are prisoners,
Although you are great and we are miserable,
Although you are rich and we are poor,
To possess another's heart is recompense.
O flowing cypress and rosebush of radiance,
Moon-beautiful and burning sun,
Receive and give, speak and listen,
These evenings are not for sleep.
This night is our solitude,
O auspicious fate and victorious fortune.
Kindle between us a candle—
Candle, do not flame,
Because there is the moonlight.
Give that wild cup to my cautious friends;
Drink down our madness,
For our drunkenness is not from wine.
Vanity is the wind;
The flash of youth is lightning.
Acquire hastily each moment what you can;
Hurry, for life speeds.
This wolf-hunger is without compassion
And never satiated.
We sons of time are grains of wheat
And the turning sky is the mill.
Saᶜdi, you will never know her
Until you brag and go closer.
O weary thirst, where have you run?
Your road is a mirage.

Is this spring wind a garden,
Or the fragrance of friends meeting?
Her eyebrows, like beautiful writing,
Carry off my heart.

O bird, taken in the heart's net,
This time, return and nest.
At night the candle and I melt,
But my fire is hidden.
My anticipation listens on the road,
And my eye is on the threshold.
When the muezzin sings
I hear the bell of a caravan.
With all your enmity, return,
For even that is friendship.
Against the strong arms of love
The hand of patience is powerless.
Leaving an intimate friend
Separates body and soul.
Sa'di, moaning sadly,
Proves the claim of friendship.
Fire burns this reed pen,
This flowing ink is smoke.

I am happy in the green world,
For the world is green because of her.
I love all the worlds,
Because every world is hers.
Breathe in, my friend, Christ's breath.
Revivify your dead heart.
You will live if the breath is hers.
Unchanging truth is possessed
Neither by heaven nor angels.
That which is in the heart's core
Of the son of Adam is from her.
With pleasure I eat poison,
When my sweet brings it.
I bear pain with devotion,
Because she is also my remedy.
If my bloody wound does not heal,
All the best! Every moment
This wound is cooled by her unguent glance.
Does wisdom distinguish joy and sorrow?
Give me wine! I rejoice

That my wound is from her.
The royal and the poor are one to me.
Everyone at this gate
Bends their back for her.
Saᶜdi, if the flood destroys this,
Sorrow's house, strengthen your heart,
For the foundation of eternity
Is strong because of her.

TRANSLATED BY R. M. REHDER

I never complained of the vicissitudes of fortune, nor murmured at the ordinances of heaven, excepting once, when my feet were bare and I had not the means of procuring myself shoes. I entered the great mosque at Cufah with a heavy heart, when I beheld a man who had no feet. I offered up praise and thanksgiving to God for His bounty, and bore with patience the want of shoes. "A broiled fowl, in the eyes of one who has satisfied his appetite, is of less estimation than a leaf of greens on a dish; but to him who hath not the means of procuring food, a boiled turnip is equal to a boiled fowl."

I saw a merchant who possessed one hundred and fifty camels laden with merchandise, and forty slaves. One night, in the island of Kish, he entertained me in his own apartment, and during the whole night did not cease talking in rambling fashion, saying: "I have such and such a partner in Turkistan, and such goods in Hindustan; these are the title-deeds of such and such a piece of ground, and, for this matter such a one is security." Sometimes he would say: "I have an inclination to go to Alexandria, the air of which is very pleasant." Then again: "No, I will not go, because the Mediterranean sea is boisterous. O Saᶜdí, I have another journey in contemplation, and after I have performed that I will pass the remainder of my life in retirement, and leave off trading." I asked what journey it was. He replied: "I want to carry Persian brimstone to China, where I have heard it bears a very high price; from thence I will transport China ware to Greece, and take the brocades of Greece to India, and Indian steel to Aleppo. The glassware of Aleppo I will convey to Yemen, and from thence go with striped cloths to Persia; after which I will leave off trade and sit down in my shop." He spoke so much of this foolishness that at length, being quite exhausted, he said: "O Saᶜdí, relate also something of what you have seen and heard." I replied: "Have you not heard that once upon a time a merchant, as he was travelling in the desert, fell from his camel? He said that the covetous eye of the worldly man is either satisfied through contentment or will be filled with the earth of the grave."

A certain king had a terrible disease, the nature of which it is not proper to mention. A number of Greek physicians agreed that there was no other remedy for this disease but the gall of a man of some particular description. The king ordered such a one to be sought for, and they found a peasant's son with the properties which the physicians had described. The king sent for the lad's father and mother, and by offering a great reward gained their consent, and the cadi gave his decision that it was lawful to shed the blood of a subject for restoring the health of the monarch. The executioner prepared to put him to death, upon which the youth turned his eyes towards heaven and laughed. The king asked what there could be in his present condition which could possibly excite mirth. He replied: "Children look to their parents for affection; a suit is referred to the cadi; and justice is expected from the monarch. Now my father and mother, deluded by vain worldly considerations, having consented to the shedding of my blood, the judge having sentenced me to die, and the king for the sake of his own health having consented to my death, where am I to seek refuge excepting in God on high? Unto whom shall I prefer my suit, since it is from you that I seek justice against you yourself?" The king's heart being troubled at these words, the tears stood in his eyes, and he said: "It is better for me to die than that the blood of an innocent person should be shed." He kissed his head and eyes, and embraced him, and after bestowing considerable gifts set him at liberty. They say, also, that in the same week the king was cured of his distemper. In application to this I recollect the verse which the elephant-driver rehearsed on the banks of the river Nile: "If you are ignorant of the state of the ant under your foot, know that it resembles your own condition under the foot of the elephant."

A person had arrived at the head of his profession in the art of wrestling: he knew three hundred and sixty capital sleights in this art, and every day exhibited something new; but having a sincere regard for a beautiful youth, one of his scholars, he taught him three hundred and fifty-nine sleights, reserving, however, one sleight to himself. The youth excelled so much in skill and in strength that no one was able to cope with him. He at length boasted, before the sultan, that the superiority which he allowed his master to maintain over him was out of respect to his years and the consideration of having been his instructor; for otherwise he was not inferior in strength, and was his equal in point of skill. The king did not approve of this disrespectful conduct, and commanded that there should be a trial of skill.

An extensive spot was appointed for the occasion. The ministers of state and other grandees of the court were in attendance. The youth, like a lustful elephant, entered with a percussion that would have removed from its base a mountain of iron. The master, being sensible that the youth was his superior in strength, attacked with the sleight which he had kept to himself. The youth not being able to repel it, the master with both hands lifted him from the ground, and raising him over his head, flung him on the earth. The multitude shouted; the king commanded that a dress and a reward in money should be bestowed on the master, and reproved and derided the youth for having presumed to put himself in competition with his benefactor, and for having failed in the attempt. He said: "O King, my master did not gain the victory over me through strength or skill; but there remained a small part in the art of wrestling which he had withheld from me, and by that small feint he got the better of me." The master observed: "I reserved it for such an occasion as the present; the sages having said, 'Put not yourself so much in the power of your friend that if he should be disposed to be inimical he may be able to effect his purpose.' Have you not heard what was said by a person who had suffered injury from one whom he had educated? 'Either there never was any gratitude in the world, or else no one at this time practices it. I never taught anyone the art of archery who in the end did not make a butt of me.' "

TRANSLATED BY REUBEN LEVY

They tell of an oppressor of the people who with a stone hit a good man on the head. The dervish did not have the power for vengeance. He kept the stone until a time when anger at the officer overcame the king, and he put him in a well. The dervish came and smashed him on the head with the stone. He said: "Who are you and why do you throw this stone at me?" He replied, "I am so-and-so and this is the same stone which on such-and-such a day you threw at me."

"Where were you all this time?"

"I used to fear your high place. Now, when I saw to where you had sunk, I counted the blessing of opportunity."

> Look, the unworthy is the friend of luck.
> The reasonable submit: choose.
> Since you do not have sharp, rending claws,
> It is wiser not to war.
> Whoever grapples steel arms
> Pains his own weak wrists.
> Wait for time to tie his hand.
> Then, for the pleasure of your friends,
> Knock out his brains.

TRANSLATED BY R. M. REHDER

ISLAM'S NEW WORLD [1350–1800]

Altered beyond any recognition of its Abbasid configuration, the Islamic world in the middle of the fourteenth century was, at any rate, peaceful. Two spacious empires, the Mamluk and the Mongol successor states, accounted between them for much of its territory. By the end of the century, however, forces were already set in motion which were to establish a "New World" for Islam at the same time that Europe, in fear of Islam's rejuvenation, discovered a "New World," both physically and spiritually, for itself.

Along the receding boundaries of the Byzantine empire in Anatolia, a vigorous new confederation of Turkish tribes called Osmanli (Ottoman) arose. But just as their territories were beginning to achieve imperial proportions, they were challenged by the forces of a fellow-Moslem, Tamerlane (Timur Lank), who not only destroyed the Anatolian basis of their empire, but incorporated it into his own, which stretched from there all the way to the borders of China. For a time Tamerlane's empire was the greatest in the world, but it was destined to shrink almost as rapidly as it had expanded, while the Ottoman empire was destined to expand and endure for many centuries.

The turn of the sixteenth century saw the rise of no less than four great new Islamic empires: the Ottoman, the Safavid, the Uzbek, and the Mughal. They were in touch and frequently at war with one another, but they produced, at least on the political plane, a degree of security and vitality unknown since much earlier days of Islam. The rise of the Ottoman empire was the most spectacular of the four. Utilizing well its virtually unique military discipline and strategy, as well as the time-honored techniques of alliance, it managed to swallow one territory after another until it was in firm control, from its capital in Istanbul (Constantinople, which fell in 1453), of an empire comprising most of the central Islamic world and constantly

reaching out into eastern Europe and Persian Iraq. In the middle of
the sixteenth century the Turks seriously threatened to occupy Austria,
and gave Europe a shock from which it did not soon recover. Before
long, Europe had entered into rather uneasy alliances with Persia (which
did slight harm to the Ottomans, but benefited both Persia and certain
European countries considerably) and the Ottoman empire itself.

The eighteenth century saw all of the Moslem empires, in varying
degrees, become flabby. While the mosques of Istanbul, Isfahan,
Samarkand, and Lahore bore matchless witness to their internal security (or rather, to the security of their interiors), an outside world
was changing and growing powerful ever more rapidly and menacingly.
New powers, such as Russia, emerged; old powers, such as Portugal,
declined. Britain and France grew stronger and more jealous of each
other. Sooner than it realized or should have liked, the Islamic world
was caught up in external power struggles in which it had little voice
and over which it had no control.

So bad is the literary reputation of this period that it is always
stigmatized, and sometimes omitted entirely, in considerations of Islamic
literature. Such a verdict must be considered unjust. During the first
century of the period, in fact, a number of masterpieces were written.
The odes of Hafiz of Shiraz could by themselves carry the period for
Persian poetry, but do not need to do so. The *masnavīs* of Jami brought
new life to Persian poetry in the fifteenth century, life enough to sustain it for centuries. In the fourteenth century, Ibn Khaldun composed
one of the greatest prose works ever written in the Arabic language.
Sometime early in this period, anonymous talents fashioned *The
Romance of Antar*, the nearest thing to an Arabic epic (and not far
from it), as well as *The Thousand and One Nights*, whose merits
Westerners seem far more eager to extol than do the Arabs themselves.

Yet it would be futile to pretend that the period was as great as
earlier ones for Islamic literature. It was not. After 1500, the Moors
were finished writing; the Arabs were numbed; the Turks were
unsuccessfully imitating the Persians; and the Persians were selling
their talents to the Mughals. A far better case could be made out that

this was the greatest of all periods for the visual arts in Islam. This prominence needs to be emphasized because it might otherwise appear that the "arts" of warfare and government had become so paramount that there was little appreciation of the fine arts at all. It could also be suggested that this period has been so poorly studied that time may yet turn up remarkable exceptions to the general picture we have of it.

What might seem the most generous view of the period is probably also the truest. These generations were appreciating the excellence of the literature they had inherited and, evidently estimating their own talents quite correctly, did little but try to imitate it. If they failed to create new forms, at least the old ones were not dishonored by their efforts.

It is appropriate that Ibn Battutah should introduce this section, for although he was very much a creature of Islam's "Old World" and, in a sense, an apologist for it, his experiences as recorded in his memoirs give one a unique picture of the dawn of Islam's "New World." It is a picture all the more valuable because it was drawn by a man who had seen more of the world than anyone else in his time, and few enough people in any time.

Like innumerable Moslems before and since, Ibn Battutah set out from his native Tangiers at the age of twenty-one, in 1325, on a pilgrimage to Mecca. Unlike them, however, he continued traveling more or less constantly for the remainder of his long life. One authority has estimated that Ibn Battutah traveled some seventy-five thousand miles, from the depths of West Africa to the seaports of China. He was able to do so because the Islamic world at that time was wide and tranquil and sufficiently homogeneous so that his profession, religious law, commanded dignity and emolument anywhere within it, and recommended him for diplomatic missions outside it.

Ibn Battutah dictated his memoirs after returning to Morocco in 1354. Some doubt has been expressed as to the reliability of many portions of the text, and it is certain that passages from other travelers were inserted to supplement the information. In the main, however, the book is an accurate record. It is written in a lively and orderly style, with many conversational digressions but almost no repetition. It carried the Arabic form of the travelogue to its highest development.

The people of the Maldive Islands are upright and pious, sound in belief and sincere in thought; their bodies are weak, they are unused to fighting, and their armour is prayer. Once when I ordered a thief's hand to be cut off, a number of those in the room fainted. The Indian pirates do not raid or molest them, as they have learned from experience that anyone who seizes anything from them speedily meets misfortune. In each island of theirs there are beautiful mosques, and most of their buildings are made of wood. They are very cleanly and avoid filth; most of them bathe twice a day to cleanse themselves, because of the extreme heat there and their profuse perspiration. They make plentiful use of perfumed oils, such as oil of sandal-wood. Their garments are simply aprons; one they tie round their waists in place of trousers, and on their backs they place other cloths resembling the pilgrim garments. Some wear a turban, others a small kerchief instead. When any of them meets the qádí, or preacher, he removes his cloth from his shoulders, uncovering his back, and accompanies him thus to his house. All, high or low, are bare-footed; their lanes are kept swept and clean and are shaded by trees, so that to walk in them is like walking in an orchard. In spite of that every person entering a house must wash his feet with water from a jar kept in a chamber in the vestibule, and wipe them with a rough towel of palm matting which he finds there. The same practice is followed on entering a mosque.

From these islands there are exported the fish we have mentioned, coconuts, cloths, and cotton turbans, as well as brass utensils, of which they have a great many, cowrie shells, and *qanbar*. This is the hairy integument of the coconut, which they tan in pits on the shore, and afterwards beat out with bars; the women then spin it and it is made into cords for sewing [the planks of] ships together. These cords are exported to India, China, and Yemen, and are better than hemp. The Indian and Yemenite ships are sewn together with them, for the Indian Ocean is full of reefs, and if a ship is nailed with iron nails it breaks up on striking the rocks, whereas if it is sewn together with cords, it is given a certain resilience and does not fall to pieces. The inhabitants of these islands use cowrie shells as money. This is an animal which they gather in the sea and place in pits, where its flesh disappears, leaving its white shell. They are used for buying and selling at the rate of four hundred thousand shells for a gold dinar, but they often fall in value to twelve hundred thousand for a dinar. They sell them in exchange for rice to the people of Bengal, who also use them as money, as well as to the Yemenites, who use them instead of sand [as ballast] in their ships. These shells are used also by the negroes in their lands; I saw them being sold at Mállí and Gawgaw at the rate of 1,150 for a gold dinar.

Their womenfolk do not cover their hands, not even their queen does so, and they comb their hair and gather it at one side. Most of them wear only

an apron from their waists to the ground, the rest of their bodies being un-
covered. When I held the qádíship there, I tried to put an end to this practice
and ordered them to wear clothes, but I met with no success. No woman was
admitted to my presence in a lawsuit unless her body was covered, but apart
from that I was unable to effect anything. I had some slave-girls who wore
garments like those worn at Delhi and who covered their heads, but it was
more of a disfigurement than an ornament in their case, since they were not
accustomed to it. A singular custom amongst them is to hire themselves out
as servants in houses at a fixed wage of five dinars or less, their employer
being responsible for their upkeep; they do not look upon this as dishonorable, and most of their girls do so. You will find ten or twenty of them in a
rich man's house. Every utensil that a girl breaks is charged up against her.
When she wishes to transfer from one house to another, her new employers
give her the sum which she owes to her former employers; she pays this to
the latter and remains so much in debt to her new employers. The chief
occupation of these hired women is spinning *qanbar*. It is easy to get married
in these islands on account of the smallness of the dowries and the pleasure
of their women's society. When ships arrive, the crew marry wives, and when
they are about to sail they divorce them. It is really a sort of temporary
marriage. The women never leave their country.

It is a strange thing about these islands that their ruler is a woman, Khadíja.
The sovereignty belonged to her grandfather, then to her father, and after
his death to her brother Shihắb ad-Dín, who was a minor. When he was
deposed and put to death some years later, none of the royal house remained
but Khadíja and her two younger sisters, so they raised Khadíja to the throne.
She was married to their preacher, Jamắl ad-Dín, who became Wazír and the
real holder of authority, but orders are issued in her name only. They write
the orders on palm leaves with a curved iron instrument resembling a knife;
they write nothing on paper but copies of the Koran and works on theology.
When a stranger comes to the islands and visits the audience-hall custom demands that he take two pieces of cloth with him. He makes obeisance towards
the Sultana and throws down one of these cloths, then to her Wazír, who is
her husband Jamắl ad-Dín, and throws down the other. Her army comprises
about a thousand men, recruited from abroad, though some are natives. They
come to the palace every day, make obeisance, and retire, and they are paid
in rice monthly. At the end of each month they come to the palace, make
obeisance, and say to the Wazír "Transmit our homage and make it known
that we have come for our pay," whereupon orders are given for it to be

issued to them. The qádí and the officials, whom they call wazírs, also present their homage daily at the palace and after the eunuchs have transmitted it they withdraw. The qádí is held in greater respect among the people than all the other functionaries; his orders are obeyed as implicitly as those of the ruler or even more so. He sits on a carpet in the palace, and enjoys the entire revenue of three islands, according to ancient custom. There is no prison in these islands; criminals are confined in wooden chambers intended for merchandise. Each of them is secured by a piece of wood, as is done amongst us [in Morocco] with Christian prisoners.

When I arrived at these islands I disembarked on one of them called Kannalús, a fine island containing many mosques, and I put up at the house of one of the pious persons there. On this island I met a man called Muhammad, belonging to Dhafár, who told me that if I entered the island of Mahal the Wazír would detain me there, because they had no qádí. Now my design was to sail from there to Maᶜbar [Coromandel], Ceylon, and Bengal, and thence on to China. When I had spent a fortnight at Kannalús, I set sail again with my companions, and having visited on our way several other islands, at which we were received with honour and hospitably entertained, arrived on the tenth day at the island of Mahal, the seat of the Sultana and her husband, and anchored in its harbour. The custom of the country is that no one may go ashore without permission. When permission was given to us I wished to repair to one of the mosques, but the attendants on shore prevented me, saying that it was imperative that I should visit the Wazír. I had previously enjoined the captain of the ship to say, if he were asked about me, "I do not know him," fearing that I should be detained by them, and ignorant of the fact that some busybody had written to them telling them about me and that I had been qádí at Delhi. On reaching the palace we halted in some porticoes by the third gateway. The qádí ᶜIsá of Yemen came up and greeted me and I greeted the Wazír. The captain brought ten pieces of cloth and made obeisance towards the Sultana, throwing down one piece, then to the Wazír, throwing down another in the same way. When he had thrown them all down he was asked about me and answered "I do not know him." Afterwards they brought out betel and rose-water to us, this being their mark of honour, and lodged us in a house, where they sent us food, consisting of a large platter of rice surrounded by plates containing salted meat, chickens, ghee, and fish. Two days later the Wazír sent me a robe, with a hospitality-gift of food and a hundred thousand cowries for my expenses.

When ten days had passed a ship arrived from Ceylon bringing some darwíshes, Arabs and Persians, who recognized me and told the Wazír's attendants who I was. This made him still more delighted to have me, and at the beginning of Ramadán he sent for me to join in a banquet attended by the amírs and ministers. Later on I asked his permission to give a banquet to the darwíshes who had come from visiting the Foot [of Adam, in Ceylon]. He gave permission, and sent me five sheep, which are rarities among them because they are imported from Maᶜbar, Mulaybár, and Maqdashaw, together with rice, chickens, ghee, and spices. I sent all this to the house of the wazír Sulaymán, who had it excellently cooked for me, and added to it besides sending carpets and brass utensils. I asked the Wazír's permission for some of the ministers to attend my banquet, and he said to me "And I shall come too." So I thanked him and on returning home to my house found him already there with the ministers and high officials. The Wazír sat in an elevated wooden pavilion, and all the amírs and ministers who came greeted him and threw down an unsewn cloth, so that there were collected about a hundred cloths, which were taken by the darwíshes. The food was then served, and when the guests had eaten, the Koran-readers chanted in beautiful voices. The darwíshes then began their ritual chants and dances. I had made ready a fire and they went into it, treading it with their feet, and some of them ate it as one eats sweetmeats, until it was extinguished. When the night came to an end, the Wazír withdrew and I went with him. As we passed by an orchard belonging to the treasury he said to me "This orchard is yours, and I shall build a house in it for you to live in." I thanked him and prayed for his happiness. Afterwards he sent me two slave-girls, some pieces of silk, and a casket of jewels.

TRANSLATED BY H. A. R. GIBB

Hafiz is honored as the greatest lyric poet of Iran and its greatest writer of *ghazals*, the form which he brought to perfection. His reputation, while he lived, spread as far as Turkestan, Iraq, and India; but he himself stayed in his native Shiraz.

We have only a very small amount of information about his life. From his poems it appears that he knew the works of Arab and other Persian authors, including some of his contemporaries, and his pen name implies that he had learned the Koran by heart. One poem states that it was written after the death of his wife; another, after the death of a son. He died in 1390.

"Hafiz wrote in the tradition of Sufism," one authority remarks, "but he was not a true Sufi, as Rumi certainly was. If there is anything divine in the love which he celebrates, that divinity must be found in the very *human* nature of it. His *Divan* is a symbolical rather than an allegorical expression of man's fate, cast as that is somewhere between the two worlds. Wine, love, and roses do not stand for some religious equivalent as in the Sufi lexicon; rather, in these very objects of nature, spirituality is to be found. . . . His poems project at once the sweetness of the joys of this world and its inadequacies."

> Soft wind, speak grace to that gazelle;
> Give her in her elegance what you gave us,
> A taste for the mountain and the wilderness.
> Sugar-seller—may your life be long!—why
> Are you not searching for your sugar-eating parrot?
> Does pride of your beauty, O Rose, not allow you
> To ask for the love-mad nightingale?
> She is able, by temper and elegance,
> To hunt the visionaries,

But with her snares she does not net the wise bird.
Why I do not know, black eyes, a slender body
And a moon face, do not show the color of friendship.
When you sit by your love measuring wine,
Remember the lovers who measure the winds.
Except this, I can speak of no flaw in your beauty:
Fidelity and honesty are not the shape of your face.
It is no wonder if in the sky, with the words of Hafiz,
The music of Venus brings the Messiah dancing.

Her hair in disarray, lips laughing;
Drunk in the sweat of revelry
Singing of love, she came, flask in hand.

Disheveled and her clothes rent
Last midnight by my bed she bent;
Her lips curved in regret.

I saw sorrow quarrel in her eyes
As her whispers spoke softly,
"Is our old love asleep?"

Given such a wine before dawn,
A lover is an infidel to love
If he does not drink.

Find no fault, anchorite, with the drinker of dregs,
For on the day of the Covenant
We were given no other gift.

We lift to our lips
Whatever he pours into the wine bowl,
The wine of Paradise or the cup of Hell.

O how many vows of repentance are undone
By the smile of wine and the tresses of a girl
Like the vows of Hafiz?

In green Heaven's fields I saw the sickle of the new moon,
Remembered my sowing and my harvest,
And said: O Fortune, you sleep and the sun blossoms.
The reply: Do not be hopeless as the past.
If you go pure and solitary as the Messiah to Heaven,
Your splendor will touch the sun.
Do not rely on the night-stealing moon,
For he stole Kaʾus's crown and Kaykhusrau's belt.
Although your ear is heavy with the red-gold ring,
The gorgeous season disappears—hear counsel.
May the evil eye be far from your beauty spot,
For on beauty's chess-board it moved a pawn
And took the prize from the moon and sun.
May the sky not sell this greatness, for in love,
They give a grain of corn for the moon's harvest,
Two for the Pleiades.
The hypocrisy of the ascetic fire
Will burn the harvest of religion.
Hafiz! Cast your cloak and go.

A rose blooms within me, wine is in my hand,
And my beloved embraced.
This day the world's king is my slave.
Bring us no candle-light at dark
Because the moon-face of love is full.
We worship wine and pour our vows, and it is
Against my law to be without your face.
My ear hears ever the speech of the reed
And the melody of lutes.
My eyes are always on red lips
And on the circulating cup.
In our assembly bring no rose perfumes,
We breathe the fragrance of your long hair.
Do not praise to me the taste of sugar,
For my desire is satisfied on your sweet lip.
As long as my grief for you is in my heart's ruins,
My place is in the tavern alley.
You speak of shame? Shame is my renown.
You speak of fame? My renown is in my shame.

We are rakes, wine-drinkers and spinning heads,
And that person who is not like us—who is he?
Do not betray his faults to the censor,
He is like us in always asking luxury.
Hafiz, do not sit one moment without your love or wine,
For these are days of rose, jasmine and celebration.

The red rose is open and the nightingale is drunk:
An invitation, Sufiyan, wine-worshippers,
To the pleasures of intoxication.
Repentance, which appeared to be stone,
Look! has been smashed by the wine-glass.
Bring wine! for in the court of independence,
Whether watchman or sultan, wise or drunk,
From this inn of two doors, one must go out.
Luxury is impossible without deep pain.
Yes, by order of the Beyond, they are bound to the Covenant.
For *is* and *not*, do not trouble your heart or happiness,
For *not* is nothing: the end of every perfection which *is*.
The magnificence of Asaf,
The horse of the wind and the language of the birds,
Went to the wind. The master showed no profit.
Do not fly from the road with feathered wings.
The arrow flies and floats but falls in the dirt.
For the language of your pen, Hafiz, what thanks from him
Who takes your words from hand to hand?

If that Shirazi Turk will take my heart in her hand
I will give up for her Bokhara and Samarqand.
Give me, Saqi, the last of the wine,
For in Paradise we will not find
The waters of Ruknabad or the meadows of Mosalla.
Alas these Luliyan torment the city with their sweet work,
Taking patience from the heart as the Turks plunder.
Her beauty is independent of my incomplete love.
What line, perfume or color does beauty need?
I, before that ever-increasing beauty which Joseph had,
Know the love which separated Zuleika from her veils.

If you curse me or swear, I am content;
The bitter answer fits your red, sugar-eating lip.
Hear, O Soul, advice from the wise man who knows,
Which is dearer than soul to the young who possess joy.
Speak music, talk wine, and as for Fortune's mystery —
As philosophy does not unravel or untie that tangle.
Your song is spoken. The pearls are strung.
Sweetly, Hafiz, sing
That heaven on your poem may scatter knots of stars.

At the head of the bazaar
They who play with life issue a proclamation.
Listen, dwellers in the alleys of pleasure, listen.
Several days have passed
Since we lost the daughter of the vine.
She went her own way, beware, be ready,
In soft ruby robes and a crown of bubbles.
She carries off reason and knowledge,
So you do not sleep safe from her.
To whoever sweetens her bitterness for me
I will give my soul as the price,
And if in Hell she is concealed or hidden,
Go to Hell for her.
This daughter wanders at night,
Impetuous and bitter.
She is the color of the rose, and drunk.
If you find her, take her to the house of Hafiz.

I do not restrain desire
Until my desire is satisfied,
Or until my body touches hers,
Or my soul from my body goes.
When I am dead, open my tomb.
You will see my heart on fire
And my shroud smoke.
Display your face and the world will despair,
Harassed by love, in wonder at your beauty.
Open the lips for which men cry.

My soul is on my lips,
In my heart is a grief
Her lips never touched;
My soul from my body sighs.
I sorrow in this narrow place
Because of her impatient mouth.
To those whom it has brought desire,
When will that mouth bring peace?
Everywhere the name, Hafiz, appears,
Lovers praise him when they meet.

When the wine sun fills the bowl of the East,
It brings to her cheeks a thousand anemones.
The wind breaks ringlets of hyacinth
Over the heads of the roses,
As among the meadows I inhale
The fragrance of her rich hair.
This does not express the night of separation,
For the fragments of her explanation
Would fill a hundred books.
You will not satisfy hunger or desire
From the tray which the sky turns.
Without the reproaches of a hundred sorrows,
You cannot have one crumb.
All your efforts will not yield you the pearl.
That is the day-dream,
And each success is a draft on the future.
If you have the patience of Noah in trouble's flood,
You may turn away calamity
To have what was desired for a thousand years.
When the wind passes with her grace
Across the grave of Hafiz,
Lamentations will rise from his dust.

Come pass me the cup quickly and hand it on;
Love first appeared easy, but trouble fell on me.
The wind discloses the musk of your hair;
My heart was twisted in that musky flame.

In my love's house, there is no peace in pleasure.
At every breath, the caravan bells cry: ride on.
Stain your prayer-rug with wine if the wise man tells you,
For that traveler knows the road's news
And the customs of its houses.
Waves, black night, and the whirlpool are my terrors.
Where do the carefree careless know me?
Their life is on the shore. All my work
Has been drawn from self-interest to infamy.
How can I conceal what they would celebrate?
Hafiz, do not give up what you desire,
For what you love, leave the world, forsake it.

TRANSLATED BY R. M. REHDER

[from *Al-Muqaddimah*, the introduction to *Kitāb al-ᶜIbar*,
The Book of Examples]

In 1375, a North African Arab aristocrat named Abd al-Rahman ibn
Khaldun, after a stormy career in politics, retired to a castle in Algeria
to write a history of the world. Before embarking on his narrative,
however, he had the courage and originality to give unhurried thought
to the nature of human history itself, to historical meaning, truth, and
method. It is this lengthy prolegomenon, or *muqaddimah*, rather than
the history itself, which has won for its author a peerage among the
world's great thinkers. Arnold Toynbee pronounced it "the greatest
work of its kind that has ever yet been created by any mind in any
time or place."

Toynbee was not exaggerating as much as one might think. Ibn
Khaldun's work is a vast encyclopedia of knowledge, brightened at
every turn by the author's tremendously gifted and exploring mind.
His original interpretations of historical phenomena in the light of
social factors have won him the title, "father of sociology." Few if
any of the provinces now claimed by the social sciences were left
unenriched by his speculation. His treatment of historical method, in
particular, has been judged uniquely perceptive. One of his most
original explanatory concepts, that of ᶜaṣabiyyah, or group solidarity,
is the subject of the following selection.

In 1382, Ibn Khaldun decided to make his pilgrimage to Mecca.
Thereafter he settled in Egypt, where he openly and successfully
competed for various high offices, including a judgeship. He revised
the introduction to his history many times. The result, in terms of
style, was a highly polished and difficult prose work more closely
resembling legal and philosophical writings than works of belles-lettres.
He took considerable pride in that style.

Human society is necessary. Philosophers express this truth by saying that man is social by nature, i.e., he needs a society, or "city" as they call it.

The reason for this is that ... each individual's capacity for acquiring food falls short of what is necessary to sustain life. Even taking a minimum, such as one day's supply of wheat, it is clear that this requires operations (grinding and kneading and baking) each of which necessitates utensils and tools, which presuppose the presence of carpenters, smiths, potmakers, and other craftsmen. Even granting that he eat the wheat unground, he can only obtain it in that state after many more operations, such as sowing and reaping and threshing, to separate the grain from the chaff, all of which processes require even more tools and crafts.

Now it is impossible for an individual to carry out all the above-mentioned work, or even part of it. Hence it becomes necessary for him to unite his efforts with those of his fellow men who by co-operating can produce enough for many times their number.

And unless he so co-operate with others he cannot obtain the food without which he cannot live, nor defend himself, for want of weapons, but will fall a prey to the beasts and his species will be extinct. Co-operation however, secures both food and weapons, thus fulfilling God's will of preserving the species. Society is therefore necessary to man ... and it is society which forms the subject of this science.

Human society having, as we have shown, been achieved and spread over the face of the earth, there arises the need of a restraining force to keep men off each other in view of their animal propensities for aggressiveness and oppression of others. Now the weapons with which they defend themselves against wild beasts cannot serve as a restraint, seeing that each man can make equal use of them. Nor can the restraint come from other than men, seeing that animals fall far short of men in their mental capacity. The restraint must therefore be constituted by one man, who wields power and authority with a firm hand and thus prevents anyone from attacking anyone else, i.e., by a sovereign. Sovereignty is therefore peculiar to man, suited to his nature and indispensable to his existence.

According to certain philosophers, sovereignty may also be found in certain animal species, such as bees and locusts, which have been observed to follow the leadership of one of their species, distinguished from the rest by its size and form. But in animals sovereignty exists in virtue of instinct and divine providence, not of reflection aiming at establishing a political organization.

The state is therefore to society as form is to matter, for the form by its nature preserves the matter and, as philosophers have shown, the two are inseparable.

For a state is inconceivable without a society; while a society without a state is well-nigh impossible, owing to the aggressive propensities of men, which require a restraint. A polity therefore arises, either theocratic or kingly, and this is what we mean by state.

The two being inseparable, any disturbance in either of them will cause a disturbance in the other; just as the disappearance of one leads to the disappearance of the other. The greatest source of disturbance is in the breakdown of such empires as the Roman, Persian, or Arab; or in [the breakdown of a whole] dynasty, such as the Omayyad or Abbasid.

The real force which operates on society is solidarity and power, which persists through [successive] rulers. Should such a solidarity disappear, and be replaced by another solidarity which acts on society, the whole Ruling Class would disappear and the disturbance thus caused be very great.

Social solidarity is found only in groups related by blood ties or by other ties which fulfil the same functions. This is because blood ties have a force binding on most men, which makes them concerned with any injury inflicted on their next of kin. Men resent the oppression of their relatives, and the impulse to ward off any harm that may befall those relatives is natural and deep rooted in men.

If the degree of kinship between two persons helping each other is very close, it is obviously the blood tie, which, by its very evidence, leads to the required solidarity. If the degree of kinship is distant, the blood tie is somewhat weakened but in its place there exists a family feeling based on the widespread knowledge of kinship. Hence each will help the other for fear of the dishonour which would arise if he failed in his duties towards one who is known by all to be related to him.

The clients and allies of a great nobleman often stand in the same relationship towards him as his kinsmen. Patron and client are ready to help each other because of the feeling of indignation which arises when the rights of a neighbour, a kinsman, or a friend are violated. In fact, the ties of clientship are almost as powerful as those of blood.

This explains the saying of the Prophet Mohammad, "Learn your genealogies to know who are your near of kin," meaning that kinship only serves a function when blood ties lead to actual co-operation and mutual aid in danger—other degrees of kinship being insignificant. The fact is that such relationship is more of an emotional than an objective fact in that it acts only by bringing together the hearts and affections of men. If the kinship is evident it acts as a natural urge leading to solidarity; if it is based on the mere knowledge of descent from a common ancestor it is weakened and has little influence on the sentiments and hence little practical effect.

Ties of kinship come out most clearly among savage peoples living in wildernesses, such as the Bedouins and other like peoples. This is because of the peculiarly hard life, poor conditions and forbidding environment which necessity has imposed upon such peoples. For their livelihood is based upon the produce of camels, and camel breeding draws them out into the wilderness where the camels graze on the bushes and plants of the desert sands; as we mentioned earlier.

Now the wilderness is a hard and hungry home, to which such men adapted their nature and character in successive generations. Other peoples, however, do not try to go out into the desert or to live with the nomads and share their fate; nay, should a nomad see the possibility of exchanging his condition for another he would not fail to do so.

As a result of all this, the genealogies of nomads are in no danger of being mixed or confused but remain clear and known to all.

Clientship and the mixing with slaves and allies can replace kinship [as the basis of solidarity]. For although kinship is natural and objective it is also emotional. For group ties are formed by such things as living together, companionship, prolonged acquaintance or friendship, growing up together, having the same foster parents, and other such matters of life and death. Such ties once formed lead to mutual help and the warding off of injuries inflicted on others; as can be commonly seen to occur. An example of this is provided by the relation of dependence. For there arises a special tie between a patron and those in his service which draws them close together so that although kinship is absent the fruits of kinship are present.

Aggressiveness and the lust for power are common characteristics of men, and whenever a man's eye dwells on the goods of his neighbour his hand is apt to follow it, unless he be checked by some restraint.

As regards towns and villages, their mutual aggressiveness is checked by the governors and the state, which restrain their subjects from attacking or oppressing each other; in other words, the power of the rulers preserves the people from oppression, unless it be the oppression of those same rulers. External aggression, for its part, is warded off by means of walls and fortifications, which protect a city by night, prevent surprises, and moreover supplement an otherwise inadequate defence; while the garrisons of the State carry out a prepared and prolonged resistance.

In nomadic societies, intragroup aggressiveness is checked by the chiefs and elders, owing to the prestige and respect with which they are regarded by the tribesmen. Aggression from outside, aimed at their possessions, is warded off by those of their young men who are noted for their bravery. And such defence can succeed only when they are united by a strong social solidarity arising out of kinship, for this greatly increases their strength.

The above [i.e., purity of race and tribal solidarity] holds true only for nomadic Arabs. The caliph Omar said: "Learn your genealogies and be not like the Nabateans of Mesopotamia who, if asked about their origin, reply: 'I come from such and such a village.'" Those Arabs who took up a more sedentary life, however, found themselves, in their quest for more fertile lands and rich pastures, crowding in on other peoples—all of which led to a mixture [of blood] and a confusion of genealogies.

This is what happened at the beginning of the Muslim era, when men began to be designated by the localities [in which they dwelt]. Thus people would refer to the military province of Qinnasrin or the military province of Damascus or that of al-ᶜAwasim. The usage then spread to Spain.

This does not mean, however, that the Arabs were no longer designated by their genealogies; they merely added to their tribal name a place-name which allowed their rulers to distinguish between them more easily. Later on, however, further mixture took place, in the cities, between Arabs and non-Arabs. This led to a complete confusion of genealogies, and a consequent weakening of that solidarity which is the fruit of tribal kinship; hence tribal names tended to be cast aside. Finally, the tribes themselves were absorbed and disappeared and with them all traces of tribal solidarity.

The nomads, however, continued as they had always been. "And God shall inherit the earth and all that are upon it."

It is evident that men are by nature in contact with and tied to each other, even where kinship is absent; though, as we have said before, in such cases such ties are weaker than where they are reinforced by kinship. Such contact may produce a solidarity nearly as powerful as that produced by kinship.

Now many city dwellers are interrelated by marriage, thus forming groups of kinsmen, divided into parties and factions, between which there exist the same relations of friendship and enmity as exist between tribes.

The end of social solidarity is sovereignty. This is because, as we have said before, it is solidarity which makes men unite their efforts for common objects, defend themselves, and repulse or overcome their enemies. We have also seen that every human society requires a restraint, and a chief who can keep men from injuring each other. Such a chief must command a powerful support, else he will not be able to carry out his restraining function. The domination he exercises is sovereignty, which exceeds the power of a tribal leader; for a tribal leader enjoys leadership and is followed by his men whom he cannot however compel. Sovereignty, on the other hand, is rule by compulsion, by means of the power at the disposal of the ruler.

[Now rulers always strive to increase their power],[1] hence a chief who secures a following will not miss the chance of transforming, if he can, his rule into sovereignty; for power is the desire of men's souls. And sovereignty can be secured only with the help of the followers on whom the ruler relies to secure the acquiescence of his people, so that kingly sovereignty is the final end to which social solidarity leads.

Kingship and dynasties can be founded only on popular support and solidarity. The reason for this is, as we have seen before, that victory, or even the mere avoidance of defeat, goes to the side which has most solidarity and whose members are readiest to fight and to die for each other. Now kingship is an honoured and coveted post, giving its holder all worldly goods as well as bodily and mental gratifications. Hence it is the object of much competition and is rarely given up willingly, but only under compulsion. Competition leads to struggle and wars and the overthrow of thrones, none of which can occur without social solidarity.

Such matters are usually unknown to, or forgotten by, the masses, who do not remember the time when the dynasty was first established, but have grown up, generation after generation, in a fixed spot, under its rule. They know nothing of the means by which God set up the dynasty; all they see is their monarchs, whose power has been consolidated and is no longer the object of dispute and who do not need to base their rule any more on social solidarity. They do not know how matters stood at first and what difficulties were encountered by the founders of the dynasty.

[1] This phrase is omitted from Quatremère's edition, but is present in other editions.

Once consolidated the state can dispense with social solidarity. The reason is that newly founded states can secure the obedience of their subjects only by much coercion and force. This is because the people have not had the time to get accustomed to the new and foreign rule.

Once kingship has been established, however, and inherited by successive generations or dynasties, the people forget their original condition, the rulers are invested with the aura of leadership, and the subjects obey them almost as they obey the precepts of their religion, and fight for them as they would fight for their faith. At this stage the rulers do not need to rely on a great armed force, since their rule is accepted as the will of God, which does not admit of change or contradiction. It is surely significant that the discussion of the Imamate is inserted [in theological books] at the end of the discussion of doctrinal beliefs, as though it formed an integral part of them.

From this time onward the authority of the king is based on the clients and freedmen of the royal household, men who have grown up under its protection; or else the king relies on foreign bands of warriors whom he attaches to himself.

An example of this is provided by the Abbaside dynasty. By the time of the Caliph Al-Muʿtaṣim and his son Al-Wāthiq, the spirit and strength of the Arabs had been weakened, so that the kings relied mainly on clients recruited from Persians, Turks, Deylamites, Seljuks, and others. These foreigners soon came to control the provinces, the Abbasides' rule being confined to the neighbourhood of Baghdad. Then the Deylamites marched on Baghdad and occupied it, holding the Caliphs under their rule. They were succeeded by the Seljuks, who were followed by the Tatars, who killed the Caliph and wiped out that dynasty.

The same is true of the Omayyad dynasty in Spain. When the spirit and solidarity of the Arabs weakened, the feudal lords pounced on the kingdom and divided it up among themselves. Each of them set himself up as supreme lord in his region and, following the example of the foreigners in the Abbaside empire, usurped the emblems and titles of sovereignty. . . . They upheld their authority by means of clients and freedmen and with the help of tribesmen recruited from the Berbers, Zenata[2] and other North Africans.

TRANSLATED BY CHARLES ISSAWI

[2] Zenata was one of the two main Berber branches, Sanhaja being the other. The Zenata, mostly nomadic, inhabited the southern parts of Algeria and Morocco. They played an important part in the history of the tenth to the thirteenth centuries, and founded the Marinid kingdom of Fez.

[from *Al-Tᶜrīf bi-ibn-Khaldūn*, Information concerning Ibn Khaldun]

Early in 1401, Ibn Khaldun, who had accompanied his sovereign, Sultan Faraj, to Damascus, met the world-conquering Tamerlane during the latter's campaign in Syria. He recorded their conversations in an autobiography uncharacteristically informal in style. It is notable that Tamerlane utilized their meeting to extract detailed information concerning North Africa, while Ibn Khaldun did not let the opportunity pass without making mention of his favorite theory of group solidarity, the subject of the foregoing selection.

When the news reached Egypt that Emir Timur [Tamerlane] had conquered Asia Minor, had destroyed Sīwās, and had returned to Syria, Sultan Faraj gathered his armies, opened the bureau of stipends, and announced to the troops the march to Syria. At that time I was out of office, but Yashbak, the Sultan's *dawādār* [chief of staff], summoned me and urged me to accompany him in the royal party. When I tried to refuse his offer he assumed a firm attitude toward me, though with gentleness of speech and considerable generosity. So I departed with them.

When I stood at the entrance [to Tamerlane's tent], permission came out to seat me there in a tent adjoining his reception tent. When my name was announced, the title "Maghribī Mālikite Cadi" was added to it;[1] he summoned me, and as I entered the audience tent to [approach] him he was reclining on his elbow while platters of food were passing before him which he was sending one after the other to groups of Mongols sitting in circles in front of his tent.

Upon entering, I spoke first, saying "Peace be upon you," and I made a gesture of humility. Thereupon he raised his head and stretched out his hand to me, which I kissed. He made a sign to me to sit down; I did so just where

---

[1] That is to say, "Judge of the Malikite school of Sunnite law from northwestern Africa." [Ed.]

I was, and he summoned from his retinue one of the erudite Ḥanafite jurists of Khwārizm, ʿAbd al-Jabbār ibn an-Nuʿmān, whom he bade sit there also to serve as interpreter between us.

He asked me from where in the Maghrib I had come, and why I had come. I replied, "I left my country in order to perform the pilgrimage [to Mecca]. I came to it [i.e., Egypt] by sea and arrived at the port of Alexandria on the day of the breaking of the Fast in the year 4 [and 80] of this seventh century, while festivities were [in progress] within their walls because aẓ-Ẓāhir [Barqūq] was sitting [in audience] on the royal throne during these ten days by count."

Timur asked me, "What did aẓ-Ẓāhir do for you?" I replied, "He was generous in giving recognition to my position; he accorded me hospitable entertainment and supplied me with provisions for the pilgrimage. Then, when I returned, he allotted me a large stipend, and I remained under his shelter and favor—may Allāh grant him mercy and recompense him."

He asked me, "How did he happen to appoint you Cadi?" I replied, "The Cadi of the Malikites had died one month before his [aẓ-Ẓāhir's] death; he thought I had the proper qualifications for the office—the pursuit of justice and right, and the rejection of outside influence—so he named me in his place. But when he died a month later, those who were in charge of the government were not pleased with my position and replaced me with another Cadi."

He said, "I desire that you write for me [a description of] the whole country of the Maghrib—its distant as well as its nearby parts, its mountains and its rivers, its villages and its cities—in such a manner that I might seem actually to see it."

I said, "That will be accomplished under your auspices."

Later, after I had departed from the audience with him, I wrote for him what he had requested, and put what was intended by it in a summary which would be the equivalent of about twelve quires of half format.

Then he gave a signal to his servants to bring from his tent some of the kind of food which they call "rishta"[2] and which they were most expert in preparing. Some dishes of it were brought in, and he made a sign that they should be set before me. I arose, took them, and drank, and liked it, and this impressed him favorably. [Then] I composed in my mind some words to say to him which, by exalting him and his government, would flatter him.

So I began by saying, "May Allāh aid you—today it is thirty or forty

---

[2] A type of macaroni soup still prepared in Syria.

years that I have longed to meet you." The interpreter, ᶜAbd al-Jabbār, asked, "And what is the reason for this?"

I replied, "Two things: the first is that you are the sultan of the universe and the ruler of the world, and I do not believe that there has appeared among men from Adam until this epoch a ruler like you. I am not one of those who speak about matters by conjecture, for I am a scholar and I will explain this, and say: Sovereignty exists only because of group loyalty [ᶜaṣabīyah], and the greater the number in the group, the greater is the extent of sovereignty. Scholars, first and last, have agreed that most of the peoples of the human race are of two groups, the Arabs and the Turks.[3] You know how the power of the Arabs was established when they became united in their religion in following their Prophet [Mohammed]. As for the Turks, their contest with the kings of Persia and the seizure of Khorāsān from their hands by Afrāsiyāb[4] is evidence of their origin from royalty; and in their group loyalty no king on earth can be compared with them, not Chosroes nor Caesar nor Alexander nor Nabuchadnezzar. . . ."

"The second reason which has led me to desire to meet him [Tamerlane] is concerned with what the prognosticators and the Muslim saints in the Maghrib used to tell," and I mentioned [some prophecies] I have related above.

The news was brought to him that the gate of the city had been opened and that the judges had gone out to fulfill their [promise of] surrender, for which, so they thought, he had generously granted them amnesty. Then he was carried away from before us, because of the trouble with his knee,[5] and was placed upon his horse; grasping the reins, he sat upright in his saddle while the bands played around him until the air shook with them; he rode toward Damascus.

When the time for Timur's journey approached and he decided to leave Damascus, I entered to him one day. After we had completed the customary greetings, he turned to me and said, "You have a mule here?"

I answered, "Yes."

---

[3] Ibn Khaldun knew better than that, but was perhaps speaking in some political sense.
[4] Afrāsiyāb was a legendary king of the Turks; he is not mentioned in Ibn Khaldun's *Muqaddimah.*
[5] Tamerlane was lamed by an arrow which wounded him in the thigh. "Lame" in Persian is *lank*, therefore *Timur-lank* and later, in European usage, Tamerlane.

He said, "Is it a good one?"

I answered, "Yes."

He said, "Will you sell it? I would buy it from you."

I replied, "May Allāh aid you—one like me does not sell to one like you; but I would offer it to you in homage, and also others like it if I had them."

He said, "I meant only that I would requite you for it with generosity."

I replied, "Is there any generosity left beyond that which you have already shown me? You have heaped favors upon me, accorded me a place in your council among your intimate followers, and shown me kindness and generosity—which I hope Allāh will repay to you in like measure."

He was silent; so was I. The mule was brought to him while I was with him at his council, and I did not see it again.

Then on another day I entered to him and he asked me: "Are you going to travel to Cairo?"

I answered, "May Allāh aid you—indeed, my desire is only [to serve] you, for you have granted me refuge and protection. If the journey to Cairo would be in your service, surely; otherwise I have no desire for it."

He said, "No, but you will return to your family and to your people."

TRANSLATED BY WALTER J. FISCHEL

The Romance of Antar is by far the most popular anonymous work in Arabic literature. It has been attributed to many authors, including Al-Asmai, an early philologist, but quite obviously does not want an author.

It is a work of pure romance—an idealization of Arab chivalry—whose hero is none other than Antarah, the pre-Islamic poet, and was formulated at a time when Arab Islam had finished reacting against its desert paternity and was inclined toward glorifying it. Our best authorities date its more permanent form from the thirteenth century, but its fierce brilliance has never been confined to any single, received text. For all that, Sir William Jones pronounced it "so lofty, so various, and so bold [in] its style that I do not hesitate to rank it amongst the most finished poems."

"What Arab art thou?" said he.

"My lord," replied Antar, "I am of the tribe of the noble Abs."

"One of its warriors," demanded Monzar, "or one of its slaves?"

"Nobility, my lord," said Antar, "amongst liberal men, is the thrust of the spear, the blow of the sword, the patience beneath the battle dust. I am the physician of the tribe of Abs when they are in sickness, their protector in disgrace, the defender of their wives when they are in trouble, and their horseman when they are in glory, and their sword when they rush to arms."

Monzar was astonished at his fluency of speech, his magnanimity, and his intrepidity, for he was then in the dishonorable state of a prisoner, and force had overpowered him. "What urged thee to this violence on my property," added Monzar, "and seizure of my camels?"

"My lord," said Antar, "the tyranny of my uncle obliged me to this act: for I was brought up with his daughter, and I had passed my life in her service. And when he saw me demand her in marriage, he asked of me as a marriage dower, a thousand Asafeer camels. I was ignorant, and knew nothing about them; so I consented to his demand, and set out in quest of them; I have out-raged you, and am consequently reduced to this miserable state."

"Hast thou then," said Monzar, "with all this fortitude and eloquence, and propriety of manners, exposed thy life to the sea of death, and endangered thine existence for the sake of an Arab girl?"

"Yes, my lord," said Antar; "it is love that emboldens to encounter dangers and horrors; and no lover is excusable but he who tastes the bitterness of absence after the sweetness of enjoyment; and there is no peril to be ap-prehended, but from a look from beneath the corner of a veil; and what mis-fortune can drive man to his destruction, but a woman who is the root and branch of it!" Then tears filled his eyes, and sighs burst from his sorrowing heart, as he thus exclaimed:

"The eyelashes of the songstress from the corner of the veil are more cutting than the edge of the cleaving scimitars; and when they wound the brave are humbled, and the corners of their eyes are flooded with tears. May God cause my uncle to drink of the draught of death at my hand! may his hand be withered, and his fingers palsied! for how could he drive one like me to destruction by his arts, and make my hopes depend on the completion of his avaricious projects. Truly Ibla, on the day of departure, bade me adieu, and said I should never return. O lightnings, waft my salutation to her, and to all the places and pastures where she dwells. O ye dwellers in the forests of tamarisks, if I die, mourn for me when my eyes are plucked out by the hungry fowls of the air. O ye steeds, mourn for a knight who could engage the lions of death in the field of battle. Alas, I am an outcast, and in sorrow. I am humbled into galling fetters, fetters that cut to my soul."

When Antar had finished, Monzar was surprised at his eloquence and fortitude and strength of mind and virtue. Now Monzar himself was one of the most eloquent of Arabs, and he was convinced that Antar was sincere in his grief; but he knew not the story of his life. Whilst Antar and Monzar were conversing, behold, the people ran away from their presence. On [Monzar's] inquiring what was the matter, "O victorious and irresistible monarch," they exclaimed, "a savage lion has appeared among us, is destroy-ing the horsemen, and dispersing the brave heroes. Spears make no impression on his carcase, and no one dares to attack him."

"Assault him," cried the King, "before he takes refuge in the forest, and cuts off the road of the travelers, and renders the ways unsafe, and we therefore be dishonored."

As soon as Antar heard this, his afflictions were relieved. "Tell your people to expose me to this lion," said he to the King, "and if he should destroy me, you will be amply revenged, and your dishonor will be cleared up: for I have slaughtered your troops, and destroyed your warriors; but should I slay the lion, reward me as I deserve, and do not refuse me justice." The King ordered the cords to be loosened: the guards came up to him and untied his hands, and were about to untie his feet also, but he cried out, "Loosen only my hands, leave my feet bound as they are, that there may be no retreat from the lion." He grasped his sword and his shield, and jumping along in his fetters, he thus exclaimed:

"Come on, thou dog of the forests and the hills! This day at my hand will I make thee drink of death. Soon wilt thou meet a knight, a lion warrior, a chief tried in battle. O then, attack not one like me, for I am a chosen hero. Attack the horsemen, thou dog of the waste, but whither wilt thou escape from me this day? Take this from my cleaving sword, that deals sorrows, deaths and pestilence from the slave of a tribe, that braves death and woe, and never fails."

Monzar was much astonished at his address to the lion, and he advanced with his attendants, to behold what Antar might do. And when they came near him, they perceived it was an immense lion, of the size of a camel, with broad nostrils and long claws; his face was wide, and ghastly was his form; his strength swelling; he grinned with his teeth clenched like a vise, and the corners of his jaws were like grappling irons. When the lion beheld Antar in his fetters, he crouched to the ground, and extended himself out; his mane bristled up; he made a spring at him: and as he approached, Antar met him with his sword, which entered by his forehead and penetrated through him, issuing out at the extremity of his backbone. "O by Abs and Adnan!" cried Antar, "I will ever be the lover of Ibla." And the lion fell down, cut in twain, and cleft into two equal portions; for the spring of the lion, and the force of the arm of the glorious warrior, just met. Then, wiping his sword on the lion, he thus spake:

"Wilt thou e'er know, O Ibla, the perils I have encountered in the land of Irak? My uncle has beguiled me with his hypocrisy and artifice, and has acted barbarously towards me in demanding the marriage dower. I plunged myself into a sea of deaths, and repaired to Irak, without friends. I drove away the camels and the shepherds singlehanded; and I was returning home burning with the flame of anxious love. I quitted them not till there arose behind me the dust of the hoofs of the high-mettled steeds. I encountered on every side the war dust, and illumined it with my thin-bladed falchion, whilst the horsemen clamored beneath it, so that I thought the thunder had let loose its uproars. As I retired, I found that my uncle had deceived me with his frauds and stratagems. But I did not fail till my horse was exhausted, and faltered in the charge and the crush of combats. Then I dismounted and drove away whole armies with my sword, as I would have driven away the camels. I rushed upon the horsemen that fiercely scoured the plain, piercing chests and eyeballs; but at the close of the day I was wearied and made captive; for my elbows and my legs were deprived of all strength. They dragged me to a noble prince, high and magnificent—May his glory endure! Then too I engaged a lion, fierce in the onset, and harsh of heart, with a face like the circumference of a shield, whose eyeballs flashed fire like hot coals. I rushed at him with my sword. I met him in my fetters, so that Monzar might bestow on me what might gratify my uncle, and favor me with the desired camels."

Monzar heard him, and beheld his acts. "This is verily a miracle of the time, and the wonder of the age and world," said he to his attendants; "his intrepidity and eloquence and perseverance are enough to confound the universe; with him I will effect with Chosroe what is the object of my wishes, and I will establish the superiority of the Arabs over the Persians."

TRANSLATED BY TERRICK HAMILTON

THE THOUSAND AND ONE NIGHTS:

THE TALE OF THE THREE APPLES

[from *Alf Laylah wa-Laylah*, One Thousand Nights and a Night]

No work of Islamic literature needs less introduction to an English reader than *The Thousand and One Nights*—and no work needs more introduction. This unwieldy anthology of stories has been greatly (one hesitates to say inordinately) appreciated in the West since Antoine Galland's French paraphrase was published, pirated, and translated in the early years of the eighteenth century. But the work has an even more complicated text-history before Galland than a translation-history after him.

In short, the kernel of the *Nights* was an old Persian book called *Hazār Afsāna* (A Thousand Tales), which also provided its thinly unifying story of Shahrazad's filibuster. That work became a matrix for innumerable other stories derived from innumerable other sources. Attempts at ordering them into their Chinese-box pattern were evidently made in the twelfth century, and they were established in something resembling their present form in Egypt in the fourteenth century.

Many types of stories and independent cycles (such as the Sinbad cycle) have been identified within the *Nights*; recent work by Gustave von Grunebaum has demonstrated that many Greco-Roman parallels can be found.[1] In general three layers of material are distinguished: the Indo-Persian archetype, which is inconspicuous; the Baghdad layer, usually recognized by its references to the reign of Caliph Harun al-Rashid; and the Cairo layer, stout and replete with topological references to Mamluk Egypt. Selections from the Baghdad and Cairo layers are included in the following pages.

[1] "Creative Borrowing: Greece in the *Arabian Nights*," *Medieval Islam* (Chicago, 1946), pp. 294–319.

It is difficult to speak of the structure of a book that keeps changing under one's nose. Less than half of the stories associated with the *Nights* are common to all of its versions. In the case of this work, above all, consideration of form must bow out in the presence of sheer delight. One of its recent editors puts it this way: "The spell of the *Nights* has possessed the imagination of mankind, and one need not read far in them to find the reason. The world which they describe is . . . one in which anything is more than likely to happen; in which almost everything does happen. The most delightful, most atrocious, most ludicrous things. It is a world of magic and reality, of sweet day-dreams and shivering awakenings, of delicate poetry and brutal horse-play. It is a world in which all the senses feast riotously, upon sights and sounds and perfumes; upon fruits and flowers and jewels; upon wines and stuffs and sweets; and upon yielding flesh, both male and female, whose beauty is incomparable. It is a world of heroic amorous encounters. . . . Romance lurks behind every shuttered window; every veiled glance begets an intrigue; and in every servant's hand nestles a scented note granting a speedy rendezvous. It is a world in which any bypath, and often the broad highway, leads straight to unexpected, unpredictable adventure; in which fate plays battledore-and-shuttlecock with men and women of high and low estate; in which no aspiration is so mad as to be unrealizable, and no day proof of what the next day may be. A world in which apes may rival men, and a butcher win the hand of a king's daughter; a world in which palaces are made of diamonds, and thrones cut from single rubies. It is a world in which all the distressingly ineluctable rules of daily living are gloriously suspended; from which individual responsibility is delightfully absent. It is the world of a legendary Damascus, a legendary Cairo, and a legendary Constantinople; the world in which a legendary Harun al-Rashid walks the streets of a legendary Baghdad. In short, it is the world of eternal fairy-tale—and there is no resisting its enchantment."[2]

[2] B. R. Redman, "Introductory Essay," *The Arabian Nights' Entertainments* (New York, 1932), pp. ix–x. The best general introduction is still Sir Richard Burton's "Terminal Essay" in *The Book of A Thousand Nights and a Night*, vol. 8 (London, 1894), pp. 59–230.

They relate, O King of the age and lord of the time and of these days, that the Caliph Harun al-Rashid summoned his Wazir Jaʾafar[3] one night and said to him, "I desire to go down into the city and question the common folk concerning the conduct of those charged with its governance; and those of whom they complain we will depose from office and those whom they commend we will promote." Quoth Jaʾafar, "Hearkening and obedience!" So the Caliph went down with Jaʾafar and Eunuch Masrur to the town and walked about the streets and markets and, as they were threading a narrow alley, they came upon a very old man with a fishing-net and crate to carry small fish on his head, and in his hands a staff; and, as he walked at a leisurely pace, he repeated these lines:—

> They say me:—Thou shinest a light to mankind
> With thy lore as the night which the Moon doth uplight!
> I answer, "A truce to your jests and your gibes;
> Without luck what is learning?—a poor-devil wight!
> If they take me to pawn with my lore in my pouch,
> With my volumes to read and my ink-case to write,
> For one day's provision they never could pledge me;
> As likely on Doomsday to draw bill at sight:"
> How poorly, indeed, doth it fare wi' the poor,
> With his pauper existence and beggarly plight:
> In summer he faileth provision to find;
> In winter the fire-pot's his only delight:
> The street-dogs with bite and with bark to him rise,
> And each losel receives him with bark and with bite:
> If he lift up his voice and complain of his wrong,
> None pities or heeds him, however he's right;
> And when sorrows and evils like these he must brave
> His happiest homestead were down in the grave.

When the Caliph heard his verses he said to Jaʾafar, "See this poor man and note his verses, for surely they point to his necessities." Then he accosted him and asked, "O Shaykh, what be thine occupation?" and the poor man answered, "O my lord, I am a fisherman with a family to keep and I have been out between midday and this time; and not a thing hath Allah made my portion wherewithal to feed my family. I cannot even pawn myself to buy them a supper and I hate and disgust my life and I hanker after death."

[3] The vizier's name would have been more accurately transliterated Jaᶜfar. [Ed.]

Quoth the Caliph, "Say me, wilt thou return with us to Tigris' bank and cast thy net on my luck, and whatsoever turneth up I will buy of thee for an hundred gold pieces?" The man rejoiced when he heard these words and said, "On my head be it! I will go back with you"; and, returning with them river-wards, made a cast and waited a while; then he hauled in the rope and dragged the net ashore and there appeared in it a chest padlocked and heavy.

The Caliph examined it and lifted it finding it weighty; so he gave the fisherman two hundred dinars and sent him about his business; whilst Masrur, aided by the Caliph, carried the chest to the palace and set it down and lighted the candles. Ja᾽afar and Masrur then broke it open and found therein a basket of palm-leaves corded with red worsted. This they cut open and saw within it a piece of carpet which they lifted out, and under it was a woman's mantilla folded in four, which they pulled out; and at the bottom of the chest they came upon a young lady, fair as a silver ingot, slain and cut into nineteen pieces.

When the Caliph looked upon her he cried, "Alas!" and tears ran down his cheeks and turning to Ja᾽afar he said, "O dog of Wazirs, shall folk be murdered in our reign and be cast into the river to be a burden and a responsibility for us on the Day of Doom? By Allah, we must avenge this woman on her murderer and he shall be made die the worst of deaths!" And presently he added, "Now, as surely as we are descended from the Sons of Abbas, if thou bring us not him who slew her, that we do her justice on him, I will hang thee at the gate of my palace, thee and forty of thy kith and kin by thy side." And the Caliph was wroth with exceeding rage. Quoth Ja᾽afar, "Grant me three days' delay"; and quoth the Caliph, "We grant thee this." So Ja᾽afar went out from before him and returned to his own house, full of sorrow and saying to himself, "How shall I find him who murdered this damsel, that I may bring him before the Caliph? If I bring other than the murderer, it will be laid to my charge by the Lord: in very sooth I wot not what to do."

He kept his house three days and on the fourth day the Caliph sent one of the Chamberlains for him and, as he came into the presence, asked him, "Where is the murderer of the damsel?" to which answered Ja᾽afar, "O Commander of the Faithful, am I inspector of murdered folk that I should ken who killed her?" The Caliph was furious at his answer and bade hang him before the palace gate and commanded that a crier cry through the streets of Baghdad, "Whoso would see the hanging of Ja᾽afar, the Barmaki, Wazir of the Caliph, with forty of the Barmecides, his cousins and kinsmen, before the palace gate, let him come and let him look!" The people flocked out from all the quarters of the city to witness the execution of Ja°afar and his kinsmen, not knowing the cause.

Then they set up the gallows and made Ja°afar and the others stand underneath in readiness for execution, but whilst every eye was looking for the Caliph's signal, and the crowd wept for Ja°afar and his cousins of the Barmecides, lo and behold! a young man fair of face and neat of dress and of favour like the moon raining light, with eyes black and bright, and brow flower-white, and cheeks red as rose and young down where the beard grows, and a mole like a grain of ambergris, pushed his way through the people till he stood immediately before the Wazir and said to him, "Safety to thee from this strait, O Prince of the Emirs and Asylum of the poor! I am the man who slew the woman ye found in the chest, so hang me for her and do her justice on me!"

When Ja°afar heard the youth's confession he rejoiced at his own deliverance, but grieved and sorrowed for the fair youth; and whilst they were yet talking, behold, another man well stricken in years pressed forwards through the people and thrust his way amid the populace till he came to Ja°afar and the youth, whom he saluted saying, "Ho thou the Wazir and Prince sans-peer! believe not the words of this youth. Of a surety none murdered the damsel but I; take her wreak on me this moment; for, an thou do not thus, I will require it of thee before Almighty Allah." Then quoth the young man, "O Wazir, this is an old man in his dotage who wotteth not whatso he saith ever, and I am he who murdered her, so do thou avenge her on me!" Quoth the old man, "O my son, thou art young and desirest the joys of the world and I am old and weary and surfeited with the world: I will offer my life as a ransom for thee and for the Wazir and his cousins. No one murdered the damsel but I, so Allah upon thee, make haste to hang me, for no life is left in me now that hers is gone."

The Wazir marvelled much at all this strangeness and, taking the young man and the old man, carried them before the Caliph, where, after kissing the ground seven times between his hands, he said, "O Commander of the Faithful, I bring thee the murderer of the damsel!" "Where is he?" asked the Caliph and Ja°afar answered, "This young man saith, I am the murderer, and this old man giving him the lie saith, I am the murderer, and behold, here are the twain standing before thee."

The Caliph looked at the old man and the young man and asked, "Which of you killed the girl?" The young man replied, "No one slew her save I"; and the old man answered, "Indeed none killed her but myself." Then said the Caliph to Ja°afar, "Take the twain and hang them both"; but Ja°afar rejoined, "Since one of them was the murderer, to hang the other were mere injustice." "By Him who raised the firmament and dispread the earth like a carpet," cried the youth, "I am he who slew the damsel"; and he went on to describe the manner of her murder and the basket, the mantilla and the bit of carpet, in fact all that the Caliph had found upon her. So the Caliph was certified that the young man was the murderer; whereat he wondered and asked him, "What was the cause of thy wrongfully doing this damsel to die and what made thee confess the murder without the bastinado, and what brought thee here to yield up thy life, and what made thee say Do her wreak upon me?"

The youth answered, "Know, O Commander of the Faithful, that this woman was my wife and the mother of my children; also my first cousin and the daughter of my paternal uncle, this old man who is my father's own brother. When I married her she was a maid and Allah blessed me with three male children by her; she loved me and served me and I saw no evil in her, for I also loved her with fondest love. Now on the first day of this month she fell ill with grievous sickness and I fetched in physicians to her; but recovery came to her little by little and, when I wished her to go to the Hammam-bath, she said:—There is a something I long for before I go to the bath and I long for it with an exceeding longing. To hear is to comply, said I. And what is it? Quoth she, I have a queasy craving for an apple, to smell it and bite a bit of it. I replied:—Hadst thou a thousand longings I would try to satisfy them! So I went on the instant into the city and sought for apples but could find none; yet, had they cost a gold piece each, would I have bought them.

"I was vexed at this and went home and said:—O daughter of my uncle, by Allah I can find none! She was distressed, being yet very weakly, and her weakness increased greatly on her that night and I felt anxious and alarmed on her account. As soon as morning dawned I went out again and made the round of the gardens, one by one, but found no apples anywhere. At last there met me an old gardener, of whom I asked about them and he answered:—O my son, this fruit is a rarity with us and is not now to be found save in the garden of the Commander of the Faithful at Bassorah, where the gardener keepeth it for the Caliph's eating.

"I returned to my house troubled by my ill-success; and my love for my wife and my affection moved me to undertake the journey. So I gat me ready and set out and travelled fifteen days and nights, going and coming, and brought her three apples which I bought from the gardener for three dinars. But when I went in to my wife and set them before her, she took no pleasure in them and let them lie by her side; for her weakness and fever had increased on her and her malady lasted without abating ten days, after which she began to recover health. So I left my house and betaking me to my shop sat there buying and selling; and about midday behold, a great ugly black slave, long as a lance and broad as a bench, passed by my shop holding in hand one of the three apples wherewith he was playing. Quoth I:—O my good slave, tell me whence thou tookest that apple, that I may get the like of it? He laughed and answered:—I got it from my mistress, for I had been absent and on my return I found her lying ill with three apples by her side, and she said to me:—My horned wittol of a husband made a journey for them to Bassorah and bought them for three dinars. So I ate and drank with her and took this one from her.

"When I heard such words from the slave, O Commander of the Faithful, the world grew black before my face, and I arose and locked up my shop and went home beside myself for excess of rage. I looked for the apples and finding only two of the three asked my wife:—O my cousin, where is the third apple?; and raising her head languidly she answered:—I wot not, O son of my uncle, where 'tis gone! This convinced me that the slave had spoken the truth, so I took a knife and coming behind her got upon her breast without a word said and cut her throat. Then I hewed off her head and her limbs in pieces and, wrapping her in her mantilla and a rag of carpet, hurriedly sewed up the whole which I set in a chest and, locking it tight, loaded it on my he-mule and threw it into the Tigris with my own hands. So Allah upon thee, O Commander of the Faithful, make haste to hang me, as I fear lest she appeal for vengeance on Resurrection Day. For, when I had thrown her into the river and one knew aught of it, as I went back home I found my eldest son crying and yet he knew naught of what I had done with his mother. I asked him:—What hath made thee weep, my boy?; and he answered:— I took one of the three apples which were by my mammy and went down into the lane to play with my brethren when behold, a big long black slave snatched it from my hand and said, Whence hadst thou this? Quoth I, My father travelled far for it, and brought it from Bassorah for my mother who was ill and two other apples for which he paid three ducats. He took no heed of my words and I asked for the apple a second and a third time, but he cuffed me and kicked me and went off with it. I was afraid lest my mother should swinge me on account of the apple, so for fear of her I went with my brother outside the city and stayed there till evening closed in upon us; and indeed I am in fear of her; and now by Allah, O my father, say nothing to her of this or it may add to her ailment!

"When I heard what my child said I knew that the slave was he who had foully slandered my wife, the daughter of my uncle, and was certified that I had slain her wrongfully. So I wept with exceeding weeping and presently this old man, my paternal uncle and her father, came in; and I told him what had happened and he sat down by my side and wept and we ceased not weeping till midnight. We have kept up mourning for her these last five days and we lamented her in the deepest sorrow for that she was unjustly done to die. This came from the gratuitous lying of the slave, the blackamoor, and this was the manner of my killing her; so I conjure thee, by the honour of thine ancestors, make haste to kill me and do her justice upon me, as there is no living for me after her!"

The Caliph marvelled at his words and said, "By Allah the young man is excusable: I will hang none but the accursed slave and I will do a deed which shall comfort the ill-at-ease and suffering, and which shall please the All-glorious King." Then he turned to Jaʾafar and said to him, "Bring before me this accursed slave who was the sole cause of this calamity; and, if thou bring him not before me within three days, thou shalt be slain in his stead." So Jaʾafar fared forth weeping and saying, "Two deaths have already beset me, nor shall the crock come off safe from every shock. In this matter craft and cunning are of no avail; but He who preserved my life the first time can preserve it a second time. By Allah, I will not leave my house during the three days of life which remain to me and let the Truth (whose perfection be praised!) do e'en as He will." So he kept his house three days, and on the fourth day he summoned the Kazis and legal witnesses and made his last will and testament, and took leave of his children weeping.

Presently in came a messenger from the Caliph and said to him, "The Commander of the Faithful is in the most violent rage that can be, and he sendeth to seek thee and he sweareth that the day shall certainly not pass without thy being hanged unless the slave be forthcoming." When Jaʾafar heard this he wept, and his children and slaves and all who were in the house wept with him. After he had bidden adieu to everybody except his youngest daughter, he proceeded to farewell her; for he loved this wee one, who was a beautiful child, more than all his other children; and he pressed her to his breast and kissed her and wept bitterly at parting from her; when he felt something round inside the bosom of her dress and asked her, "O my little maid, what is in thy bosom pocket?"; "O my father," she replied, "it is an apple with the name of our Lord the Caliph written upon it. Rayhan our slave brought it to me four days ago and would not let me have it till I gave him two dinars for it."

When Ja²afar heard speak of the slave and the apple, he was glad and put his hand into his child's pocket and drew out the apple and knew it and rejoiced saying, "O ready Dispeller of trouble!" Then he bade them bring the slave and said to him, "Fie upon thee, Rayhan! whence haddest thou this apple?" "By Allah, O my master," he replied, "though a lie may get a man once off, yet may truth get him off, and well off, again and again. I did not steal this apple from thy palace nor from the gardens of the Commander of the Faithful. The fact is that five days ago, as I was walking along one of the alleys of this city, I saw some little ones at play and this apple in hand of one of them. So I snatched it from him and beat him and he cried and said, O youth this apple is my mother's and she is ill. She told my father how she longed for an apple, so he travelled to Bassorah and bought her three apples for three gold pieces, and I took one of them to play withal. He wept again, but I paid no heed to what he said and carried it off and brought it here, and my little lady bought it of me for two dinars of gold. And this is the whole story."

When Ja²afar heard his words he marvelled that the murder of the damsel and all this misery should have been caused by his slave; he grieved for the relation of the slave to himself, while rejoicing over his own deliverance, and he repeated these lines:—

> If ill betide thee through thy slave,
> Make him forthright thy sacrifice;
> A many serviles thou shalt find,
> But life comes once and never twice.

Then he took the slave's hand and, leading him to the Caliph, related the story from first to last and the Caliph marvelled with extreme astonishment, and laughed till he fell on his back and ordered that the story be recorded and be made public amongst the people. But Ja²afar said, "Marvel not, O Commander of the Faithful, at this adventure, for it is not more wondrous than the History of the Wazir Nur al-Din Ali of Egypt and his brother Shams al-Din Mohammed." Quoth the Caliph, "Out with it; but what can be stranger than this story?" And Ja²afar answered, "O Commander of the Faithful, I will not tell it thee, save on condition that thou pardon my slave"; and the Caliph rejoined, "If it be indeed more wondrous than that of the three apples, I grant thee his blood, and if not I will surely slay thy slave." So Ja²afar began in these words the Tale of Nur al-Din Ali and his son Badr al-Din Hasan.

MARUF THE COBBLER

There dwelt once upon a time in the God-guarded city of Cairo a cobbler who lived by patching old shoes. His name was Ma³aruf[1] and he had a wife called Fatimah, whom the folk had nicknamed "The Dung"; for that she was a whorish, worthless wretch, scanty of shame and mickle of mischief. She ruled her spouse and used to abuse him and curse him a thousand times a day; and he feared her malice and dreaded her misdoings; for that he was a sensible man and careful of his repute, but poor-conditioned. When he earned much, he spent it on her, and when he gained little, she revenged herself on his body that night, leaving him no peace and making his night black as her book; for she was even as of one like her saith the poet:—

> How manifold nights have I passed with my wife
> In the saddest plight with all misery rife:
> Would Heaven when first I went in to her
> With a cup of cold poison I'd taken her life.

Amongst other afflictions which befell him from her one day she said to him, "O Ma³aruf, I wish thee to bring me this night a vermicelli-cake dressed with bees' honey." He replied, "So Allah Almighty aid me to its price, I will bring it thee. By Allah, I have no dirhams to-day, but our Lord will make things easy." She rejoined, "I wot naught of these words; whether He aid thee or aid thee not, look thou come not to me save with the vermicelli and bees' honey; and if thou come without it I will make thy night black as thy fortune whenas thou marriedst me and fellest into my hand." Quoth he, "Allah is bountiful!" and going out with grief scattering itself from his body, prayed the dawn prayer and opened his shop, saying, "I beseech thee, O Lord, to vouchsafe me the price of the Kunafah and ward off from me the mischief of yonder wicked woman this night!" After which he sat in the shop till noon, but no work came to him and his fear of his wife redoubled.

Then he arose and locking his shop, went out perplexed as to how he should do in the matter of the vermicelli-cake, seeing he had not even the where-withal to buy bread. Presently he came up to the shop of the Kunafah-seller and stood before it distraught, whilst his eyes brimmed with tears. The pastry cook glanced at him and said, "O Master Ma³aruf, why dost thou weep? Tell me what hath befallen thee." So he acquainted him with his case,

---

[1] The cobbler's name would have been more accurately transliterated Maᶜrūf. [Ed.]

saying, "My wife is a shrew, a virago who would have me bring her a Kunafah; but I have sat in my shop till past midday and have not gained even the price of bread; wherefore I am in fear of her." The cook laughed and said, "No harm shall come to thee. How many pounds wilt thou have?" "Five pounds," answered Maᵓaruf. So the man weighed him out five pounds of vermicelli-cake and said to him, "I have clarified butter, but no bees' honey. Here is drip-honey, however, which is better than bees' honey; and what harm will there be, if it be with drip-honey?" Maᵓaruf was ashamed to object, because the pastry cook was to have patience with him for the price, and said, "Give it me with drip-honey." So he fried a vermicelli-cake for him with butter and drenched it with drip-honey, till it was fit to present to Kings. Then he asked him, "Dost thou want bread and cheese?"; and Maᵓaruf answered, "Yes." So he gave him four half dirhams worth of bread and one of cheese, and the vermicelli was ten nusfs. Then said he, "Know, O Maᵓaruf, that thou owest me fifteen nusfs; so go to thy wife and make merry and take this nusf for the Hammam; and thou shalt have credit for a day or two or three till Allah provide thee with thy daily bread. And straiten not thy wife, for I will have patience with thee till such time as thou shalt have dirhams to spare." So Maᵓaruf took the vermicelli-cake and bread and cheese and went away, with a heart at ease, blessing the pastry cook and saying, "Extolled be Thy perfection, O my Lord! How bountiful art Thou!"

When he came home, his wife enquired of him, "Hast thou brought the vermicelli-cake?"; and, replying "Yes," he set it before her. She looked at it and seeing it was dressed with cane-honey, said to him, "Did I not bid thee bring it with bees' honey? Wilt thou contrary my wish and have it dressed with cane-honey?" He excused himself to her, saying, "I bought it not save on credit"; but said she, "This talk is idle; I will not eat Kunafah save with bees' honey." And she was wroth with it and threw it in his face, saying, "Begone, thou pimp, and bring me other than this!" Then she dealt him a buffet on the cheek and knocked out one of his teeth. The blood ran down upon his breast and for stress of anger he smote her on the head a single blow and a slight; whereupon she clutched his beard and fell to shouting out and saying, "Help, O Moslems!" So the neighbours came in and freed his beard from her grip; then they reproved and reproached her, saying, "We are all content to eat Kunafah with cane-honey. Why, then, wilt thou oppress this poor man thus? Verily, this is disgraceful in thee!" And they went on to soothe her till they made peace between her and him.

But, when the folk were gone, she sware that she would not eat of the vermicelli, and Ma³aruf, burning with hunger, said in himself, "She sweareth that she will not eat; so I will e'en eat." Then he ate, and when she saw him eating, she said, "Inshallah, may the eating of it be poison to destroy the far one's body." Quoth he, "It shall not be at thy bidding," and went on eating, laughing and saying, "Thou swarest that thou wouldst not eat of this; but Allah is bountiful, and tomorrow night, an the Lord decree, I will bring thee Kunafah dressed with bees' honey, and thou shalt eat it alone." And he applied himself to appeasing her, whilst she called down curses upon him; and she ceased not to rail at him and revile him with gross abuse till the morning, when she bared her forearm to beat him. Quoth he, "Give me time and I will bring thee other vermicelli-cake."

Then he went out to the mosque and prayed, after which he betook himself to his shop and opening it, sat down; but hardly had he done this when up came two runners from the Kazi's court and said to him, "Up with thee, speak with the Kazi, for thy wife hath complained of thee to him and her favour is thus and thus." He recognised her by their description; and saying, "May Allah Almighty torment her!" walked with them till he came to the Kazi's presence, where he found Fatimah standing with her arm bound up and her face-veil besmeared with blood; and she was weeping and wiping away her tears. Quoth the Kazi, "Ho man, hast thou no fear of Allah the Most High? Why hast thou beaten this good woman and broken her forearm and knocked out her tooth and entreated her thus?" And quoth Ma³aruf, "If I beat her or put out her tooth, sentence me to what thou wilt; but in truth the case was thus and thus and the neighbours made peace between me and her." And he told him the story from first to last.

Now this Kazi was a benevolent man; so he brought out to him a quarter dinar, saying, "O man, take this and get her Kunafah with bees' honey and do ye make peace, thou and she." Quoth Ma³aruf, "Give it to her." So she took it and the Kazi made peace between them, saying, "O wife, obey thy husband; and thou, O man, deal kindly with her." Then they left the court, reconciled at the Kazi's hands, and the woman went one way, whilst her husband returned by another way to his shop and sat there, when, behold, the runners came up to him and said, "Give us our fee." Quoth he, "The Kazi took not of me aught; on the contrary, he gave me a quarter dinar." But quoth they, " 'Tis no concern of ours whether the Kazi took of thee or gave to thee, and if thou give us not our fee, we will exact it in despite of thee." And they fell to dragging him about the market; so he sold his tools and gave them half a dinar, whereupon they let him go and went away, whilst he put his hand to his cheek and sat sorrowful, for that he had no tools wherewith to work.

Presently, up came two ill-favoured fellows and said to them, "Come, O man, and speak with the Kazi; for thy wife hath complained of thee to him." Said he, "He made peace between us just now." But said they, "We come from another Kazi, and thy wife hath complained of thee to our Kazi." So he arose and went with them to their Kazi, calling on Allah for aid against her; and when he saw her, he said to her, "Did we not make peace, good woman?" Whereupon she cried, "There abideth no peace between me and thee." Accordingly he came forward and told the Kazi his story, adding, "And indeed the Kazi Such-an-one made peace between us this very hour." Whereupon the Kazi said to her, "O strumpet, since ye two have made peace with each other, why comest thou to me complaining?" Quoth she, "He beat me after that"; but quoth the Kazi, "Make peace each with other, and beat her not again, and she will cross thee no more." So they made peace and the Kazi said to Maᵓaruf, "Give the runners their fee." So he gave them their fee and going back to his shop, opened it and sat down, as he were a drunken man for excess of the chagrin which befell him.

Presently, while he was still sitting, behold, a man came up to him and said, "O Maᵓaruf, rise and hide thyself, for thy wife hath complained of thee to the High Court and Abu Tabak is after thee." So he shut his shop and fled towards the Gate of Victory. He had five nusfs of silver left of the price of the lasts and gear; and therewith he bought four worth of bread and one of cheese, as he fled from her. Now it was the winter season and the hour of midafternoon prayer; so, when he came out among the rubbish-mounds the rain descended upon him, like water from the mouths of water-skins, and his clothes were drenched. He therefore entered the ᵓAdiliyah, where he saw a ruined place and therein a deserted cell without a door; and in it he took refuge and found shelter from the rain. The tears streamed from his eyelids, and he fell to complaining of what had betided him and saying, "Whither shall I flee from this whore? I beseech Thee, O Lord, to vouchsafe me one who shall conduct me to a far country, where she shall not know the way to me!"

Now while he sat weeping, behold, the wall clave and there came forth to him therefrom one of tall stature, whose aspect caused his body-pile to bristle and his flesh to creep, and said to him, "O man, what aileth thee that thou disturbest me this night? These two hundred years have I dwelt here and have never seen any enter this place and do as thou dost. Tell me what thou wishest and I will accomplish thy need, as ruth for thee hath got hold upon my heart." Quoth Maᵓaruf, "Who and what art thou?"; and quoth he, "I am the Haunter of this place." So Maᵓaruf told him all that had befallen him with his wife and he said, "Wilt thou have me convey thee to a country, where thy wife shall know no way to thee?" "Yes," said Maᵓaruf; and the other, "Then mount my back." So he mounted on his back and he flew with him from after suppertide till daybreak, when he set him down on the top of a high mountain and said to him, "O mortal, descend this mountain and thou wilt see the gate of a city. Enter it, for therein thy wife cannot come at thee." He then left him and went his way, whilst Maᵓaruf abode in amazement and perplexity till the sun rose, when he said to himself, "I will up with me and go down into the city: indeed there is no profit in my abiding upon this highland."

So he descended to the mountain-foot and saw a city girt by towering walls, full of lofty palaces and gold-adorned buildings which was a delight to beholders. He entered in at the gate and found it a place such as lightened the grieving heart; but, as he walked through the streets the townsfolk stared at him as a curiosity and gathered about him, marvelling at his dress, for it was unlike theirs. Presently, one of them said to him, "O man, art thou a stranger?" "Yes." "What countryman art Thou?" "I am from the city of Cairo the Auspicious." "And when didst thou leave Cairo?" "I left it yesterday, at the hour of afternoon prayer." Whereupon the man laughed at him and cried out, saying, "Come look, O folk, at this man and hear what he saith!" Quoth they, "What doth he say?"; and quoth the townsman, "He pretendeth that he cometh from Cairo and left it yesterday at the hour of afternoon prayer!" At this they all laughed and gathering round Maᵓaruf, said to him, "O man, art thou mad to talk thus? How canst thou pretend that thou leftest Cairo at midafternoon yesterday and foundest thyself this morning here, when the truth is that between our city and Cairo lieth a full year's journey?" Quoth he, "None is mad but you. As for me, I speak sooth, for here is bread which I brought with me from Cairo, and see, 'tis yet new." Then he showed them the bread and they stared at it, for it was unlike their country bread. So the crowd increased about him and they said one to another, "This is Cairo bread: look at it"; and he became a gazing-stock in the city and some believed him, whilst others gave him the lie and made mock of him.

Whilst this was going on, behold, up came a merchant riding on a she-mule and followed by two black slaves, and brake a way through the people, saying,

"O folk, are ye not ashamed to mob this stranger and make mock of him and scoff at him?" And he went on to rate them, till he drave them away from Maʾaruf, and none could make him any answer. Then he said to the stranger, "Come, O my brother, no harm shall betide thee from these folk. Verily they have no shame." So he took him and carrying him to a spacious and richly-adorned house, seated him in a speak-room fit for a King, whilst he gave an order to his slaves, who opened a chest and brought out to him a dress such as might be worn by a merchant worth a thousand. He clad him therewith and Maʾaruf, being a seemly man, became as he were Consul to the merchants. Then his host called for food and they set before them a tray full of all manner exquisite viands.

The twain ate and drank and the merchant said to Maʾaruf, "O my brother, what is thy name?" "My name is Maʾaruf and I'm a cobbler by trade and patch old shoes." "What countryman art thou?" "I am from Cairo." "What quarter? Dost thou know Cairo?" "I am of its children. I come from the Red Street." "And whom dost thou know in the Red Street?" "I know such an one and such an one," answered Maʾaruf and named several people to him. Quoth the other, "Knowest thou Shaykh Ahmad the druggist?" "He was my next neighbour, wall to wall." "Is he well?" "Yes." "How many sons hath he?" "Three, Mustafa, Mohammed and Ali." "And what hath Allah done with them?" "As for Mustafa, he is well and he is a learned man, a professor: Mohammed is a druggist and opened him a shop beside that of his father, after he had married, and his wife hath borne him a son named Hasan." "Allah gladden thee with good news!" said the merchant; and Maʾaruf continued, "As for Ali, he was my friend, when we were boys, and we always played together, I and he. We used to go in the guise of the children of the Nazarenes and enter the church and steal the books of the Christians and sell them and buy food with the price. It chanced once that the Nazarenes caught us with a book, whereupon they complained of us to our folk and said to Ali's father:—An thou hinder not thy son from troubling us, we will complain of thee to the King. So he appeased them and gave Ali a thrashing; wherefore he ran away none knew whither and he hath now been absent twenty years and no man hath brought news of him." Quoth the host, "I am that very Ali, son of Shaykh Ahmad the druggist, and thou art my play-mate Maʾaruf."

So they saluted each other and after the salam Ali said, "Tell me why, O Maʾaruf, thou camest from Cairo to this city." Then he told him all that had befallen him of ill-doing with this wife Fatimah the Dung and said, "So, when her annoy waxed on me, I fled from her towards the Gate of Victory and went forth the city. Presently, the rain fell heavy on me; so I entered a ruined cell in the ꝰAdiliyah and sat there, weeping; whereupon there came forth to me the Haunter of the place, which was an Ifrit of the Jinn, and questioned me. I acquainted him with my case and he took me on his back and flew with me all night between heaven and earth, till he set me down on yonder mountain and gave me to know of this city. So I came down from the mountain and entered the city, when the people crowded about me and questioned me. I told them that I had left Cairo yesterday, but they believed me not, and presently thou camest up and driving the folk away from me, carriedst me to this house. Such, then, is the cause of my quitting Cairo; and thou, what object brought thee hither?"

Quoth Ali, "The giddiness of folly turned my head when I was seven years old, from which time I wandered from land to land and city to city, till I came to this city, the name whereof is Ikhtiyan al-Khatan. I found its people an hospitable folk and a kindly, compassionate for the poor man and selling to him on credit and believing all he said. So quoth I to them:—I am a merchant and have preceded my packs and I need a place wherein to bestow my baggage. And they believed me and assigned me a lodging. Then quoth I to them:—Is there any of you will lend me a thousand dinars, till my loads arrive, when I will repay it to him; for I am in want of certain things before my goods come? They gave me what I asked and I went to the merchants' bazaar, where, seeing goods, I bought them and sold them next day at a profit of fifty gold pieces and bought others. And I consorted with the folk and treated them liberally, so that they loved me, and I continued to sell and buy, till I grew rich. Know, O my brother, that the proverb saith, The world is show and trickery: and the land where none wotteth thee, there do whatso liketh thee. Thou too, an thou say to all who ask thee, I'm a cobbler by trade and poor withal, and I fled from my wife and left Cairo yesterday, they will not believe thee and thou wilt be a laughing-stock among them as long as thou abidest in the city; whilst, an thou tell them, An Ifrit brought me hither, they will take fright at thee and none will come near thee; for they will say, This man is possessed of an Ifrit and harm will betide whoso approacheth him. And such public report will be dishonouring both to thee and to me, because they ken I come from Cairo."

Maꝰaruf asked:—"How then shall I do?" and Ali answered, "I will tell thee how thou shalt do, Inshallah! Tomorrow I will give thee a thousand dinars and a she-mule to ride and a black slave, who shall walk before thee and guide thee to the gate of the merchants' bazaar; and do thou go in to them. I will be there sitting amongst them, and when I see thee, I will rise to thee and salute thee with the salam and kiss thy hand and make a great man of thee. Whenever I ask thee of any kind of stuff, saying, Hast thou brought with thee aught of such a kind? do thou answer, Plenty. And if they question me of thee, I will praise thee and magnify thee in their eyes and say to them, Get him a storehouse and a shop. I also will give thee out for a man of great wealth and generosity; and if a beggar come to thee, bestow upon him what thou mayst; so will they put faith in what I say and believe in thy greatness and generosity and love thee. Then will I invite thee to my house and invite all the merchants on thy account and bring together thee and them, so that all may know thee and thou know them, whereby thou shalt sell and buy and take and give with them; nor will it be long ere thou become a man of money."

Accordingly, on the morrow he gave him a thousand dinars and a suit of clothes and a black slave and mounting him on a she-mule, said to him, "Allah give thee quittance of responsibility for all this, inasmuch as thou art my friend and it behoveth me to deal generously with thee. Have no care; but put away from thee the thought of thy wife's misways and name her not to any." "Allah requite thee with good!" replied Maᵓaruf and rode on, preceded by his blackamoor till the slave brought him to the gate of the merchants' bazaar, where they were all seated, and amongst them Ali, who when he saw him, rose and threw himself upon him, crying, "A blessed day, O Merchant Maᵓaruf, O man of good works and kindness!" And he kissed his hand before the merchants and said to them, "Our brothers, ye are honoured by knowing the merchant Maᵓaruf." So they saluted him, and Ali signed to them to make much of him, wherefore he was magnified in their eyes. Then Ali helped him to dismount from his she-mule and saluted him with the salam; after which he took the merchants apart, one after other, and vaunted Maᵓaruf to them. They asked, "Is this man a merchant?"; and he answered, "Yes; and indeed he is the chiefest of merchants, there liveth not a wealthier than he; for his wealth and the riches of his father and forefathers are famous among the merchants of Cairo. He hath partners in Hind and Sind and Al-Yaman and is high in repute for generosity. So know ye his rank and exalt ye his degree and do him service, and wot also that his coming to your city is not for the sake of traffic, and none other save to divert himself with the sight of folks' countries: indeed, he hath no need of strangerhood for the sake of gain and profit, having wealth that fires cannot consume, and I am one of his servants."

And he ceased not to extol him, till they set him above their heads and began to tell one another of his qualities.

Then they gathered round him and offered him junkets and sherbets, and even the Consul of the Merchants came to him and saluted him; whilst Ali proceeded to ask him, in the presence of the traders, "O my lord, haply thou hast brought with thee somewhat of such and such a stuff?"; and Maʾaruf answered, "Plenty." Now Ali had that day shown him various kinds of costly cloths and had taught him the names of the different stuffs, dear and cheap. Then said one of the merchants, "O my lord, hast thou brought with thee yellow broad cloth?"; and Maʾaruf said, "Plenty"! Quoth another, "And gazelles' blood red?"; and quoth the Cobbler, "Plenty"; and as often as he asked him of aught, he made him the same answer. So the other said, "O Merchant Ali, had thy countryman a mind to transport a thousand loads of costly stuffs, he could do so"; and Ali said, "He would take them from a single one of his storehouses, and miss naught thereof."

Now whilst they were sitting, behold, up came a beggar and went the round of the merchants. One gave him a half dirham and another a copper, but most of them gave him nothing, till he came to Maʾaruf who pulled out a handful of gold and gave it to him, whereupon he blessed him and went his ways. The merchants marvelled at this and said, "Verily, this is a King's bestowal for he gave the beggar gold without count, and were he not a man of vast wealth and money without end, he had not given a beggar a handful of gold." After a while, there came to him a poor woman and he gave her a handful of gold; whereupon she went away, blessing him, and told the other beggars, who came to him, one after other, and he gave them each a handful of gold, till he disbursed the thousand dinars. Then he struck hand upon hand and said, "Allah is our sufficient aid and excellent is the Agent!" Quoth the Consul, "What aileth thee, O Merchant Maʾaruf?"; and quoth he, "It seemeth that the most part of the people of this city are poor and needy; had I known their misery I would have brought with me a large sum of money in my saddle-bags and given largesse thereof to the poor. I fear me I may be long abroad and 'tis not in my nature to baulk a beggar; and I have no gold left: so, if a pauper come to me, what shall I say to him?" Quoth the Consul, "Say, Allah will send thee thy daily bread!"; but Maʾaruf replied, "That is not my practice and I am care-ridden because of this. Would I had other thousand dinars, wherewith to give alms till my baggage come!" "Have no care for that," quoth the Consul and sending one of his dependents for a thousand dinars, handed them to Maʾaruf, who went on giving them to every beggar who passed till the call to noon prayer. Then they entered the Cathedral mosque and prayed the noon prayers, and what was left him of the thousand gold pieces he scattered on the heads of the worshippers. This drew the people's attention to him and they blessed him, whilst the merchants marvelled at the abundance of his generosity and openhandedness. Then he turned to another trader and borrowing of him other thousand ducats, gave these also away, whilst Merchant Ali looked on at what he did, but could not speak. He ceased not to do this till the call to midafternoon prayer, when he entered the mosque and prayed and distributed the rest of the money. On this wise, by the time they locked the doors of the bazaar, he had borrowed five thousand sequins and given them away, saying to every one of whom he took aught, "Wait till my baggage come when, if thou desire gold I will give thee gold, and if thou desire stuffs, thou shalt have stuffs; for I have no end of them."

At eventide Merchant Ali invited Maᵓaruf and the rest of the traders to an entertainment and seated him in the upper end, the place of honour, where he talked of nothing but cloths and jewels, and whenever they made mention to him of aught, he said, "I have plenty of it." Next day, he again repaired to the market street where he showed a friendly bias towards the merchants and borrowed of them more money, which he distributed to the poor: nor did he leave doing thus twenty days, till he had borrowed threescore thousand dinars, and still there came no baggage, no, nor a burning plague. At last folk began to clamour for their money and say, "The merchant Maᵓaruf's baggage cometh not. How long will he take people's monies and give them to the poor?" And quoth one of them, "My rede is that we speak to Merchant Ali." So they went to him and said, "O Merchant Ali, Merchant Maᵓaruf's baggage cometh not." Said he, "Have patience, it cannot fail to come soon." Then he took Maᵓaruf aside and said to him, "O Maᵓaruf, what fashion is this? Did I bid thee brown the bread or burn it? The merchants clamour for their coin and tell me that thou owest them sixty thousand dinars, which thou hast borrowed and given away to the poor. How wilt thou satisfy the folk, seeing that thou neither sellest nor buyest?" Said Maᵓaruf, "What matters it; and what are threescore thousand dinars? When my baggage shall come, I will pay them in stuffs or in gold and silver, as they will." Quoth Merchant Ali, "Allah is Most Great! Hast thou then any baggage?"; and he said, "Plenty." Cried the other, "Allah and the Hallows requite thee thine impudence! Did I teach thee this saying, that thou shouldst repeat it to me? But I will acquaint the folk with thee." Maᵓaruf rejoined, "Begone and prate no more! Am I a poor man? I have endless wealth in my baggage and as soon as it cometh, they shall have their money's worth, two for one. I have no need of them." At this Merchant Ali waxed wroth and said, "Unmannerly wight that thou art, I will teach thee to lie to me and not be ashamed!" Said Maᵓaruf, "E'en work the worst thy hand can do! They must wait till my baggage come, when they shall have their due and more."

So Ali left him and went away, saying in himself, "I praised him whilome and if I blame him now, I make myself out a liar and become of those of whom it is said:—Whoso praiseth and then blameth lieth twice." And he knew not what to do. Presently, the traders came to him and said, "O Merchant Ali, hast thou spoken to him?" Said he, "O folk, I am ashamed and, though he owe me a thousand dinars, I cannot speak to him. When ye lent him your money ye consulted me not; so ye have no claim on me. Dun him yourselves, and if he pay you not, complain of him to the King of the city, saying:—He is an impostor who hath imposed upon us. And he will deliver you from the plague of him."

Accordingly, they repaired to the King and told him what had passed, saying, "O King of the age, we are perplexed anent this merchant, whose generosity is excessive; for he doeth thus and thus, and all he borroweth, he giveth away to the poor by handful. Were he a man of naught, his sense would not suffer him to lavish gold on this wise; and were he a man of wealth, his good faith had been made manifest to us by the coming of his baggage; but we see none of his luggage, although he avoucheth that he hath a baggage train and hath preceded it. Now some time hath past, but there appeareth no sign of his baggage train, and he oweth us sixty thousand gold pieces, all of which he hath given away in alms." And they went on to praise him and extol his generosity.

Now this King was a very covetous man, a more covetous than Ashᵓab; and when he heard tell of Maᵓaruf's generosity and openhandedness, greed of gain got the better of him and he said to his Wazir, "Were not this merchant a man of immense wealth, he had not shown all this munificence. His baggage train will assuredly come, whereupon these merchants will flock to him and he will scatter amongst them riches galore. Now I have more right to this money than they; wherefore I have a mind to make friends with him and profess affection for him, so that, when his baggage cometh whatso the merchants would have had I shall get of him; and I will give him my daughter to wife and join his wealth to my wealth." Replied the Wazir, "O King of the age, methinks he is naught but an impostor, and 'tis the impostor who

ruineth the house of the covetous." The King said, "O Wazir, I will prove
him and soon know if he be an impostor or a true man and whether he be a
rearling of Fortune or not." The Wazir asked, "And how wilt thou prove
him?"; and the King answered, "I will send for him to the presence and entreat
him with honour and give him a jewel which I have. An he know it and wot
its price, he is a man of worth and wealth; but an he know it not, he is an
impostor and an upstart and I will do him die by the foulest fashion of deaths."

So he sent for Ma'aruf, who came and saluted him. The King returned his
salam and seating him beside himself, said to him, "Art thou the merchant
Ma'aruf?" and said he, "Yes." Quoth the King, "The merchants declare that
thou owest them sixty thousand ducats. Is this true?" "Yes," quoth he.
Asked the King, "Then why dost thou not give them their money?"; and he
answered, "Let them wait till my baggage come and I will repay them twofold.
An they wish for gold, they shall have gold; and should they wish for silver,
they shall have silver; or an they prefer for merchandise, I will give them
merchandise; and to whom I owe a thousand I will give two thousand in
requital of that wherewith he hath veiled my face before the poor; for I
have plenty."

Then said the King, "O merchant, take this and look what is its kind and
value." And he gave him a jewel the bigness of a hazelnut, which he had
bought for a thousand sequins and not having its fellow, prized it highly.
Ma'aruf took it and pressing it between his thumb and forefinger brake it,
for it was brittle and would not brook the squeeze. Quoth the King, "Why
hast thou broken the jewel?"; and Ma'aruf laughed and said, "O King of the
age, this is no jewel. This is but a bittock of mineral worth a thousand dinars;
why dost thou style it a jewel? A jewel I call such as is worth threescore and
ten thousand gold pieces and this is called but a piece of stone. A jewel that
is not of the bigness of a walnut hath no worth in my eyes and I take no
account thereof. How cometh it, then, that thou, who art King, stylest this
thing a jewel, when 'tis but a bit of mineral worth a thousand dinars? But ye
are excusable, for that ye are poor folk and have not in your possession things
of price." The King asked, "O merchant, hast thou jewels such as those
whereof thou speakest?"; and he answered, "Plenty." Whereupon avarice
overcame the King and he said, "Wilt thou give me real jewels?" Said
Ma'aruf, "When my baggage train shall come, I will give thee no end of
jewels; and all that thou canst desire I have in plenty and will give thee,
without price."

At this the King rejoiced and said to the traders, "Wend your ways and have patience with him, till his baggage arrive, when do ye come to me and receive your monies from me." So they fared forth and the King turned to his Wazir and said to him, "Pay court to Merchant Maʾaruf and take and give with him in talk and bespeak him of my daughter, Princess Dunya, that he may wed her and so we gain these riches he hath." Said the Wazir, "O King of the age, this man's fashion misliketh me and methinks he is an impostor and a liar; so leave this whereof thou speakest lest thou lose thy daughter for naught." Now this Minister had sued the King aforetime to give him his daughter to wife and he was willing to do so, but when she heard of it she consented not to marry him. Accordingly, the King said to him, "O traitor, thou desirest no good for me, because in past time thou soughtest my daughter in wedlock, but she would none of thee; so now thou wouldst cut off the way of her marriage and wouldst have the Princess lie fallow, that thou mayst take her; but hear from me one word. Thou hast no concern in this matter. How can he be an impostor and a liar, seeing that he knew the price of the jewel, even that for which I bought it, and brake it because it pleased him not? He hath jewels in plenty, and when he goeth in to my daughter and seeth her to be beautiful, she will captivate his reason and he will love her and give her jewels and things of price: but, as for thee, thou wouldst forbid my daughter and myself these good things."

So the Minister was silent, for fear of the King's anger, and said to himself, "Set the curs on the cattle!" Then with show of friendly bias he betook himself to Maʾaruf and said to him, "His highness the King loveth thee and hath a daughter, a winsome lady and a lovesome, to whom he is minded to marry thee. What sayst thou?" Said he, "No harm in that; but let him wait till my baggage come, for marriage settlements on Kings' daughters are large and their rank demandeth that they be not endowed save with a dowry befitting their degree. At this present I have no money with me till the coming of my baggage, for I have wealth in plenty and needs must I make her marriage portion five thousand purses. Then I shall need a thousand purses to distribute amongst the poor and needy on my wedding night, and other thousand to give those who walk in the bridal procession and yet other thousand wherewith to provide provaunt for the troops and others; and I shall want an hundred jewels to give to the Princess on the wedding morning and other hundred gems to distribute among the slave-girls and eunuchs, for I must give each of them a jewel in honour of the bride; and I need wherewithal to clothe a thousand naked paupers, and alms too needs must be given. All this cannot be done till my baggage come; but I have plenty and, once it is here, I shall make no account of all this outlay."

The Wazir returned to the King and told him what Maʾaruf said, whereupon quoth he, "Since this is his wish, how canst thou style him impostor and liar?" Replied the Minister, "And I cease not to say this." But the King chid him angrily and threatened him, saying, "By the life of my head, an thou cease not this talk, I will slay thee! Go back to him and fetch him to me and I will manage matters with him myself." "So the Wazir returned to Maʾaruf and said to him, "Come and speak with the King." "I hear and obey," said Maʾaruf and went in to the King, who said to him, "Thou shalt not put me off with these excuses, for my treasury is full; so take the keys and spend all thou needest and give what thou wilt and clothe the poor and do thy desire and have no care for the girl and the handmaids. When the baggage shall come, do what thou wilt with thy wife, by way of generosity, and we will have patience with thee anent the marriage portion till then, for there is no manner of difference betwixt me and thee; none at all." Then he sent for the Shaykh Al-Islam and bade him write out the marriage contract between his daughter and Merchant Maʾaruf, and he did so; after which the King gave the signal for beginning the wedding festivities and bade decorate the city. The kettle drums beat and the tables were spread with meats of all kinds and there came performers who paraded their tricks. Merchant Maʾaruf sat upon a throne in a parlour and the players and gymnasts and effeminates and dancing men of wondrous movements and posture-makers of marvellous cunning came before him, whilst he called out to the treasurer and said to him, "Bring gold and silver." So he brought gold and silver and Maʾaruf went round among the spectators and largessed each performer by the handful; and he gave alms to the poor and needy and clothes to the naked and it was a clamorous festival and a right merry. The treasurer could not bring money fast enough from the treasury, and the Wazir's heart was like to burst for rage; but he dared not say a word, whilst Merchant Ali marvelled at this waste of wealth and said to Merchant Maʾaruf, "Allah and the Hallows visit this upon thy head-sides! Doth it not suffice thee to squander the traders' money, but thou must squander that of the King to boot?" Replied Maʾaruf, "'Tis none of thy concern: whenas my baggage shall come, I will requite the King manifold." And he went on lavishing money and saying in himself, "A burning plague! What will happen will happen and there is no flying from that which is foreordained."

The festivities ceased not for the space of forty days, and on the one-and-fortieth day, they made the bride's cortège and all the Emirs and troops

walked before her. When they brought her in before Maᵓaruf, he began
scattering gold on the people's heads, and they made her a mighty fine procession, whilst Maᵓaruf expended in her honour vast sums of money. Then they
brought him in to Princess Dunya and he sat down on the high divan; after
which they let fall the curtains and shut the doors and withdrew, leaving
him alone with his bride; whereupon he smote hand upon hand and sat awhile
sorrowful and saying, "There is no Majesty and there is no Might save in
Allah, the Glorious, the Great!" Quoth the Princess, "O my lord, Allah
preserve thee! What aileth thee that thou art troubled?" Quoth he, "And
how should I be other than troubled, seeing that thy father hath embarrassed
me and done with me a deed which is like the burning of green corn?" She
asked, "And what hath my father done with thee? Tell me!"; and he answered,
"He hath brought me in to thee before the coming of my baggage, and I want
at very least an hundred jewels to distribute among thy handmaids, to each a
jewel, so she might rejoice therein and say, My lord gave me a jewel on the
night of his going in to my lady. This good deed would I have done in honour
of thy station and for the increase of thy dignity; and I have no need to stint
myself in lavishing jewels, for I have of them great plenty." Rejoined she,
"Be not concerned for that. As for me, trouble not thyself about me, for I will
have patience with thee till thy baggage shall come, and as for my women
have no care for them. Rise, doff thy clothes and take thy pleasure; and when
the baggage cometh we shall get the jewels and the rest."

So he arose and putting off his clothes sat down on the bed and sought
love-liesse and they fell to toying with each other. He laid his hand on her knee
and she sat down in his lap and thrust her lip like a titbit of meat into his
mouth, and that hour was such as maketh a man to forget his father and his
mother. And merchant Maᵓaruf abated her maidenhead and that night was
one not to be counted among lives for that which it comprised of the enjoyment
of the fair, till the dawn of day, when he arose and entered the Hammam
whence, after donning a suit for sovrans suitable he betook himself to the
King's Divan. All who were there rose to him and received him with honour
and worship, giving him joy and invoking blessings upon him; and he sat
down by the King's side and asked, "Where is the treasurer?" They answered,
"Here he is, before thee," and he said to him, "Bring robes of honour for all
the Wazirs and Emirs and dignitaries and clothe them therewith." The
treasurer brought him all he sought and he sat giving to all who came to him
and lavishing largesse upon every man according to his station.

On this wise he abode twenty days, whilst no baggage appeared for him nor aught else, till the treasurer was straitened by him to the uttermost and going in to the King, as he sat alone with the Wazir in Ma᾽aruf's absence, kissed ground between his hands and said, "O King of the age, I must tell thee somewhat, lest haply thou blame me for not acquainting thee therewith. Know that the treasury is being exhausted; there is none but a little money left in it and in ten days more we shall shut it upon emptiness." Quoth the King, "O Wazir, verily my son-in-law's baggage train tarrieth long and there appeareth no news thereof." The Minister laughed and said, "Allah be gracious to thee, O King of the age! Thou art none other but heedless with respect to this impostor, this liar. As thy head liveth, there is no baggage for him, no, nor a burning plague to rid us of him! Nay, he hath but imposed on thee without surcease, so that he hath wasted thy treasures and married thy daughter for naught. How long therefore wilt thou be heedless of this liar?"

Then quoth the King, "O Wazir, how shall we do to learn the truth of his case?"; and quoth the Wazir, "O King of the age, none may come at a man's secret but his wife; so send for thy daughter and let her come behind the curtain, that I may question her of the truth of his estate, to the intent that she may make question of him and acquaint us with his case." Cried the King, "There is no harm in that; and as my head liveth, if it be proved that he is a liar and an impostor, I will verily do him die by the foulest of deaths!" Then he carried the Wazir into the sitting-chamber and sent for his daughter, who came behind the curtain, her husband being absent, and said, "What wouldst thou, O my father?" Said he, "Speak with the Wazir." So she asked, "Ho thou, the Wazir, what is thy will?"; and he answered, "O my lady, thou must know that thy husband hath squandered thy father's substance and married thee without a dower; and he ceaseth not to promise us and break his promises, nor cometh there any tidings of his baggage; in short we would have thee inform us concerning him." Quoth she, "Indeed his words be many, and he still cometh and promiseth me jewels and treasures and costly stuffs; but I see nothing." Quoth the Wazir, "O my lady, canst thou this night take and give with him in talk and whisper to him:—Say me sooth and fear from me naught, for thou art become my husband and I will not transgress against thee. So tell me the truth of the matter and I will devise thee a device whereby thou shalt be set at rest. And do thou play near and far with him in words and profess love to him and win him to confess and after tell us the facts of his case." And she answered, "O my papa, I know how I will make proof of him."

Then she went away and after supper her husband came in to her, according to his wont, whereupon Princess Dunya rose to him and took him under the armpit and wheedled him with winsomest wheedling (and all-sufficient are woman's wiles whenas she would aught of men); and she ceased not to caress him and beguile him with speech sweeter than the honey till she stole his reason; and when she saw that he altogether inclined to her, she said to him, "O my beloved, O coolth of my eyes and fruit of my vitals, Allah never desolate me by less of thee nor Time sunder us twain me and thee! Indeed, the love of thee hath homed in my heart and the fire of passion hath consumed my liver, nor will I ever forsake thee or transgress against thee. But I would have thee tell me the truth, for that the sleights of falsehood profit not, nor do they secure credit at all seasons. How long wilt thou impose upon my father and lie to him? I fear lest thine affair be discovered to him, ere we can devise some device and he lay violent hands upon thee. So acquaint me with the facts of the case for naught shall befall thee save that which shall begladden thee; and, when thou shalt have spoken sooth, fear not harm shall betide thee. How often wilt thou declare that thou art a merchant and a man of money and hast a luggage train? This long while past thou sayest, My baggage! my baggage! but there appeareth no sign of thy baggage, and visible in thy face is anxiety on this account. So an there be no worth in thy words, tell me and I will contrive thee a contrivance whereby thou shalt come off safe, Inshallah!"

He replied, "I will tell thee the truth, and do then thou whatso thou wilt." Rejoined she, "Speak and look thou speak soothly; for sooth is the ark of safety, and beware of lying, for it dishonoureth the liar." He said, "Know, then, O my lady, that I am no merchant and have no baggage, no, nor a burning plague; nay, I was but a cobbler in my own country and had a wife called Fatimah the Dung, with whom there befell me this and that." And he told her his story from beginning to end; whereat she laughed and said, "Verily, thou art clever in the practice of lying and imposture!" whereto he answered, "O my lady, may Allah Almighty preserve thee to veil sins and countervail chagrins!" Rejoined she, "Know, that thou imposedst upon my sire and deceivedst him by dint of thy deluding vaunts, so that of his greed for gain he married me to thee. Then thou squanderedst his wealth and the Wazir beareth thee a grudge for this. How many a time hath he spoken against thee to my father, saying, Indeed, he is an impostor, a liar! But my sire hearkened not to his say, for that he had sought me in wedlock and I consented not that he be baron and I femme. However, the time grew longsome upon my sire and he became straitened and said to me, Make him confess. So I have made thee confess and that which was covered is discovered. Now my father purposeth thee a mischief because of this; but thou art become my husband and I will never transgress against thee. An I told my father what I have learnt from thee, he would be certified of thy falsehood and imposture and that thou imposest upon Kings' daughters and squanderest royal wealth: so would thine offense find with him no pardon and he would slay thee sans a doubt: wherefore it would be bruited among the folk that I married a man who was a liar, an impostor, and this would smirch mine honour. Furthermore an he kill thee, most like he will require me to wed another, and to such thing I will never consent; no, nqt though I die! So rise now and don a Mameluke's dress and take these fifty thousand dinars of my monies, and mount a swift steed and get thee to a land whither the rule of my father does not reach. Then make thee a merchant and send me a letter by a courier who shall bring it privily to me, that I may know in what land thou art, so I may send thee all my hand can attain. Thus shall thy wealth wax great and if my father die, I will send for thee, and thou shalt return in respect and honour; and if we die, thou or I, and go to the mercy of God the Most Great, the Resurrection shall unite us. This, then, is the rede that is right: and while we both abide alive and well, I will not cease to send thee letters and monies. Arise ere the day wax bright and thou be in perplexed plight and perdition upon thy head alight!"

Quoth he, "O my lady, I beseech thee of thy favour to bid me farewell with thine embracement"; and quoth she, "No harm in that." So he embraced her and knew her carnally; after which he made the Ghusl-ablution; then, donning the dress of a white slave, he bade the syces saddle him a thorough-bred steed. Accordingly, they saddled him a courser and he mounted and farewelling his wife, rode forth the city at the last of the night, whilst all who saw him deemed him one of the Mamelukes of the Sultan going abroad on some business.

Next morning, the King and his Wazir repaired to the sitting-chamber and sent for Princess Dunya who came behind the curtain; and her father said to her, "O my daughter, what sayst thou?" Said she, "I say, Allah blacken thy Wazir's face, because he would have blackened my face in my husband's eyes!" Asked the King, "How so?"; and she answered, "He came in to me yesterday; but, before I could name the matter to him, behold, in walked Faraj the Chief Eunuch, letter in hand, and said:—Ten white slaves stand under the palace window and have given me this letter, saying:—Kiss for us the hands of our lord, Merchant Maᵖaruf, and give him this letter, for we are of his Mamelukes with the baggage, and it hath reached us that he hath wedded the King's daughter, so we are come to acquaint him with that which befell us by the way. Accordingly I took the letter and read as follows:— From the five hundred Mamelukes to his highness our lord Merchant Maʾaruf. But further. We give thee to know that, after thou quittedst us, the Arabs came out upon us and attacked us. They were two thousand horse and we five hundred mounted slaves and there befell a mighty sore fight between us and them. They hindered us from the road thirty days doing battle with them and this is the cause of our tarrying from thee. They also took from us of the luggage two hundred loads of cloth and slew of us fifty Mamelukes. When the news reached my husband, he cried, Allah disappoint them! What ailed them to wage war with the Arabs for the sake of two hundred loads of merchandise? What are two hundred loads? It behoved them not to tarry on that account, for verily the value of the two hundred loads is only some seven thousand dinars. But needs must I go to them and hasten them. As for that which the Arabs have taken, 'twill not be missed from the baggage, nor doth it weigh with me a whit, for I reckon it as if I had given it to them by way of alms. Then he went down from me, laughing and taking no concern for the wastage of his wealth nor the slaughter of his slaves. As soon as he was gone, I looked out from the lattice and saw the ten Mamelukes who had brought him the letter, as they were moons, each clad in a suit of clothes worth two thousand dinars, there is not with my father a chattel to match one of them. He went forth with them to bring up his baggage and hallowed be Allah who hindered me from saying to him aught of that thou badest me, for he would have made mock of me and thee, and haply he would have eyed me with the eye of disparagement and hated me. But the fault is all with thy Wazir, who speaketh against my husband words that befit him not."

Replied the King, "O my daughter, thy husband's wealth is indeed endless and he recketh not of it; for, from the day he entered our city, he hath done naught but give alms to the poor. Inshallah, he will speedily return with the baggage, and good in plenty shall betide us from him." And he went on to appease her and menace the Wazir, being duped by her device.

So fared it with the King; but as regards Merchant Maʾaruf he rode on into waste lands, perplexed and knowing not to what quarter he should betake him; and for the anguish of parting he lamented and wept with sore weeping, for indeed the ways were walled up before his face and death seemed to him better than dreeing life, and he walked on like a drunken man for stress of distraction, and stayed not till noontide, when he came to a little town and saw a plougher hard by, ploughing with a yoke of bulls. Now hunger was sore upon him; and he went up to the ploughman and said to him, "Peace be with thee!"; and he returned his salam and said to him, "Welcome, O my lord! Art thou one of the Sultan's Mamelukes?" Quoth Ma²aruf, "Yes"; and the other said, "Alight with me for a guest-meal." Whereupon Ma²aruf knew him to be of the liberal and said to him, "O my brother, I see with thee naught with which thou mayst feed me: how is it, then, that thou invitest me?" Answered the husbandman, "O my lord, weal is well nigh. Dismount thee here: the town is near hand and I will go and fetch thee dinner and fodder for thy stallion." Rejoined Ma²aruf, "Since the town is near at hand, I can go thither as quickly as thou canst and buy me what I have a mind to in the bazaar and eat." The peasant replied, "O my lord, the place is but a little village and there is no bazaar there, neither selling nor buying. So I conjure thee by Allah, alight here with me and hearten my heart, and I will run thither and return to thee in haste."

Accordingly he dismounted and the Fellah left him and went off to the village, to fetch dinner for him whilst Ma²aruf sat awaiting him. Presently he said in himself, "I have taken this poor man away from his work; but I will arise and plough in his stead, till he come back, to make up for having hindered him from his work." Then he took the plough and started the bulls, ploughed a little, till the share struck against something and the beasts stopped. He goaded them on, but they could not move the plough; so he looked at the share and finding it caught in a ring of gold, cleared away the soil and saw that it was set centre-most a slab of alabaster, the size of the nether millstone. He strave at the stone till he pulled it from its place, when there appeared beneath it a souterrain with a stair. Presently he descended the flight of steps and came to a place like a Hammam, with four daïses, the first full of gold, from floor to roof, the second full of emeralds and pearls and coral also from ground to ceiling; the third of jacinths and rubies and turquoises and the fourth of diamonds and all manner other preciousest stones. At the upper end of the place stood a coffer of clearest crystal, full of union-gems each the size of a walnut, and upon the coffer lay a casket of gold, the bigness of a lemon.

When he saw this, he marvelled and rejoiced with joy exceeding and said to himself, "I wonder what is in this casket?" So he opened it and found therein a seal-ring of gold, whereon were graven names and talismans, as they were the tracks of creeping ants. He rubbed the ring and behold, a voice said, "Adsum! Here am I, at thy service, O my lord! Ask and it shall be given unto thee. Wilt thou raise a city or ruin a capital or kill a king or dig a river-channel or aught of the kind? Whatso thou seekest, it shall come to pass, by leave of the King of All-might, Creator of day and night." Ma³aruf asked, "O creature of my lord, who and what art thou?"; and the other answered, "I am the slave of this seal-ring standing in the service of him who possesseth it. Whatsoever he seeketh, that I accomplish for him, and I have no excuse in neglecting that he biddeth me do; because I am Sultan over two-and-seventy tribes of the Jinn, each two-and-seventy thousand in number, every one of which thousand ruleth over a thousand Marids, each Marid over a thousand Ifrits, each Ifrit over a thousand Satans and each Satan over a thousand Jinn: and they are all under command of me and may not gainsay me. As for me, I am spelled to this seal-ring and may not thwart whoso holdeth it. Lo! thou hast gotten hold of it and I am become thy slave; so ask what thou wilt, for I hearken to thy word and obey thy bidding; and if thou have need of me at any time, by land or by sea, rub the signet-ring and thou wilt find me with thee. But beware of rubbing it twice in succession, or thou wilt consume me with the fire of the names graven thereon; and thus wouldst thou lose me and after regret me. Now I have acquainted thee with my case and—the Peace!"

The Merchant asked him, "What is thy name?" and the Jinni answered, "My name is Abu al-Sa³adat." Quoth Ma³aruf, "O Abu al-Sa³adat, what is this place and who enchanted thee in this casket?"; and quoth he, "O my lord, this is a treasure called the Hoard of Shaddad son of Ad, him who the base of 'Many-columned Iram laid, the like of which in the lands was never made.' I was his slave in his lifetime and this is his seal-ring, which he laid up in his treasure; but it hath fallen to thy lot." Ma³aruf enquired, "Canst thou transport that which is in this hoard to the surface of the earth?"; and the Jinni replied, "Yes! Nothing were easier." Said Ma³aruf, "Bring it forth and leave naught." So the Jinni signed with his hand to the ground, which clave asunder, and he sank and was absent a little while. Presently, there came forth young boys full of grace, and fair of face bearing golden baskets filled with gold which they emptied out and going away, returned with more; nor did they cease to transport the gold and jewels, till ere an hour had sped they said, "Naught is left in the hoard." Thereupon out came Abu al-Sa³adat and said to Ma³aruf, "O my lord, thou seest that we have brought forth all that was in the hoard." Ma³aruf asked, "Who be these beautiful boys?" and the Jinni answered, "They are my sons. This matter merited not that I should muster for it the Marids, wherefore my sons have done thy desire and are honoured by such service. So ask what thou wilt beside this."

Quoth Ma³aruf, "Canst thou bring me he-mules and chests and fill the chests with the treasure and load them on the mules?" Quoth Abu al-Sa²adat, "Nothing easier," and cried a great cry; whereupon his sons presented themselves before him, to the number of eight hundred, and he said to them, "Let some of you take the semblance of he-mules and others of muleteers and handsome Mamelukes, the like of the least of whom is not found with any of the Kings; and others of you be transmewed to muleteers, and the rest to menials." So seven hundred of them changed themselves into bat-mules and other hundred took the shape of slaves. Then Abu al-Sa²adat called upon his Marids, who presented themselves between his hands and he commanded some of them to assume the aspect of horses saddled with saddles of gold crusted with jewels. And when Ma²aruf saw them do as he bade he cried, "Where be the chests?" They brought them before him and he said, "Pack the gold and the stones, each sort by itself." So they packed them and loaded three hundred he-mules with them. Then asked Ma²aruf, "O Abu al-Sa²adat, canst thou bring me some loads of costly stuffs?"; and the Jinni answered, "Wilt thou have Egyptian stuffs or Syrian or Persian or Indian or Greek?" Ma²aruf said, "Bring me an hundred loads of each kind, on five hundred mules"; and Abu al-Sa²adat, "O my lord, accord me delay that I may dispose my Marids for this and send a company of them to each country to fetch an hundred loads of its stuffs and then take the form of he-mules and return, carrying the stuffs." Ma²aruf enquired, "What time dost thou want?"; and Abu al-Sa²adat replied, "The time of the blackness of the night, and day shall not dawn ere thou have all thou desirest." Said Ma²aruf, "I grant thee this time," and bade them pitch him a pavilion. So they pitched it and he sat down therein and they brought him a table of food.

Then said Abu al-Sa²adat to him, "O my lord, tarry thou in this tent and these my sons shall guard thee: so fear thou nothing; for I go to muster my Marids and despatch them to do thy desire." So saying, he departed, leaving Ma²aruf seated in the pavilion, with the table before him and the Jinni's sons attending upon him, in the guise of slaves and servants and suite.

And while he sat in this state behold, up came the husbandman, with a great porringer of lentils and a nose-bag full of barley and seeing the pavilion pitched and the Mamelukes standing, hands upon breasts, thought that the Sultan was come and had halted on that stead. So he stood open-mouthed and said in himself, "Would I had killed a couple of chickens and fried them red with clarified cow-butter for the Sultan!" And he would have turned back to kill the chickens as a regale for the Sultan; but Ma²aruf saw him and cried

out to him and said to the Mamelukes, "Bring him hither." So they brought
him and his porringer of lentils before Ma²aruf, who said to him, "What is
this?" Said the peasant, "This is thy dinner and thy horse's fodder! Excuse
me, for I thought not that the Sultan would come hither; and, had I known
that, I would have killed a couple of chickens and entertained him in goodly
guise." Quoth Ma²aruf, "The Sultan is not come. I am his son-in-law and I
was vexed with him. However he hath sent his officers to make his peace with
me, and now I am minded to return to city. But thou hast made me this
guest-meal without knowing me, and I accept it from thee, lentils though it
be, and will not eat save of thy cheer." Accordingly he bade him set the
porringer amiddlemost the table and ate of it his sufficiency, whilst the Fellah
filled his belly with those rich meats. Then Ma²aruf washed his hands and
gave the Mamelukes leave to eat; so they fell upon the remains of the meal
and ate; and, when the porringer was empty, he filled it with gold and gave
it to the peasant, saying, "Carry this to thy dwelling and come to me in the
city, and I will entreat thee with honour." Thereupon the peasant took the
porringer full of gold and returned to the village, driving the bulls before him
and deeming himself akin to the King. Meanwhile, they brought Ma²aruf
girls of the Brides of the Treasure, who smote on instruments of music and
danced before him, and he passed that night in joyance and delight, a night
not to be reckoned among lives.

Hardly had dawned the day when there arose a great cloud of dust which
presently lifting, discovered seven hundred mules laden with stuffs and attended by muleteers and baggage-tenders and cresset-bearers. With them came
Abu al-Sa²adat, riding on a she-mule, in the guise of a caravan-leader, and
before him was a travelling-litter, with four corner-terminals of glittering
red gold, set with gems. When Abu al-Sa²adat came up to the tent, he dismounted and kissing the earth, said to Ma²aruf, "O my lord, thy desire hath
been done to the uttermost and in the litter is a treasure-suit which hath not
its match among Kings' raiment: so don it and mount the litter and bid us do
what thou wilt." Quoth Ma²aruf, "O Abu al-Sa²adat, I wish thee to go to
the city of Ikhtiyan al-Khutan and present thyself to my father-in-law the
King; and go thou not in to him but in the guise of a mortal courier;" and
quoth he, "To hear is to obey." So Ma²aruf wrote a letter to the Sultan and
sealed it and Abu al-Sa²adat took it and set out with it; and when he arrived,
he found the King saying, "O Wazir, indeed my heart is concerned for my
son-in-law and I fear lest the Arabs slay him. Would Heaven I wot whither
he was bound, that I might have followed him with the troops! Would he

had told me his destination!" Said the Wazir, "Allah be merciful to thee for this thy heedlessness! As thy head liveth, the wight saw that we were awake to him and feared dishonour and fled, for he is nothing but an impostor, a liar."

And behold, at this moment in came the courier and kissing ground before the King, wished him permanent glory and prosperity and length of life. Asked the King, "Who art thou and what is thy business?" "I am a courier," answered the Jinni, "and thy son-in-law who is come with the baggage sendeth me to thee with a letter, and here it is!" So he took the letter and read therein these words, "After salutations galore to our uncle the glorious King! Know that I am at hand with the baggage train: so come thou forth to meet me with the troops." Cried the King, "Allah blacken thy brow, O Wazir! How often wilt thou defame my son-in-law's name and call him liar and impostor? Behold, he is come with the baggage train and thou art naught but a traitor." The Minister hung his head groundwards in shame and confusion and replied, "O King of the age, I said not this save because of the long delay of the baggage and because I feared the loss of the wealth he hath wasted." The King exclaimed, "O traitor, what are my riches! Now that his baggage is come he will give me great plenty in their stead." Then he bade decorate the city and going in to his daughter, said to her, "Good news for thee! Thy husband will be here anon with his baggage; for he hath sent me a letter to that effect and here am I now going forth to meet him." The Princess Dunya marvelled at this and said in herself, "This is a wondrous thing! Was he laughing at me and making mock of me, or had he a mind to try me, when he told me that he was a pauper? But Alhamdolillah, Glory to God, for that I failed not of my duty to him!"

On this wise fared it in the Palace; but as regards Merchant Ali, the Cairene, when he saw the decoration of the city and asked the cause thereof, they said to him, "The baggage train of Merchant Ma³aruf, the King's son-in-law, is come." Said he, "Allah is Almighty! What a calamity is this man! He came to me, fleeing from his wife, and he was a poor man. Whence then should he get a baggage train? But haply this is a device which the King's daughter hath contrived for him, fearing his disgrace, and Kings are not unable to do anything. May Allah the Most High veil his fame and not bring him to public shame!" And all the merchants rejoiced and were glad for that they would get their monies.

Then the King assembled his troops and rode forth, whilst Abu al-Sa³adat returned to Ma³aruf and acquainted him with the delivering of the letter. Quoth Ma³aruf, "Bind on the loads"; and when they had done so, he donned the treasure-suit and mounting the litter became a thousand times greater and more majestic than the King. Then he set forward; but, when he had gone half-way, behold, the King met him with the troops, and seeing him riding in the Takhtrawan and clad in the dress aforesaid, threw himself upon him and saluted him, and giving him joy of his safety, greeted him with the greeting of peace. Then all the Lords of the land saluted him and it was made manifest that he had spoken the truth and that in him there was no lie. Presently he entered the city in such state procession as would have caused the gall-bladder of the lion to burst for envy and the traders pressed up to him and kissed his hands, whilst Merchant Ali said to him, "Thou hast played off this trick and it hath prospered to thy hand, O Shaykh of Impostors! But thou deservest it and may Allah the Most High increase thee of His bounty!"; whereupon Maᵇaruf laughed.

Then he entered the palace and sitting down on the throne said, "Carry the loads of gold into the treasury of my uncle the King and bring me the bales of cloth." So they brought them to him and opened them before him, bale after bale, till they had unpacked the seven hundred loads, whereof he chose out the best and said, "Bear these to Princess Dunya that she may distribute them among her slave-girls; and carry her also this coffer of jewels, that she may divide them among her handmaids and eunuchs." Then he proceeded to make over to the merchants in whose debt he was stuffs by way of payment for their arrears, giving him whose due was a thousand, stuffs worth two thousand or more; after which he fell to distributing to the poor and needy, whilst the King looked on with greedy eyes and could not hinder him; nor did he cease largesse till he had made an end of the seven hundred loads, when he turned to the troops and proceeded to apportion amongst them emeralds and rubies and pearls and coral and other jewels by handsful, without count, till the King said to him, "Enough of this giving, O my son! There is but little left of the baggage." But he said, "I have plenty." Then indeed, his good faith was become manifest and none could give him the lie; and he had come to reck not of giving, for that the Slave of the Seal-ring brought him whatsoever he sought.

Presently, the treasurer came in to the King and said, "O King of the age, the treasury is full indeed and will not hold the rest of the loads. Where shall we lay that which is left of the gold and jewels?" And he assigned to him another place. As for the Princess Dunya when she saw this, her joy redoubled and she marvelled and said in herself, "Would I wot how came he by all this wealth!" In like manner the traders rejoiced in that which he had given them and blessed him; whilst Merchant Ali marvelled and said to himself, "I wonder how he hath lied and swindled that he hath gotten him all these treasures? Had they come from the King's daughter, he had not wasted them on this wise! But how excellent is his saying who said:—

> When the Kings' King giveth, in reverence pause
> And venture not to enquire the cause:
> Allah gives His gifts unto whom He will,
> So respect and abide by His Holy Laws!"

So far concerning him; but as regards the King, he also marvelled with passing marvel at that which he saw of Ma²aruf's generosity and open-handedness in the largesse of wealth. Then the Merchant went in to his wife, who met him, smiling and laughing-lipped and kissed his hand, saying, "Didst thou mock me or hadst thou a mind to prove me with thy saying:—I am a poor man and a fugitive from my wife? Praised be Allah for that I failed not of my duty to thee! For thou art my beloved and there is none dearer to me than thou, whether thou be rich or poor. But I would have thee tell me what didst thou design by these words." Said Ma²aruf, "I wished to prove thee and see whether thy love were sincere or for the sake of wealth and the greed of worldly good. But now 'tis become manifest to me that thine affection is sincere and as thou art a true woman, so welcome to thee! I know thy worth."

Then he went apart into a place by himself and rubbed the seal-ring, whereupon Abu al-Sa²adat presented himself and said to him, "Adsum at thy service! Ask what thou wilt." Quoth Ma²aruf, "I want a treasure-suit and treasure-trinkets for my wife, including a necklace of forty unique jewels." Quoth the Jinni, "To hear is to obey," and brought him what he sought, whereupon Ma²aruf dismissed him and carrying the dress and ornaments in to his wife, laid them before her and said, "Take these and put them on and welcome!" When she saw this, her wits fled for joy, and she found among the ornaments a pair of anklets of gold set with jewels of the handiwork of the magicians, and bracelets and earrings and a belt such as no money could buy. So she donned the dress and ornaments and said to Ma²aruf, "O my lord, I will treasure these up for holidays and festivals." But he answered, "Wear them always, for I have others in plenty." And when she put them on and her women beheld her, they rejoiced and bussed his hands.

Then he left them and going apart by himself, rubbed the seal-ring whereupon its slave appeared and he said to him, "Bring me an hundred suits of apparel, with their ornaments of gold." "Hearing and obeying," answered Abu al Saʾadat and brought him the hundred suits, each with its ornaments wrapped up within it. Maʾaruf took them and called aloud to the slave-girls, who came to him and he gave them each a suit: so they donned them and became like the black-eyed girls of Paradise, whilst the Princess Dunya shone amongst them as the moon among the stars. One of the handmaids told the King of this and he came in to his daughter and saw her and her women dazzling all who beheld them; whereat he wondered with passing wonderment. Then he went out and calling his Wazir, said to him, "O Wazir, such and such things have happened; what sayst thou now of this affair?" Said he, "O King of the age, this be no merchant's fashion; for a merchant keepeth a piece of linen by him for years and selleth it not but at a profit. How should a merchant have generosity such as this generosity, and whence should he get the like of these monies and jewels, of which but a slight matter is found with the Kings? So how should loads thereof be found with merchants? Needs must there be a cause for this; but, an thou wilt hearken to me, I will make the truth of the case manifest to thee."

Answered the King, "O Wazir, I will do thy bidding." Rejoined the Minister, "Do thou foregather with thy son-in-law and make a show of affect to him and talk with him and say:—O my son-in-law, I have a mind to go, I and thou and the Wazir but no more, to a flower-garden that we may take our pleasure there. When we come to the garden, we will set on the table wine; and I will ply him therewith and compel him to drink; for, when he shall have drunken, he will lose his reason and his judgment will forsake him. Then we will question him of the truth of his case and he will discover to us his secrets, for wine is a traitor and Allah-gifted is he who said:—

> When we drank the wine, and it crept its way
> To the place of Secrets, I cried, "O stay!"
> In my fear lest its influence stint my wits
> And my friends spy matters that hidden lay.

When he hath told us the truth we shall ken his case and may deal with him as we will; because I fear for thee the consequences of this his present fashion: haply he will covet the kingship and win over the troops by generosity and lavishing money and so despose thee and take the kingdom from thee." The King said to him, "Thou hast spoken sooth!"; and they passed the night on this agreement.

And when morning morrowed the King went forth and sat in the guest-chamber, when lo, and behold! the grooms and serving-men came in to him in dismay. Quoth he, "What hath befallen you?"; and quoth they, "O King of the age, the syces curried the horses and foddered them and the he-mules which brought the baggage; but, when we arose in the morning, we found that thy son-in-law's Mamelukes had stolen the horses and mules. We searched the stables, but found neither horse nor mule; so we entered the lodging of the Mamelukes and found none there, nor know we how they fled." The King marvelled at this, unknowing that the horses and Mamelukes were all Ifrits, the subjects of the Slave of the Spell, and asked the grooms, "O accursed, how could a thousand beasts and five hundred slaves and servants flee without your knowledge?" Answered they, "We know not how it happened," and he cried, "Go, and when your lord cometh forth of the Harim, tell him the case." So they went out from before the King and sat down bewildered, till Ma'aruf came out and, seeing them chagrined enquired of them, "What may be the matter?" They told him all that had happened and he said, "What is their worth that ye should be concerned for them? Wend your ways." And he sat laughing and was neither angry nor grieved concerning the case; whereupon the King looked in the Wazir's face and said to him, "What manner of man is this, with whom wealth is of no worth? Needs must there be a reason for this."

Then they talked with him awhile and the King said to him, "O my son-in-law, I have a mind to go, I, thou and the Wazir, to a garden, where we may divert ourselves." "No harm in that," said Ma'aruf. So they went forth to a flower-garden, wherein every sort of fruit was of kinds twain and its waters were flowing and its trees towering and its birds carolling. There they entered a pavilion, whose sight did away sorrow from the soul, and sat talking, whilst the Minister entertained them with rare tales and quoted merry quips and mirth-provoking sayings and Ma'aruf attentively listened, till the time of dinner came, when they set on a tray of meats and a flagon of wine. When they had eaten and washed hands, the Wazir filled the cup and gave it to the King, who drank it off; then he filled a second and handed it to Ma'aruf, saying, "Take the cup of the drink to which Reason boweth neck in reverence." Quoth Ma'aruf, "What is this, O Wazir?"; and quoth he, "This is the grizzled virgin and the old maid long kept at home, the giver of joy to hearts, whereof said the poet:—

> The feet of sturdy Miscreants went trampling heavy tread,
> And she hath ta'en a vengeance dire on every Arab's head.

> A Kafir youth like fullest moon in darkness hands her round
> Whose eyne are strongest cause of sin by him inspirited.

And Allah-gifted is he who said:—

> 'Tis as if wine and he who bears the bowl,
> Rising to show her charms for man to see,
> Were dancing undurn-Sun whose face the moon
> Of night adorned with stars of Gemini.
> So subtle is her essence it would seem
> Through every limb like course of soul runs she.

And yet another;—

> Wine-cup and ruby-wine high worship claim;
> Dishonour 'twere to see their honour waste:
> Bury me, when I'm dead, by side of vine
> Whose veins shall moisten bones in clay misplaced;
> Nor bury me in wold and wild, for I
> Dread only after death no wine to taste."

And he ceased not to egg him on to the drink, naming to him such of the virtues of wine as he thought well and reciting to him what occurred to him of poetry and pleasantries on the subject, till Ma²aruf addressed himself to sucking the cup-lips and cared no longer for aught else. The Wazir ceased not to fill for him and he to drink and enjoy himself and make merry, till his wits wandered and he could not distinguish right from wrong.

When the Minister saw that drunkenness had attained in him to the utterest and the bounds transgressed, he said to him, "By Allah, O Merchant Ma²aruf, I admire whence thou gottest these jewels whose like the Kings of the Chosroes possess not! In all our lives never saw we a merchant that had heaped up riches like unto thine or more generous than thou, for thy doings are the doings of Kings and not merchants' doings. Wherefore, Allah upon thee, do thou acquaint me with this, that I may know thy rank and condition." And he went on to test him with questions and cajole him, till Ma²aruf, being reft of reason, said to him, "I'm neither merchant nor King," and told him his whole story from first to last. Then said the Wazir, "I conjure thee by Allah, O my lord Ma²aruf, show us the ring, that we may see its make." So, in his drunkenness, he pulled off the ring and said, "Take it and look upon it." The Minister took it and turning it over, said, "If I rub it, will its slave appear?" Replied Ma²aruf, "Yes. Rub it and he will appear to thee, and do thou divert thyself with the sight of him." Thereupon the Wazir rubbed the ring and behold forthright appeared the Jinni and said, "Adsum, at thy service, O my lord! Ask and it shall be given to thee. Wilt thou ruin a city or raise a capital or kill a king? Whatso thou seekest, I will do for thee, sans fail."

The Wazir pointed to Maᵓaruf and said, "Take up yonder wretch and cast him down in the most desolate of desert lands, where he shall find nothing to eat nor drink, so he may die of hunger and perish miserably, and none know of him." Accordingly, the Jinni snatched him up and flew with him betwixt heaven and earth, which when Maᵓaruf saw, he made sure of destruction and wept and said, "O Abu al-Saᵓadat, whither goest thou with me?" Replied the Jinni, "I go to cast thee down in the Desert Quarter, O ill-bred wight of gross wits. Shall one have the like of this talisman and give it to the folk to gaze at? Verily, thou deservest that which hath befallen thee; and but that I fear Allah, I would let thee fall from a height of a thousand fathoms, nor shouldst thou reach the earth, till the winds had torn thee to shreds." Maᵓaruf was silent and did not again bespeak him till he reached the Desert Quarter and casting him down there went away and left him in that horrible place.

So much concerning him; but returning to the Wazir who was now in possession of the talisman, he said to the King, "How deemest thou now? Did I not tell thee that this fellow was a liar, an impostor, but thou wouldst not credit me?" Replied the King, "Thou wast in the right, O my Wazir, Allah grant thee weal! But give me the ring, that I may solace myself with the sight." The Minister looked at him angrily and spat in his face, saying, "O lackwits, how shall I give it to thee and abide thy servant, after I am become thy master? But I will spare thee no more on life." Then he rubbed the seal-ring and said to the Slave, "Take up this ill-mannered churl and cast him down by his son-in-law the swindlerman." So the Jinni took him up and flew off with him, whereupon quoth the King to him, "O creature of my Lord, what is my crime?" Abu al-Saᵓadat replied, "That wot I not, but my master hath commanded me and I cannot cross whoso hath compassed the enchanted ring." Then he flew on with him, till he came to the Desert Quarter and, casting him down where he had cast Maᵓaruf, left him and returned. The King hearing Maᵓaruf weeping, went up to him and acquainted him with his case; and they sat weeping over that which had befallen them and found neither meat nor drink.

Meanwhile the Minister, after driving father-in-law and son-in-law from the country, went forth from the garden and summoning all the troops held a Divan, and told them what he had done with the King and Maᵃaruf and acquainted them with the affair of the talisman, adding, "Unless ye make me Sultan over you, I will bid the Slave of the Seal-ring take you up one and all and cast you down in the Desert Quarter where you shall die of hunger and thirst." They replied, "Do us no damage, for we accept thee as Sultan over us and will not anywise gainsay thy bidding." So they agreed, in their own despite, to his being Sultan over them, and he bestowed on them robes of honour, seeking all he had a mind to of Abu al-Saᵃadat, who brought it to him forthwith.

Then he sat down on the throne and the troops did homage to him; and he sent to Princess Dunya, the King's daughter, saying, "Make thee ready, for I mean to come in unto thee this night, because I long for thee with love." When she heard this, she wept, for the case of her husband and father was grievous to her, and sent to him saying, "Have patience with me till my period of widowhood be ended: then draw up thy contract of marriage with me and go in to me according to law." But he sent back to say to her, "I know neither period of widowhood nor to delay have I a mood; and I need not a contract nor know I lawful from unlawful; but needs must I go unto thee this night." She answered him saying, "So be it, then, and welcome to thee!"; but this was a trick on her part. When the answer reached the Wazir, he rejoiced and his breast was broadened, for that he was passionately in love with her. He bade set food before all the folk, saying, "Eat; this is my bride-feast; for I purpose to go in to the Princess Dunya this night." Quoth the Shaykh al-Islam, "It is not lawful for thee to go in unto her till her days of widowhood be ended and thou have drawn up thy contract of marriage with her." But he answered, "I know neither days of widowhood nor other period; so multiply not words on me." The Shaykh al-Islam was silent, fearing his mischief, and said to the troops, "Verily, this man is a kafir, a Miscreant, and hath neither creed nor religious conduct."

As soon as it was evenfall, he went in to her and found her robed in her richest raiment and decked with her goodliest adornments. When she saw him, she came to meet him, laughing and said, "A blessed night! But hadst thou slain my father and my husband, it had been more to my mind." And he said, "There is no help but I slay them." Then she made him sit down and began to jest with him and make show of love caressing him and smiling in his face so that his reason fled; but she cajoled him with her coaxing and cunning only that she might get possession of the ring and change his joy into calamity on the mother of his forehead: nor did she deal thus with him but after the rede of him who said:—

> I attained by my wits
> What no sword had obtained,
> And return wi' the spoils
> Whose sweet pluckings I gained.

When he saw her caress him and smile upon him, desire surged up in him and he besought her of carnal knowledge; but, when he approached her, she drew away from him and burst into tears, saying, "O my lord, seest thou not the man who is looking at us? I conjure thee by Allah, screen me from his eyes! How canst thou know me while he looketh on us?" When he heard this, he was angry and asked, "Where is the man?"; and answered she, "There he is, in the bezel of the ring! putting out his head and staring at us." He thought that the Jinni was looking at them and said laughing, "Fear not; this is the Slave of the Seal-ring, and he is subject to me." Quoth she, "I am afraid of Ifrits; pull it off and throw it afar from me." So he plucked if off and laying it on the cushion, drew near to her, but she dealt him a kick, her foot striking him full in the stomach, and he fell over on his back senseless; whereupon she cried out to her attendants, who came to her in haste, and said to them, "Seize him!" So forty slave-girls laid hold on him, whilst she hurriedly snatched up the ring from the cushion and rubbed it; whereupon Abu al-Sa'adat presented himself, saying, "Adsum, at thy service, O my mistress." Cried she, "Take up yonder Infidel and clap him in jail and shackle him heavily." So he took him and throwing him into the Prison of Wrath returned and reported, "I have laid him in limbo." Quoth she, "Whither wentest thou with my father and my husband?"; and quoth he, "I cast them down in the Desert Quarter." Then cried she, "I command thee to fetch them to me forthwith." He replied, "I hear and I obey," and taking flight at once, stayed not till he reached the Desert Quarter, where he lighted down upon them and found them sitting weeping and complaining each to other. Quoth he, "Fear not, for relief is come to you"; and he told them what the Wazir had done, adding, "Indeed I imprisoned him with my own hands in obedience to her, and she hath bidden me bear you back." And they rejoiced in his news.

Then he took them both up and flew home with them; nor was it more than an hour before he brought them in to Princess Dunya, who rose and saluted sire and spouse. Then she made them sit down and brought them food and sweetmeats, and they passed the rest of the night with her. On the next day she clad them in rich clothing and said to the King, "O my papa, sit thou upon thy throne and be King as before and make my husband thy Wazir of the Right and tell thy troops that which hath happened. Then send for the Minister out of prison and do him die, and after burn him, for that he is a Miscreant, and would have gone in unto me in the way of lewdness, without the rites of wedlock and he hath testified against himself that he is an Infidel and believeth in no religion. And do tenderly by thy son-in-law, whom thou makest thy Wazir of the Right." He replied, "Hearing and obeying, O my daughter. But do thou give me the ring or give it to thy husband." Quoth she, "It behoveth not that either thou or he have the ring. I will keep the ring myself, and belike I shall be more careful of it than you. Whatso ye wish seek it of me and I will demand it for you of the Slave of the Seal-ring. So fear no harm so long as I live and after my death, do what ye twain will with the ring." Quoth the King, "This is the right rede, O my daughter," and taking his son-in-law went forth to the Divan.

Now the troops had passed the night in sore chagrin for Princess Dunya and that which the Wazir had done with her, in going to her after the way of lewdness, without marriage-rites, and for his ill-usage of the King and Maʾaruf, and they feared lest the law of Al-Islam be dishonoured, because it was manifest to them that he was a Kafir. So they assembled in the Divan and fell to reproaching the Shaykh al-Islam, saying "Why didst thou not forbid him from going in to the Princess in the way of lewdness?" Said he, "O folk, the man is a Miscreant and hath gotten possession of the ring and I and you may not prevail against him. But Almighty Allah will requite him his deed, and be ye silent, lest he slay you." And as the host was thus engaged in talk, behold the King and Maʾaruf entered the Divan.

Then the King bade decorate the city and sent to fetch the Wazir from the place of duresse. So they brought him, and as he passed by the troops, they cursed him and abused him and menaced him, till he came to the King, who commanded to do him dead by the vilest of deaths. Accordingly, they slew him and after burned his body, and he went to Hell after the foulest of plights. The King made Maʾaruf his Wazir of the Right and the times were pleasant to them and their joys were untroubled. They abode thus five years till, in the sixth year, the King died and Princess Dunya made Maʾaruf Sultan in her father's stead, but she gave him not the seal-ring. During this time she had conceived by him and borne him a boy of passing loveliness, excelling in beauty and perfection, who ceased not to be reared in the laps of nurses till he reached the age of five, when his mother fell sick of a deadly sickness and calling her husband to her, said to him, "I am ill." Quoth he, "Allah preserve thee, O dearling of my heart!" But quoth she, "Haply I shall die and thou needst not that I commend to thy care thy son: wherefore I charge thee but be careful of the ring, for thine own sake and for the sake of this thy boy." And he answered, "No harm shall befall him whom Allah preserveth!" Then she pulled off the ring and gave it to him, and on the morrow she was admitted to the mercy of Allah the Most High, whilst Ma'aruf abode in possession of the kingship and applied himself to the business of governing.

Now it chanced that one day, as he shook the handkerchief and the troops withdrew to their places that he betook himself to the sitting-chamber, where he sat till the day departed and the night advanced with murks bedight. Then came in to him his cup-companions of the notables according to their custom, and sat with by way of solace and diversion, till midnight, when they craved permission to withdraw. He gave them leave and they retired to their houses; after which there came in to him a slave-girl affected to the service of his bed, who spread him the mattress and doffing his apparel, clad him in his sleeping-gown. Then he lay down and she kneaded his feet, till sleep overpowered him; whereupon she withdrew to her own chamber and slept.

But suddenly he felt something beside him in the bed and awaking started up in alarm and cried, "I seek refuge with Allah from Satan the stoned!" Then he opened his eyes and seeing by his side a woman foul of favour, said to her, "Who art thou?" Said she, "Fear not, I am thy wife Fatimah al-Urrah." Whereupon he looked in her face and knew her by her loathly form and the length of her dog-teeth: so he asked her, "Whence camest thou in to me and who brought thee to this country?" "In what country art thou at this present?" "In the city of Ikhtiyan al-Khutan. But thou, when didst thou leave Cairo?" "But now." "How can that be?" "Know," said she, "that, when I fell out with thee and Satan prompted me to do thee a damage, I complained of thee to the magistrates, who sought for thee and the Kazis enquired of thee, but found thee not. When two days were past, repentance gat hold upon me and I knew that the fault was with me; but penitence availed me not, and I abode for some days weeping for thy loss, till what was in my hand failed and I was obliged to beg my bread. So I fell to begging of all, from the courted rich to the contemned poor, and since thou leftest me, I have eaten of the bitterness of beggary and have been in the sorriest of conditions. Every night I sat beweeping our separation and that which I suffered, since thy departure, of humiliation and ignominy, of abjection and misery." And she went on to tell him what had befallen her whilst he stared at her in amazement, till she said, "Yesterday, I went about begging all day but none gave me aught; and as often as I accosted any one and craved of him a crust of bread, he reviled me and gave me naught. When night came, I went to bed supperless, and hunger burned me and sore on me was that which I suffered: and I sat weeping when, behold, one appeared to me and said, O woman why weepest thou? Said I, erst I had a husband who used to provide for me and fulfil my wishes; but he is lost to me and I know not whither he went and have been in sore straits since he left me. Asked he, What is thy husband's name? and I answered, His name is Ma²aruf. Quoth he, I ken him. Know that thy husband is now Sultan in a certain city, and if thou wilt, I will carry thee to him. Cried I, I am under thy protection: of thy bounty bring me to him! So he took me up and flew with me between heaven and earth, till he brought me to this pavilion and said to me:—Enter yonder chamber, and thou shalt see thy husband asleep on the couch. Accordingly I entered and found thee in this state of lordship. Indeed I had not thought thou wouldst forsake me, who am thy mate, and praised be Allah who hath united thee with me!"

Quoth Ma²aruf, "Did I forsake thee or thou me? Thou complainedst of me from Kazi to Kazi and endedst by denouncing me to the High Court and bringing down on me Abu Tabak from the Citadel: so I fled in mine own despite." And he went on to tell her all that had befallen him and how he was become Sultan and had married the King's daughter and how his beloved Dunya had died, leaving him a son who was then seven years old. She rejoined, "That which happened was foreordained of Allah; but I repent me and I place myself under thy protection beseeching thee not to abandon me, but suffer me eat bread with thee by way of an alms." And she ceased not to humble herself to him and to supplicate him till his heart relented towards her and he said, "Repent from mischief and abide with me, and naught shall betide thee save what shall pleasure thee: but, an thou work any wickedness, I will slay thee nor fear any one. And fancy not that thou canst complain of me to the High Court and that Abu Tabak will come down on me from the Citadel; for I am become Sultan and the folk dread me: but I fear none save Allah Almighty, because I have a talismanic ring which when I rub, the Slave of the Signet appeareth to me. His name is Abu al-Sa²adat, and whatsoever I demand of him he bringeth to me. So, an thou desire to return to thine own country, I will give thee what shall suffice thee all thy life long and will send thee thither speedily; but, an thou desire to abide with me, I will clear for thee a palace and furnish it with the choicest of silks and appoint thee twenty slave-girls to serve thee and provide thee with dainty dishes and sumptuous suits, and thou shalt be a Queen and live in all delight till thou die or I die. What sayest thou of this?" "I wish to abide with thee," she answered and kissed his hand and vowed repentance from frowardness. Accordingly he set apart a palace for her sole use and gave her slave-girls and eunuchs, and she became a Queen.

The young Prince used to visit her as he visited his sire; but she hated him for that he was not her son; and when the boy saw that she looked on him with the eye of aversion and anger, he shunned her and took a dislike to her. As for Maᵓaruf, he occupied himself with the love of fair handmaidens and bethought him not of his wife Fatimah the Dung, for that she was grown a grizzled old fright, foul-favoured to the sight, a bald-headed blight, loathlier than the snake speckled black and white; the more that she had beyond measure evil entreated him aforetime; and as saith the adage, "Ill-usage the root of desire disparts and sows hate in the soil of hearts"; and God-gifted is he who saith:—

> Beware of losing hearts of men by thine injurious deed;
> For when Aversion takes his place none may dear Love restore:
> Hearts, when affection flies from them, are likest unto glass
> Which broken, cannot whole be made,—'tis breached forevermore.

And indeed Maᵓaruf had not given her shelter by reason of any praiseworthy quality in her, but he dealt with her thus generously only of desire for the approval of Allah Almighty—

—Here[2] Dunyazad interrupted her sister Shahrazad, saying, "How winsome are these words of thine which win hold of the heart more forcibly than enchanters' eyne; and how beautiful are these wondrous books thou hast cited and the marvellous and singular tales thou hast recited!" Quoth Shahrazad, "And where is all this compared with what I shall relate to thee on the coming night, an I live and the King deign spare my days?" So when morning morrowed and the day brake in its sheen and shone, the King arose from his couch with breast broadened and in high expectation for the rest of the tale and saying, "By Allah, I will not slay her till I hear the last of her story," repaired to his Durbar while the Wazir, as was his wont, presented himself at the Palace, shroud under arm. Shahriyar tarried abroad all the day, bidding and forbidding between man and man; after which he returned to his Harim and, according to his custom, went in to his wife Shahrazad.

---

[2] At this point the narrative returns to the unifying story of Shahrazad. [Ed.]

Now when it was the Thousand and First Night,

Dunyazad said to her sister, "Do thou finish for us the History of Maᵖaruf!" She replied, "With love and goodly gree, an my lord deign permit me recount it." Quoth the King, "I permit thee; for that I am fain of hearing it." So she said:—It hath reached me, O auspicious King, that Maᵖaruf would have naught to do with his wife by way of conjugal duty. Now when she saw that he held aloof from her bed and occupied himself with other women, she hated him and jealousy gat the mastery of her and Iblis prompted her to take the seal-ring from him and slay him and make herself Queen in his stead. So she went forth one night from her pavilion, intending for that in which was her husband King Maᵖaruf; and it chanced by decree of the Decreer and His written destiny, that Maᵖaruf lay that night with one of his concubines; a damsel endowed with beauty and loveliness, symmetry and a stature all grace. And it was his wont, of the excellence of his piety, that, when he was minded to have to lie with a woman, he would doff the enchanted seal-ring from his finger, in reverence to the Holy Names graven thereon, and lay it on the pillow, nor would he don it again till he had purified himself by the Ghusl-ablution. Moreover, when he had lain with a woman, he was used to order her go forth from him before daybreak, of his fear for the seal-ring; and when he went to the Hammam he locked the door of the pavilion till his return, when he put on the ring, and after this, all were free to enter according to custom.

His wife Fatimah the Dung knew of all this and went not forth from her place till she had certified herself of the case. So she sallied out, when the night was dark, purposing to go in to him, whilst he was drowned in sleep, and steal the ring, unseen of him. Now it chanced at this time that the King's son had gone out, without light, to the Chapel of Ease for an occasion, and sat down over the marble slab of the jakes in the dark, leaving the door open. Presently, he saw Fatimah come forth of her pavilion and make stealthily for that of his father and said in himself, "What aileth this witch to leave her lodging in the dead of the night and make for my father's pavilion? Needs must there be some reason for this"; so he went out after her and followed in her steps unseen of her.

Now he had a short sword of watered steel, which he held so dear that he went not to his father's Divan, except he were girt therewith; and his father used to laugh at him and exclaim, "Mashallah! This is a mighty fine sword of thine, O my son! But thou hast not gone down with it to battle nor cut off a head therewith." Whereupon the boy would reply, "I will not fail to cut off with it some head which deserveth cutting." And Maʾaruf would laugh at his words. Now when treading in her track, he drew the sword from its sheath and he followed her till she came to his father's pavilion and entered, whilst he stood and watched her from the door. He saw her searching about and heard her say to herself, "Where hath he laid the seal-ring?"; whereby he knew that she was looking for the ring and he waited till she found it and said, "Here it is." Then she picked it up and turned to go out; but he hid behind the door. As she came forth, she looked at the ring and turned it about in her grasp. But when she was about to rub it, he raised his hand with the sword and smote her on the neck; and she cried a single cry and fell down dead.

With this Maʾaruf awoke and seeing his wife strown on the ground, with her blood flowing, and his son standing with the drawn sword in his hand, said to him, "What is this, O my son?" He replied, "O my father, how often hast thou said to me, Thou hast a mighty fine sword; but thou hast not gone down with it to battle nor cut off a head. And I have answered thee, saying, I will not fail to cut off with it a head which deserveth cutting. And now, behold, I have therewith cut off for thee a head well worth the cutting!" And he told him what had passed. Maʾaruf sought for the Seal-ring, but found it not; so he searched the dead woman's body till he saw her hand closed upon it; whereupon he took it from her grasp and said to the boy, "Thou art indeed my very son, without doubt or dispute; Allah ease thee in this world and the next, even as thou hast eased me of this vile woman! Her attempt led only to her own destruction, and Allah-gifted is he who said:—

> When forwards Allah's aid a man's intent,
> His wish in every case shall find consent:
> But an that aid of Allah be refused,
> His first attempt shall do him damagement."

Then King Maʾaruf called aloud to some of his attendants, who came in haste, and he told them what his wife Fatimah the Dung had done and bade them to take her and lay her in a place till the morning. They did his bidding, and next day he gave her in charge to a number of eunuchs, who washed her and shrouded her and made her a tomb and buried her. Thus her coming from Cairo was but to her grave, and Allah-gifted is he who said:—

> We trod the steps appointed for us: and he whose steps are appointed must tread them.
> He whose death is decreed to take place in our land shall not die in any land but that.

After this, King Ma'aruf sent for the husbandman, whose guest he had been, when he was a fugitive, and made him his Wazir of the Right and his Chief Counsellor. Then, learning that he had a daughter of passing beauty and loveliness, of qualities nature-ennobled at birth and exalted of worth, he took her to wife; and in due time he married his son. So they abode awhile in all solace of life and its delight and their days were serene and their joys untroubled, till there came to them the Destroyer of delights and the Sunderer of societies, the Depopulator of populous places and the Orphaner of sons and daughters. And glory be to the Living who dieth not and in whose hand are the Keys of the Seen and the Unseen!

TRANSLATED BY RICHARD F. BURTON

[from *Yūsuf u Zulaikhā*, Joseph and Zulaikha]

Jami, born in 1414 in a village near Samarkand, is commonly considered the last great classical Persian writer. While he lived, he was highly praised, and his work had great authority and many imitators after he died. He was a member of the Naqshbandi order, and one of his more famous works is a book of Sufi biographies. He was versatile, prolific, and proud. He wrote: "I have found no master with whom I have read superior to myself. On the contrary, I have invariably found that in argument I could defeat them all. I acknowledge, therefore, the obligations of a pupil to his master to none of them; for if I am a pupil of anyone it is of my own father, who taught me the language."

He was, first and foremost, a poet, writing many poems of many kinds. He collected three separate *dīvāns* of his poems, not including his seven *masnavīs*. The theme of Joseph and Potiphar's wife (known as Zulaykha in Islamic tradition) was an extremely popular one with the Persian poets. Embellishing the Koranic account, they turned it into a tragic love story, exonerating Zulaykha on the ground that Joseph's beauty was irresistible. Jami's poem on the subject is one of his best works and one of the best treatments of it in all of Islamic literature. The episode described in the following selection was derived from the two verses in the Koran 12.30–31.

> Love is ill suited with peace and rest:
> Scorn and reproaches become him best.
> Rebuke gives strength to his tongue, and blame
> Wakes the dull spark to a brighter flame.
> Blame is the censor of Love's bazaar:
> It suffers no rust the pure splendour to mar.
> Blame is the whip whose impending blow

Speeds the willing lover and wakes the slow;
And the weary steed who can hardly crawl
Is swift of foot when reproaches fall.
When the rose of the secret had opened and blown,
The voice of reproach was a bulbul in tone.[1]

The women of Memphis, who heard the tale first,
The whispered slander received and nursed.
Then, attacking Zulaikha for right and wrong,
Their uttered reproaches were loud and long:
"Heedless of honour and name she gave
The love of her heart to the Hebrew slave,
Who lies so deep in her soul enshrined
That to sense and religion her eyes are blind.
She loves her servant. 'Tis strange to think
That erring folly so low can sink;
But stranger still that the slave she woos
Should scorn her suit and her love refuse.
His cold eye to hers he never will raise;
He never will walk in the path where she strays.
He stops if before him her form he sees;
If she lingers a moment he turns and flees.
When her lifted veil leaves her cheek exposed,
With the stud of his eyelash his eye is closed.
If she weeps in her sorrow he laughs at her pain,
And closes each door that she opens in vain.
It may be that her form is not fair in his eyes,
And his cold heart refuses the proffered prize.
If once her beloved one sat with us
He would sit with us ever, not treat us thus.
Our sweet society ne'er would he leave,
But joy unending would give and receive.
But not all have this gift in their hands: to enthral
The heart they would win is not given to all.
There is many a woman, fair, good, and kind,
To whom never the heart of a man inclined;
And many a Laila with soft black eye.
The tears of whose heart-blood are never dry."

[1] An allusion to the bulbul's love of the rose, whose beauty, according to Persian legend, he sings.

Zulaikha heard, and resentment woke
To punish the dames for the words they spoke.
She summoned them all from the city to share
A sumptuous feast which she bade prepare.
A delicate banquet meet for kings
Was spread with the choicest of dainty things.
Cups filled with sherbet of every hue
Shone as rifts in a cloud when the sun gleams through.
There were goblets of purest crystal filled
With wine and sweet odours with art distilled.
The golden cloth blazed like the sunlight; a whole
Cluster of stars was each silver bowl.
From goblet and charger rare odours came;
There was strength for the spirit and food for the frame.
All daintiest fare that your lip would taste,
From fish to fowl, on the cloth was placed.
It seemed that the fairest their teeth had lent
For almonds, their lips for the sugar sent.
A mimic palace rose fair to view
Of a thousand sweets of each varied hue,
Where instead of a carpet the floor was made
With bricks of candy and marmalade.
Fruit in profusion, of sorts most rare,
Piled in baskets, bloomed fresh and fair.
Those who looked on their soft transparency felt
That the delicate pulp would dissolve and melt.
Bands of boys and young maidens, fine
As mincing peacocks, were ranged in line;
And the fair dames of Memphis, like Peris eyed,
In a ring on their couches sat side by side.
They tasted of all that they fancied, and each
Was courteous in manner and gentle in speech.

The feast was ended; the cloth was raised,
And Zulaikha sweetly each lady praised.
Then she set, as she planned in her wily breast,
A knife and an orange beside each guest:
An orange, to purge the dark thoughts within
Each jaundiced heart with its golden skin.
One hand, as she bade them, the orange clasped,
The knife in the other was firmly grasped.

Thus she addressed them: "Dames fair and sweet,
Most lovely of all when the fairest meet,
Why should my pleasure your hearts annoy?
Why blame me for loving my Hebrew boy?
If your eyes with the light of his eyes were filled,
Each tongue that blames me were hushed and stilled.
I will bid him forth, if you all agree,
And bring him near for your eyes to see."
"This, even this," cried each eager dame,
"Is the dearest wish that our hearts can frame.
Bid him come; let us look on the lovely face
That shall stir our hearts with its youthful grace.
Already charmed, though our eyes never fell
On the youth we long for, we love him well.
These oranges still in our hands we hold,
To sweeten the spleen with their skins of gold.
But they please us not, for he is not here:
Let not one be cut till the boy appear."

She sent the nurse to address him thus:
"Come, free-waving cypress, come forth to us.
Let us worship the ground which thy dear feet press,
And bow down at the sight of thy loveliness.
Let our love-stricken hearts be thy chosen retreat,
And our eyes a soft carpet beneath thy feet."

But he came not forth, like a lingering rose
Which the spell of the charmer has failed to unclose.
Then Zulaikha flew to the house where he dwelt,
And in fond entreaty before him knelt:
"My darling, the light of these longing eyes,
Hope of my heart," thus she spoke with sighs,
"I fed on the hope which thy words had given;
But that hope from my breast by despair is driven.
For thee have I forfeited all: my name
Through thee has been made a reproach and shame.
I have found no favour: thou wouldst not fling
One pitying look on so mean a thing.
Yet let not the women of Memphis see
That I am so hated and scorned by thee.
Come, sprinkle the salt of thy lip to cure

The wounds of my heart and the pain I endure.
Let the salt be sacred: repay the debt
Of the faithful love thou shouldst never forget."

The heart of Yusuf grew soft at the spell
Of her gentle words, for she charmed so well.
Swift as the wind from her knees she rose,
And decked him gay with the garb she chose.
Over his shoulders she drew with care,
The scented locks of his curling hair,
Like serpents of jet-black lustre seen
With their twisted coils where the grass is green.
A girdle gleaming with gold, round the waist
That itself was fine as a hair, she braced.
I marvel so dainty a waist could bear
The weight of the jewels that glittered there.
She girt his brow with bright gems; each stone
Of wondrous beauty enhanced his own.
On his shoes were rubies and many a gem,
And pearls on the latchets that fastened them.
A scarf, on whose every thread was strung
A loving heart, on his arm was hung.
A golden ewer she gave him to hold,
And a maid brow-bound with a fillet of gold
In her hand a basin of silver bore,
And shadow-like moved as he walked before.
If a damsel had looked, she at once had resigned
All joy of her life, all the peace of her mind.
Too weak were my tongue if it tried to express
The charm of his wonderful loveliness.

Like a bed of roses in perfect bloom
The secret treasure appeared in the room.
The women of Memphis beheld him, and took
From that garden of glory the rose of a look.
One glance at his beauty o'erpowered each soul
And drew from their fingers the reins of control.
Each lady would cut through the orange she held,
As she gazed on that beauty unparalleled.
But she wounded her finger, so moved in her heart,
That she knew not her hand and the orange apart.

One made a pen of her finger, to write
On her soul his name who had ravished her sight—
A reed which, struck with the point of the knife,
Poured out a red flood from each joint in the strife.
One scored a calendar's lines in red
On the silver sheet of her palm outspread,
And each column, marked with the blood-drops, showed
Like a brook when the stream o'er the bank has flowed.

   When they saw that youth in his beauty's pride:
"No mortal is he," in amaze they cried.
"No clay and water composed his frame,
But, a holy angel, from heaven he came."
" 'Tis my peerless boy," cried Zulaikha, "long
For him have I suffered reproach and wrong.
I told him my love for him, called him the whole
Aim and desire of my heart and soul.
He looked on me coldly; I bent not his will
To give me his love and my hope fulfill.
He still rebelled: I was forced to send
To prison the boy whom I could not bend.
In trouble and toil, under lock and chain,
He passed long days in affliction and pain.
But his spirit was tamed by the woe he felt,
And the heart that was hardened began to melt.
Keep your wild bird in a cage and see
How soon he forgets that he once was free."

   Of those who wounded their hands, a part
Lost reason and patience, and mind and heart.
To weak the sharp sword of his love to stay,
They gave up their souls ere they moved away.
The reason of others grew dark and dim,
And madness possessed them for love of him.
Bare-headed, bare-footed, they fled amain,
And the light that had vanished ne'er kindled again.
To some their senses at length returned,
But their hearts were wounded, their bosoms burned.
They were drunk with the cup which was full to the brim.
And the birds of their hearts were ensnared by him.
Nay, Yusuf's love was a mighty bowl

With varied power to move the soul.
One drank the wine till her senses reeled;
To another, life had no joy to yield;
One offered her soul his least wish to fulfil;
One dreamed of him ever, but mute and still.
But only the woman to whom no share
Of the wine was vouchsafed could be pitied there.

TRANSLATED BY RALPH T. H. GRIFFITH

[from *Bābur-nāmeh*, The Book of Babur]

The founder of the Mughal empire of India, Zahir al-Din Muhammad Babur (1483–1530), was a king at the age of twelve, but he was soon caught up in dynastic and other struggles in central Asia, and found himself without a kingdom. He then set about creating an empire for himself. After innumerable defeats, operating out of a stronghold in Afghanistan, he began his conquest of India. In five campaigns, each steadily more successful, his empire was assured.

Remarkably, he left to posterity a record of his life in Chagatay Turkish, which has considerable literary value above and apart from its historical importance.[1] "Instead of the stately, systematic, artificial character that seems to belong to the throne in Asia," his translator wrote, "we find him natural, lively, affectionate, simple, retaining on the throne all the best feelings and affections of common life."

Two excerpts from the work are included: the first represents a stage in Babur's early time of troubles; the second, his reflections after the most decisive of his victories.

The Year 1502

While I remained at Tâshkend at this time, I endured great distress and misery. I had no country, nor hopes of a country. Most of my servants had left me from absolute want; the few who still remained with me, were unable to accompany me on my journeys from sheer poverty. When I went to my uncle the Khan's Divan, I was attended sometimes by one person, sometimes by two; but I was fortunate in one respect, that this did not happen among strangers, but with my own kinsmen. After having paid my compliments to the Khan my uncle, I went in to wait on Shah Begum, bare-

---

[1] See S. M. Edwardes, *Babur: Diarist and Despot* (London, n.d.).

headed and bare-foot, with as much freedom as a person would do at home in his own house.

At length, however, I was worn out with this unsettled state, and with having no house nor home, and became tired of living. I said to myself, rather than pass my life in such wretchedness and misery, it were better to take my way and retire into some corner where I might live unknown and undistinguished; and rather than exhibit myself in this distress and debasement, far better were it to flee away from the sight of man, as far as my feet can carry me. I thought of going to Khitâ, and resolved to shape my course in that direction; as from my infancy I had always had a strong desire to visit Khitâ, but had never been able to accomplish my wish, from my being a King, and from my duty to my relations and connexions. Now my kingship was gone, my mother was safe with her mother and younger brother; in short, every obstacle to my journey was removed, and all my difficulties were at an end.

The Year 1526

I placed my foot in the stirrup of resolution, and my hand on the reins of confidence-in-God, and marched against Sultan Ibrâhim, the son of Sultan Iskander, the son of Sultan Behlûl Lodi Afghân, in whose possession the throne of Delhi and the dominions of Hindustân [India] at that time were.

The army of the enemy opposed to us was estimated at one hundred thousand men; the elephants of the emperor and his officers were said to amount to nearly a thousand. He possessed the accumulated treasures of his father and grandfather, in current coin, ready for use. It is an usage in Hindustân, in situations similar to that in which the enemy now were, to expend sums of money in bringing together troops who engage to serve for hire. These men are called Bedhindi. Had he chosen to adopt this plan, he might have engaged one or two hundred thousand more troops. But God Almighty directed everything for the best. He had not the heart to satisfy even his own army; and would not part with any of his treasure. Indeed, how was it possible that he should satisfy his troops, when he was himself miserly to the last degree, and beyond measure avaricious in accumulating pelf? He was a young man of no experience. He was negligent in all his movements; he marched without order; retired or halted without plan, and engaged in battle without foresight. . . .

They made one or two very poor charges on our right and left divisions. My troops making use of their bows, plied them with arrows, and drove them in upon their centre. The troops on the right and left of their centre, being huddled together in one place, such confusion ensued, that the enemy, while totally unable to advance, found also no road by which they could flee. The sun had mounted spear-high when the onset of battle began, and the combat lasted till midday, when the enemy were completely broken and routed, and my friends victorious and exulting. By the grace and mercy of Almighty God, this arduous undertaking was rendered easy for me, and this mighty army, in the space of half a day, laid in the dust. Five or six thousand men were discovered lying slain, in one spot, near Ibrâhim. We reckoned that the number lying slain, in different parts of this field of battle, amounted to fifteen or sixteen thousand men. On reaching Agra, we found, from the accounts of the natives of Hindustân, that forty or fifty thousand men had fallen in this field. After routing the enemy, we continued the pursuit, slaughtering, and making them prisoners. Those who were ahead, began to bring in the Amîrs and Afghâns as prisoners. They brought in a very great number of elephants with their drivers, and offered them to me as peshkesh. Having pursued the enemy to some distance, and supposing that Ibrâhim had escaped from the battle, I appointed Kismâi Mirza, Bâba Chihreh, and Bujkeh, with a party of my immediate adherents, to follow him in close pursuit down as far as Agra. Having passed through the middle of Ibrâhim's camp, and visited his pavilions and accommodations, we encamped on the banks of the Siâh-ab.

It was now afternoon prayers when Tahir Taberi, the younger brother of Khalîfeh, having found Ibrâhim lying dead amidst a number of slain, cut off his head, and brought it in. . . .

On Thursday, the 28th of Rejeb, about the hour of afternoon prayers, I entered Agra, and took up my residence at Sultan Ibrâhim's palace. From the time when I conquered the country of Kâbul, which was in the year 910, till the present time, I had always been bent on subduing Hindustân. Sometimes, however, from the misconduct of my Amîrs and their dislike of the plan, sometimes from the cabals and opposition of my brothers, I was prevented from prosecuting any expedition into that country, and its provinces escaped being overrun. At length these obstacles were removed. There was now no one left, great or small, noble or private man, who could dare to utter a word in opposition to the enterprise. In the year 925 I collected an army, and having taken the fort of Bajour by storm in two or three geris, put all the garrison to the sword. I next advanced into Behreh, where I prevented all marauding and plunder, imposed a contribution on the inhabitants, and having levied it to the amount of four hundred thousand shahrokhis in money and goods, divided the proceeds among the troops who were in my service, and returned back to Kâbul. From that time till the year 932, I attached myself in a peculiar degree to the affairs of Hindustân, and in the space of these seven or eight years entered it five times at the head of an army. The fifth time, the Most High God, of his grace and mercy, cast down and defeated an enemy so mighty as Sultan Ibrâhim, and made me the master and conqueror of the powerful empire of Hindustân. From the time of the blessed Prophet, (on whom and on his family be peace and salvation!) down to the present time, three foreign kings had subdued the country, and acquired the sovereignty of Hindustân. One of these was Sultan Mahmûd Ghazi, whose family long continued to fill the throne of that country. The second was Sultan Shehâbeddîn Ghûri, and for many years his slaves and dependents swayed the sceptre of these realms. I am the third. But my achievement is not to be put on the same level with theirs; for Sultan Mahmûd, at the time when he conquered Hindustân, occupied the throne of Khorasân, and had absolute power and dominion over the Sultans of Khwârizm and the surrounding chiefs. The King of Samarkand, too, was subject to him. If his army did not amount to two hundred thousand, yet grant that it was only one hundred thousand, and it is plain that the comparison between the two conquests must cease. Moreover, his enemies were Rajas. All Hindustân was not at that period subject to a single Emperor: every Raja set up for a Monarch on his own account, in his own petty territories. Again, though Sultan Shehâbeddîn Ghûri did not himself enjoy the sovereignty of Khorasân, yet his elder brother, Sultan Ghiaseddîn Ghûri, held it. In the Tabakât-e-Nâsiri it is said that on one occasion he marched into Hindustân with one hundred and twenty thousand cataphract horse. His enemies, too, were Rais and Rajas; a single monarch did not govern the whole of Hindustân. When I marched into Behreh, we might amount to one thousand five hundred, or two thousand men at the utmost. When I invaded the country for the fifth time, overthrew Sultan Ibrâhim, and subdued the empire of Hindustân, I had a larger army than I had ever before brought into it. My servants, the merchants and their servants, and the followers of all descriptions that were in the camp along with me, were numbered, and amounted to twelve thousand men. The kingdoms that depended on me were Badakhshan, Kundez, Kâbul, and Kandahâr; but these countries did not furnish me with assistance equal to their resources; and, indeed, some of them, from their vicinity to the enemy, were so circumstanced, that, far from affording me assistance, I was obliged to send them extensive supplies from my other territories. Besides this, all Mâweralnaher was occupied by the Khans and Sultans of the Uzbeks, whose armies were calculated to amount to about a hundred thousand men, and who were my ancient foes. Finally, the whole empire of Hindustân, from Behreh to Behâr, was in the hands of the Afghâns. Their prince, Sultan Ibrâhim, from the resources of his kingdom, could bring into the field an army of five hundred thousand men. At that time some of the Amîrs to the east were, in a state of rebellion. His army on foot was computed to be a hundred thousand strong; his own elephants, with those of his Amîrs, were reckoned at nearly a thousand. Yet, under such circumstances, and in spite of this power, placing my trust in God, and leaving behind me my old and inveterate enemy the Uzbeks, who had an army of a hundred thousand men, I advanced to meet so powerful a prince as Sultan Ibrâhim, the lord of numerous armies, and emperor of extensive territories. In consideration of my confidence in Divine aid, the Most High God did not suffer the distress and hardships that I had undergone to be thrown away, but defeated my formidable enemy, and made me the conqueror of the noble country of Hindustân. This success I do not ascribe to my own strength, nor did this good fortune flow from my own efforts, but from the fountain of the favour and mercy of God.

TRANSLATED BY JOHN LEYDEN AND WILLIAM ERSKINE

MUGHAL POETRY

During the reigns of Babur's grandson Akbar (ruled 1556–1605) and his successors, Jehangir and Shah Jahan (who built the Taj Mahal), the Mughal empire established itself as one of the three principal centers of power within the Islamic world. Culturally the Mughal empire was heavily under the influence of Iran, and most of its important early literature was written in Persian. Mughal literature is renowned, in fact, for its Persian poetry. The Mughal courts so recognized and rewarded poetic talent that for more than two centuries the best Persian poets migrated to India.

The Persian poets of Mughal India did not, in general, attempt the lengthy *masnavī* form, but contented themselves with the *ghazal* and even single couplets, in which they excelled. It is said that one of the first of the Mughal Persian couplets was uttered by a parrot. In the original it is quite fine:

> Men have gone past;
> aren't you going on?

Babur

The new year, the spring, the wine, and the beloved are pleasing;
Enjoy them, Babur, for the world is not to be had a second time.

Mir Ali Shir

Give justice, O blue sky,
Which of these two walked more beautifully;
Either thy world-illuminating sun from the side of Morn,
Or my world-traversing moon from the side of Eve.

349

Kabir

Do not go to the garden,
O brother go not there,
In thy *self* is the garden,
Take thy seat on the petals
Of the lotus, and then behold,
The Eternal beauty.

None but a sane man will hear
The melody which arises in the sky.
He who is the source of all melody
Fills all vessels with music,
And sits in fullness Himself.

Clouds thicken in the sky,
O, listen to their roarings,
The rain comes from the East,
With its thundrous roar.
Take care of the fences and the fields,
Lest the rain make a flood over there.

Gadai Dehlevi

Sometimes the soul was the abode of love, sometimes the heart;
I carry thy love from place to place.
Be not remiss to the need of one grief-stricken,
For he forgets not thee for a moment.
I tied my infatuated heart to thy curly lock;
I am ensnared in that musky chain.
If by surrendering one's life the task would become easy,
To lovers no difficulty would have remained.
O Gadāī, life ended with failure;
My object was not achieved from the ruby lips of the beloved.

TRANSLATED BY M. A. GHANI

Saib

Stealing a kiss is a wonderful theft; how pleasing the end in any case!
For should it be taken back, it is doubled!

Mulla Shaida

Night and day our master Talib
Is running after this carcass of the world.
Perhaps he remembers not the words of the Prophet:
"This world is a carrion and he who hankers after it is a dog."

Nur Jahan

The ruby button that glistens on thy silk shirt
Is the drop of my blood that has caught you by the collar.

Muizzi

The King beheld the *fire* which in me blazed:
Me from the *earth* above the moon he raised:
From me a verse, like *water* fluent, heard,
And swift as *wind* a noble steed conferred.

TRANSLATED BY R. P. MASANI

[from *Mīzān al-Ḥaqq*, The Balance of Truth]

Katib Chelebi, who later called himself Hajji Khalifah, was a Turkish writer of the seventeenth century. He served the Ottoman state as an official in the control of the cavalry, and participated in several military campaigns. After 1635, a substantial inheritance enabled him to pursue a life of scholarship, which he preferred, although he did not completely retire from public service. He devoted more than twenty years to the compilation of his *Kashf al-Ẓunūn* (The Removal of Doubts), a vast encyclopedia and bibliography.

The Balance of Truth was his last work. It consists of a number of essays on controversial points of Islamic doctrine and practice, concluding with a brief autobiography. It well illustrates how current questions could be treated within the traditional form of legal exposition. "It breathes a spirit of liberalism and good sense," its translator says, "enlivened with a mordant humour." Hajji Khalifah died in Istanbul in 1657, while drinking a cup of coffee.

Tobacco

At one time I drafted an essay on the tobacco-smoking now practised by all mankind, but I never made a fair copy of it. What is offered here is a rough draft embodying the gist of that essay. Before we examine the matter, what was the cause of the appearance of this practice? Let us explain this in a didactic passage.

The Facts. Some time in the latter half of the ninth century of the Hijra, after some Spanish ships had discovered the New World, the Portuguese and English were exploring its shores to find a passage from the Eastern to the Western Ocean. They came to an island close to the mainland, called in the *Atlas* "Gineyā." A ship's doctor, who had been smitten with a lymphatic disorder, due to the influence of the sea air on his natural temperament, decided to try and cure it with hot and dry things, in accordance with the laws of treatment by opposites. When his ship reached that island, he noticed a kind of leaf was burning. He smelled it, and as it was hot of scent he began to inhale it, using an instrument resembling a pipe. It did him good, so he took a large quantity of the leaf and used it throughout their stay. The ship's company saw this and, regarding it as a beneficial medicine, followed the doctor's example and loaded themselves up with the leaf. One saw another and they all began to smoke. When the ship arrived in England, the habit spread, through France to the other lands. People tried it, not knowing its origin, and not considering that it was smoked for a serious purpose. Many became addicts, putting it in the category of stimulating drugs. It has become a thing common to East and West, and no one has succeeded in suppressing it.

From its first appearance in Turkey, which was about the year 1010/1601, to the present day, various preachers have spoken against it individually, and many of the Ulema have written tracts concerning it, some claiming that it is a thing forbidden, some that it is disapproved. Its addicts have replied to the effect that it is permissible. After some time had elapsed, the eminent surgeon Ibrāhīm Efendi devoted much care and attention to the matter, conducting great debates in the Abode of the Sultanate, that is, in the city of Islambol,[1] giving warning talks at a special public meeting in the mosque of Sultan Mehmed, and sticking copies of fetwas onto walls. He troubled himself to no purpose. The more he spoke, the more people persisted in smoking. Seeing that it was fruitless, he abandoned his efforts. After that, the late Sultan Murad IV, towards the end of his reign, closed down the coffeehouses in order to shut the gate of iniquity, and also banned smoking, in consequence of certain outbreaks of fire.[2] People being undeterred, the imperial anger necessitated the chastisement of those who, by smoking, committed the sin of disobedience to the imperial command. Gradually His

[1] Islambol is Turkish for "Islam abounding," and was a common punning variant for the name of the Ottoman capital.

[2] Murad IV (1623–1640) had come to the throne when barely twelve years old, in a period of anarchy, and had been obliged to take ruthless measures against the mutinous Janissaries. He closed the coffeehouses and forbade smoking on pain of death, on September 16, 1633, a fortnight after the great fire which destroyed one-fifth of Istanbul. The coffeehouses were breeding places of disaffection. The reason for the Sultan's objection to smoking is less obvious: some say he was persuaded to outlaw tobacco by Qādīzāde Mehmed Efendi, who regarded it as a sinful innovation. According to the historians, the great fire was not due to a careless smoker, but started in a shipyard where calking was going on.

Majesty's severity in suppression increased, and so did people's desire to smoke, in accordance with the saying, "Men desire what is forbidden," and many thousands of men were sent to the abode of nothingness.

When the Sultan was going on the expedition against Baghdad, at one halting-place fifteen or twenty leading men of the Army were arrested on a charge of smoking, and were put to death with the severest torture in the imperial presence. Some of the soldiers carried short pipes in their sleeves, some in their pockets, and they found an opportunity to smoke even during the executions. At Istanbul, no end of soldiers used to go into the barracks and smoke in the privies. Even during this rigorous prohibition, the number of smokers exceeded that of the non-smokers.

After that Sultan's death, the practice was sometimes forbidden and sometimes allowed, until the Sheykh al-Islam, the late Bahāʾī Efendi, gave a fetwa ruling that it was permissible, and the practice won renewed popularity among the people of the world. Occasional reprimands from the Throne to smokers have generally been disregarded, and smoking is at present practised all over the habitable globe. Such are the vicissitudes undergone by tobacco.

Now there are a number of possible ways of considering the subject, which we shall briefly set forth.

(1) The first possibility is that the people may be effectively prevented from smoking and may give it up. This possibility must be set aside, for custom is second nature. Addicts are not made to give up in this way. The suggestion should be put to them. If they say "And what purpose will prohibition serve?"—great men have recommended "Let the rulers not stint the rod on the backs of the common people." Consequently it is the rulers' duty, publicly to prohibit and chastise; thus do they perform their part. As for the people, their duty, if they are addicted to such things, is to refrain from committing a breach of good order by using them in the streets. But in his own house every man may do as he pleases. Then, if the rulers interfere, they will be taking upon themselves more than they should:

"What work for the censor within a man's home?"

(2) Is this tobacco found to be good or bad by the intelligence? If we set aside the fact that addicts think it good, common sense judges it to be bad. The criterion of goodness and badness may be either the intelligence or the sacred law. By either criterion it is bad, for the conditions necessary for intellectual approval are lacking in it, while the grounds for canonical dis-

approval are present in it. Yet if certain of the lacking conditions are fulfilled, it may then be found good; for example, if it be used medicinally. The fact that it is not used by judges in law courts, at council meetings, in mosques or other places of worship, is a consequence of its being found bad by the criterion of intelligence.

(3) Its good and harmful effects. As to its harmful effects there is no doubt. It ends by becoming a basic need of the addict, who does not consider its evil consequences. Its harmful physical effect too is established, for tobacco is medically noxious in that it makes turbid the aerial essence. Eventually, to him who is habituated to its use, custom becomes second nature, and thus he keeps its noxious effects at bay. The craving of addiction and nature's disposition towards the use of tobacco have a protective quality whereby, when the defiled air is sniffed up, it does not affect the heart. So when certain invalids eat the noxious food they crave it does not harm them so very much, and may even work an occasional cure. Craving and desire give a strength which repels the disease. The influence exerted on the body by such things depends on the nature's disposition or aversion. If a man does not use tobacco, declares it to be harmful and feels a natural repugnance towards it, the inhaling of tobacco-smoke does him more harm and has a greater effect.

Apart from the noxious effects of the corruption of the aerial essence, the smoker must belong to one of two classes: he is either of moist temperament or of dry. In either case his temperament may be either healthy or out of sorts. If the man of moist temperament is healthy, smoking is suitable and agreeable to him. But certainly for most people some dryness is necessary. If he be out of sorts, and if this be due to excessive moisture, smoking will act as a remedy for him. For the man of dry temperament, however, it is in no wise permissible. It will increase his dryness and will constantly desiccate the moisture of his lungs. There is absolutely no foundation for the claim some people make that it is good for scurvy; this is idle chatter which has no point of contact with the circle of the laws of medicine.

(4) Is it innovation? It may be conceded that it is innovation in the eyes of the sacred law, for it appeared in recent times, nor is it possible to class it as "good innovation." That it is innovation in the light of intelligence is sure, for it is not a thing that has been seen or heard of by the intelligent ever since the time of Adam. There is a tale that it first appeared in the

hallowed time of ᶜUmar (God be pleased with him) and that many thousands of men were killed because of it. This is without foundation, a fiction of the fanatical.

(5) Is it abominable? There is no word of justification for this, in reason or in law. This view is accepted by the generality of people. For a thing to reach the stage of the abominable, it is an essential condition that it be used to excess. The scent of tobacco-smoke and the scent of the tobacco-leaf are not intrinsically abominable. It is perhaps not irrelevant to point out that the scent of burning tobacco has curative uses as an inhalant. But an evil odour arises in the mouth of the heavy smoker, by comparison with which, in the nostrils of the non-smoker, halitosis is as aloes-wood and ambergris.

To sum up, just as there is abomination in the eating of raw onion, garlic, and leek, which inevitably produce an abominable odour in the mouth, so also heavy smoking is disapproved as producing a smell in the mouth, the body, and the clothing. And the reason is that there is incontestable offence in both cases. Just as the prohibition against sexual intercourse during menstruation, on account of uncleanliness and offensiveness, has given rise to an analogous prohibition against pederasty, so too the use of such foods and of tobacco comes under a common disapproval.

The conclusion must be to recommend abstention. The fact that addicts do not concede this scent to be disapproved is irrelevant and not to be taken into consideration. For they are at liberty not to disapprove the smell of one another's mouths.

The purpose of all this is to demonstrate the facts: there is no question of interference with those who have the addiction. To try to put them off is not a practical possibility, and is generally agreed to be in the category of preaching to the winds.

(6) Is it canonically forbidden? It is written in the manuals of jurisprudence that in any particular matter where there is no decisive ruling in the law, the jurisconsult may exercise his own discretion. He may, according to one point of view, bring together all relevant circumstances, consider them, and make his own deductions. Yet the following course is preferable: not to declare things forbidden, but always to have recourse to any legal principle that justifies declaring them permitted, thus preserving the people from being laden with sins and persisting in what has been prohibited.

(7) Is it canonically indifferent? As the rise of smoking is of recent occurrence, there is no explicit treatment or mention of it in the legal manuals. This being so, some say that in accordance with the principle that permissibility is the norm—i. e., that in the absence of a clear prohibition things are permitted—smoking is permitted and lawful.

The great doctors of the law have in former times pronounced it disapproved, while certain provincial muftis have declared it forbidden. More recently, the late Bahāʾī Efendi pronounced it lawful, not out of regard for his own addiction but because he considered what was best suited to the condition of the people and because he held fast to the principle that permissibility is the norm. For the rule about fetwas is to base them on a tradition from one of the four Founders of the Law. In the absence of such a tradition, it is necessary to go back to first principles.

Although the prevalence of smoking, together with all the attendant circumstances, does not suffice to put it in the class of permissibles, yet an objection arises against pronouncing it forbidden or disapproved, which overrides any consideration of its undesirable qualities. And what is that objection? It is that the people will persist in using the forbidden thing, with baneful results. Further, declaring it to be lawful is in the general interest, as being an act of compassion towards the addict and protecting the public from sin. For this reason the preference has been given to declaring it permitted. As most Muslims are addicted to it, they have become inseparably attached to the practice, and will in no circumstance be deterred from it or abandon it, and it has taken hold of the whole world. In matters of this kind, judge and mufti must give their decisions and rulings according to what the sacred law allows, so that men be not driven into sin. For a fetwa has been given which says "Persistence in a practice which is adjudged by contemporary authority to be forbidden and disapproved, is canonically indifferent"; it is not like persistence in a practice expressly prohibited by the sacred law. The latter is pure bane, but in the former there is no harm.

The judge who decides on the basis of some such legal principle as "Choose the lesser of the two evils" is committing no sin and may perhaps acquire merit and reward for delivering a believer from sin.

The late Bahāʾī Efendi was a man of right nature and sound sense. Had he studied hard "in accordance with the *qānūn*," and had he not been addicted to narcotics, he would have become one of the most eminent scholars in Turkey. But he did have a talent for deduction, and by his natural ability he used to display his cleverness everywhere. In the matter under discussion he had regard for the condition of mankind and was compassionate. May God be compassionate to him. There has never been a mufti like him since the late ʿAbd al-Rahīm Efendi.[3]

Admonition. Some may ask, Can one thing be simultaneously indifferent, disapproved, and forbidden? Is this not self-contradictory? The answer is that it is possible, with a change of aspect and viewpoint. For example, while it is permissible to eat *baklava*, it is forbidden to do so when one is sated, as this is harmful.

Hereafter the most necessary and useful thing for the rulers of the Muslims to do is this: they should farm out exclusive concessions to deal in tobacco-leaf in every part of the Guarded Domains, appointing custodians. Tobacco will bear a fixed contribution to the Treasury of 20 piastres per *okka*. It should be sold in one appointed place in every city and should not be allowed in the markets at large. This will yield 100 million aspers a year.

During the rigorous prohibition enforced under the late Ghazi Sultan Murad, many people, not daring to smoke tobacco in pipes, used to repel the craving by crushing the leaf and snuffing it up their noses, but subsequently they have abandoned this foolishness, for smoking without fear has become possible. Next, there are certain God-fearing men who themselves piously refrain, but do not interfere with smokers. Some again find that it does not agree with them, and for that reason do not smoke, like the present writer.

The fool may interfere, saying:
"Scatter the stupidity of smoking with the wind of fortitude
For it has obstructed with its heat the sun of the mind."
The addict replies:
"The joy and savour of tobacco are not found in honey and sugar,"

and goes on smoking, quite undismayed. The best course is not to interfere with anyone in this respect, and that is all there is to it.

---

[3] Hajji ʿAbd al-Rahīm Efendi was Bahāʾī Efendi's immediate predecessor as Sheykh al-Islam, 1647–1649. The compliment is not so empty as it may seem: there had been six other incumbents of the office between Bahāʾī Efendi's first dismissal, in May 1651, and November, 1656, when the *Balance of Truth* was completed.

Coffee

This matter too was much disputed in the old days. It originated in Yemen and has spread, like tobacco, all over the world. Certain sheykhs, who lived with their dervishes in the mountains of Yemen, used to crush and eat the berries, which they called *qalb wabūn*, of a certain tree. Some would roast them and drink their water. Coffee is a cold dry food, suited to the ascetic life and sedative of lust. The people of Yemen learned of it from one another, and sheykhs, Sufis, and others used it.

It came to Asia Minor by sea, about 950/1543, and met with a hostile reception, fetwas being delivered against it. For they said, Apart from its being roasted,[4] the fact that it is drunk in gatherings, passed from hand to hand, is suggestive of loose living. It is related of Abuʾl-Suʿūd Efendi that he had holes bored in the ships that brought it, plunging their cargoes of coffee into the sea. But these strictures and prohibitions availed nothing. The fetwas, the talk, made no impression on the people. One coffeehouse was opened after another, and men would gather together, with great eagerness and enthusiasm, to drink. Drug addicts in particular, finding it a life-giving thing, which increased their pleasure, were willing to die for a cup.

Since then, muftis pronounced it permissible. The late Bostānzāde delivered a detailed fetwa, in verse.[5] Thus coffeehouses experienced varying fortunes for several years, now banned, now permitted. After the year 1000/1591–1592, they ceased to be prohibited. They were opened everywhere, freely: on every street corner a coffeehouse appeared.

Storytellers and musicians diverted the people from their employments, and working for one's living fell into disfavour. Moreover the people, from prince to beggar, amused themselves with knifing one another. Towards the end of 1042/1633, the late Ghazi Sultan Murad, becoming aware of the situation, promulgated an edict, out of regard and compassion for the people, to this effect: Coffeehouses throughout the Guarded Domains shall be dismantled and not opened hereafter. Since then, the coffeehouses of the capital

[4] Part of one of these fetwas, quoted in R. E. Koçu's *Osmanlı Tarihinde Yasaklar* (Istanbul, 1950), runs: "Whatsoever reaches the level of carbonization, that is, becomes charcoal, is absolutely forbidden." An *ad hoc* rule?
[5] Bostānzāde Mehmed Efendi was Sheykh al-Islam from April, 1589, to May, 1592, and again from July, 1593, till his death in April, 1598. He wrote verses in Arabic and Turkish.

have been as desolate as the heart of the ignorant. In the hope that they might be reopened, their proprietors did not dismantle them for a while, but merely closed them. Later the majority, if not all of them, were dismantled and turned into other kinds of shops. But in cities and towns outside Istanbul, they are opened just as before. As has been said above, such things do not admit of a perpetual ban.

Now let us come to the description of coffee itself. Coffee is indubitably cold and dry: Dā'ūd of Antioch's statement, in the *Tadhkira*, that it is hot and dry, is not generally accepted.[6] Even when it is boiled in water and an infusion made of it, its coldness does not depart; perhaps it increases, for water too is cold. That is why coffee quenches thirst, and does not burn if poured on a limb, for its heat is a strange heat, with no effect.

But a certain abatement comes to its dryness: for instance, in itself it is of the third degree of dryness but, when mixed with moisture of the second degree of cold, one degree of its dryness goes, leaving it in the second degree of dryness. By the dryness it repels sleep. It has a positive diuretic effect, varying with the temperament.

To those of dry temperament, especially to the man of melancholic temperament, large quantities are unsuitable, and may be repugnant. Taken in excess, it causes insomnia and melancholic anxiety. If drunk at all, it should be drunk with sugar.

To those of moist temperament, and especially to women, it is highly suited. They should drink a great deal of strong coffee. Excess of it will do them no harm, so long as they are not melancholic.

TRANSLATED BY G. L. LEWIS

[6] *Tadhkirat uli'l-albāb* ("Reminder for People of Understanding"), a celebrated treatise on medicine by Dā'ūd ibn 'Umar al-Antākī (d. *ca.* 1597).

[from *Nasā'iḥ al-Vuzarā' v-al-Umarā'*, Counsel
for Viziers and Governors]

During his career as treasurer to the Ottoman Sultan Ahmed III
(ruled 1703–1730), Sari Mehmed Pasha wrote a handbook of Ottoman
statecraft in the tradition of Nizam al-Mulk's *Book of Government*.
While it cannot be contended that this book advanced the literary
form very significantly, it illustrated the Turks' fondness for such
traditional forms and the resiliency of the form itself.

Sari Mehmed Pasha worked his way up to the highest position in
the treasury department, and held the post five times. Apparently he
aspired to the office of Grand Vizier, but was not sufficiently subtle
in the methods he employed to advance his candidacy. As a result he
was disgraced and soon executed by the government he had served
for nearly fifty years.

In his work "we see the rare spectacle of a man who is himself a
part of the vast machine of the Ottoman state and is yet able to look
at it objectively, measuring its defects and planning to remedy them,"
as the translator puts it. As was the case with Nizam al-Mulk's work,
Sari Mehmed Pasha's chapters were not limited merely to repetition
of precepts and wise sayings couched in the literary form deemed
appropriate, but were meant to illuminate contemporary problems, to
instill a right attitude toward government, and to suggest reforms.
He often paints a black picture of conditions, and his work is regarded
as a valuable indication of the state of the Ottoman empire as it began
its long decline. This particular selection has a special irony in view
of the author's subsequent fate.

It is a most necessary essential for all the ministers of the government
to know what the conduct and behavior of officeholders should be, and [to
know] in what manner they should live with the population of the [various]
districts, and to act accordingly. First of all it is necessary to inquire dili-

gently about the condition of affairs among the officeholders who are outside [Istānbūl] and to know how they behave. One or two complaints do not necessitate the removal of a provincial governor. Rather let a letter imparting advice be sent him from his excellency the grand vezir, and let him be warned and admonished. If he accept not this advice and complaints come again, and if his oppression be evident, he should be removed. Let the position be given to a man of consequence, and let it not be given to those who are uninformed regarding the honored law and the conditions of the world, nor to those unable to acquit themselves of the duty. And let it not be given because of interceding or pleading or bribing. It is generally agreed that the wound of adversity to the country, and the temptation to revolt among the people of all governments which have gone before, have come through neglecting to act in accordance with the precept: "Give back the trust to its owner."[1] There is very great advantage in not flinging into the corner of oblivion, as being powerless, the men who are good workers, experienced and moderate, but in appointing such men to suitable government positions.

It is essential to be on guard against giving office through bribery to the unfit and to tyrannical oppressors. For the giving of office to such as these because of bribes means the giving of permission to plunder the property of the subject people. An equivalent for the bribe which is given must be had. In addition to what is given as bribe, he must make a profit for himself and his followers. Bribery is the beginning and root of all illegality and tyranny, the source and fountain of every sort of disturbance and sedition, the most vast of evils, and greatest of calamities. It is the mine of corruption than which there is nothing whatever more calamitous to the people of Islām or more destructive to the foundations of religion and government. Than this there is no more powerful engine of injustice and cruelty, for bribery destroys both faith and state. An act which is entirely destitute of benefit, whose harm may so endure and extend itself as perhaps both to necessitate public ignominy in this world and to become the object of bitter punishment in that to come—is this the act of a wise man? It is not! The Prophet of God (on whom be the commendation and salutation of God) has said: "May God curse the briber and the taker of bribes."[2]

[1] Koran 4.58.
[2] A tradition quoted in Ahmad ibn-Hanbal, *Musnad*, Vol. 2, p. 387.

[Verses]:

> Most tyrannies come from bribes.
> No position is given justly to the briber.
> The Prophet has said:
> "The souls of both briber and bribed are cursed by God."

If it becomes necessary to give a position because of bribes, in this way its holder has permission from the government for every sort of oppression. Stretching out the hand of violence and tyranny against the poor subjects along his route [of travel] and spreading fire among the poor, he destroys the wretched peasants and ruins the cultivated lands. As the fields and villages become empty of husbandmen, day by day weakness comes to land and property, which remain destitute of profits and revenues and harvest and benefit. In addition to the fact that it causes a decline in the productivity of the subjects and in the revenues of the Treasury, through neglect of the employment of tilling and lack of the work of agriculture, there is the greatest probability (may God—exalted is He—forfend!) that it will cause scarcity and dearth and mishaps and calamities.

The fear of removal should be driven away from the Ottoman offices of state. Those of the rulers who persevere in tyranny and dare to act oppressively should be killed by the stroke of the sword of punishment. With the promise of menace the positions should be given freely and gratuitously to those who are deserving. No person has need of taking great pains to seek after and trouble himself over the high position which he [really] deserves, nor of offering money and presents and bribes [for it]. When high officials act in accordance with right and use justice in appointing those who deserve positions, bribery is not necessary. For example, in the case of a position connected with the science of accounting, they should cause to be found someone well versed in that art, and assign him to the duties of keeper of accounts. Moreover, through abundant increase of knowledge and skill, he becomes absolute master of the subject. Longing for nothing else, he neither runs about after anything nor has inordinate ambitions, and there is no likelihood that he will give bribes.

If, on the other hand, a person unskilled in accounting come from outside and say: "By all means employ me in this work. So and so much money I will give as a bribe," and if they yield to his design, though in outward form there is no inference beyond their taking of the bribe money, nevertheless because of his ignorance of the art and lack of skill he is unable to succeed in his work, and consequently becomes the source of great mistakes. In short, the person to whom an office is given should previously have performed services useful to the Exalted Government and should be known by everybody as one who will bestow perfect care on the business to which he is assigned. It is essential to have experienced persons who will not be heedless of the details of government business. To give office to the unfit because of bribery is a very great sin.

If neither the grand vezir nor the vezirs who are rulers of the provinces in a country, nor the governors nor the commanders nor the other civil authorities, cast a glance from the corner of their eye at the bribe which is offered by a person in exchange for something contrary to the honored law or opposed to the imperial ordinance, and if they be deadly and jealous enemies to the vain and frustrated briber, there is no chance that anyone whatever among their attendants and other stewards will dare to covet wealth or the means of fulfilling a mania for tyranny and evil. If a just vezir, though doing no other pious deed, yet abstain from bribery, it suffices. This vast work of universal benefit is greater in merit than the value of the world.

At the present time some among the judges also give bribes the title of "income" and do not execute the laws of God. They decide (may the Most High God forfend!) in favor of whichever side shows the greater bribe. If they wish, the debtor comes off creditor and his bankruptcy becomes as the wealth of Korah.[3] To gain the favor of God—exalted is He—let them strive and endeavor to make diligent inquiry with perfect care about this sort of persons, that they may be expelled and driven away from the aforementioned path. Even as it has been said regarding these [verses]:

> Cursed be the money for which thou sellest the law.
> Thou castest the commandment of God to the wilderness.
> For a bribe thou annullest the word of truth.
> Thou exchangest religion for worldly wealth.
> Of this thou thinkest not, O erring one,
> That this is glorious, this Law of God.
> With it Gabriel, the trusted one,
> Reverently adorned the face of the earth.

[3] The biblical Korah was fabled in Islamic tradition for his wealth.

God defend us, for there is no sin greater than [that of] giving, because of bribes, another form to measures whose execution is required by the law, and of committing acts contrary to the glorious canons.

To government officials the disease of bribery is one whose cure [is hard to determine. Perhaps it has no cure.][4] [Yet] there is no disease without remedy. This must be considered in all its aspects and absolutely eschewed and avoided. And yet, should one's own friend bring a gift, there is no harm in taking the present. It must not be with any implication, but rather with the purpose of causing an increase in friendship.

Consultation should be held with the chiefs of the *ᶜulema* regarding the teachers of the law and the religious officials, and their positions should be assigned in accordance with the communications and opinions of the former. To what they say against each other no attention should be paid.

And once again, if the *eyalets* and *sanjaqs* situated in the divinely protected dominions be always presented and given to useful, celebrated, and veteran *beylerbeys* and *sanjaq beys*[5] who have come by the straight road, and if the punishment of those from whom great sins issue be given according to the law, and if they undergo their deserts without fail, if the grand *mullahs* and judges be examined and those who are ignorant and unfit be expelled and their offices be given to men of knowledge and superiority, if orders be issued and the ancient law be carried out that not one day from the days of their terms of office be subtracted or added—[if all this be done]—to whom will the briber give his bribes, and from whom can those who desire bribes get the bribes? Thus, when bribery is cured and remedied and the rulers are just, the subjects will be neither oppressed nor ill treated. And it is to be expected that the peasants who have been scattered from certain regions will of their own free will return to their ancient homes and settle permanently.

TRANSLATED BY WALTER LIVINGSTON WRIGHT

---

[4] This passage was erased from the principal manuscript on which the translation was based, but is found in all the other manuscripts.

[5] *Eyalets* and *sanjaqs* were provinces and sub-provinces of the Ottoman empire; and *beylerbeys* and *sanjaq beys*, their governors and lieutenant governors.

The Ottoman poets do not rank among the most famous or the best of Islamic poets, but they must not be discounted. Many of them wrote in Persian, and some in Arabic. The adaptation of the *qaṣīdah* and *ghazal* forms to Turkish was itself no small accomplishment. Ottoman poetry is judged harshly because it is full of clichés and conceits. Yet there is much good Sufi poetry, and its best creations, perhaps, are the less inhibited *ghazals* of love, reminiscent of Hafiz.

Nejati: From the Winter Qasidah

Locust-like down from the sky the snowflakes wing their way;
From the green-plumaged bird, Delight, O heart! hope not for lay.
Like drunken camels, spatter now the clouds earth's winding sheet;
Laded the caravan of mirth and glee, and passed away.
With lighted lamps in daytime seek the people for the sun;
Yet scarce, with trouble, a dim, fitful spark discover they.

The Moon in Sign of Bounteousness! the Shade of Allah's grace!
The King, star-armied! he in aspect fair as Hermes' ray—
The Khān Muhammad! at the portal of whose sphere of might
To wait as servants would Darius and Key-Khusrev pray!
E'en should the sun till the Last Day it measure with gold beam,
Nor shore nor depth could e'er it find to th' ocean of his sway!

Quatrains

O handkerchief! I send thee—off to yonder maid of grace;
Around thee I my eyelashes will make the fringe of lace;
I will the black point of my eye rub up to paint therewith;
To yon coquettish beauty go—go look thou in her face.

O handkerchief! the loved one's hand take, kiss her lip so sweet,
Her chin, which mocks at apple and at orange, kissing greet;
If sudden any dust should light upon her blessed heart,
Fall down before her, kiss her sandal's sole, beneath her feet.

A sample of my tears of blood thou, handkerchief, wilt show.
Through these within a moment would a thousand crimson grow;
Thou'lt be in company with her, while I am sad with grief;
To me no longer life may be, if things continue so.

Mesihi: From the Spring Qasidah

Up from indolent sleep the eyes of the flowers to awake,
Over their faces each dawn the cloudlets of spring water shake.
Denizens all of the mead now with new life are so filled,
That were its foot not secured, into dancing the cypress would break.
Roses' fair cheeks to describe, all of their beauty to tell,
Lines on the clear river's page rain-drops and light ripples make.
Silvery rings, thou would'st say, they hung in the bright water's ear,
When the fresh rain-drops of spring fall on the stretch of the lake.
Since the ring-dove, who aloft sits on the cypress, its praise
Sings, were it strange if he be sad and love-sick for its sake?

Fuzuli: Mukhammes

Attar within vase of crystal, such thy fair form silken-gowned;
And thy breast is gleaming water, where the bubbles clear abound;
Thou so bright none who may gaze upon thee on the earth is found;
Bold wert thou to cast the veil off, standing forth with garland crowned·
  Not a doubt but woe and ruin all the wide world must confound!

Lures the heart thy gilded palace, points it to thy lips the way;
Eagerly the ear doth listen for the words thy rubies say;
Near thy hair the comb remaineth, I despairing far away;
Bites the comb, each curling ringlet, when it through thy locks doth stray:
  Jealous at its sight, my heart's thread agonized goes curling round.

Selīmī: Ghazal

Hand in hand thy mole hath plotted with thy hair,
Many hearts made captive have they in their snare.
Thou in nature art an angel whom the Lord
In his might the human form hath caused to wear.
When he dealt out 'mongst his creatures union's tray,
Absence from thee, God to me gave as my share.
Thou would'st deem that Power, the limner, for thy brows,
O'er the lights, thine eyes, two *nūns*[1] had painted fair.
O Selīmī, on the sweetheart's cheek the down
Is thy sighs' fume, which, alas, hath rested there.

Baqi: Ghazal

Tulip-cheeked ones over rosy field and plain stray all around;
Mead and garden cross they, looking wistful each way, all around.
These the lovers true of radiant faces, aye, but who the fair?
Lisson Cypress, thou it is whom eager seek they all around.
Band on band Woe's legions camped before the City of the Heart,
There, together leagued, sat Sorrow, Pain, Strife, Dismay, all around.
From my weeping flows the river of my tears on every side,
Like an ocean 'tis again, a sea that casts spray all around.
Forth through all the Seven Climates have the words of Bāqī gone;
This refulgent verse recited shall be always, all around.

Ghazal

From thine own beauty's radiant sun doth light flow;
How lustrously doth now the crystal glass show!
Thy friend's the beaker, and the cup's thy comrade;
Like to the dregs why dost thou me aside throw?
Hearts longing for thy beauty can resist not;
Hold, none can bear the dazzling vision's bright glow!
United now the lover, and now parted;
This world is sometimes pleasure and sometimes woe.
Bound in the spell of thy locks' chain is Bāqī.
Mad he, my Liege, and to the mad they grace show.

---

[1] A letter of the Arabic alphabet, which rather resembles an eye. [Ed.]

Fazil Beg: Ghazal

The trees and flowers their turbans roll of black and white and red;
The garden fastens on its stole of black and white and red.
With sable eve and ermine dawn and fez of sunset bright,
The sky doth all its pomp unroll of black and white and red.
The pupils of my eyes are points upon the gleaming page,
With tears of blood I've writ a scroll of black and white and red.
The youthful Magian's locks and breast were shadowed in the wine;
It seemed as though they filled the bowl with black and white and red.
Is't ambergris, or is it pearl, or coral, Fazil, say,
This poesy thy reed doth troll, of black and white and red?

Circassian Women

Ah! her cheek doth rob the fair sun of its sight,
And her sweet grace envy brings to Venus bright.
Like to moons are the Circassian damsels fair;
Whatsoe'er the lover seeks he findeth there.
Like to tall palm-trees their slender forms in grace,
Or a ladder to the clear moon of the face.
With the two feet of the eyes doth one ascend,
But the vision of the mind too one must bend.
Since their lips and cheeks are taverns of wine,
Is it strange their eyes inebriate should shine?
Since like rubies are created their two lips,
Doubly seared the lover's heart, like the tulip's.
Since their bodies are distilled from moon and sun,
How an equal to their pure frame find can one?

Greek Women

Source of being! if a mistress thou should seek,
Then, I pray thee, let thy loved one be a Greek.
Unto her fancies of the joyous bend,
For there's leave to woo the Grecian girl, my friend.
Caskets of coquetry are the Grecian maids,
And their grace the rest of womankind degrades.

What that slender waist so delicate and slight!
What those gentle words the sweet tongue doth indite!
What those blandishments, that heart-attracting talk!
What that elegance, that heart-attracting walk!
What that figure, as the cypress tall and free—
In the park of God's creation a young tree!
Other women seek to imitate her grace,
As their pride and frontispiece she holds her place.

TRANSLATED BY E. J. W. GIBB

[from *Kanlı Kavak*, The Bloody Poplar]

Sophisticated theatrical drama did not develop in the Islamic world until modern times, but various forms of popular theater were enjoyed, especially in the Ottoman period. Three general types of popular theater can be distinguished. One was an open-air classic mime, known to have existed in Seljuk times, which was, much later, influenced by the *commedia dell'arte*. A second type, presumed to have originated among the Arabs, was a panegyric, or a story, of a saint, recited by a single actor to the accompaniment of music. The third type, usually called *karagöz* (black-eyed), from the name of its principal character, was the puppet theater. Possibly of Chinese origin, it was known in the Islamic world in the thirteenth century, and became popular at royal courts and village squares alike. Its form was that of a dialogue between the two characters Karagöz and Hadjeivat, who appear, like the protagonists in Al-Hariri's *Assemblies*, in an endless variety of disguises.

The Bloody Poplar was one of the favorite plays in the *karagöz* repertory.

HADJEIVAT: Is it possible to a belle to be such a coquette?
Is it possible to retouch thus the blue eyes?
Is it possible to love a beauty secretly?
Oh, my life's quintessence, come and embrace me once!
Where are you, temptress, whither must I guide myself?
By whom may I be informed?
Let me look once at your face,
Oh, my life's quintessence, come and embrace me once!

(*Appears on the screen and pronounces the perde gazeli.*)[1] This is the performance of shadows. It is an enigma for men of knowledge. You, looking at it with the eye of the spectator, stand amazed by its brilliance and try to understand its meaning; if you cannot understand, they say to you—it is a mystery. (*Goes to the door of Karagöz.*) Come down, Karagöz!

[1] The *perde gazeli* is the "curtain poem" which precedes the play. [Ed.]

371

KARAGÖZ: For what purpose did you call me?

HADJEIVAT: Welcome, pilaw zerde! (*pilaw—boiled rice, prepared with butter, broth, etc.; zerde—with a sauce of saffron*)

KARAGÖZ: How do you do, tahta perde! (*tahta—a board, plank; tahta perde—a fence or partition of boards*)

HADJEIVAT: What a joker you are. You give rhymed answers.

KARAGÖZ: Yes, if you wish, I will reply to one word—five or fifteen rhymes.

HADJEIVAT: Well, let me say something once more, and you give answer. (*Karagöz and Hadjeivat continue to say rhymed jokes without any sense.*) Hello, skimmer!

KARAGÖZ: Hello, post-horse!

HADJEIVAT: When the boat breaks its prow, it means the end of pleasure! Let me say one more thing; answer!

KARAGÖZ: Say it!

HADJEIVAT: Hello, the spring of the watch-maker!

KARAGÖZ: Hello, the gipsy from Sulu-kule (*a village*).

HADJEIVAT: How are you, Karagöz, rich or poor?

KARAGÖZ: Brother, I am as empty now as the water in a pitcher.

HADJEIVAT: It is impossible, brother; let us start a business.

KARAGÖZ: And what will we do?

HADJEIVAT: As we have many friends, we shall be ice cream makers.

KARAGÖZ: But I have not one instrument.

HADJEIVAT: Don't worry, I have them. Let us go home, I shall give you all. (*They go to the house of Hadjeivat.*) Take this. Bring this vat for ice cream out to the street, and come back. (*Karagöz brings it out and returns.*) Take some snow and bring this cover-cloth also. (*Karagöz brings this out and returns.*) Take this package of salt, a shovel, a can of milk; bring everything out, and I shall come immediately. (*Comes to Karagöz.*) Take the cover from the vat and crumble in some snow.

KARAGÖZ: All right. (*Crumbles snow.*)

HADJEIVAT: Did you crumble?

KARAGÖZ: I did.

HADJEIVAT: Press the snow down compactly in the vat. Now put in salt, and turn. (*Karagöz turns carefully.*) Is it ready? open the cover, I shall see if it is sweet enough. (*He tastes, it is salted.*) It seems that you strewed salt in the milk?

KARAGÖZ: You said put salt in the vat, and I did.

HADJEIVAT: I ordered you to strew it around, but not in the middle. Have you never seen how they make ice cream? How can we sell the salted ice cream now?

KARAGÖZ: That is not your business. I'll sell it.

HADJEIVAT: Wipe off some plates, put everything on your shoulder; let us go, but be careful, don't break the plates, they are expensive.

KARAGÖZ: Do not worry, I shall not break them.

HADJEIVAT: Put it on your shoulder. (*Karagöz raises them up, some fall down and are broken.*) Wah, but you broke them! (*Strikes him.*)

KARAGÖZ: (*cries*) Here is good ice cream, cherry, vanilla! (*To Hadjeivat*) How many kinds do we have?

HADJEIVAT: What is the matter?

KARAGÖZ: But we have one kind only—the salted one?

HADJEIVAT: Do not tell that or they will not want to buy.

KARAGÖZ: Can I be a liar; I shall tell the truth.

WOMEN (*their voices call*): Ice cream seller!

HADJEIVAT: What do you want?

KARAGÖZ (*also cries*): What do you want?

HADJEIVAT: Shut up!

KARAGÖZ: No, you shut up!

HADJEIVAT: No, you!

KARAGÖZ: But I am the owner.

HADJEIVAT: No, I am (*They dispute.*)

WOMEN: Bring ice cream quickly!

HADJEIVAT: With pleasure! Just a moment, I am bringing it. (*He puts ice cream on the plates, places them on the tray and gives it to Karagöz.*) Take it, bring it to them. (*He brings it.*)

WOMEN: What kind of ice cream is it?

KARAGÖZ: Salted.

WOMEN: But does one eat salted ice cream? (*They strike Karagöz and throw everything out. Karagöz weeps and goes to Hadjeivat.*)

HADJEIVAT: Where is the tray and money?

KARAGÖZ: They asked me what is this ice cream, and I said salted. They struck me and threw everything out.

HADJEIVAT: Is it possible to say to buyers that it is salted? (*Strikes Karagöz again; he, weeping, goes home.*)

WOMEN: Hadjeivat Chelebi, take 50 medjidies (*a big silver or a small gold coin*) and send to your comrade, we shall give him more.

HADJEIVAT: With pleasure! (*Calls Karagöz.*) Ei, Karagöz, come here, they are giving bakshish (*English—tips*).

KARAGÖZ: I was there just now and received two strikes of bakshish; it is enough, I wept and went home. (*Disappears. Haialdji begins to sing "sharki"; a poplar grows on the screen. Karagöz, knowing nothing, hits against it.*)

KARAGÖZ: What is this? (*Looks at it, some terrible monsters look out.*) Ai-wai, what is this? I am afraid of that! (*Calls Hadjeivat.*)

HADJEIVAT: You cannot understand, brother? You, do not walk here too much!

KARAGÖZ: Why?

HADJEIVAT: This is the dangerous, so-called Bloody Poplar, which is usually situated in the iaila Tobzak between Seres and Salonika. (*Iaila is a summer camp of nomads and shepherds; Seres was a river in old Turkey and now is in modern Rumania; Salonika is a well-known city and port in the Balkan peninsula.*) It is peopled by evil spirits; don't walk here, they can do you great damage.

KARAGÖZ: And how much one okka?

HADJEIVAT: One okka of what?

KARAGÖZ: Of sweet pumpkin. (*Sweet pumpkin—balli kabak. Karagöz confuses it with kanli kavak, i. e., bloody poplar.*)

HADJEIVAT: Not balli kabak, but the Bloody Poplar; it can harm you. (*Goes away.*)

KARAGÖZ: Ei, Balli Kabak! What are you doing here? (*The monsters appear again.*) But Hadjeivat spoke truly. (*Goes home. Ashik Hasan and Muslu come singing a gazel.*)

ASHIK:

> Your summer is like winter,
> You are like a head covered with grief,
> Or like a sad drunkard,
> You, mystically intoxicated mountains!
> Mountains, mountains, solitary mountains,
> Which make us weep as if in separation from friends;
> Let us go, Ashik Hasan,
> Let us take evil for good,
> Let us go away from death in these mountains,

Where before we enjoyed ourselves,
Which make us weep in separation from friends!

(*Goes with his child.*) Ah, my baby, do you see this? Before us is the cruel Bloody Poplar. Hold on tightly to my skirt; we shall save ourselves. For if anybody enters here with another, he goes out alone, and if anybody comes here alone, he goes out never. I shall read a gazel—and let us go.

Day and night to sigh
Is enough for me.
Offend me, oh cruel,
To perish is enough for me.
But this joyful friend,
Have mercy on him for my sake.
I was inflamed with the fire of love,
To flame is enough for me.

(*A monster comes out of the poplar and seizes the child.*)

Ashik (*seeing that the child is gone, calls him*): Oh, my dear child, Muslu, Muslu!

Karagöz (*looking out of the window*): Ei, uncle with a washbasin, what is the matter, do you want to wash your face? (*Muslu is a proper name; Karagöz for a joke, says "musluk," i. e., washbasin.*)

Ashik: Leave me alone! Oh, cruel poplar, you thought that I have many children, did you? Now I shall read a gazel for each branch of yours, let me beat my head on your trunk, let me perish.

You, poplar, that is standing here,
That gives nobody passage,
Why did you take my Muslu, where did you carry him?
Oh, cruel poplar, what did you do with my Muslu?
You are poplar, your name is bloody,
You give sorrow, because of you
Lamentations go up to heaven's vault;
You ruin passengers;
Bloody poplar, what did you do with my Muslu?

(*Meanwhile the spirits bring the child back.*) Oh, my little child, where were you? (*Embraces him.*)

KARAGÖZ: What? The washbasin came back? From a tinner, maybe?

ASHIK (*to Karagöz*): Come here, my uncle. This is my child, whom you call washbasin. Take measures please against this poplar. (*Goes out.*)

KARAGÖZ (*to the poplar*): Ei, you, Balli Kabak, get out of here! Why do you not give rest to the passengers? (*Somebody strikes Karagöz from behind; a monster appears, approaches him, and notwithstanding his cries, brings him to the poplar, bends his arms and legs and throws him.*) What has happened to me? I cannot move either arms or legs. (*Hadjeivat enters.*)

HADJEIVAT: It seems to me that they threw a cock in a ditch here.

KARAGÖZ: Did they make a cock of me?

HADJEIVAT: And the voice is well known to me. Karagöz!

KARAGÖZ: Who is this?

HADJEIVAT: What is the matter with you, brother?

KARAGÖZ: I wanted to drive away Balli Kabak, but suddenly a monster appeared, dragged me off, and I do not know what happened to me afterwards.

HADJEIVAT: They curved you into a bow.

KARAGÖZ: Oh, am I broken? (*to Hadjeivat*), Help, Hadjeivat, in any way.

HADJEIVAT: I shall devise something; but you must swear that you will never raise up your hand against me.

KARAGÖZ: My little lamb Hadjeivat, I shall do nothing against you.

HADJEIVAT: If that is so, I will try to implore the monsters. (*He im_ plores, they straighten out Karagöz and carry him aside.*) Brother, come on, do not walk here! (*They go home. Karagöz takes an axe and climbs on the poplar.*)

KARAGÖZ: Well, Balli Kabak, I have no wood at home; let me cut your branches. I shall bring them home. (*He cuts and sings.*)

> One poplar is higher than another.
> On the vine the grapes ripen.
> My friend, my two little eyes,
> Clap the palms of your hands,
> I am very anxious.
> On the poplar the voice of the crane resounds.
> My girl-friend has a pretty fez.
> It is a great sorrow to be separated from a friend.
> Clap the palms of your hands.
> I am deeply sorry.

(Having cut a branch, he begins to cut the one on which he is sitting. Hadjeivat enters.)

HADJEIVAT: Why, brother, are you cutting the branch on which you are sitting? You will fall immediately.

KARAGÖZ: Go ahead, pass on, I want to bring wood home. *(Cuts this branch and falls down.)* If Hadjeivat knew that I was going to fall, it means he knows when I will die. *(He meets two Arnauts who are coming; Karagöz hides the axe in his hand.)*

ARNAUT: Who cut the poplar?

KARAGÖZ: I do not know.

ARNAUT: You cut it, you, dog!

KARAGÖZ: I did not cut it. *(Suddenly the Arnauts perceive the axe in his hand.)*

ARNAUTS: Catch him! *(They attack Karagöz, take him, attach a rope to his nose, drag him around on all sides and say):* That is for you, that is for you! *(Karagöz tears the rope and saving himself, escapes.)*

The play ends.

TRANSLATED BY NICHOLAS MARTINOVITCH

SHORT BIBLIOGRAPHY

This bibliography is included for the purpose of directing the interested general reader toward more information about Islam, its history, and its literature. It does not list original texts or even works in foreign languages, although many of the best works on these subjects are written in foreign languages. The reader who wishes to trace the complete translations of works included in this anthology may do so by consulting the list of acknowledgements on pages v–vii.

ISLAM

ARBERRY, A. J. *Sufism*. London, 1950.

DONALDSON, D. M. *The Shi'ite Religion*. London, 1933.

GARDET, L. *Mohammedanism*, tr. by W. Burridge. New York, 1961.

GIBB, H. A. R. *Mohammedanism*. London, 1949.

———. *Modern Trends in Islam*. Chicago, 1947.

———, and KRAMERS, J. H. *Shorter Encyclopaedia of Islam*. Leiden, 1953.

JEFFERY, A., ed. *Islam*. New York, 1958.

LAMMENS, H. *Islam*. Tr. by F. D. Ross. London, 1929.

MACDONALD, D. B. *Development of Muslim Theology, Jurisprudence, and Constitutional Theory*. London, 1903.

MARGOLIOUTH, D. S. *The Early Development of Mohammedanism*. London, 1914.

MASSÉ, H. *Islam*. Tr. by H. Edib. New York, 1938.

TRITTON, A. S. *Muslim Theology*. London, 1947.

WATT, W. M. *Muhammad at Mecca*. Oxford, 1953.

———. *Muhammad at Medina*. Oxford, 1956.

WENSINCK, A. J. *The Muslim Creed*. Cambridge, 1932.

WILLIAMS, J. A., ed. *Islam*. New York, 1961.

ISLAMIC HISTORY

ARBERRY, A. J., ed. *The Legacy of Persia*. Oxford, 1953.
ARNOLD, T. W. *The Caliphate*. Oxford, 1924.
———, and GUILLAUME, A., eds. *The Legacy of Islam*. London, 1931.
BROCKELMANN, C. *History of the Islamic Peoples*. Tr. by J. Carmichael and M. Perlmann. New York, 1947.
FARIS, N., ed. *The Arab Heritage*. Princeton, 1946.
GIBB, H. A. R. *Studies on the Civilization of Islam*, ed. by S. Shaw and W. Polk Boston, 1962.
———, and BOWEN, H. *Islamic Society and the West*. 2 vols. London, 1950–1957.
GRUNEBAUM, G. E. VON. *Medieval Islam*. Chicago, 1947.
———. *Islam*. London, 1955.
———, ed. *Unity and Variety in Muslim Civilization*. Chicago, 1955.
HAZARD, H. W., and COOKE, H. L. *Atlas of Islamic History*. Princeton, 1954.
HITTI, P. K. *History of the Arabs*. 6th ed. London, 1956.
———. *The Near East in History*. Princeton, 1961.
KIRK, G. *A Short History of the Middle East*. New York, 1959.
KRITZECK, J., and WINDER, R. B., eds. *The World of Islam*. 3rd ed. London, 1960.
LEVY, R. *An Introduction to the Sociology of Islam*. 2 vols. London, 1933.
LEWIS, B. *The Arabs in History*. London, 1950.
SMITH, W. C. *Islam in Modern History*. Princeton, 1957.
SYKES, P. M. *A History of Persia*. 3rd ed. 2 vols. London, 1950.
YOUNG, T. C., ed. *Near Eastern Culture and Society*. Princeton, 1951.

ISLAMIC LITERATURE

ARBERRY, A. J. *Persian Poems*. London, 1954.
———. *Classical Persian Literature*. London, 1958.
BROWNE, E. G. *A Literary History of Persia*. 4 vols. London, 1924–1930.
GIBB, E. J. W. *A History of Ottoman Poetry*. 6 vols. London, 1900–1909.
GIBB, H. A. R. *Arabic Literature*. 2nd ed. Oxford, 1963.
LANDAU, J. M. *Studies in the Arab Theater and Cinema*. Philadelphia, 1958.
LEVY, R. *Persian Literature*. London, 1928.
MARTINOVITCH, N. N. *The Turkish Theatre*. New York, 1933.
NICHOLSON, R. A. *Studies in Islamic Poetry*. Cambridge, 1921.
———. *Eastern Poetry and Prose*. Cambridge, 1922.
———. *A Literary History of the Arabs*. 3rd ed. Cambridge, 1953.
ULLAH, NAJIB. *Islamic Literature*. New York, 1963.

JAMES KRITZECK

is Professor of Oriental Languages and History at Notre Dame University and Director of the Institute for Advanced Religious Studies. In addition to the companion to this volume, *Modern Islamic Literature* (available in a Mentor edition), he has published *Islam in Africa, Sons of Abraham, Peter the Venerable and Islam*, and *The World of Islam*.